DB

# *The* REUNION

Amy Silver is a writer and freelance journalist living in London. This is her fourth novel.

# The
# REUNION

## Amy Silver

arrow books

Published by Arrow Books 2013

2 4 6 8 10 9 7 5 3 1

First published in Great Britain in 2013 by
Arrow Books
Random House, 20 Vauxhall Bridge Road,
London SW1V 2SA

www.randomhouse.co.uk

Addresses for companies within The Random House Group Limited can be found at:
www.randomhouse.co.uk/offices.htm
The Random House Group Limited Reg. No. 954009

A CIP catalogue record for this book
is available from the British Library

ISBN 9780099574491

The Random House Group Limited supports the Forest Stewardship Council® (FSC®),
the leading international forest-certification organisation. Our books carrying the FSC label
are printed on FSC®-certified paper. FSC is the only forest-certification scheme supported
by the leading environmental organisations, including Greenpeace. Our paper procurement
policy can be found at: www.randomhouse.co.uk/environment

Typeset in Fournier MT 12.5/15pt by Palimpsest Book Production Ltd,
Falkirk, Stirlingshire
Printed and bound by CPI Group (UK) Ltd, Croydon, CR0 4YY

*For Mum, with all my love*

I would like to thank Lizzy Kremer and Gillian Holmes for their helpful insights and endless patience. My thanks also to Harriet Moore, Lettie Smythers, Glynne Hawkins and Jamie Wilding.

# *Prologue*

*Hey beautiful,*

*Hello from rainy Cork. I hope you're doing OK.*

*Just wanted to get some words down for you. After I got your message last night, I lay awake for ages, thinking about what an idiot I am and how lucky I am to have you in my life and how sorry I am that I made you cry. God, I'm so sorry.*

*So last night, I couldn't sleep, I couldn't stop thinking about how upset you were, and I wanted to call you again, I wanted to hear your voice but I was worried that you'd already gone to bed and I'd wake you up. So eventually I got up and went downstairs, found an open bottle of Bushmills in the kitchen cupboard and drank the lot of it. I assume it was Ronan's. He's going to kill me. I probably ought to leave town before he finds out.*

*I digress. The point is, I was sitting there in the dark in the kitchen and I was thinking about all the ways you make me happy.*

*I went back to bed and I still couldn't sleep so I did that thing I do, when I replay things over in my head, start to finish. Sometimes I do* Godfather II *or the whole of* Goodfellas, *scene by scene. Last night I thought about us. I thought about the last day at the French house, the day before we had to come home.*

*It had been glorious all summer, and then on the last day it had to rain — the thunder started up that morning and the heavens opened and I was convinced that the roof wouldn't hold out and we'd all get soaked. Last night I thought about that day and I played it out in my head, scene by scene.*

*It turned cold, suddenly, overnight, so we lit the fire in the morning. There was barely any wood left, so someone had to go out to the shed in the slashing rain to get more, and poor Andrew drew the short straw. Wrecked he was, from the night before, do you remember? All he wanted to do was go back to bed, but Lilah wouldn't have it and so out he went and he slipped and fell on the way back and cut his hand and we heard about it all bloody afternoon.*

*It was all right, though, wasn't it, because that farmer, the grumpy bugger down the way, had brought us sausages and eggs (glad to see the back of us, I'm sure he was), so we did a big fry-up and we just sat there, drinking pots of coffee and talking nonsense because there was nothing else to do and not one of us who didn't have a hangover. We were making plans, already looking forward to the next summer, when we'd be back again. Fire roaring in the grate, windows steaming up, the smell of sausages and coffee and the sound of the rain pounding down outside. And you, sitting there, holding my hand under the table, looking gorgeous, just lush, this after you'd drunk almost your own weight in red wine the night before and slept for less than three hours. How d'you do it? You're a sorceress, aren't you? That must be it.*

*God, I didn't want to leave that place. And now I can't wait to get back there. Less than four months now.*

*At some point (I think it may have been after we decided it was late enough to open a bottle of wine), Nat decided that she couldn't possibly return to England the same girl that left it, so she demanded that Lilah cut all her hair off. Do you remember that; you were horrified? All that long brown hair lying in clumps on the floor, Lilah wielding those scissors like some sort of evil mad woman, and then she was done, and Nat looked gorgeous, a tiny pixie with enormous green eyes. Dan and Andrew were gobsmacked, just staring at her like they'd never seen her before.*

*Eventually, the rain stopped, and Dan forced us all to go outside so that he could take photographs of us, the house, us in front of the house, us on the stone wall, us with the valley as backdrop, with the mountain as backdrop, us, us, us. You three girls, you and Lilah and Natalie posing on the wall like supermodels, you three beautiful girls, and Andrew lying on the wet grass moaning about his terrible head and his injured hand, the lightweight. Do you have those pictures, now? I don't think I ever saw them. I want to get those pictures, put them up on the wall.*

*It started to rain again. You took my hand and gripped it hard – you said you felt dizzy, you had a case of the weirds, the way you do when you're hung over, and I said you'd feel better with another drink in you. So we all went back inside and drank red wine and the rest of that God-awful cider and we danced to Gainsbourg and Donna Summer. Do you remember, when we went to bed that night, when we lay down on the mattress in the back room, we were sore, bellies aching from laughing so much? (Have I told you, by the way, that you've the most beautiful laugh I've ever heard?)*

*That was the best of days, wasn't it? Nothing really happened, nothing special. We just ate and drank and danced and laughed and I've never felt happier.*

*I played that day over in my head, last night, and when I woke up this morning my head was full of you. I don't want ever to forget what*

*we were like that day, the way we felt, you and me and all of us. We*
*should hold on to that. I'm told it doesn't always last.*

   *Ma sends love.*

   *Can't wait to see you pretty girl, I ache for you.*


*All my love, always,*


*Conor*

# Part One

# Chapter One

~

*December 2012*

As she climbed the stairs for what seemed like the fourteenth time that afternoon, Jen noticed a drop of blood on one of the stone steps. She made a mental note to clean it up. Later. After she'd finished getting the bedrooms ready, after she'd checked the bathrooms were spotless, after she'd straightened the bedspreads and dusted the sills, after she'd made sure there was dry firewood in the kitchen and the living room, after she'd placed flowers in vases. White tea roses for Andrew and Natalie, blood-red orchids for Lilah. She'd driven all the way to a posh florist in Draguignan to buy them, close to a two-hour drive there and back. Ridiculous, really, but it had seemed important that morning. To make the place feel welcoming. She hadn't been sure what to buy for Dan: peonies seemed too feminine, lilies funereal, carnations too cheap. In the end she bought a little pot of black velvet petunias which she placed on the desk below the window, the one looking up to the thicket of trees behind the house, and to the mountain beyond.

After buying the flowers, she'd ended up spending more than

300 euros, buying brightly coloured throws for the beds and the sofa downstairs, scatter cushions covered with vibrant African prints, an oxblood rug for the living room. It was beyond stupid, she'd only have to pack it all up in a couple of weeks' time. And do what with it? She wasn't even sure where she was going. And now, placing the roses on the chest in the second bedroom, the one she'd given to Andrew and Natalie, she wondered if it might all be for nothing. She stood at the window looking out across the valley and shivered; it was three o'clock in the afternoon and the light was almost gone, threatening charcoal-grey clouds moving inexorably towards her. She'd had the radio on downstairs; the forecast had changed. The bad weather they had been predicting for the middle of the following week had been brought forward, to the weekend, but looking at the sky now even that seemed optimistic. It seemed as though the storm were almost upon her. Snow lay thick on the ground from the last heavy fall, a couple of days previously, but for now the roads were clear. If the storm came early, if the snow fell too soon, the road would be blocked and her guests would never get there.

Flowers done, she went into the bathroom, soaked a cloth and cleaned the blood from the stairs. She'd cut her finger French-trimming the rack of lamb for dinner. A banal enough explanation, but for some reason the action of wiping away blood seemed to herald something sinister. The hair on the back of her neck stood up and out of the corner of her eye she seemed to catch movement in the half-light of the house; she felt afraid. She went downstairs and stoked up the fire in the living room, she turned on all the lights.

Even with the lights on, the fire lit, the bright new throws and the cushions, despite all her attempts to make the house feel lived in, it felt cold, empty. Before she'd arrived, two months prior, it had been unoccupied for over a year and it hadn't lost its sense of abandonment. That took time, she imagined, and people, and possessions. She'd brought very little from Paris: clothes and books and kitchenware, a laptop and the radio, not much else. The rest was all still there, packed up in boxes marked with her name, awaiting a destination.

It wasn't just the loneliness, though, it was the season. The wind fairly screamed up the valley, whipping through the place, whistling through gaps under doors, rattling against the old leaded windows. This was the first time Jen had ever come here in winter, and she found herself wandering around with a blanket permanently wrapped around her shoulders.

The entire character of the place was different in winter. It was so quiet. In summer, you would hear the clang of bells on cows, sheep bleating in the fields, tractors in the distance, birdsong. In winter there was nothing, the deepest calm interrupted on the rarest of occasions by the sound of a triporteur, one of those funny little three-wheeled vans, chugging past on the road below, or a sudden crackle from the fire, which always made her jump. It was unnerving, this silence, it rang in her ears. She had to put the radio on to drown it. And at night, she kept the radio on to drown out the other noises, the ones that kept her awake: wooden beams creaking, the wind in the trees behind, whispering or howling, the foxes with their horrible cries, like infants abandoned to the elements.

You could smell the cold. In summer, the air was full of the scent of the lavender and rosemary that grew in the beds along the front of the house. There used to be climbing roses, too, although they were gone now. The essence of wood smoke remained, of course, but underneath that was something else, damp, untouched, the smell of cold stone, like a tomb. The quality of the light was also different. She remembered the house as it was in July, all the windows and doors flung open, shutters hooked back, sunshine streaming in along with the scent of the flowers and herbs. Now it felt as though there were parts of each room which light never touched, as though she were living in permanent shadow.

And there were ghosts. No neighbours (Villefranche, the nearest village, population 1,489, was a five-minute drive down the mountain; further up, there was nothing but shepherd's huts and, much further on, a farmhouse or two). Only ghosts. They sat around the kitchen table, they searched for firewood in the stand of trees behind the house, gently caressed Jen's shoulder blade when she stood at the mirror in the bathroom brushing her teeth. There was Conor, standing on a ladder, stripped to the waist, hammering nails into a beam, Natalie and Lilah sunning themselves on the lawn out front, Andrew listening to the World Service in the kitchen, Dan sitting on the dry stone wall with his notebook, cigarette dangling from his lower lip.

And now, this afternoon, weather permitting, they'd be back for real, those of them that could make it. And in her mind they would be exactly the same. People don't really change that much, do they? Her own life had been turned upside down, once, twice, three times, and she still felt pretty much the same as she had when she was twenty-one. A little worn around the edges, rounder and slower, but essentially not much different. The same convictions, the same passions – she still loved words and language, Offenbach, sailing; she loved the sea but hated beaches; she loved dogs but not the ones Parisians have, the ones that fit into handbags. She wasn't sure whether this was a failing or something to be proud of, this sameness. She liked to think of it as suggesting a certain strength of character, but sometimes she wondered if it just meant she was stuck.

She was nervous, she couldn't settle. Now, arrivals imminent, she almost wished it *would* snow. She was suddenly frightened, to think of them all, here in France, making their way here, to her. There was no going back. She felt a flutter in her belly, butterflies or baby, she wasn't sure. She couldn't escape the feeling that she might have made a terrible mistake. She went into the kitchen and poured herself a glass of red, trying not to feel guilty about it. After all, she'd been in this country the best part of twenty years, and French women think nothing of it.

A couple of hundred miles south, in a hotel room in Nice, a skinny girl lay on a bed, propped up against the headboard, her long blonde hair not quite covering her breasts. She watched her lover haphazardly throwing clothes into a suitcase.

'You should stay tonight,' the blonde girl said. 'It's going to be snowing in the mountains and you'll get stuck on the roads. Stay with me.' As she said this, she raised her left knee slightly and, grasping the sheet which covered her between her toes, pulled it a little lower, exposing a few inches more of her pale flesh. Her teeth grazed her lower lip. Her eyes held his. Dan laughed.

'I can't stay, Claudia, my friend's expecting me. In any case your plane leaves at midnight.'

'That's hours away,' she replied, giving him her most enticing little-girl pout. She drew her left leg up higher still and pushed the sheet all the way down to the bottom of the bed, leaving her totally exposed.

Dan sat down on the edge of the bed, leaned over her body, lowered himself to kiss her. She grabbed hold of him tightly, wrapping her arms around his waist, pulling his body against hers. No denying it was tempting, she was tempting. She was more than that, she was special.

They'd been in Nice three days. There was a film festival, a mini one, lots of worthy indies and angry documentaries made by 23-year-olds with extravagant facial hair. In comparison he was an old man, and, relatively speaking, wildly successful, which in their eyes, of course, meant sell-out. They'd learn. In any case, it was hard to feel aggrieved when you were staying in a suite at the Palais de la Mediterranée with the most beautiful girl in Nice.

The idea of staying with her, even for just a few hours more, was almost irresistible. Almost. He had to go. No, it was more than that; he wanted to go. To say that his interest was piqued by Jen's email, received quite out of the blue a month previous, was an understatement. Jennifer Donleavy, the girl who ran away, the one who got away. The girl he hadn't seen in, what was it, sixteen years? She wanted to see him, she'd invited him, and the others of course, back to the French house. It was being sold, she said, and she thought they might like to see it one last time.

If ever there were an offer he couldn't refuse, this was it. A chance to go back to that house, the place, he still felt, where his career pretty much started. He got all his best ideas, wrote all his best lines sitting on the stone wall overlooking the valley with his fancy leather-bound notebook (a present from Jen for his birthday), smoking Gauloises Blondes. He grinned at the memory. There was no denying it, he'd been a pretentious wanker back then. He wondered what it would stir up, being back there, walking through those rooms, whether there was any inspiration left.

And he couldn't wait to drive his brand-new Audi on those incredible winding mountain roads. Music up loud, adrenaline rushing as he took the corners, space to think. He hadn't had that in a while, it would do him good. Get the creative juices flowing. Plus, it wouldn't be a bad thing for him and Claudia to be apart for a few days; it would sweeten the reunion, heighten its passion.

But above all that, there was Jen. He didn't allow himself to think about her much, he hadn't done for a long time, but how could he pass up the chance to see her again, to find out where she had been all this time, what she was now? She had been off the radar, no Facebook page, no Twitter he could locate, not a single hit on Google. He'd dug out some old photos when he first got her email, pictures he hadn't looked at in a decade. He was dying to see what she looked like now: was she still beautiful? Had she got fat? It was a chance to see all the others too; and he had to admit that he was looking forward to seeing how a reunion between Natalie and Lilah would play out. He had a feeling it would be worth getting the popcorn out for that one.

'I told Jen I'd be there today,' he said to Claudia. 'I can't just not turn up. I'm not even sure I have the right number for her, she'll think something's happened to me. And I'll see you in three days, in Paris. In three days we can be together properly. Can't we?'

'Of course,' Claudia said, lips pushed into a perfect little moue. She pulled the sheet back up to her waist and rolled away from him, affording him the perfect view of her creamy, lightly freckled back.

'Christmas Eve in Paris,' Dan said, reaching out to touch the smooth blade of her shoulder.

'Of course,' Claudia said again, but she didn't look back at him.

It took them more than forty-five minutes to get to the front of the hire-car queue and by the time they actually found their silver Citroën in the middle of a football field-sized car park full of silver Citroëns, it was almost dark and starting to rain. They got lost trying to get out of Marseilles, mostly because Natalie was too busy fiddling with her phone to read the road signs. Andrew didn't say anything, because the last thing they needed now was to get into a fight.

'I wonder if we should stop somewhere, just stay in a hotel for tonight?' Natalie asked him. Her left arm was pressed against her upper body, her hand gripping her seat belt, knuckles white. With every sharp corner, every lane change, her right hand shot out and grabbed the dashboard. Every time she did it, Andrew tried not to flinch. Natalie didn't like driving in bad weather.

'Do you remember what it was like up there? The roads are dreadful. Scenic, I think, is the euphemism, meaning winding, narrow, along the edge of a bloody great cliff. And you know how the French drive. It'll be a nightmare. Plus, we don't have snow tyres. We should have asked for them, shouldn't we?'

'It'll be OK, Nat. I'll drive slowly. We're in no hurry.'

She gave a little sigh. 'Why don't we just stop somewhere? And we can drive to Jennifer's tomorrow, when it's light, and the weather's better? If we stop somewhere, I could phone the girls, I don't seem to have any signal at the moment.'

Andrew drew a deep breath. 'Jen's expecting us, Nat,' he said, giving his wife a tight little smile. 'And we rang the girls from Heathrow, they were fine.'

Just as they'd been fine that morning when he and Natalie

10

left them at their grandparents' place in Shepton. Fine was an understatement, in fact; they were delighted to see the back of Mum and Dad and didn't bother hiding it, high-fiving each other as they watched their parents' car pull out of the driveway, looking forward to four days of endless pre-Christmas shopping trips financed by Grandpa's credit card and being allowed a glass of sparkling wine before dinner.

Natalie didn't like driving in bad weather, it was true, but Andrew was well aware that there was more to her reluctance to take this trip than just that. She hadn't wanted to leave the girls so close to Christmas and she didn't share his desire to see the house again. It had taken a fair bit of persuasion to get her to agree to being in the same room as Dan again, too.

Andrew couldn't wait. Not to see Dan, though he didn't mind that. He didn't harbour grudges with quite the same tenacity as his wife did. He didn't feel he had the energy. Dan simply wasn't that important to him any longer. For Andrew, this trip was all about Jen. He felt that he had somehow neglected a duty of care towards her, although Natalie never wasted any time in pointing out that this was ridiculous. It was Jen who had made it impossible for them to be in her life, just as she'd failed to be in theirs. Even so, Andrew couldn't get past the feeling that there were other things he could have done, should have done. They didn't talk about it much, because conversations about what happened back then invariably ended in arguments, but when the subject did come up, Natalie always insisted that Jen was not Andrew's responsibility, and Andrew never once managed to succeed in demonstrating to his wife why he thought that she was.

More than that, though, he just wanted to see her again, those warm brown eyes, full of laughter. And to see her in that place, too. That would be something.

'I really think,' Natalie was saying, 'that we ought to call the girls to let them know that we've arrived safely.'

'We'll call them from Jen's place,' Andrew said, 'when we actually have arrived safely.' He regretted the words as soon as they came out of his mouth. It wasn't what he meant, but he'd made it sound as though some other outcome might be a possibility. He reached over and gave her thigh a comforting squeeze. 'They're probably not at home anyway, your mum's almost certainly taken them shopping already.'

'Keep your hands on the wheel, Andrew,' Natalie said. There were tears in her voice and the overreaction irritated him, but he didn't say so. Dutifully arranging his hands in the ten to two position, he repeated: 'It'll be fine, Nat. I'll drive slowly.'

The Moroccan taxi driver was called Khalid. He had a winning smile and the confidence of a Formula One driver.

'I come from Imlil, you know this place? In the mountains of Atlas. Toubkal, you know this place? These roads here like autoroutes compared to there.'

'Great,' Lilah said, taking another furtive sip from the half jack of vodka they'd bought at duty free. She offered it to Zac, who shook his head.

'You nervous?' he asked her. She gave a little shrug.

'No need to be afraid,' Khalid said cheerily. 'I never have accidents in this country.'

She was nervous, but not about the driving. The whole situation was a little bizarre. About a month ago, she'd received a letter written in a hand she'd known immediately. Jen, writing to tell her that the French house was on the market, and wondering would she like to come and see it, one last time. She'd invited the others, too – she felt a reunion was long overdue. Lilah's first reaction had been to throw it in the bin. She retrieved it, hours later, and read and reread. It would be lovely to see Jen after all this time. But all of them? In one house? Blood would be spilled.

She talked it over with Zac when he came home from work. Old friends, a get-together at a house we went to one year. We spent the summer doing it up for Jen's dad. She's selling it now, and she's invited us out there, to visit.

'Sounds like fun, babe,' he said, but what did he know?

Now, sitting in the car, she was certain that this was a terrible idea. What were they all going to say to each other, after the initial hellos and how've you beens? It was going to be like Facebook, where you make contact with people from your past, only this would be like real-world Facebook where you couldn't just turn off your laptop and walk away when you realised that actually there was a perfectly good reason why you weren't friends with these people any more.

Zac reached over to her, grazed the side of her face with his fingers, nudged her chin gently towards him.

'You look so worried, babe.'

'It's just weird, you know, her contacting me after so long. I mean, we used to send Christmas cards and stuff but I haven't actually laid eyes on her in about fifteen years. I can't believe this is just about the house.'

'Didn't you ask? When you emailed her, to accept?'

'I did. She just said she wanted to see us. Christ, I hope she isn't dying.'

'Lilah.'

'Well, you never know, do you? Although I suppose she wouldn't have invited a plus one if she was dying, would she?'

'I'm sure she's not dying.'

'No, probably not. I'm excited to see her,' she said, hoping to convince herself as much as her boyfriend. 'I really am.'

She shifted up closer to Zac and hooked one leg over his, so that she was almost sitting on his lap.

Khalid watched them in the rear-view mirror. 'This is honeymoon?' he asked.

Lilah laughed. 'It's not a honeymoon. Just a dirty weekend.'

'Dirty?'

'It's just a little holiday,' Zac said.

Thank God for Zac. Even if it was awful and awkward, at least she had Zac, a human buffer zone. He was so ridiculously affable, so likeable, so very nice to look at, that he had a soothing effect on those around him, a tendency to calm troubled waters. He should be a UN peace envoy or a hostage negotiator or something. Not that he wasn't a damn fine fitness instructor. Such a shame there was bugger-all money in it.

There. She'd gone there and now the thought was in her head, the one she'd had just before she'd retrieved Jen's letter from the waste-paper basket. Money. She was broke, and she was tired of it. Poverty didn't suit her, never had. She didn't know about Jen or Andrew or Nat (and she would never ask them, anyway), but Dan had money. She knew Dan had money and frankly, he owed her.

It was dark by the time they got there, and they almost missed the turning, a sharp bend to the right, up the hill. You couldn't actually see the house from the road – it wasn't until you got halfway up the drive that it appeared, looking deceptively small against the rise of the mountain behind. They pulled up out front as the snow was starting to fall. Lilah, determined that if she was going to have to face the past she was going to face it in style, was wearing boots with four-inch heels and open toes; Zac had to carry her to the front door while Khalid took their bags out of the boot.

Zac deposited Lilah on the doorstep.

'Thank you, baby,' she purred, and gave him a kiss with lots of tongue, trying to exude a confidence she didn't feel. She took a hand mirror out of her bag and checked her face. She pinched the skin over her cheekbones and bit her lower lip to redden it. She put the mirror back into her bag and took out the small bottle of vodka. One quick swig, a run of her hand through her hair and she was ready.

'Let's do this,' she said, and pressed the doorbell.

They got there in the end, no thanks to a taxi driver who almost ran them off the road as they turned out of Villefranche, a speeding Mercedes overtaking a lorry as it careened down the hill. Natalie's yelp of fear caught in her throat, and she'd barely made a sound since. She gripped the door handle, her chin resting on her chest – she didn't dare look up. They crawled up the hill. She had been right about the roads, narrow and winding. He should have listened to her.

When she did look up, she tried to keep her eyes front, on the road, or to the right-hand side, the mountain side, where a bank of snow piled a metre high served as testament to weeks of heavy snowfalls. But she couldn't help herself: every now and again she would glance to her left, where the snow had fallen away, over the edge of the mountain into the ravine below. Andrew turned on the radio. Natalie turned it off again.

'Just concentrate on the road,' she said, wishing she didn't sound quite so peevish, so plaintive.

The problem was, she felt peevish and plaintive. What were

they doing, flying and then driving all the way out here, to the middle of nowhere for three days? It would have made so much more sense for Jen to come to them. She could have stayed for Christmas. (Christ, Christmas. She had a million things to do, this trip really couldn't have come at a less convenient time.) She would have put her foot down, point blank refused, only she could see that it meant so much to Andrew, to come back to the old place. The summer they'd spent at the house had been raised, in his mind, almost to the level of myth, it shone golden in his memory. She understood, but she couldn't help but feel a little sad about it; for her, as sweet as that summer was, it was bitter too. Her feelings about it were always going to be mixed.

And Dan was going to be there, the weasel. She'd promised Andrew that she'd be nice, but it was going to take iron self-control not to give the little git a slap.

And oh God, she wished they could have made this journey in daylight, preferably without snow. Still. Finally, mercifully, there were there. She hadn't expected it, but she felt a surge of happiness looking up at the house, beautiful in its dusting of white, an idyll standing all alone on the hillside. Lonely, but welcoming, pine-scented wood smoke billowing from chimneys at either end of the roof, a warm glow spilling out onto fresh snow.

'God,' Natalie said, 'it's so lovely.' She turned to Andrew and smiled, and he looked so incredibly relieved, she felt awful for being so snappy with him on the way here, for making things so difficult.

'Sorry, love,' she said, reaching for his hand.

'Nothing to be sorry for,' he said, and squeezed her hand and leaned over to kiss her on the lips.

Andrew fetched their bags from the boot of the car. Natalie

stood on the doorstep, her back to the door, gazing out across the valley and to the mountains beyond, white caps illuminated by moonlight. She could hear voices inside the house, laughter. She felt nervous all of a sudden, wished she'd thought harder about interesting things to say, and, looking down at her bootcut jeans, trainers and khaki parka, she wished that she'd made a bit more of an effort. She could at least have had her hair cut.

'OK, love?'

She nodded and took his hand again, then lifted the iron knocker and let it fall. The sound rang out alarmingly loud, splitting the silence.

'Here we go,' a voice called out. 'I'll get that, shall I?'

Natalie's heart did a little flip in her chest. That wasn't Jen's voice. She looked over at Andrew; he was looking back at her, his eyes widening. Natalie shook her head a little, something wasn't right, she knew, they both did, and she brought her hand up to cover her mouth which had fallen open, aghast. The door flew open and there she was, rail-thin and ice-blonde, a smear of vermillion lipstick on her mouth. Lilah.

'Hello, you two,' she said, a voice to cut glass, an assassin's smile. 'We were just wondering where you'd got to. How the devil are you?'

*Dear Nat,*

*I'm sorry I didn't make it to see you at the weekend. I was all set to drive down yesterday, but Lilah came home in the early hours in a bad way and I couldn't leave her on her own. Pupils like saucers, chattering and shivering and scared of her own shadow, talking the most unbelievable shit. She couldn't sleep, wouldn't eat anything. She'd been out with the guys from work. She doesn't handle drugs nearly as well as she thinks she does.*

*She's asleep now, finally. I think she'll be in bed all day. Viva bank holidays. I rang her mum this morning, she seems to think it's post-traumatic stress from the accident, but that doesn't really make sense. This has been going on a while, hasn't it? I mean, I know it's been worse of late, but the bingeing and the secretiveness, that goes back further. I don't know what the hell to do. Neither of us are happy in this relationship any longer, but I can't leave her like this. I've suggested counselling, I guess you can imagine how that goes down.*

*I'm sorry she hasn't been down to see you these past few weeks, you know it's not that she doesn't care. She talks about you all the time. She's just not facing up to the here and now particularly well.*

*God, listen to me whinge.*

*How are you, Nat? I hope the physio's going better. I know (what do I know? I know nothing) – I understand that you're working so hard, and I hope that it won't be long until you're back on your feet, strong again, like you were. That ridiculously handsome nurse must be easing the pain a little!*

*How are you getting on with* Infinite Jest? *I found it hard going at first, but I think it's worth sticking with it. (Lilah doesn't. She had a quick flick through it and said, 'What on earth would she want to read*

18

*that for? Doesn't she have enough on her plate?' Then she called me a pseudo-intellectual wanker and went to get herself a drink. She may have a point. She suggested I bring you* Bridget Jones' Diary, *which she thinks is hilarious. I read a few pages and have to admit, it is quite funny. I'll bring it for you when I come next.)*

*I haven't seen Dan in a couple of weeks, though he rang last week and claims to be working very hard. He and Lilah cross paths in Soho from time to time. He said he was planning to get down to see you soon. Perhaps I'll bring him the weekend after next? I think this weekend I want you all to myself.*

*I've heard nothing from Jen. I wrote to her mother and she sent back a very short note saying that Jen was no longer in England. No further details. They're obviously still very angry with me. I wonder whether Jen's with Maggie, in Cork? As kind as Maggie's been to me, I can't help but think I'm the last person she wants to speak to right now. Perhaps you could drop her a line? We'll talk about it when I see you.*

*I think about you, all the time. I know I shouldn't. I can't help myself. I'm counting the minutes until I'm by your side, it's the only place that makes sense to me right now.*

*With all my love,*

*Andrew*

*P.S. I have a court date, by the way. It's 12 December, just in time for Christmas. Frankly, the sooner the better, I just want it over.*

## Chapter Two

~

Nothing went the way she'd imagined it would, and yet, as it played out, Jen kept thinking, well of course this was the way this was going to go, how stupid of me to think otherwise. She'd expected, based on where they were all coming from, Andrew and Natalie to be the first to arrive. Jen had estimated that she would have a good half an hour with the two of them before Lilah got there, which would give her ample time to explain that she hadn't been 100 per cent honest about the guest list. If she broke it to them gently, just the two of them, over a glass of wine, it would be all right.

But it didn't happen like that. Dan was first to arrive. He pulled up outside the house in a flashy silver car, and she watched from the living-room window as he climbed out, looked up, turned to look down the valley, and then back towards the house. He stood there, hands on hips, the trace of a smile on his face, looking ludicrously boyish. His hair was cropped close to his head, the skin over his nose a little freckled, like he'd spent some time in the sun.

When she opened the door, he looked almost as though

he were surprised to see her, as though he'd been expecting someone else. He seemed lost for words. And she was taken aback, too, because he wasn't what she'd been expecting. She'd read about his films and his success, she'd seen him 'linked' with any number of women and she'd expected him to be brasher, bolder, louder than the old Dan, and yet there he was, smiling diffidently at her, stumbling over his words when he said hello, shyly kissing her on the cheek. She remembered why he'd got to her the way he did. The lost boy.

He stepped inside and she closed the door behind them, and they stood there for a moment, just looking at each other, not saying anything, Dan's face a little flushed, and Jen started laughing and offered him a drink. She didn't have time to get it, though, because it was just then that she heard another car pull up, heard doors slamming and laughter and a loud, confident knock. She smiled at Dan and took a deep breath, opened the door and was knocked back by a blast of cold air and by Lilah, hurling herself into Jen's arms.

'Jen! Oh God, Jen!' Lilah was laughing and crying at the same time, her arms wrapped tightly around Jen's body. She clung to her, and Jen couldn't say a word, she could barely breathe, she just stood there, locked in an embrace, feeling the sharp edges of Lilah's scapulae rising and falling. It was like hugging a skeleton. Eventually, Lilah pulled away.

She laughed, wiping the tears from her cheeks, smearing mascara towards her hairline.

'Jen! Oh my God. Look at you! You've put on weight.' She laughed again, pulling Jen towards her. 'It suits you! No, it does, I mean it. You look wonderful.'

'And you look exactly the same,' Jen said, although this wasn't quite true. Lilah was even thinner, even blonder than before, her blue eyes huge above razor-sharp cheekbones. She looked almost other-worldly, a caricature of herself.

'Oh, you are kind,' she said, flicking her hair over her shoulder in a parody of coyness. 'This,' she said, waving her arm grandly in the direction of the man she'd brought with her, 'is Zac.' Zac, who was extremely handsome and looked around twenty-five, shook hands with Jen and then with Dan, while Lilah inspected the place, making funny little noises of exclamation. After a few moments she acknowledged Dan's presence, greeting him not quite coldly but not warmly either.

Jen was in the kitchen pouring drinks when she heard the third car arrive, and halfway through uncorking a bottle of red wine when she heard Lilah call out, should she get that? And before Jen had time to step in, Lilah had flung open the front door, Natalie and Andrew were standing on the doorstep, open-mouthed, shocked, and when Andrew at last looked over at Jen, he looked like he'd been punched in the gut.

Natalie was furious and even to her own ears Jen's apologies sounded trite and mealy-mouthed.

'I just wanted you all to be here,' she heard herself simper, 'and I knew, Nat, I knew you wouldn't want to come if . . .'

'If what?' Lilah snapped, wasting no time to jump into the fray. 'They wouldn't come if they knew *I* was coming?' She lit a cigarette, her cheeks sunken as she dragged on it furiously. 'Bloody cheek.'

'I'm sorry,' Jen said. 'I really am. This was a mistake.'

'I think it probably was,' Andrew said quietly. He was reaching for his wife's hand, eyes dipped, unable to meet Jen's eye; he looked crestfallen. Jen felt as though she might burst into tears. 'Perhaps it would be better,' Andrew said, 'if Nat and I went down to the village for the night.'

'No!' Natalie's refusal was loud and vehement. 'I'm not driving anywhere else tonight, Andrew. Absolutely not. We'll stay here tonight and leave in the morning.'

Feeling silly and sheepish, Jen took the couples to their rooms. Lilah, determined to outdo Natalie in the huffiness stakes, stomped off with her man and slammed the door behind them; Jen was left to accompany a silent Andrew and Natalie. She opened the door and beamed at them, feeling rather like a hotel porter angling for a tip. Natalie bustled past her and disappeared straight into the bathroom, muttering something about needing a bath. Andrew stood in the doorway, his hand resting on the frame. He rapped it once with his knuckle.

'Held up all right, didn't they?' he said; there was a small smile on his lips, pride, or remembrance. That summer, way back when, the summer of the renovation, Andrew and Conor had repaired most of the door frames up here on the first floor. They'd fixed sagging joists and repaired the roof, shored up the vast oak beams, rescued the place from collapse.

'They held up great,' Jen said. She was perched on the edge of the bed, watching him, waiting for him to look at her; to *really* look at her.

But Andrew was admiring his old handiwork, running his hands over the walls and testing the floorboards as though he were looking for subsidence or dry rot. He took a good look at the beams in the ceiling, inspected the window frames and finally, his survey complete, he turned towards her. He stood tall, hands on hips, looking her directly in the eye for the first time since he'd arrived.

'The place looks great,' he said, and before she could reply he went on: 'I can't believe you're selling it.'

Jen sighed, got to her feet, and stood in front of him. She'd known he'd be upset, but looking at him now, seeing the satisfaction it gave him to see the house again, to stand here in the place they'd worked so hard, she realised that it was going to be harder than she'd imagined.

'I never use it. Obviously I'm here now, but this is the first time in ages. And now, Dad's gone and Mum certainly doesn't want to come here . . .' She shrugged. They smiled at each other awkwardly for a second. She couldn't think of anything else to say, she could hardly believe that he was actually here, standing in front of her. It didn't seem real.

'Andrew!' Natalie called him from the bathroom. 'Can you come in here for a second?'

Andrew shrugged, holding his hands out, palms up.

'I'm sorry,' Jen said, voice little more than a whisper, 'about the thing with Lilah.'

Andrew shook his head, waving the apology away. 'It's OK,' he said. 'We'll talk in the morning.' He smiled at her and for a second he looked like his old self, or at least he looked to her as though his old self might be in there, somewhere, behind the mask of an old man.

Jen paused, halfway down the stairs, resting her hand against the cold stone wall. She felt breathless, her heart beating a little too fast. As she steadied herself she looked down and realised she'd missed another drop of blood.

'Out, damned spot,' she muttered as she continued downstairs and into the kitchen. Dan was waiting for her, leaning against the counter, drinking a beer and checking his phone. He looked at once at home and completely out of place, the dissonance made her head spin. She couldn't allow herself to dwell on it too much. Not yet, things to do.

'Sorry,' she said to him, 'I thought it would be best to get the others settled in first.'

He looked up and smiled, then went back to his phone.

'Would you like to go through and see your room now?'

She took him through the back door, across the yard to what was once the barn, now a low-slung modernist apartment with sliding glass doors, a bedroom on the mezzanine level and a wet room.

'Bloody hell,' he said. 'This is an improvement.'

'Well,' she said, giving him a smile. 'It's not every day I have a famous film director to stay.'

He shot her a look, there was a flicker of defensiveness in his eyes as though he thought she might be taking the piss.

'I'm joking,' she said quickly. 'It was the tenant. This writer from Paris, quite famous actually, long tomes of rather awful pop philosophy.' She was babbling, sentences running into one another. 'Anyway, he rented the place for ages, years and years. He used to come here for half the year, use it to write, you know, and to entertain women. This was his writing studio.'

'So you haven't been using the house?' Dan looked surprised.

'No. It was supposed to be Mum and Dad's bolthole, but that never happened because they never actually wanted to go anywhere together. Then they got divorced, and after that Dad got ill. I didn't really want to come back here. Not all alone. So Dad decided to rent it out and Delacourt – that's the writer – just kept taking it, year after year. He eventually bought a place of his own a couple of years ago, so it's been empty since then. Well, until I got here.'

'And now your dad wants to sell it?'

'It's mine now, actually. Dad died last year.'

'Oh, I'm sorry.'

The words were spoken completely without emotion. The diffident, lost boy who'd appeared on the doorstep just a few minutes ago was gone, now, replaced by a different Dan, rather controlled, curiously blank, disconnected. He seemed to be trying not to meet her eye. Jen waited for a second, for him to say something.

'I'll leave you to it then, shall I? Come through and have some dinner when you're ready. OK?'

'Great. Thanks, Jen.' He was looking at his phone again.

Jen went back to the kitchen, laid the table and opened a bottle of red to let it breathe. She took a moment to breathe herself. You couldn't say it was a disaster, not yet. Everyone just needed a moment or two to adjust. She heard a creak of floorboards in the hallway and looked up. Andrew was standing in the doorway, watching her.

'Drink?' she asked.

'Ah, Jen. Nat's really not feeling so well, she's lying down, so . . . Sorry, we're going to give dinner a miss.'

Jen smiled through gritted teeth.

'Shall I bring something up to you?'

'That's all right,' he said. 'We're fine.' He was embarrassed, eager to get away. Jen let it go, this was all her fault anyway. So maybe this weekend was going to be a disaster after all.

*7 September 1999*

*Email, from Dan to Lilah, Andrew, Natalie*

*Dear all*

*I'm sorry things turned out the way they did the other night. I didn't set out to hurt or offend anyone, you must know that. I wish you'd given me some time to explain.*

*First, the film is fiction. I know there are places and people and events that look familiar, but it's not supposed to be an accurate reflection of those places or people or events. They were my inspiration. You were my inspiration. But that's all. I wasn't making a film about you or about the accident.*

*Second, and I know this sounds like a lame excuse, but the final edit was not done by me. There were some scenes, particularly at the end, that I objected to. I fought to have some scenes included and others left out, and I lost.*

*I'd like to see you, all of you, to talk to you face to face and to explain exactly what I intended and what I did not intend. Please allow me that.*

*Most of all, please know that I never wanted to hurt any of you. You are my family, you know that.*

*Dan*

27

## Chapter Three

～

Dan had the feeling that this weekend was going to turn into a total disaster. Dinner was painful, no two ways about it. It was the kind of scene which would have been difficult to watch if it had been in a movie, the kind that made you cringe, slide down in your seat and close your eyes; living through it was excruciating. Minute upon minute of insufferable silence as they chewed their food (a good rack of lamb, actually, along with the wine, the only positive point about the evening), Lilah sulking, her Action Man boyfriend uttering the occasional platitude, Jen looking pale and tense.

It fell to Dan to attempt to rescue the evening. He did his best. He told them about Claudia, the beautiful German actress, the new Audi he'd driven all the way from London to Nice, the holiday home he was thinking of buying; finally he talked about his plans for Christmas, the suite he'd booked at the Ritz, where he planned to meet up with Claudia (once she'd broken the bad news to her husband).

He might as well have been talking to himself. Oh, Jen nodded and smiled and actively listened, but he could tell she wasn't really engaging with what he was saying. It was frustrating. It was disappointing. If he was perfectly honest he expected everyone to be rather impressed. His girlfriend was a *film star*, for God's sake.

Lilah didn't appear to have listened to him at all, because the second he stopped talking, she changed the subject, launching into an attack on Jen for setting up this weird reunion in the first place.

'You should at least have told *me* that you weren't telling *them*,' she said to Jen, arranging her face into a perfect pout. 'That was really awkward. And in any case, I don't get why she gets to be pissed off. *She* ran off with *my* boyfriend. *I* should be the one throwing hissy fits.'

'You used to go out with *him*?' the boyfriend asked, an amused expression on his face. 'That bloke upstairs?'

'Yes, she used to go out with *him*,' Dan snapped, instantly feeling defensive of Andrew, who he felt was being insulted in some way. 'What of it?'

'Leave Zac alone,' Lilah said, reaching out to stroke her boyfriend's neck. 'He was only asking.' Lilah leaned forward, interlocking her fingers in front of her face and cocking her head to one side. She flashed him her killer smile and he felt his bowels contract. He shouldn't have said anything; now he'd only gone and drawn her fire.

'Mr Parker,' she said, taking a slurp of her wine. 'The great film director. I haven't seen you for . . . ooh, I don't know. How long has it been, Dan?'

Dan swallowed. 'You know very well how long it's been, Lilah. Thirteen years.'

'Lucky for some,' she said. She picked up the wine bottle and poured the last few drops into her glass. She turned to Zac and said: 'The last time I saw Dan was for the première of his first

29

film. *One Day in June*. It was quite successful, wasn't it, Dan? You must have made quite a bit of money.'

Dan nodded. He kept his eyes on Lilah's face because he couldn't bear to look at Jen's. Of course, he'd known this was coming. He'd prepared himself for a discussion about that film at some point. He'd just hoped there would be a gentler run-in, not Lilah with daggers drawn, on the offensive. He'd hoped to be able to talk to Jen about it alone.

'What was the film about?' Zac asked politely, and Dan wanted dearly at that moment to punch him in the face.

He took a deep breath. 'Well, it was . . .'

'It was supposed to be about Dan's miserable childhood,' Lilah cut in loudly. She picked up the wine bottle and then put it down again. Jen got to her feet to fetch another one. 'But in fact, it wasn't really about him at all. It was about us, about some things that happened to us, and about what terrible people we all were and how wonderful Dan was . . .'

'That is *not* true, Lilah.'

Jen came back to the table with another bottle.

'Am I being unfair, Jen? What did you think of it?'

Dan could hardly bear to look up at her, but when he did, he didn't see anger or sadness, he saw embarrassment.

'Well, I thought . . .'

She hadn't seen it. It had never occurred to him before that she wouldn't have watched it, but right then, he knew. 'Well, the thing is . . .' she tried again.

'You haven't seen it, have you?' Dan asked her.

She shook her head. 'It wasn't shown in the cinema in France,' she said with an apologetic smile. It was, actually, but he didn't bother to correct her, he just smiled and let her pour him another glass of wine.

He ought to feel relieved. He wasn't sure how she'd have reacted to it, she might have hated it. The others did, after all. But he wasn't relieved, he was disappointed. He wanted to know what she felt when she watched it, if she recognised the scenes that she'd influenced, all that time ago, when they'd spent all those nights talking about it. Lilah was right that he'd made a lot of money from the film; it had opened doors for him, it had set his career in motion. It cost him though, he'd paid a price. And if she hadn't seen it, never even wanted to see it, well. Perhaps the price looked a little high.

Dan pushed his seat back, about to make his excuses, get to his feet, go to his room out back, away from them all, to call Claudia, forget about this whole wash of an evening, but Lilah wasn't finished.

'I can't believe you haven't seen his film, Jen,' she said, lighting a cigarette.

'Well, you know, as I said . . .'

'It's available on DVD,' Lilah said cheerfully. 'I think you'll find it interesting.'

'Lilah,' Dan said, 'let's just leave this now, OK?'

'No, why? It's your *masterpiece*. And Jen comes out of it pretty well, doesn't she? A little fickle, I suppose, a bit flighty . . .' The look on Lilah's face was pure malice. 'Hopping from one thing to another . . .'

'Lilah, come on.'

'*I*, on the other hand, come across as a vacuous, drug-addled bitch, don't I?'

'Jesus, Lilah!' Dan got to his feet. 'It's fiction! Jen's not in the film, and neither are you. *Fiction*, OK? It even says so at the beginning: all resemblance to personages living or dead, blah, blah, blah.'

31

'If you say so, Dan,' Lilah said, a thin smile on her lips, one eyebrow raised. She leaned forward and tapped her cigarette on the edge of his glass, flicking the ash into his wine.

An hour later he lay on the bed in the barn listening to the sound of the building creaking. The wind was getting up. He shivered despite the warmth of the room, imagining what it must be like to be out in this weather, up on the hills behind the house or in the woods. He slipped off the bed and clambered down the ladder to make sure that the sliding door was locked, trying vainly to push from his mind a hundred horror movie images, things coming in from the cold, looking for warmth, looking for food. He'd always had a somewhat overactive imagination.

Dan looked at his phone to check the time. It was almost midnight. He was mildly disappointed that he'd no missed calls and no texts, no love notes from Claudia, not even a message asking if he'd got there safely which, when you thought about it, was pretty remiss of her. He had been driving up to the snowy mountains in a fast car, after all. He thought about calling her, but decided that by this time she'd probably be on the plane anyway. And he didn't want to look needy.

He had to force himself to play it cool, always had done. He wasn't very good at it. He thought about his arrival just a few hours earlier, how he'd had all these things in his head that he wanted to say to Jen, to everyone, how he'd wanted to breeze in, nonchalant, clap Andrew on the back and give Lilah a wink and a kiss, and then he'd turned up and there was no one else there and he'd stammered an awkward hello and blushed and not known whether to hug Jen or kiss her, and of course he should have kissed her, but he went for the hug and it was awkward and just . . . ugh. He could feel his face colouring at the memory.

And so he overcompensated, as he always had, withdrawn into himself, so when she'd shown him out here to the barn and told him that her dad had died, he didn't say anything, he barely reacted, he didn't take her in his arms and give her a kiss as he should have done, as a normal person would, as an old friend would. He just froze up and looked away and, Christ, what must she think?

He picked up his phone again and rang Claudia's number. Straight to voicemail, obviously, but then he thought, perhaps she was on the phone when he was calling, perhaps she was dialling him at that very moment, so he rang her again and it went to voicemail again, and now she was going to have two missed calls from him and he was going to look needy.

The wind shrieked and he jumped. There was no way he was getting to sleep without another drink.

*Hi Dan,*

*How's it going? I can't believe Norwich is really as terrible as you claim.*

*Or perhaps it is, because you can't have been going out very much — you've written loads. And it's really good — I'm so impressed. You are a total star. Can't believe how much it's come on since last summer. My detailed notes are enclosed . . .*

*As you'll see, I can't really find all that much wrong with it, although I can't help feeling that it's missing a scene or two. I know that you've written it in your achingly cool, European, slice-of-life style, and I like that, I just wonder whether one moment of drama — something frightening, life-changing, heartbreaking — wouldn't make it more complete? I'm not suggesting you turn it into classic blockbuster, beginning-middle-end stuff. Anyway, as I said, notes enclosed, I think I explain it better in there.*

*How goes the search for funding? I saw Lilah on the weekend, she was saying that she'd be happy to volunteer to help you pitch to City boys — she seems to think she has what it takes to sell to them. I think she might be right. She seemed better, by the way, a little less manic, although she did get really pissed at dinner. Things still seem tense with Andrew, she bit his head off when he suggested they go straight home after closing. Parties to go to, people to see, apparently.*

*Talking of people to see, do you want to come to London this weekend? They're showing A* Night on Earth *at the BFI from this Friday, and you're the only other person I know who actually likes that film. Plus, Conor's going to Ireland (again) to work on his brother's house. Apparently they're almost finished. I've been hearing that since last October . . .*

Conor's well, although he's working incredibly hard, so with that and all the trips to Ireland I feel like we hardly ever get to see each other. My work is heinous. The boss is the biggest bitch I've ever met. Thank God it's only till the summer.

Cannot wait until the summer! Do you think you're going to be able to make it over to France this year? I hope so. I miss hanging out with you.

How's your love life, player? Get up to anything fun on Valentine's Day?

If you're not up to anything fun on the weekend, come and play. And we can talk film stuff.

Lots of love

Jen

# Chapter Four

～

Natalie couldn't sleep. She'd been lying there in the dark, watching the snow fall, listening to Andrew's breathing getting deeper and slower as he drifted further into sleep. She was wide awake, limbs restless, blood throbbing in her head. She could turn on the light. Andrew wouldn't mind, he'd just roll over and go straight back to sleep, and even if he didn't go back to sleep, he wouldn't get pissed off. He'd snuggle in closer and hold her as she read, she knew he would. She didn't feel like reading, though, and she felt even less like being held. In the pit of her stomach, anger roiled like acid.

Her rage at Jen's duplicity had abated not one iota over the past few hours. Throwing them all together unexpectedly was cruel to her, Andrew, and even to Lilah. The worst of it was, she hadn't been able to express these sentiments out loud, not in the forceful way she wanted to. Because in this, Andrew would not be on her side. He would see her point, but he would make allowances. He would forgive. Andrew would always forgive Jen. No one was supposed to get angry with Jen. All this time had passed, rivers, lakes, oceans of water under the bridge, and still, she wasn't supposed to get pissed off with Jen.

Nat was angry, restless and absolutely starving. They hadn't had anything to eat since the Pret a Manger sandwiches they'd bought for the flight, and she'd eaten hers in the departure lounge, couldn't even wait until they'd got onto the plane. She sat up, slowly, trying not to wake Andrew. Carefully, she swung one leg at a time over the edge of the bed, placing her feet on the pleasantly warm wooden floor. She sat up very straight, then twisted her torso gently from side to side, loosening out the muscles and the joints in her back. She ached. Her back was always worse after a journey. Finally, she got to her feet, grabbing one of Andrew's sweatshirts from the suitcase (she'd refused to let him unpack – there was no point as they were *definitely* going to leave the next morning) and crept out onto the landing. The doors to Jen's and Lilah's bedrooms were closed, the lights out. She padded along to the top of the stairs and peered down: there was a warm glow coming from somewhere. The fire still burning, presumably. Running her hand along the wall for guidance, she tiptoed down the stairs, the stone floor cold underfoot.

The fire was burning in the living-room hearth, but the lights were out. Mercifully, there was no one in the kitchen either, so she raided the fridge, helping herself to a wedge of Brie and some crackers which she found in a cupboard. The house was perfectly silent, save for the occasional crackle from the dying fire next door. She ate hurriedly, standing at the kitchen counter, in the dark. She ate a second biscuit, a third, a fourth. She breathed deeply, exhaled.

She felt comforted. She had an emotional relationship with food, that's what her mother told her. Had done for years and years, ever since she spent all that time in hospital. When she came out, she ate. Nat argued that it was better than drink, or an addiction to painkillers. Her mother always smiled at that, said, 'Of course it is, darling,' then went back to her green salad. Her mother was a size eight and liked to talk about the fact that she could still fit into the suit she'd worn as her going-away outfit at her wedding.

The corrosive feeling in her gut subsided; she could almost feel her blood sugar rising, the tension ebbing out of her neck and shoulders. She piled a few more biscuits onto her plate and took her bounty through to the living room, still dimly lit by a few hot coals in the grate. She sat down in one of the battered leather armchairs, her plate balanced on her knees, and ate.

They used to cook on the fire, the summer they spent here. There wasn't a stove back then, just a hotplate they bought from Leclerc, so they either barbecued out back or cooked on the fire, in here. They toasted bread and baked potatoes, cooked fish wrapped in foil. This was the room they lived in. They even used to sleep here, sometimes, when it rained. They couldn't go upstairs because the roof was leaking and, in any case, it wasn't entirely safe upstairs in the early days. Natalie and Lilah always had to be closest to the fire, because they were always coldest. Andrew would lie at Lilah's back, his arms around her. Jen and Conor used to curl up in the corner underneath the window; Dan liked to lie against the opposite wall. He was paranoid about sparks from the fire setting his sleeping bag alight.

The memory of it brought a lump to her throat. She remembered waking in the grey dawn light, opening her eyes, and the first thing she would see in the morning would be Lilah's face, long lashes against her skin, her blonde hair falling over her shoulders. And if Natalie raised herself up a little, to rest on one elbow, the next thing she would see would be Andrew, his face half hidden in Lilah's neck. Sometimes, he'd be awake too, and he'd look up at her and smile, mouth 'morning', silently.

The bitter and the sweet. Spending all summer with her best friend, falling hopelessly for her best friend's boyfriend, trying with everything she had not to want him. Failing. Trying again. Andrew didn't have complicated memories of this place: when he thought of the French house, he thought of Conor, long summer days, the two of them working side by side, up on the rafters, fixing the roof or drinking ice-cold beers on the front lawn, beautiful girlfriends in bikinis at their sides. Natalie had been just a friend to him then. She was Lilah's sidekick, quiet and bookish, sitting under the oak trees in the shade in case she got sunburnt.

Natalie's feelings about the French house were wound tightly up in knots, impossible to unravel. There were flashes of intense happiness wound up with memories of desperate, hopeless longing, and the sting of guilt.

She'd liked the early mornings best, before the sun got too strong. It became her habit to walk to the village first thing, often leaving the others sleeping, to buy fresh bread or croissants. It was just under six miles there and back, a good hour and a half's walk, brisk on the way down, slower back up. Six miles! She could barely do two these days. Sometimes Andrew used to join her; sometimes he used to walk down with her and then run back up – he'd been a keen sportsman at university and didn't want to get out of shape. They would argue politics or talk books, occasionally just walking in companionable silence, the beauty of the Alpine foothills in summertime stretching out in front of them.

There were times on those walks when Natalie imagined she

saw something in Andrew's expression, or heard something in the tone of his voice, that suggested that his feelings for her weren't purely platonic any more.

Sometimes, if she'd landed a particularly devastating verbal punch or made an especially astute observation, he'd stop and turn to her and smile or shake his head with a look in his eyes that suggested something like awe, and her heart would race.

Back at the house, she'd watch Lilah sanding a floor or varnishing one of the doors, beautiful even with paint on her face, dripping with sweat, always laughing about something, loud, undeniable. Natalie would look at her then and think: how ridiculous, even for a second, to imagine that Andrew could want her when he had Lilah. She'd think how awful she was, to imagine such things. She'd think how empty her life would be, how drab, without Lilah in it. Sometimes the guilt grabbed her around the throat and shook her, crushed her trachea, stopped her breathing.

Natalie felt the itch of salt water on her skin and realised that she had started to cry. She got to her feet, took her empty plate into the kitchen, her eyes taking a moment to readjust to the darkness. Through the back window she thought she saw movement outside in the courtyard and she gasped. There was someone there – she heard the noise of someone trying the door handle. A cry caught in her throat. The door opened, the light came on.

'Jesus!' Dan literally jumped into the air when he saw her. 'What are you doing skulking around in the dark?'

'I couldn't sleep.'

'You nearly gave me a heart attack.'

'I didn't realise you were out there. I thought . . .' She stopped herself because it sounded too stupid to say out loud. She saw

40

the shadow and she thought of Conor, thought of him creeping in late at night after he'd been out back, working in the shed.

'I just fancied another beer. I'm not used to going to bed so early.' It was just after two in the morning. Dan made his way over to the fridge, seeming a little unsteady on his feet, as though this beer might be the latest in a series. 'Join me, Nat?'

She'd forgotten, in her fright, to be cross with him. Now, hearing him say her name, she remembered.

'No, I won't have a beer. I'll leave you to it,' she said.

'Oh, come on Nat.' He grinned at her, the cheeky boyish grin, coupled with the single raised eyebrow, that she remembered so well. He had used it, in the past, with considerable success.

Never on Natalie, though. She fixed him with a stern look. 'Don't. Don't talk to me like we're friends.'

'Nat. Come on.' He took two beers out of the fridge, held one out to her. 'Please? Have a drink with me.'

Against her better judgement, she took it. They went into the living room and sat by the fire. Dan tried to make small talk.

'How're the kids, Nat? They getting on OK? How old are they now? Eight or nine, must be?'

'They're twelve.'

'No. Really?'

'Yes, Dan, really.'

'Amazing.' A pause. 'So, you look well. Everything all right?' It was painful. He started to babble on, apologising to her for not getting in touch for such a long time, for not coming to see them. He'd been very busy, working, travelling. Nat was only half listening. All she could think was, what was she doing there?

'How many years has it been?' Dan's question caught her attention.

'Seven.'

'No. Really? Seven years? Amazing.'

'We had dinner, remember? You took us to Nobu. You were with that actress, the Spanish one. Emaciated, coked-up. Can't remember her name.'

'Elena.'

'That's it.'

'It was a good night, wasn't it?'

'No, Dan, it wasn't. Your actress obviously thought Andrew and I were insufferably boring, talking about banalities like our kids and our jobs, you spent the night looking around the room to see if you could spot any of your famous friends, and Andrew ended up with food poisoning.'

'Oh. I'm sorry.' He looked hurt. 'I remember us having a good time.'

'You always were rather good at rewriting history.'

'Ah, Nat.'

She knew what he was thinking, so she cut him off. 'I'm not talking about the film. Forget the bloody film, I have. I'm talking about this—' She gestured around her. 'All this. What are we even doing here? I don't understand why we're trying to turn the clock back, this whole nostalgia trip. It's about pretending we're all still friends, isn't it?'

'We are still friends.'

'No, we're not. You can't even remember the ages of my children. We're not friends. And you know what, I'm not even sure we ever were. I was best friends with Lilah, who was going out with Andrew, who was Conor's best friend, and Conor was going out with Jen. I'm not really sure how you came into it.'

As the words came out of her mouth she regretted them, even before she saw Dan wince.

'That isn't fair. You were very important to me, all of you. You were my family.'

Like a killer feeling the knife slide in, past the point of no return, she blundered on. 'OK, at college, there was a kind of closeness, I admit that. You used to try to sleep with me, in between girlfriends, just because I wasn't sleeping with anyone else. I think you might have pitied me.'

Dan shook his head. 'That isn't true,' he said, 'that is not true.'

'But now? What are we now? Any of us? What's left to hold us together? I'm no longer friends with Lilah, who's no longer going out with Andrew, who has no best friend because Conor's dead. So what's left?'

*Dearest Jen,*

*I'm sending this to you care of your parents. I don't know where you are. I don't know whether they will pass this on to you.*

*I am so sorry.*

*The words seem as meaningless written down as they sound when I saw them. But you know, only you know, how sorry I am. He's gone, three weeks and six days. It seems impossible.*

*My mother lost her father when she was just a teenager. She came to see me yesterday and told me that the hardest thing was this: once the funeral was over, and an 'appropriate' length of time had passed, people expect you to get on. Get up, get dressed, brush your teeth, go to work. It seems impossible.*

*My parents have been kind. I know they are disappointed, they are heartbroken, I know they are ashamed, desperately ashamed. They hide it well. I am going to go and stay with them, as soon as I get Lilah settled with her mother. I can't leave her alone.*

*Ronan came to see me last weekend. He was very kind, too. He brought me some things – photographs, Conor's collection of electro on vinyl, things he thought Conor might want me to have. It was unbearable. I wished, I longed for him to hit me, to ball his fists, to hit me and keep on hitting me, until there was nothing left.*

*We went for a pint at the Greyhound. When he left, he shook my hand, clapped me on the back, and said, 'Will I be seeing you, then?' If I'd closed my eyes at that moment, if I'd just listened to his voice, his intonation, I would have sworn it was Conor. Nothing on this earth could have persuaded me otherwise. I couldn't say anything, I just walked away.*

*I replay it, in my head, every night. Everything I did, didn't do, every wrong decision. I would give my life to take it back.*

*I don't know where you are. Please come back.*

*I am so sorry.*


*With love,*


*Andrew*


*P.S. Nat is awake. She came out of the coma ten days ago, and is now speaking normally and there are no signs of brain damage. The doctors are still unsure about whether or not she will regain a full range of movement. She asks after you. She told me that she dreamed you came to see her. I said that you did, while she was unconscious. Perhaps you spoke to her? Perhaps she could hear you.*

# Chapter Five

~

Andrew lay on his side, his eyes fixed on the group of freckles on Natalie's neck, just below her hairline. His wife lay with her back to him, facing the window. The curtains were drawn, but a bright sliver of sunlight, slicing through a gap between the drapes, fell across the bed, across Natalie's shoulder, illuminating the tip of the scar which started at the base of her neck and traced halfway down her back, running parallel to her spine. He wanted to touch her, but he daren't. He didn't want to wake her. Assuming she was still asleep – and he hoped, fervently hoped that she was still sleeping, although he doubted it was possible, what with all the noise.

On the other side of the wall behind their headboard, Lilah and her boyfriend were having loud and enthusiastic sex. They had been at it for some time now, and yet Andrew was pretty sure they still had a way to go. It may have been more than fifteen years since he'd last heard them, but Andrew remembered Lilah's sex noises and he knew that she wasn't quite there yet.

It didn't help that, aside from Lilah's ecstatic cries, the house was in perfect silence. No birdsong, no traffic, no aeroplanes overhead, no police sirens. The whole world muffled and muted by snow. Andrew desperately wanted to press his fingers into his ears to drown out the din, but he didn't dare move because then Natalie would know for sure that he was awake and that the two of them had been lying there, listening to a kind of passion and excitement which they now seemed incapable of finding together, and he didn't want to do that to her. He wanted her to be able to pretend that he was sleeping too.

But then the moaning started. It wasn't Lilah, he was sure, it was the boyfriend, and that was even worse. It was horrible, a guttural, animal sound somewhere between pain and pleasure and Andrew couldn't stand it for another second. He whipped the duvet back and jumped out of bed, grabbed his sweatshirt that for some reason was hanging over the chair next to the bedroom door, and made his exit as quickly as possible, without looking back at his wife.

Downstairs, Jennifer, wearing jeans and a voluminous poncho-type jumper thing with an apron on top, was standing next to the range oven, frying sausages, listening to the radio which was playing some kind of awful French pop. She was singing along, her voice soft and tuneless. For a moment he just stood at the foot of the stairs, watching her: her raven hair, long and lustrous, curling down her back, the line of her neck, her pale, creamy skin, as youthful as he remembered. She was still so lovely. She looked back at him over her shoulder and caught him staring.

'Smells delicious,' he said, striding into the kitchen.

Jen put down the fork she was holding and turned to greet him, cocking her head a little and giving him a smile, a deep dimple appearing in her left cheek. He wanted to give her a hug, but he didn't, he just froze, overwhelmed by the most intense rush of happiness combined with a sense of regret so powerful it brought a lump to his throat. He had to turn away.

On the other side of the kitchen counter was a table, a square slab of pale ash, solid as a butcher's block. He stared at it, took a step forward, traced his fingers along its smooth surface. He could feel Jen's eyes on him. He turned back to her and they both smiled.

'Hello, big brother,' she said.

'Hey, little sister.'

Jen wiped her hands on her apron and came over to him, wrapping her arms around him. They stood there, holding each other, for a long time. The brother/sister thing started at university, a silly joke, their way of mocking Conor's briefly held fear that his best friend and his girlfriend had become a little too close.

She let him go.

'You want coffee?' she asked. 'Eggs, sausages?'

'Yes to all.'

'Good. Still take your coffee black?'

'Actually, I'm embarrassed to say that I'm more a herbal tea than a coffee person these days, but I'll take it as it comes.'

She laughed. 'Herbal tea? Good Lord, what has she done to you?' Then he laughed too, but the silence that followed was awkward, the unnamed 'she' hanging in the air.

Jen placed the coffee on a coaster in front of him. He took a sip; it was strong and bitter, it sent a prickle over his skin. It tasted wonderful, like cigarettes and cheap red wine; it tasted of youth. He slipped his hand underneath the table, ran his finger along the ridges underneath, crisp carved lettering. He traced the grooves with his forefinger, spelling out a name. Jennifer. This was her spot.

'What will you do,' he asked, looking up at Jen, 'with this? With all the furniture? When you sell?'

'Depends on who I sell it to, I suppose. It's most likely going to be a holiday home so I imagine they'll want to keep quite a bit of it. The armchairs and the sofa are probably ready for a skip, though.' She either didn't realise what he was asking or was purposefully ignoring it.

'Isn't it hard,' he asked, gentle still, tentative, moving around the subject, 'to think of selling the place?'

'It's harder to live here.' She stopped moving for a moment, put down her kitchen utensils, wiped her hands, the expression on her face intense. 'I think, with time, I would grow to love it again. I think I would. But there are circumstances,' she said mysteriously, 'which prevent me from staying here long enough to find out.'

Andrew imagined for a moment something sinister, a *Jean de Florette* situation, someone attempting to drive away the pesky English interloper.

'And I'm afraid. I feel afraid when I'm here.'

It was something sinister, he was sure of it.

'Oh, don't look like that!' she said, smiling at him. 'It's nothing terrible. It's just lonely up here. It's creepy at night, when you're all by yourself – everything creaks and the wind howls, and it's just so isolated. I lie in bed thinking about how I might be chopped to bits with an axe and no one would hear me scream.' She laughed again and he did too; it was impossible not to, her laugh was like music. 'I think if I stayed here I'd end up turning into Jack Nicholson in *The Shining*, seeing creepy children everywhere.'

'That was his son.'

'Sorry?'

'His son saw the creepy twins. He went nuts and tried to kill

49

everyone. And wrote what can only be described as a very dull book.'

'Oh, yes. All work and no play . . .' Jen selected the largest and most lethal-looking of the knives in the rack on the counter and brandished it at him. 'Now you know my real intention behind inviting you here . . .'

There was a small sound from around the corner, the clearing of a throat. Jen immediately put down the knife and stopped giggling. Andrew leaned to one side to get a look: Natalie was standing there, suitcase beside her, looking less than amused.

'Oh, hello darling,' he said. 'Come and have a cup of coffee.' She didn't move.

'Milk and sugar, Nat?' Jen asked her.

Natalie passed her hand over her eyes. 'OK,' she said. 'But just a quick one. Andrew and I need to get going.'

'Nat,' Jen pleaded. 'Please stay.'

'No, Jen. Not under these circumstances. Don't you see that's it's completely unfair, what you did, bringing us here under false pretences . . .'

'That's a bit strong,' Andrew said, and almost instantly regretted it. Natalie turned to him and threw her hands up, shaking her head.

'What a surprise. You're taking her side.'

'There aren't any sides, Nat. I just think that now we're here . . .'

'We can enjoy the reunion? No. I don't want a reunion. I don't want a walk down memory lane. I came here for you, Andrew, because you wanted to come, but to come here and find we've been lied to . . .'

Jen walked over to her and took Natalie's hands in her own. Nat tried for a moment to pull away, but gave up.

'I'm sorry, Nat. I was wrong. I actually can't quite believe I did that. After I did, I kept trying to think of ways to tell you that Lilah would be here too without you cancelling. I chickened out. I thought that once you got here, and you saw everyone, once you were here at the house . . .'

'That we'd forgive you. Well, you were half right.'

'Stay for lunch. You have to stay for lunch.'

'We don't *have* to . . .'

'No, you really do. Have you looked outside?' As one, they turned and looked out of the window, where virgin snow lay inches thick on the window sills and the lawn outside. 'We must have had a foot of snow last night. You're not going anywhere for a good few hours. There is a snow plough in the village, it usually does this road, but it might not be until this afternoon. You're stuck here, for the moment. Sorry.'

Natalie cleared her throat. She sighed. 'Can I use your landline then?' Her voice was tight, as though something was pressing against her throat. 'Or the internet? Do you have internet access? I can't get a signal and I want to contact my daughters.'

'Of course you can. The phone's upstairs, or there's a laptop in my room.' As Natalie turned to walk upstairs, Jen shot Andrew an anxious glance, gave him a guilty little shrug, a half-smile.

He let it go. He knew what Jen was thinking. Had Nat always been so tightly wound? Did she always have such a bad temper? Well, no, she didn't. And it wasn't temper now. It was a lot more complicated than that. The thing was, with Nat, that you had to learn to read the signs. Anyone else looking at her, the stiffness of her movements, the way she stood with her arms folded across her body, hands on opposite elbows, would think that she was tense, defensive, closed off. They would listen to her voice and hear that strained tone and imagine that she was about to throw a tantrum.

But Andrew didn't hear plaintive, he heard exhausted. And he could see, from the way she turned to speak to him – the way she turned her whole body, not just her head – that her back was bothering her, more than usual. She held her arms like that to remind herself to stand straight, which eased the strain on her spine and helped, in a small way, to alleviate her pain. The thing you had to realise with Natalie was that she lived with pain. Some days were worse than others. But what other people didn't realise about Natalie was that she was the bravest person Andrew knew.

So when Natalie talked about 'her daughters', he let it slide. When she turned on her heel and stomped off upstairs to try to call them, he smiled at Jen and said, 'It'll be all right. Once she's spoken to the girls and had something to eat, she'll start to feel better. Her back, you know.'

'I know. Some days are worse than others.'

So he'd said it to her before. He must have said it in letters, he couldn't remember saying it to her face. There were, after all, only a handful of occasions on which he could have said it; they had seen each other only a couple of times in the past sixteen years, just twice since the funeral. Andrew and Natalie visited her once, in Paris, when the girls were about five or six, and Jen was living with her then-husband, an other-wordly academic old enough to be her father. They'd seen each other briefly when Jen's father died. But they had not attended Jen's wedding, and Jen had not attended theirs, she had not been there when his children were born, or when they were christened, or for his fortieth birthday party. He'd asked, but Jen didn't like coming back to England, she was obstinate on this point, and Natalie hated to travel. After a while, he'd resigned himself sadly to the fact that his relationship with Jen would be conducted by letter.

Jen set a plate of eggs and sausages down in front of him.

'I hope you can persuade her to stay,' she said. 'It's been too long, Andrew. We've left it much too long.'

Maybe it was the defensiveness he felt about Natalie, maybe it was just the rush from the caffeine making him light-headed, but he had to bite back the urge to snap: 'And whose fault is that, Jen?' Instead, he asked her:

'How long have you been living here? *Are* you living here, or are you still in Paris? Is this just a holiday?' The questions made his point. I don't know anything about your life.

Jen sat down opposite him, a cup of coffee cradled between her hands, her head bent, hair falling forward so he couldn't read her expression.

'I've decided to move back to England,' she said softly. 'I don't want to be here any more. And I don't mean here, exactly, I mean in France. As for here, in this house, as I said. It's so isolated, it's not the right sort of place . . . It's lonely. And everywhere I look, in every room, on every wall, in every joist and hinge and door handle, at the table we're sitting at, there are reminders, of what it once was. That once upon a time it was anything but lonely, when it was so full of us.' She looked up at him and smiled. 'But more than that, it's just not practical. So I've decided to sell up and move to England. And I want . . .' she hesitated, her voice cracking a little. 'Look, I know I don't deserve this, but I want to be part of your lives again. I want you to be part of mine. I want to know your daughters' – she held up her hand to stop him talking – 'and yes, I know, it's a bit late for that, but I'm asking anyway. I'm asking you to forgive me.'

*Dear Andrew,*

*I should have done this ages ago, I've tried so many times to put down in words how sorry I am for leaving the way I did, for abandoning you. I find it impossible.*

*My mother has forwarded the letters that you wrote to me. Thank you.*

*I am starting over. Trying to start over. I saw no other way.*

*I am all right. I am living in France now, working in the translation department at one of the big advertisers. It's not thrilling, but it is absorbing, as well as really hard work. Absorption and exhaustion, I think, have been good for me. I imagined, when I left, that I would be gone for a matter of months and here I am eighteen months on and still trying to start over.*

*I think that I did the right thing, by leaving, though I understand if you don't see it that way. I think about you all the time, you and Lilah and Nat and Dan. I think about you, but I cannot imagine how I would cope with being around you again, without him there with me. I cannot imagine it, just the thought of it sends me into a panic, it closes my throat.*

*My life here is quite solitary, and although I am lonely, I don't mind it all that much. I work all week and on the weekends I shop and cook, but mostly I walk. I feel I know every inch of Paris now, every park from Luxembourg to Buttes Chaumont, every cobbled street and every market. One day, when things are better, I would love to show it to you.*

*I was not in the least surprised to hear that you and Nat are together now. I think that the two of you were always going to end up together, no matter what. I think we all did, even Lilah. I imagine she took it hard, but she falls on her feet, that girl. She will forgive you.*

*If you see him, will you give Dan my love?*

*I hope you don't think me too selfish, I know you must think me
weak. I don't know what to say. Only, every night I have the same
nightmare, and every morning I wake up to find out that it's true.*

*I love you, dearest friend. I miss you.*

*Jen*

## Chapter Six

~

About a quarter way up the stairs, Lilah stood silently, eavesdropping. Straining to hear what was being said, trying to gauge the mood. She could hear Andrew and Jen, no one else. Jen was talking about selling up and moving to England. Oh Christ, maybe she *was* dying. She didn't look like she was dying, though. She looked positively Rubenesque. Lilah tiptoed down a couple more steps. Now Jen was apologising to Andrew.

What for? It couldn't just be for inviting him here without giving him the full guest list, surely? She must be talking about before. Leaving the way she did. It had been cold, sure enough, but Lilah might well have done the same thing herself, had she been in Jen's shoes. Just get away, start over. Nothing worse than the post-mortem, the endless dissection and reconstruction of events. Better to just put it somewhere, store it away and try to forget. She doubted Andrew would understand. He had the opposite reaction to momentous events: he wanted to examine everything in minute detail, as though somehow meaning could be found there.

She decided to slip outside for a preparatory cigarette before she faced the others. Stealthily she crept past the entrance to the kitchen, her red silk kimono swishing gently against the stone walls, lifted the heavy latch on the front door and snuck out into the snow.

The cold took her breath away; it was like having a bucket of ice water thrown in her face. It was almost painfully light, the sun reflecting bright and harsh as steel off the snow. She regretted leaving her sunglasses upstairs, she regretted not getting properly dressed before coming out here: underwear, a scant layer of silk and Ugg boots were not appropriate attire. Still. She lit a cigarette, inhaling deeply and feeling, for the first time since she'd arrived, that it had been a good idea to come.

She didn't think about it much, but if you'd told her all of a sudden that the French house had been sold, she could never go back there, it would have made her sad. She would have regretted never again having the chance to stand on this step and look out over the sweep of the front lawn, down to the dry stone wall and beyond. It triggered something in her. No, the wrong expression – being here was like lifting a veil, giving her once more a clear view of things long ago obscured. It brought back fragments of memory, like echoes, flickering images, a silent movie on a wall.

She remembered, for the first time in forever, having a row with Andrew in the kitchen, something minor, something ludicrously petty, like her retuning the radio to Mélodie FM when he wanted to listen to the World Service. The row had escalated, and eventually Lilah had stomped off upstairs in a sulk, throwing herself on the bed, pulling the sheet up over her head. She just wanted to be somewhere else. She was sick of this place, sick of the unrelenting heat, sick of the dust and cobwebs and back-breaking bloody work. She wanted to be in

Juans-les-Pins, where she used to go with her mum when she was younger, before the money ran out. She wanted to be on the private beach at the Hotel Belles Rives. Did they really have to spend the entire summer in this place, Jen's dad's unpaid lackeys?

There was a soft knock on the door.

'Piss off!' she'd yelled.

'Lilo?' It was Natalie.

'Sorry, Nat,' she called out, the sheet still pulled over her head. 'Thought you were Arsehole.'

Natalie pushed the door open gently. 'Oh, don't be like that. You know how he is if he can't get his daily fix of current events.'

Lilah groaned. 'I'm just so sick of it here. Can't we go somewhere else?' She pulled the sheet off her head and sat up straight. 'I know! Let's nick Andrew's car and drive to the coast.'

'Lilah, we can't do that . . .'

'We can! Just for a day, or two. We can go swimming in the Med, pick up sexy French boys . . . We deserve it!'

Natalie clambered onto the bed next to her, getting under the sheet and pulling it back up over their heads, like a tent. 'We can't do that. And you don't want to pick up French boys, you're just cross.' Lilah rolled onto her side, draping her arm over Natalie's body.

'Don't you long for it sometimes, though? The idea of being elsewhere.'

Natalie rolled onto her side too, so they were facing, their noses almost touching.

'I'm happy here.'

Nat went into the room next door and robbed a spliff out of Dan's cigarette case. They sat on the bed and smoked it, and

58

then Nat decided that, because Lilah had been denied the joys of Radio Mélodie FM, she would sing French pop songs, to cheer her up. They lay on the bed and laughed and laughed until tears ran down their faces, until they were gasping for breath. All of a sudden Nat leapt up, scrambling to get off the bed. She just about made it to the door and then she stood there, bent over a little, her knees knocking inwards, her face red turning to puce.

'Nat? Are you all right? Nat? Are you peeing yourself?'

Seventeen years later, Lilah stood on the doorstep and laughed out loud. She flicked her cigarette butt into the snow, desperate all of a sudden to run inside and say, 'Do you remember the time Nat peed herself?' But she couldn't, of course, because she was sworn to secrecy on pain of death, so the only people who knew that Nat had peed herself were Nat and Lilah. And she had a feeling Nat wouldn't find it funny any more.

She was too cold to stand outside any longer, so she pushed the front door open and crept back inside.

'Good morning,' she said, popping her head around the kitchen doorway. 'Any coffee going?'

'Lilah! Jesus. You're blue, do you know that?' Jen looked horrified. 'Were you outside? I thought I heard the door go – what on earth were you doing?' Jen caught hold of her wrist and pulled her over next to the wood burner. 'Sit there. I'll get you a cup of coffee.'

Lilah allowed herself to be dragged over to the fire; she flashed Andrew her best naughty little girl smile.

'Went out for a fag, innit?' She gave him a wink. 'How are you, Drew? You look knackered.'

'Thank you, Lilah. You look . . . freezing.' Lilah sat down and crossed her legs, allowing her kimono to slip off her thighs. From underneath lowered lids, she looked up at him.

'Oh, come on. I look better than that, don't I?'

He shook his head impatiently, as though dealing with a naughty child, but she could see the blush creeping up from the neckline of his sweatshirt.

Fights over radio stations notwithstanding, they had been very happy here, she and Andrew. Yes, she would have liked to escape to the Riviera to drink cocktails and go dancing every once in a while, but most of the time she was content, working on the house and working on her tan, playing volleyball on the lawn, making love with Andrew on steamy afternoons in the bedroom upstairs, the two of them bronzed and fit, as perfectly, beautifully athletic as they were ever going to be. Looking at him now, greying, a little overweight, his shoulders a little hunched, his jaw just a bit too heavy, the contrast with that Andrew might have been shocking. Only Lilah wasn't shocked, because the grey, and the exhaustion, and the slope of his shoulders, that hadn't taken the best part of twenty years. That came pretty much overnight, and she'd been there to witness it.

Dan and Nat entered the room, from opposite directions, at almost exactly the same time. Lilah smiled at Natalie, who ignored her, and went over to speak to Andrew in hushed tones. Lilah sighed loudly.

'Do you have tomato juice, Jen? I fancy a Bloody Mary. Dan? Can I tempt you?'

Dan shrugged, then nodded. His eyes were only half open and bloodshot, he looked like he hadn't had much sleep.

'Bloody Mary, Jen?' She declined. 'How about you two?' she asked, addressing Andrew and Natalie.

Natalie looked up at her, face expressionless, mouth set in a line.

'Ummm . . .' Andrew said.

60

'No, thank you, we're fine,' Natalie said. Nothing. Not the slightest flicker of emotion.

Lilah lowered her eyes, looking over her shoulder at Andrew, a half-smile on her lips. 'You sure? Drew?' She could see the muscle tense in Nat's jaw, but she didn't say anything. Lilah was a little disappointed, she thought that one would have landed for sure. After all, no one but Lilah had ever called him Drew: to them he was always Andrew. She'd just have to push harder. 'Come on,' she said, grin widening. 'You know you want to.' She slid one leg off the other and got up to make the cocktails. She could feel Natalie's eyes boring into her back and her adrenaline starting to rise.

Lilah turned her attention to Dan, who was eyeing her a little nervously. He was thinking about what she'd said the night before, she could tell. He was wondering whether she was going to start up again, to give him a hard time. She smiled at him sweetly as she handed him his drink.

'You sleep OK, sweetie?' she asked.

'Uh. Yeah, fine, thanks.' He looked puzzled, which was just the way she wanted him. She needed to throw him off his game, wrong-foot him. Start off mean, then go charming. Like negging, only backwards. That's the way to get what you want from them. She sat down at Dan's side, directly opposite Andrew, diagonally opposite Natalie. Jen buzzed around them, bringing food, pouring coffee. The fire crackled, the sun shone. Lilah raised her glass.

'Cheers, everyone,' she said with a smile. 'It really is lovely to see you all again.'

They clinked. Lilah enjoyed their slightly bemused expressions.

'Is your . . . uh . . . is Zac not joining us for breakfast?' Jen asked her, placing a large jug of orange juice in the centre of the table.

'He's still in bed,' Lilah replied. 'Let him sleep,' she went on coyly, keeping her eyes down. 'I think I may have worn him out.' She looked up at Andrew and smiled.

Andrew's cheeks reddened again, Natalie rolled her eyes, exhaling through pursed lips.

Lilah wasn't looking for the eyeroll, though, she didn't just want an exasperated sigh. She wanted Natalie to say something, she wanted her to react. Any sort of reaction would do, even a furious one. She just couldn't bear *this*, the silence, the sense of being ignored, the utter disconnect. Even last night, when Natalie was angry, she was angry with Jen, she engaged with *Jen*. Lilah got the feeling that all Natalie wanted of her was to go away.

There had been a time when she and Nat had lived each other's lives, shared every joy and failure, finished each other's sentences. They used to talk for hours and hours into the night, planning their glorious futures. They were going to share a flat together in London; Nat would be working on her novel, Lilah, with visions of Sam Jones in her head, would make a fortune in PR. They were going to travel to the Far East, to South America, drive across the United States or Australia. Sometimes Andrew was going to come with them, sometimes he was curiously absent. They had such plans, before the fall. Before.

*14 January 1996*
*Email, from Natalie to Lilah*

*Hi Lilo,*

*I hope you're feeling better. I thought I'd write this down, as we don't seem to be getting anywhere on the phone.*

*I'm worried. This isn't like you, it isn't like you to not show up when we've arranged to meet, or to ignore my calls.*

*I know you said it was nothing I'd done, but I can't help but feel that it must be: why else wouldn't you talk to me? You always talk to me. Sometimes even when I don't want you to . . . !*

*I know you're feeling bad about the office party, but come on. Everyone behaves like an idiot at office parties. Don't feel too bad. I'm sure you weren't the worst.*

*I was thinking, maybe we could do a January health kick thing together. I am huge (134 pounds! Aaargh), and I could really do with a fitness buddy. We can stay off the booze for a bit, eat healthy, go running . . . It'll be fun. OK, it'll be hell, but we'll find a way to make it fun.*

*Love you*

*X Nat*

*15 January 1996*
*Email, from Lilah to Natalie*

*Hi darling. In haste, at work with hangover from hell, trying not to catch my colleagues' eyes as there was a bit of an indiscretion last*

63

*night. Again. I know. Bad, bad Lilah. No way in hell am I going teetotal in January. I'd rather die. Talk soon xxx*

*Lilo*


15 January 1996
Email, from Natalie to Lilah

*Lilah, come on. You need to sort this, you can't keep doing this. And I don't want to know, I don't want to be told these things. Andrew is my friend, you know very well how much I care about him. Don't treat him like this. Come round tonight? We'll have a quiet night in, talk a bit.*

*X Nat*


17 January 1996
Email, from Lilah to Natalie

*Hello. Sorry I didn't get back to you, it's mad busy here. Don't go mental! When I say indiscretion, I don't mean that kind of indiscretion. Just a bit of silly flirting and then I felt like an idiot the next day. Same old, same old. And yes, I know you love Andrew. I love Andrew too, but oh God, Nat. I need to talk to you because things are just going badly and I don't know what to do, stick or twist. When I think about it clearly, I think it might be over. Can we meet up? You free on Tuesday? I have to go to a cocktail thing in Soho but we could do something after xx Lilo*

*17 January 1996*
*Email, from Natalie to Lilah*


*You don't mean that, Lilo. It's not over.*


*19 January 1996*
*Email, from Lilah to Natalie*


*Nat, I need to cancel tonight. Sorry sorry sorry. Had a very late one last night, feeling totally ragged, just have to sleep. And you're right, I didn't mean it. I need him so much right now, sometimes I feel like he's the only thing anchoring me to the earth.*

*Xx Lilo*

# Chapter Seven

~

Jen wasn't sure the Bloody Marys were a very good idea. She wasn't sure that alcohol before lunchtime was ever a great idea, but in a situation this delicately balanced, it was almost certain to cause trouble. Unless, of course, it served to lubricate away the friction. So far, it was difficult to tell. Lilah was being oddly charming to Dan, with whom she'd been so sharp the previous night, and predictably spiky with Nat, obviously trying to bait her by flirting with Andrew. So far, Natalie had maintained a dignified, tight-lipped silence, but Jen couldn't see that lasting.

They needed a distraction. Jen needed to wrest control of the conversation from Lilah. She sat down at the table, topped up everyone's coffee, and cleared her throat, as though about to give a speech. They all looked up at her, expectant.

'I know that you must all think it odd, this sudden urge to get the old gang back together. It *is* odd. And, of course, it isn't just about this house. It's hard for me to explain, but I wanted to apologise to you, all of you.' She was looking at Andrew as she said this. 'I never meant for things to turn out the way they did, I never meant for my absence to be so permanent.' Andrew covered her hand with his, but she didn't look up at the others, she needed to get this said. 'When I left, I thought it best that I just had some time, a little while, cut off. Not just from you – from London, from England, from everything he touched, everywhere we'd been together. I meant to come back. Only, I got stuck. It's difficult to explain. I said that already, didn't I?'

She looked up at their faces, all of them were watching her intently, expressions ranging from the compassionate to the quizzical. 'You think this is ridiculous. It sounds so self-indulgent.' Jen couldn't miss the dip of Natalie's eyes, silent acquiescence. 'I just wanted to tell you that I'm sorry. For running away. For making things worse.'

There was a moment of silence, then Lilah spoke.

'So what happened? We heard you went to Ireland, to stay with Conor's mother. Which, to be honest, Jen, doesn't sound much like *getting away from everything he touched*.'

'That was only for a few weeks, Lilah. I went back to my parents after that, and then I got a job offer in Paris and it sounded like the perfect thing. I could go for six months, a year, get my head straight, come back. We could pick up again, we would be together again.'

'Only you didn't come back.' Dan had that look again, that cool detachment, as though he were watching her at one remove.

'As I said, I was stuck. The story I'd written for myself, about what happened, to us, to Conor, about how I was going to live with it, to cope, it became this inescapable thing, as though it had its own life. It took over mine.'

'But you did move on, didn't you?' Natalie said. 'You got married to Jean-Luc, you made a life for yourself.'

'And it didn't work out. It felt as though I wasn't on the right road, as though I'd taken a diversion. And it wasn't fair on him. He was a good man and I made him unhappy. So the marriage ended, and I tried to start again.' She turned her coffee cup in her hands, round and round. 'There was someone else. I met someone else, a long time after Jean-Luc. Nicolas. It felt different this time, it felt real, as real as anything I've felt since Conor.'

She ran the fingers of her right hand along the surface of the table, all the way to the corner.

'Do you remember the grand unveiling?' she asked them. Dan looked down, surprised.

'This is it? This is Conor's table? It's still here? God, I didn't realise . . .'

'He worked on it all summer,' Nat said, she too now touching its surface with her fingertips. 'It was supposed to be a secret, only everyone found out apart from Jen.'

'And we all had to act really surprised when he uncovered it,' Lilah went on, 'but it was totally obvious we all knew what it was because we were really rubbish actors.'

'But we didn't know what was underneath,' Andrew said. One by one, they all slipped down off their chairs until the five of them were crouched beneath the table, necks bent at awkward angles, trying to get a look at the carving in the underside of the wood. Around the edges, their names: Jennifer Donleavy, Andrew Moorcroft, Lilah Lewis, Dan Parker, Natalie Hewson, Conor Sheridan; and in the centre, 'For all of us, forever', and the date: 21 August 1995.

Andrew banged his head crawling back out from under the table. There were tears in his eyes and Jen wondered if he'd knocked his head on purpose, so that the others wouldn't see him crying. Nat put her arm around his shoulders and gave him a kiss on the cheek.

'Do you remember,' she said, 'he'd set up a kind of workshop in that old woodshed out back – I don't think it's there any longer, is it?'

'No, it must have been knocked down at some point,' Jen said. 'There's a new, smarter one now.'

'He used to sneak out there all the time, often late at night, and he'd get really, really arsey if you tried to get a look inside.'

'We called it his wanking shed,' Lilah said, and she caught Nat's eye and they both started to giggle.

'I remember the night we carried the table in here,' Dan said, turning to Andrew.

'And you and I were supposed to carry the thing without realising what it was. We'd both been on the beers that afternoon, and you dropped it on Conor's foot. God, he was in a rage.' Everyone was laughing now. 'He was hopping around out back there, cursing us, calling us eejits, stupid articles . . .'

'He always did go very Irish when he was pissed off,' Jen said, smiling. 'But it was like a tropical storm, wasn't it, that temper. Blew up, blew out, all in about five minutes flat.'

'Mmm. Unlike some people.' Andrew was giving Nat the side eye, a wry little smile on his face.

'Oh God, yes, the rows you and Conor used to get into . . .' Jen started laughing.

'Well, he was always so bossy,' Natalie protested.

'*He* was bossy?' Now Andrew and Dan were laughing, too, even Lilah's lips twitched.

'And then afterwards you'd be in a sulk for *hours* . . .' Andrew said, putting his arm around Nat's shoulders.

'I would not!' she replied huffily, but she didn't push him away, and just in that instant, Jen saw that it wasn't a disaster, bringing them together.

Jen poured more coffee, Lilah made some more Bloody Marys, singing softly to herself as she did, but by the time she sat back down at the table she was looking tearful.

'What is it, sweetheart?' Jen asked her, putting her hand up to touch Lilah's cheek. Lilah took her hand and held it.

'I was just reminiscing,' she said, sitting back down at the table. 'Oh, God. Do you remember how he used to do that thing, at college . . . This always kills me . . .' she tailed off, but Nat knew where she was going. 'With the books, you mean?' She was welling up too. 'The notes he used to leave for you, Jen?' Lilah nodded, sniffing. 'He used to come and get the reading list for the week off me, and then he'd go into the library and find the books he knew you'd have to read, and then he'd leave little notes for you in them, just hoping that you'd get the copy he'd chosen.'

'And sometimes I did,' Jen said, a smile on her lips. 'It used to make going to the library so much more interesting.'

When Zac finally came down for breakfast, he found them all dabbing at their eyes. Jen got to her feet quickly, fussing around him, getting him a plate of food. When he asked Lilah what was wrong she just purred, 'Nothing, baby,' and gave him a kiss and that seemed to satisfy him. Jen got the impression that he probably wasn't the most challenging of partners, but she could see the attraction. When he yawned, stretching his arms up into the air, his sweatshirt rose up to reveal an impressive six-pack, and below it a starkly defined iliac crest. Lilah caught her looking, raised an eyebrow and grinned, Jen laughed and looked away.

'You never finished your story,' Lilah said to her, 'the man you met. The one you fell in love with. Why isn't he joining in our happy little reunion?'

'Nicolas,' Jen said, fanning her face with one hand, as though it were the heat of the stove giving her colour. 'Well, he turned out to be, you know. French.'

'Meaning?'

'Incapable of fidelity. Not incapable so much, actually, just of the mind that fidelity was an unnecessary, undesirable state of affairs. If you'll excuse the pun. I put up with it for a while, but in the end I decided I couldn't. I left him, packed up my stuff, moved down here. I didn't really know where else to go. That was a couple of months ago. It was only when I got here that I realised I really couldn't stay. This can't be the place I start over, this could only ever be temporary.'

'Why?' Andrew asked her. 'What's wrong with this place? You could work here, freelance I mean . . . I know it's selfish of me, but selling this place? It doesn't seem right.'

'I know how you feel about it, Andrew. I do. But I can't stay here. It's really no place to raise a child.'

Everyone stopped what they were doing, stopped sipping and stirring and stared at her.

'A child?' Andrew asked.

'Oh, yes,' Jen said, a small, shy smile on her lips. 'Did I not mention? I'm pregnant.'

*14 May 1995*

*J*

*I've been thinking about LAF (Life After Finals), and this is what I think
we should do:*

1. *Leave college (obviously).*
2. *Move to the Big Smoke, earn a bit of cash.*
3. *Move in together.*
4. *Go to Asia for a bit. Thailand, Vietnam, you know the sort of thing.
   Teach English, take hallucinogenics.*
5. *Come back to the UK, earn a bit more cash.*
6. *Get married.*
7. *Move to the French house. I will make beautiful pieces of furniture in the
   barn. You will translate great works of literature into French.*
8. *Have lots of babies.*

*What d'ya think?*

*Love you.*

*C*

*P.S. Enjoy* The German Ideology. *Looks deathly if you ask me.*

## Chapter Eight

Outside, in the converted barn, Dan sat on the bed on the mezzanine, his head bowed. He rang Claudia's number. It went to voicemail. He wondered whether she had spoken to her husband yet, whether she was speaking to him right now. He imagined them in the middle of a screaming match, tears running down her perfectly angled cheekbones, along the sharp line of her jaw, down her neck. In his head, she looked impossibly beautiful even in the most arduous of circumstances, including the act of leaving her husband. Dan had never actually met the husband, he hadn't come to the set. Dan hoped he didn't have too fiery a temper. He doubted it – the guy was a director of some charitable foundation. Plus, he was German, which meant that by rights he should have ice in his veins. Still, you never could tell. He rang Claudia's number again, listened to her voice, low and throaty, as she told him, first in German and then in English, that he should leave a message. He didn't.

He opened his suitcase and finished the unpacking he'd half-heartedly begun the night before. His suits were already hanging in the closet. He'd brought the good ones, the Paul

Smith and the Richard James (he liked to wear English tailoring, none of this Gucci or D&G nonsense). That was as far as he'd got, however, what with the beer and the wine and dinner and Lilah and Natalie. His shirts lay crumpled in his bag.

He clambered down the ladder to the main part of the apartment. He hung his 100 per cent lambskin APC bomber jacket over the back of the desk chair in the corner of the room and set about unpacking his toiletries in the wet room, lining them up carefully on the shelf: Marc Jacobs eau de toilette, REN Glycolactic Radiance Renewal Mask, Lab Series Restorative Shampoo, Kerastase conditioner, Gilette Fusion ProGlide Styler.

He left his running gear and trainers in the bag; it was unlikely he was going to be able to get out this weekend, not in this weather. Usually, he liked to keep to a five-mile-per-day, five-days-a-week minimum. In the business he was in, ridiculous though it seemed, looks mattered, even if you were only behind the camera. So he took care of himself, he moisturised, he exercised. And he knew, even though no one had ever said as much, that he looked better than he had in his twenties. He'd been so slight then, so insubstantial. His frame was still narrow, but he had meat on his bones now, sinewy and hard. His dark hair was greying, but he preferred it like that, it suited him, bestowing upon him a gravitas which his face, pale and youthful and lightly freckled, had always denied him.

He heard a door slam outside, laughter. Lilah and her himbo walking hand in hand in the snow towards the woodshed. Dan wondered what, apart from the obvious, she saw in him. And he wondered what the others would have thought of Claudia. The girls would have been jealous, she was so young, so beautiful. But would they have liked her? He wasn't entirely sure. She was brilliant and talented, passionate and eccentric, but she wasn't particularly warm. She was a man's woman. He reached for his phone again, rang Claudia again, listened to the voicemail again.

He stood at the French windows and gazed glumly out into the bright sunlight. It was hard to admit, but he'd always preferred bad weather. There was something boring about sunshine. Still, it would be gone soon; the wind was picking up, clouds gathering, matching his mood. He tried to persuade himself that this sense of unease and unhappiness was all about Claudia. He took a deep breath and shook out his arms, rolled his shoulders, tried to relax. He should go back inside and have a drink. It was almost Christmas, getting drunk in the morning was a perfectly acceptable thing to do. But he didn't want to go back inside because this unease . . . it wasn't all about Claudia. That little bite of anguish he'd felt when Jen talked about her husband, he knew exactly what that was about.

Nineteen ninety-six. He was twenty-three years old. He met her in Richmond, at the train station. He hadn't been sure what to expect, but he could remember, even now, sixteen years later, the feeling of excitement, the swarm of butterflies in his gut. They walked down to the river and turned left, passing under the bridge and skirting around a field full of caramel-coloured cows, Jerseys with huge, liquid brown eyes. It was early spring, chilly, the weather just about to turn. The sky, though blue, still had that wintry touch of pale. They talked about the others for a little while, and then, all of a sudden, Jen took his arm and stepped out in front of him, stopped him right there on the path and said:

'It can't happen, you know it can't. I've only ever been in love with one person. I only ever will be. I know it seems silly, but we really are that rarest of things, two people who are meant for each other, only for each other. That's how we are, Conor and I. I'm never going to love anyone else.'

He'd handled it beautifully. He'd cocked his head to one side and smiled and given her a hug, picked her up, twirled her round, held her as tight as he could. He didn't let her see that he was hurt. He didn't give her a hard time, he didn't make her feel bad. He wasn't angry, not in the slightest, because he believed her. He *really* believed her, he did then and he'd continued to believe her, for all this time it had made it easier not to think about her. And now he finds out it wasn't true after all.

She had fallen in love. She'd been married. She'd made a whole other life for herself and now she was going to have a baby. And so what? What had he thought was going to happen? That she'd never move on? That one day, somewhere down the line, he'd get his chance? That one day he would finally be good enough? He felt a laugh rising in his throat. This was ridiculous. What on earth did it matter? It was a million years ago. It was just he would have liked the chance. That was all. He felt like he was always missing chances, as though his shot at real happiness was always obscured in some way. As though he was being unfairly disadvantaged.

But he thought he'd made his peace with that. By choosing Claudia, he'd acknowledged that there would be no family, not with her. She alone would be enough. He just needed to talk to Claudia, to hear her voice, to know that they were on track and that in a couple of days' time their life together would start, for real. That would be enough.

He rang her again (just the one more time), and let the phone ring and ring and, finally, she answered.

'What is it?' she asked him in a whisper. 'It's not a good time now.'

'He's there?'

'Yes, he's here, obviously. We are at home.'

'Are you OK?'

'I'm fine.'

'Have you spoken to him?'

'Not yet, I'm waiting for the right time.'

'I miss you.'

Silence.

'Claudia? Are you there?'

'I'm here, yes.'

Dan didn't want to know, but for some reason he couldn't help himself, and he asked her: 'Have you slept with him?'

'Dan!'

'Well, have you?'

'I'm his wife, and I've been away from him for five weeks. What do you think?'

'Jesus, Claudia.'

'Listen, I have to go. He's coming now, we're going to lunch. Just . . . be patient, OK?'

She ended the call.

Dan sat back down on the desk chair, his elbows on his knees, his head in his hands. He felt nauseous. Why did she tell him that? Why did he ask? Bloody idiot. Suddenly he was beyond furious; he leapt to his feet, grabbed the stupid little pot with the stupid little purple flower in it and made to hurl it against the wall. He stopped himself in time. He put the pot back down and carefully brushed the bit of soil which had spilled out under the rug. He sat down on the floor, crossing his legs and resting the backs of his hands on his knees, thumb lightly touching the third finger. He closed his eyes and breathed, in and out. He felt a little better. He tried to clear his mind, to forget the here and now, but the sick feeling in his stomach wouldn't go away and he couldn't banish the image from his head of Claudia's head thrown back, white throat exposed, someone else moving on top of her.

*Dear Jen,*

*I don't know if this will reach you. Andrew says he sends his letters to you care of your parents, but isn't sure if they pass them on.*

*It's been almost five months. I waited, because I knew you'd need time, I knew you'd probably want to be left alone. But I didn't want you to think that I wasn't thinking of you, spending every moment wondering where you are and what you're doing. Wondering whether you'll be OK, whether you'll ever come back.*

*I understand why you went, but please come back.*

*There is no reason for you to feel guilty. None of this was your fault. It was mine, mine and Andrew's: we were the ones who were driving too fast. The terrible part of it is that I have escaped without punishment. Without formal punishment, anyway.*

*Andrew will not be so lucky. His sentencing is next month. His legal career will be over, though they think he will escape a custodial sentence. Nat is doing better. Still at her parents' place, but she's out of the chair most of the time now, which I think is a huge relief. She talks about coming back to London, taking up her old job. I haven't seen much of Lilah. I don't think she's doing too well. It's hard to tell because she won't talk about it. She isn't strong, though. She isn't strong like you.*

*We miss you, Jen.*

*I can't know what you're feeling, but I know that mixed in with all the grief there will be something else, and I know I am the cause of that. Can I be sorry without feeling regret? Because I can't, Jen, I can't regret it, I wish that I could, that I could wish it had never happened, but I can't. I can't bring myself to wish for that.*

*Please, give me a chance to help you through this, Jen. I just want a chance.*

*Come back.*

*Dan*

# Chapter Nine

～

They were running low on firewood and Zac volunteered to fetch more. Lilah jumped at the chance to go with him, to have a cigarette and get away from baby talk. She'd never been good at enthusing about maternity. Zac went upstairs to get their coats and they went out the back door, past the barn and up the hill, hand in hand, towards the woodshed. They squinted into the sunshine.

'You want to go back for your sunglasses?' Zac asked her.

'It's OK,' she said, raising a hand to shield her eyes. They were looking up towards a clump of trees halfway up the hill, beyond the shed. Suddenly, Lilah stopped dead.

'What is it?'

'Nothing,' she said, and started to walk again. Just for the briefest of moments, she'd thought she saw someone moving, just beyond the tree line. It gave her a fright. She blinked hard into the brightness, but there was nothing there. No one there. Still, it made her feel a little strange. There was something about those woods, something frightening and yet alluring. She gripped Zac's hand a little harder; he turned to her and smiled, and kissed the top of her head.

'Beautiful girl,' he said and at once she was safe.

Zac filled a basket with logs while Lilah sat on a tree stump and smoked. There weren't many decent-sized logs left, so Zac opted to chop some more. He took off his jacket, picked up an axe and grinned at Lilah, who was taking pictures with her phone.

'There you go, baby. Very Tom of Finland.'

'Tom who?'

She just smiled at him and shook her head.

After a couple of minutes he stopped chopping, wiped the film of sweat from his forehead with the back of his glove. Shielding his eyes from the glare, he looked down over the house and into the valley.

'Gorgeous, isn't it?'

'Mm-hmm,' she murmured, but she was looking at him rather than the view.

'Look at it, Lilah! It's incredible. All this space. This clean air!' Lilah took a long drag on her cigarette; Zac raised his eyes to the sky. 'You're hopeless. I have to say, I agree with Andrew,' he said, picking up his axe again, readying himself for another swing. 'Jen's mad to sell this place.'

'I wouldn't want to be out here all alone,' Lilah said, shivering a little. 'Not in winter, anyway. It's different in summer, though. It was lovely in the summer.'

'Ah, the fabled summer of . . . what was it? Ninety-eight?'

'Ninety-five. You were still at school,' she said, eyebrow arched. 'Running around in short trousers.'

'And you were with Andrew.'

'I was.'

'He seems like a nice bloke, but I just can't quite see it, you and him.'

'He was different, then. Very different.'

'Different how?'

'More . . . alpha. He was very much the alpha male.'

'Andrew? Andrew in the comfy jumper? He was never the alpha male.'

Lilah laughed, ran her fingers through her hair, flicked her cigarette away. 'Oh, he was. When we were at university, Andrew was the golden boy. He was gorgeous and clever and good at everything – captain of the rugby team, editor of the college newspaper, all that crap. He was also friendly and outgoing and everyone liked him. If we'd been at an American high school, he'd have been the one voted most likely to succeed, most likely to marry well, get rich, be happy ever after.'

She lit another cigarette, looked up at Zac who was watching her expectantly, waiting for her to go on. She shrugged. 'Things didn't turn out so well for him. It wasn't his fault, there were . . . circumstances.'

'Oh. What circumstances?'

'It's a long story.'

Zac went back to chopping; he didn't press the point, he never did. Which suited her perfectly. Never one for analysing the past, she'd always found it less painful to let things slip away. She knew that this was cowardice. It was her way of not facing up to things, her way of shirking responsibility. Most people did, in some way, she supposed: Jen ran away, Dan made up stories and rewrote history.

Not Andrew, though. It still amazed Lilah, all these years on, that there was never a moment when Andrew had hidden from what had happened. If it had been her, behind the wheel, there is no way in hell that she could have gone to the funeral. But it never crossed Andrew's mind not to go. Lilah was terrified that there might be a scene – she had melodramatic visions of

Conor's mother flinging herself at Andrew, calling him a killer. Andrew said that if he was asked to leave, he would. But of course no one did ask him to leave. When they arrived at the church, Conor's mum was standing outside and she'd greeted them like friends, kissing them and telling them how much her son had loved them both. She asked them to sit with her, at the front of the chapel. Lilah could remember walking up the aisle, holding Andrew's hand, stupidly, drunkenly (because she'd already started, that morning, in the bathroom), wondering if they'd ever take that walk in the opposite direction, with her in white not black. She remembered looking for Natalie before realising that of course she wouldn't be there because she was lying in a hospital bed, unconscious, possibly crippled, possibly brain damaged. She'd stumbled halfway up, and Andrew had caught her arm. She'd turned towards him but he wasn't looking at her, his eyes were fixed ahead of them. He'd told her not to wear such high heels, they weren't practical.

Zac had stopped chopping again and he was looking at her, a small smile on his lips.

'What?'

'Nothing. You just look pretty today, sitting there on your stump, lost in your thoughts.' She laughed, shaking her head. 'I think he must have been bonkers,' he said.

'Who's bonkers?'

'Andrew. Leaving you for Natalie. I mean, I'm sure she's a nice girl and everything, bit high strung for my tastes, lovely eyes, I must say, but . . . compared to you? Absolutely bonkers.'

Lilah got to her feet, went over to him and kissed him on the mouth. 'You are lovely, my darling, but you don't know the half of it.'

'What do you mean?'

83

She turned away from him, looked down at the house, picture-postcard pretty blanketed in snow, smoke curling from the chimneys. 'It's all much more complicated than you think. These things always are. I was hurt, obviously, I was very hurt by everything that happened, but with hindsight, with the wisdom that my advanced years have afforded me, it all makes sense to me that he would fall in love with her.'

Zac shook his head. 'I don't know how you can say that.'

'I was hard to love, Zac. Sometimes, I was very hard to love.'

He put the axe down and took her hand. 'You could never be hard to love.'

Lilah laughed out loud. 'Oh, you know that's bullshit!' she said.

'No, it isn't,' he said crossly, 'you are *not* hard to love.'

'Oh, darling,' she purred, 'you are so sweet,' and she gave him a shy smile, looking up from beneath lowered lashes. She could almost see him melt.

They walked back down the hill, carrying a basket of wood each. As they passed the barn, they noticed Dan, sitting on the floor, legs crossed, eyes closed. He seemed to be doing some sort of yogic breathing.

'Ommmm,' Zac said, and Lilah giggled.

Inside the house, Jen had put some music on, something folksy and gentle. She was talking to Andrew, animated: they were laughing, she watched him reach out and place his hand on her belly. Her big brother, that's what he used to call himself. The sight of them together made Lilah feel happy and bereft all at once; guilty too. The iPod shuffled, the track changed and a new song came on, 'Can't Be Sure'. Instantly Lilah was transported back in time and space to a campsite in St-Malo, a muddy field on the side of a hill, sitting inside the tent because it was raining, drinking wine out of a plastic bottle, listening to The Sundays.

The previous day, Nat had been dumped by a monosyllabic northerner with bad hair and an even worse attitude and Lilah had persuaded her to leave college immediately in search of 'cathartic adventure'. They'd borrowed Jen's car and driven south through the night, arriving at Dover in the early hours, finally getting to rainy, miserable northern France around lunchtime, with no adventure in sight and nothing to do but get drunk and listen to The Sundays, so that's what they did, for two days running. *Did you know, desire's a terrible thing?* Natalie, washing up in the kitchen, looked over at her, and Lilah smiled. Natalie looked away.

*15 April 1999*
*Email, from Lilah to Natalie*

*Dear Natalie,*

*No, I bloody well do not want to come to your wedding.*
  *Did you honestly think there was a chance I would?*

*Lilah*

# Chapter Ten

~

They were staying. He'd managed to persuade her. Or, she was persuaded, in any case, by the snow or the baby or just the fact that it would be embarrassing to leave now. Andrew carried their case back upstairs, and they unpacked.

'What did the girls say?' Andrew asked her. 'Are they having a good time at your parents'?'

'Seem to be,' Natalie replied. She was standing with her back to him, refolding his boxer shorts, placing them neatly in the top drawer of the oak dresser.

'Did you speak to both of them?'

'Mmm-hmm.'

'Has Grace been practising her violin?'

'So she says.'

'Good.' He waited a moment, for her to turn back to him, so that he could see her face. He could tell, from the way she was standing, the set of her shoulders, that she was hurting. He put the empty suitcase on the floor and approached her, placing a hand gently between her shoulder blades. 'Are you all right?'

'I'm fine,' she said, but he could tell by her voice, thin, a little high, that she was struggling. He took the last of the clothes from her hands and put them in the drawer, steered her back to the bed. She allowed him to manipulate her, silent, supine. She lay down, facing away from him, and he kicked off his shoes and lay behind her, his hand placed on her lower back. She liked the warmth, it seemed to ease the tension.

'I wish,' she said softly, after a few minutes, 'I wish we could just let all this go. I wish you could let it all go.'

'I know.' But he couldn't, he would not be persuaded.

'It feels like poison.'

'What do you mean?'

'I don't know . . .' Her voice was breaking a little.

'You need your pills?'

'Please.' Her voice was tiny, trapped at the base of her throat.

Andrew got to his feet and went into the bathroom, rooted through her toiletry bag for her painkillers, the strong ones. There they were, six of twelve left, stamped into their silver sheet, the reverse of which bore a warning about addiction. Not Nat, she was too strong. She didn't take them often, but today was a bad day. It was the plane, yesterday, the driving, the tension. She'd be better tomorrow. He poured her a glass of water and took it through to her. She propped herself up on one elbow and swallowed two pills in quick succession, jerking her head back as she took them, eyes shut, throat exposed.

She lay back down, reaching one arm back, a signal for him to join her. He lay down behind her, slipped his hand under her top, gently massaging her lower back. 'Our life is good,' she said softly. 'We have family and work and each other. I don't want all this . . . the past, I don't want it to poison our well. That's what I mean. There's too much sadness and too much hurt and too much blame. We moved on, we made our lives. It is not our fault, not *your* fault, that others failed.'

'Nat . . .'

'No. Let me say this. Jen and Lilah will always be the women you hurt. You can't see them any other way. But . . .' Carefully, she rolled over so that she could face him, as he watched the pain cross her face like a shadow. 'You've already paid, in full, one, two, three hundred times over, for anything you did wrong. Only you can't see that. All you can ever be with them is guilty. You still want them to forgive you. I don't want you to spend the rest of your life asking for forgiveness. You don't deserve that.' She closed her eyes and he kissed her, lightly, on her lips. He tried to think of a response, but she wasn't done. Eyes still shut, she said: 'I want our life to be about us, to be about now.' Her voice faltered a little. 'I don't want to live with ghosts.'

He reached around her and pulled her closer. 'I know you don't, love.'

He'd never quite been able to explain to her that he *did* want to live with ghosts. It was his way of accepting what happened, his path to redemption. And it wasn't about torturing himself, which is exactly what Nat would have thought. Every day, he thought of him. That was how he coped. That was how he lived with it.

He didn't think, at first, that he would be able to. He gave himself a week. Get through that week and then we'll see. The morning of the funeral, six days after the accident, he got up early. He and Lilah were staying in a grubby B&B in the centre of Cork, the room was cramped and too warm with no air conditioning. When they opened the windows the sounds from the street made it impossible to sleep. Lilah slept. She had some pills she'd got from her mother.

Andrew took one of her cigarettes and leaned out over the railing, looking down two storeys to the street below, and smoked. The sun shone maddeningly bright, it was warm already, even at seven in the morning, and it was loud, too: the noise of bottles clinking, the thump of beer barrels slamming onto the street. The cigarette made him retch, he only ever touched them when he was drunk and that morning he was terrifyingly sober. He felt hyper-aware: of the unpleasant tickle of nicotine on the inside of his mouth, his T-shirt clinging to his lower back with sweat, the sound of Lilah breathing behind him, the sense of terror rising, from the pit of his stomach, into his chest and then to his throat. He thought of Jen, whom he hadn't seen in five days, not since the morning after, at the hospital. He thought of Natalie, still unconscious. He thought of Maggie, Conor's mother. He thought, briefly, of the fact that with a minimum of effort he could pitch forward over this railing and it would be over.

Later, as he tried to tie his shoelaces with shaking hands, he realised that after this week, there would be another one, and another one after that, and that he would have to try to find a way to get through all those days and weeks, because he knew in his heart that he would not be pitching himself over any railings, not today or any other day. Lilah came out of the bathroom, knelt at his feet and kissed him. He could smell the alcohol on her breath. It was quarter to nine in the morning. 'You sure about this?' she asked him.

He wasn't, he was terrified, but he went anyway. He didn't have everything figured out, not until later, and not without help. But that day was the starting point. Since he was never going to be able to live without it, he had to live with it. And, ridiculous as it sounded, he now lived if not comfortably, then at the very least peacefully with Conor's ghost.

Nat's eyes were closed – the pills made her drowsy, he thought she might have drifted off to sleep – but when he tried to move away, she slipped her arm around him. He drew her in closer, whispered into her hair.

'There was more to us, you know, than sadness and hurt and blame, wasn't there? Don't you remember? How we once were?'

*Dearest Andrew,*

*I hope this letter finds you well. I have just finished writing another, which will be sent to the trial judge as a reference of your character. Since I want, as best I can, to ease the suffering that you are feeling, I thought I would let you know what I have said.*

*The judge will know, of course, that you are now and have always been an honest, law-abiding, hard-working young man. They don't need me to tell them that. There are records, I've no doubt, of your academic and other achievements, those achievements that can be measured with grades or rewarded with prizes. Some things, though, aren't so easily quantified.*

*So I have told them of your goodness. That you were a loyal friend to my son, a man he looked up to, a man he counted on. I told them that of Conor's group of friends, I would identify you not only as the kindest among them, but the most responsible. I know full well that you made a terrible mistake that day, but I know that you were not alone in that mistake.*

*Difficult as it may be for you to imagine, I was young once too. I dimly recall what it feels like, to be on the cusp of adulthood, those few years when the world stretches out before you and you feel yourself to be utterly invincible. Yes, of course, it is an illusion, but there can be few amongst us (including, I assume, the trial judge) who didn't feel it, who cannot look back and remember that we once took stupid risks and laughed at our own audacity later. For most of us, the very great, lucky majority, those risks don't cost us, or at least don't cost us much. You were not lucky, neither was my son.*

*Most important, though, as I have written in my letter, is that the last thing, the very last thing on earth that my son would have wanted,* would have been to see you punished any more than you have already been. The idea of you going to prison would have been horrifying to him, as it is to me.

That, Andrew, is more or less what I have written to be presented as evidence to the judge. This is what I have to say to you. This thing you have done, it could destroy you. It could ruin your life. It has taken your best friend, it has taken your career. I imagine it has taken a lot more besides.

You could let it destroy you. I hope you will not. You could let it define you, too, and I'm not entirely sure that would be a bad thing. It sounds rather trite to say to you: make sure that something good comes out of this, but that is what I want you to do. Don't run away from it, don't hide from it. Let it sit with you. Let it become a part of you.

Live a good life, whatever that means to you. Find someone to love, someone who loves you. I don't know if that'll be that tall blonde drink of water you're knocking around with right now, or whether it'll be someone else. Make it someone who values you.

Don't fight it. Let it define you, just don't let it consume you. It's a fine line, I'm sure. I hope that you can find it.

Now, I know you have enough guilt to be getting on with, so listen to me: don't you worry about me. I have Ronan, and I have a wonderful daughter-in-law in Clara, and soon there's to be a baby, too – I'm to be a grandmother and I can't tell you how excited I am about that. I'll survive this. So will you. Conor wouldn't have it any other way.

Good luck.

All my love,

Maggie

# Chapter Eleven

Natalie left Andrew sitting on the edge of the bed, texting. She closed the bathroom door and ran herself a bath. She'd already had a shower that morning, but sometimes a hot bath was all that would do it. Andrew was chatting to the girls, something he managed quite happily by text. Nat couldn't bear the text speak, the 'how r u', the punctuated smiley faces. She liked to speak in full sentences, to spell and punctuate correctly, even when communicating electronically. These things were important.

Andrew was better at going with the flow, which was probably why Grace and Charlotte's preference appeared to have switched from mother to father over the past couple of years. Natalie tried not to be hurt by this. It was inevitable, really; Andrew had always been the cooler one. Not that that was difficult. Natalie was steadfastly, resolutely uncool. Always had been. It was the coolest thing about her, Andrew always said. He, however, had found a way to be *ironically* down with the kids without generating the kind of gold medal-winning eye rolling which Nat was greeted with when she tried to communicate with them on their level.

She lowered herself gently into the bath. One of her greatest pleasures, this. She liked to get into the bath when there was barely any water in it, lie as flat as she could, feel the heat build around her. She let her head slip down, so that her ears were underwater and the sound of her breathing was amplified. Beyond that there were other sounds, unidentifiable sounds, people moving around the house, walking up and down the stairs, something else, deeper, further away, a voice, low and steady. She splashed water over her chest and torso, wriggled her hips a little, feeling the tension in her body seep out into the water. Her head was buzzing slightly from the pills – they gave her the merest hint of a high, made her throat dry, made her feel like she wanted a cigarette.

She hadn't smoked a cigarette in sixteen years; she gave up in hospital. Didn't have much choice really. Unconscious for ten days, unable to get out of bed for another forty-one. Being forced to quit smoking was the silver lining, her mother said. Her mother liked to look for the silver lining. On one occasion, a birthday or a Christmas, something boozy, her mother announced to her guests that her Natalie had been in a terrible accident, but something good came out of it: she got Andrew.

When all the guests were gone, Natalie called mother cruel and ridiculous, and they didn't speak for days. It *was* ridiculous. What, after all, did her mother really know about it? She hadn't been there. She hadn't seen the way Andrew had started to look at her, that summer at the French house, and then afterwards too. Sometimes she caught it, just out of the corner of her eye, when they were walking back from the cinema or having lunch together in the pub, she'd catch him watching her. Natalie's mother hadn't been privy to the conversations that they had, late into the night, night after night, when Lilah was out getting wasted, careening off the rails, when Andrew didn't know what to do with her.

Her mother didn't know. But if she didn't know, if she was so ridiculous, then why was Natalie so rattled by it? Why did it hurt her so much? In the deepest, secret part of her, she knew, although she never allowed the thought to coalesce, to force itself to the forefront. She knew that even if she didn't believe it, others did. Lilah certainly did. Jen might, she wasn't sure.

Nat let herself slide back under the water, closing her eyes, listening once more to the murmurs of the house. She thought she could hear chatter, noises from the kitchen, pots and pans clanging against each other, faint, deep music, Lilah's jagged laughter. Uneven, the laughter of an hysteric, a laugh that made everyone in the room look around.

Natalie first saw Lilah at a party, a rather formal event, at the beginning of their first year of university. A meet-the-dean type of affair, people dressed up and chatting politely with professors. Lilah wore leather trousers and sat in the corner smoking and whispering into the ear of some guy. And every now and then, that laugh. Natalie thought she was ridiculous. Ridiculous, terrifying, impossibly beautiful.

And beautiful she was, head-turning. It was impossible to go anywhere with her for a girly night out, because within minutes there would be someone making a play. It was effortless then, too, she was a different woman from the one here now. Then she was glowing, athletic. Not this rather strange, stick-like creation, skin a shade too dark, hair a shade too blonde. It was rather sad, really, Natalie thought. She looked down, contemplating the soft white mound of her belly, the mottled skin over her heavy breasts. All right, so not all *that* sad.

Natalie didn't meet Lilah properly until weeks, possibly months after that first formal. It was at a rugby match. She'd been invited to go and watch by the handsome Irishman on her corridor, one Conor Sheridan, on whom Natalie had nursed the briefest of crushes before she first saw him with his girlfriend, who looked like she'd wandered out of a Renoir, all porcelain skin and raven hair. Natalie wasn't much into sports, but she was keen to have a rounded college experience, and she was very keen to meet some promising boys, the ones on her course proving to be insufficiently stimulating.

They were sitting at the edge of the stands, three of them: Conor, flanked by his girlfriend on one side and Lilah on the other. Lilah was wearing jeans and knee-high boots with an enormous wedge heel, and was leaning forward, elbows on knees, chewing on a fingernail, not watching the match. When Conor caught sight of Natalie, he smiled and waved, beckoning her over to join them. The girlfriend smiled too. Lilah just looked at her, blankly.

There was no space to sit next to them, so Natalie had to sit in front of them, at their feet. Every now and again, Conor and his girlfriend, whose name was Jen, would leap to their feet and cheer. Then Conor would sit down and lean forward and explain to her what had just happened, Jen would lean forward and offer her a lemon drop, but what Natalie was most aware of was Lilah's foot, tapping constantly at her side. It was annoying. At some point in the second half, she couldn't stand it any longer. She turned around and said: 'Sorry, but could you stop doing that? It's driving me mental.'

Lilah stopped, looking at her curiously. 'What was your name again?' she asked.

'Natalie.'

'Right. You have amazing eyes, Natalie,' she said, and she smiled, and it was like the sun coming out. Natalie turned back to the game, but Lilah nudged her gently with her foot. 'Are you enjoying this?' she asked.

'I'm not really sure I understand the rules,' Natalie replied.

'Me neither. It's fucking boring, isn't it? You want to go get a drink?'

'OK.'

'Great, we have to be quick though, my boyfriend's playing and he'll be pissed off if he thinks I haven't stayed to the end. We need to be back by the time he gets off the field. Field? Pitch? Whatever it is.'

By the time they got to the beer tent and back, Natalie knew Lilah's life story. Born in London, brought up in a house on Charles Street in Mayfair. Daddy drove a white Rolls-Royce. When Lilah was eleven years old, Daddy bought a Maserati and drove off into the sunset with a 25-year-old, leaving Lilah and her mother to pay off the debts. They moved to Enfield. 'It was, like, hell,' Lilah said. Or: 'It was like hell.' Natalie couldn't tell; Lilah's words and sentences ran together, she had so much to tell. They struggled for years, financially. 'It's a miracle I'm here at all,' Lilah said. 'Double miracle, actually: financial and academic.' They were walking, arms linked, as though they were the oldest of friends. Lilah leaned in and whispered in Natalie's ear: 'Don't tell anyone, but I'm not all that bright.'

Lilah was cynical and optimistic at the same time, savagely self-deprecating, generous to a fault. She counted her blessings. It made Natalie laugh, but she actually did, she enumerated them, wrote them down.

'My mother made me do this. You have to start with the really basic stuff, like: I have a roof over my head, I have running water, I have food in the fridge. I have booze in the fridge. And then you go up and up, to the more exceptional things: I have a boyfriend who loves me, I have good friends, I am getting a university education. I have legs that are forty inches hip to toe.'

Natalie could hear banging, a muffled voice, rising. She raised her head.

'Nat?' Andrew was knocking at the door. 'You all right in there? Natalie?'

'I'm all right,' she called back.

'You swimming?'

'Uh-huh.'

'You need me?'

'I'm OK.'

Count your blessings, young lady. You have a roof over your head, you have running water, you have food in the fridge. Money in the bank. You have a husband who loves you, two beautiful children. And right now, right at this moment, you are not in pain.

Downstairs, she found Jen making lunch, flanked by Andrew and Zac, giving instructions.

'Right, so for the marinade, you need to chop up some rosemary and thyme and mix that into the olive oil, and add in two or three cloves of garlic, chopped fine, plus a tablespoon of mustard seed. Then you really need to massage that into the meat, OK?'

Zac was quite the sous-chef, knife zipping along the chopping board. Andrew was peeling potatoes, slowly.

'Can I do anything?' Natalie asked.

'Help yourself to a drink,' Jen said. 'We've got it covered.'

Nat wandered into the living room, pulled one of the armchairs over to the window and sat there with her feet up on the sill. Outside, the wind was whipping up the valley, blowing a fine spray of snow off the top of the garden wall. The sunlight, which had been so bright just an hour or two ago, had turned pale and watery, like melting ice. In the distance, the sky was the colour of slate.

She pulled her feet up onto the chair and wrapped her arms around her legs, her chin resting on her knees. She could hear the others laughing in the kitchen, a cheering contrast to the wildness of the weather outside, the emptiness of the landscape. Natalie thought about the previous inhabitants of this house, before they came, before the sheep and the rats. She could scarcely imagine how lonely it must have felt, how cold and how frightening, before tarred roads and electricity. She wondered about the families who'd lived here a hundred years ago, about their children, whether they were happy. For herself, she wouldn't want to live here. She understood why Andrew loved this place so much – there was no denying its beauty – but Natalie could not imagine a life here, could not imagine raising a child here. Despite expectations to the contrary, she liked suburbia. She liked normality, the reassurance of the school run and dinner on the table at half past seven.

She could hear Andrew and Jen chattering in the kitchen, Andrew asking questions about the baby, when was she due, did she have the scan? She was asking about his career, about Nat's work. Is she still writing? Her cheeriness deserting her, Natalie felt a hot little prickle of anger at the back of her neck. You should know this stuff. If you really were our friend, you *would* know this stuff. And where were *you*, Jennifer, when I got *my* scan? She took deep breaths and tried to let it all roll off her.

Lunch was delicious. A rib of beef, roasted on a bed of vegetables, accompanied by a rich, creamy boulangère. The wine was a deep cherry Pinot Noir. Conversation ebbed and flowed, swirling along gently before hitting rapids. They discussed Jen's plans, where she would live, what she would do. Only she didn't seem to have made any plans, just knew that she wanted to return to England, that Paris was done for her now.

'What about the baby's father?' Andrew asked her. 'Will he not want to be a part of all this? Is he OK with you picking up and taking off?'

'I think he may have forfeited his right to have any say in the matter,' Jen said, chin jutting out, mouth a firm line.

'Really? You don't want him to have anything to do with the baby at all?' There was a note of disapproval in Andrew's voice, probably inaudible to the others around the table, but Natalie caught it and she smiled. Of the many things which Andrew took seriously, fatherhood topped the list.

'I forgave him his first infidelity, and his second,' Jen said quietly. 'After that, I tried to turn a blind eye. But when I discovered that he had continued an affair even after I told him I was pregnant, I decided enough was enough.'

'Jen, that's awful, but it's still his child . . .'

Natalie leaned back in her seat, trying not to enjoy too much the fact that her husband was, for once, standing up to her.

'It's not that unusual, though, is it?' Dan cut in, spoiling the moment.

'What isn't?'

'Well,' he went on, thoughtfully stroking the touchpad of his mobile phone, 'I think it's just more common over here, isn't it? In Europe, I mean. On the continent. They have a more . . . relaxed attitude to fidelity. Possibly a more mature attitude . . .'

'Oh, for Christ's sake,' Andrew muttered, downing the rest of his wine. Dan looked up at him, a little surprised.

'What?'

'Where do you people get this idea that it's in some way adult or sophisticated to betray the person you've promised to be with?'

'That's not really what I meant . . .'

'You said it was mature. That infidelity was mature. So failure to stick with your commitments is a sign of maturity to you, is it?'

Dan shrugged and shook his head and went back to his food. Natalie looked at the colour rising in her husband's cheeks and felt herself flush with pride.

It amused her, too, how quickly Dan backed down. After all these years, with all those oceans of water under the bridge, their relationships to each other hadn't actually changed all that much. Dan, the big movie director, still deferred to Andrew, the teacher. Andrew was still the moral compass, still the principled one, to the point of self-righteousness, to a fault. Jen still looked to the men (Andrew first, then Dan) for affirmation of her actions, she couldn't help herself. And when Lilah found something funny, she looked at Natalie, because she knew that Nat would be laughing too. They always had exactly the same sense of humour.

Natalie wondered whether their dynamic was still the same because their friendship had formed with Conor at its centre. Since he couldn't evolve, neither could they. Or perhaps it was just like with family: you can't help but revert to your formative state, the way Natalie started acting like a fifteen-year-old the second she was under her mother's roof.

She herself, though, she *had* changed. Somewhere along the line, she had become an outsider.

It was not a role she cherished. It didn't come naturally to her. Andrew had said it to her, that morning: why can't you remember the good stuff? She could, she could remember it, it was just that she didn't seem to be able to feel it any more, even to remember how it had felt, to love them all.

'Jen,' Natalie said, attempting to step back into the circle of friends, 'do you ever hear from Maggie at all? Or Ronan?'

'I haven't spoken to Ronan in a long while, I think he moved to Dubai or something. But Maggie and I are in touch. I'm thinking of actually going over to Ireland once I've got everything sorted out here, spending some time with her before the baby's born.'

'Sorry,' Zac interrupted, 'Maggie is?'

'Conor's mum,' Jen replied. 'And Ronan's his brother.'

'OK. So you must have been very close to the family,' Zac said, 'to stay in touch for all this time, I mean.'

'Oh, yes. Very much so. I've known them since I was sixteen, so . . .' she tailed off, got to her feet and began clearing away the plates. Natalie got to her feet to help. She rinsed the plates and loaded them into the dishwasher while Jen prepared the dessert.

'It was a drunk driver, wasn't it?' Zac said as Jen laid a dish of apricot tarte tatin in front of him. 'That caused the accident I mean.' Natalie watched two spots of red appear high on Jen's cheeks; she could feel the colour drain from her own.

'No, no, it wasn't,' Jen said, turning away.

'Oh. I'm sorry,' Zac said, confusion on his face. He turned to Lilah. 'I thought that's what you said . . .'

'Let's drop it, shall we?' Lilah said, her voice low.

Natalie sat back down at the table, her eyes on Lilah's face.

'You told him Conor was killed by a drunk driver?' she asked.

'No, I didn't, I said that . . .'

'Well, he was,' Andrew piped up. He looked Zac directly in the eye. 'It was me. I was driving. I *was* over the limit. There was an accident. Conor was killed.' His voice was steady and even.

'Oh, Christ, I'm sorry . . .'

'It wasn't Andrew's fault,' Jen said. 'He wasn't over the limit. They did a blood test. He wasn't over the limit. It was just an accident.'

'It was my fault, Jen, we all know that. The blood test was hours later,' Andrew said softly, giving her a small, sad smile, and Natalie felt a sob bubble up in her throat. She hated this, hated seeing him take everything on his shoulders.

'I'm sorry,' Zac said. 'I shouldn't have said anything.'

'No,' Dan said quietly. 'You probably shouldn't have.'

'It's all right,' Andrew said. 'It was a long time ago. We've all dealt with it in our own ways, haven't we?'

He tried to smile at Natalie, but she could sense the effort it took, to hold his head up, his shoulders back. He looked so exhausted. Her heart contracted. Sometimes, especially when she was away from the girls, or when the pain was very bad, or when she sat at her desk on a Sunday, watching Andrew dutifully washing their crappy old car in their crappy old driveway on their crappy old street, she felt as though her heart were getting smaller and smaller, beat by beat. Then something would happen: Grace would play her a new piece on the violin, Charlotte would tell her something hilarious that happened at school, Andrew would smile at her in his old, secret way, and whoosh! It just expanded again, it filled up, her heart, and she felt whole.

Now, she felt it get smaller and smaller, and she listened as Jen steered the conversation elsewhere, away from dangerous ground; she listened to Lilah's brittle laughter at something Dan said and she was overwhelmed by anger. A righteous anger. Sitting there at that table, her fingernails digging into her palms, she had a sudden, irresistible urge to tell the truth. Not history rewritten, not the past through rose-tinted spectacles, not the sanitised version of the story they'd all been telling themselves for years and years, but the truth she'd been carrying around all this time, a secret, with all its potency.

'I'm not sure,' Natalie said, loud and abrupt, interrupting Dan who was telling everyone a story about shooting a film in Australia, 'that we have all dealt with it. Not very well, anyway.'

'Nat, let's just leave it now,' Andrew said.

'I don't want to leave it.'

'Please, Natalie . . .' Jen said, imploring.

'No, Jen, I'm sorry, but I'm just not prepared to leave it at that. I'm not prepared to allow Lilah to tell her boyfriend that Conor was killed by a drunk driver . . .'

'That isn't what I told him,' Lilah snapped.

'So what did you tell him? Did you tell him about the race? Did you mention that Dan in his flash new car was so desperate to get Andrew to race him?' Natalie looked over at him, but Dan didn't meet her eye. 'You probably didn't. After all, he missed that bit out in his own *fictional* account of what happened that day.'

'Please, Nat.' Andrew reached over the table to take her hand, but she withdrew it.

'No, Andrew, I'm sorry. It's about time everyone here really did face up to things. Like the fact that Conor wasn't a saint, or the fact that Jen punished us, *all* of us, by leaving the way she did . . .' Jen looked stricken, but Natalie didn't care. She was past caring, she was tired of feeling sorry for Jen, for Jen's loss. What about her husband's loss? No one ever talked about that. Andrew's loss was just as deep, unfathomable, endless. His best friend, his career, his prospects, his future, the wonderful life he should have led, the one he deserved.

'I didn't mean to punish anyone, Nat,' Jen said, her voice just starting to waver. 'That really wasn't what I intended. It wasn't rational. I broke down. I'm so sorry that you feel as though I punished you, or Andrew, I'm so sorry . . .'

'Jesus Christ,' Lilah snapped. 'Jen, you don't have to apologise, not to her, not to anyone. For God's sake, Natalie. What is wrong with you?'

Natalie pushed her chair back and got to her feet. She was shaking a little, she thought that she had better leave the room, right away. She wanted to get away from them, she wanted to be outside, in the cold, to hear the wind screaming rather than the voice in her head, her own voice, shrill, hectoring, ugly. She wanted to feel the snow on her skin, cleansing and pure, like an ice bath.

'Honestly!' Lilah exclaimed. Natalie could hear the scrape of chair legs on stone, the click, hiss of a cigarette lighter. 'You ought to be ashamed.'

Natalie stopped, halfway between the dining room table and the back door. For a few moments, she didn't move a muscle, then slowly, deliberately, she turned to face Lilah.

'I'm sorry?' she asked, her voice dangerously soft. 'What did you say?'

Lilah simply shook her head, didn't reply.

'I should be ashamed? What should I be ashamed of, Lilah?' No answer. The rage surged through her, bitter, like bile. That secret she'd been keeping, that power she had, it was time to wield it, and damn the consequences. If she didn't say something now, she'd carry it forever, and it would stay there, lodged in her chest, heavy as lead, corrosive like acid. 'It's funny to me, it really is, to hear you talk about shame,' Natalie said. 'You of all people, Lilah.' Lilah got to her feet, walked around the table and came to stand in front of Natalie, barely two feet away. Her chin was tilted up a little, defiant, but Natalie could see that her hands were shaking.

Natalie gave Lilah a cold, bloodless smile. 'She says she

doesn't, but I think Jen blames Andrew for what happened. I think she blames Dan, too. I don't think she blames you though, does she?' Lilah couldn't hold Natalie's gaze any longer, she looked away. There, she was vulnerable now. If Natalie really wanted to, she could rip her throat out.

She wanted to. 'I blame you, though,' Natalie said. She watched the shadow pass over Lilah's face, the panic; she looked like a woman drowning, a woman sinking into quicksand. There was an odd silence in the room, as though time had stopped. No one was moving. It was so still that, even from a couple of feet away, she could hear Lilah's breathing, shallow, raspy, catching. Like a death rattle. 'I blame you, Lilah, because Andrew wasn't supposed to be driving the car that afternoon, was he? It was his celebration, remember? So you were the designated driver. Only you couldn't drive, could you, Lilah, because you'd been sneaking double vodkas into your orange juice and snorting coke in the ladies. Did you know that, Jen? Did she ever tell you about that?' Jen said nothing, she didn't move. 'No, I bet she didn't. I don't think she told anyone about it. She certainly didn't mention it to anyone when Andrew was being sentenced for causing death by careless driving. Not that it would have changed the verdict, I understand that. It might have changed some people's views on things, though, mightn't it? At the very least people would know that Andrew didn't just get behind the wheel after two pints because he was a fucking idiot. He did it because he knew that he was in a better state to drive than the person who'd told everyone she'd stay sober.'

The tears were sliding freely down Lilah's face now; her shoulders slumped. Natalie wasn't ready to stop yet.

'I would have said something about it at the hearing, obviously, had I remembered. I didn't though, because of the memory loss after the accident. Post-traumatic stress or retrograde amnesia, they said. There was a lot I couldn't remember about that day. It was years later that it came to me, the truth. After the girls were born, after we were married. At first I thought I must have mis-remembered, that it was something I'd dreamt up in my imagination, because she wouldn't do that, would she? Surely not even at her most selfish could Lilah do that?'

Andrew got to his feet, walked across to them and took Lilah's arm. He was at Lilah's side. 'Please, Nat. That's enough. Please just stop now.'

He was at Lilah's side. On Lilah's side. On Jen's side. Why wasn't he on her side? Why was he never on her side? She was always on his side, Jesus Christ, she was doing this, saying all these things, to make them see who was really responsible. To make them understand that Andrew shouldn't have borne all that guilt. It was too much. She shook her head, her eyes never leaving Lilah's face.

'Do you ever think about what might have happened if you hadn't got drunk that day? If you hadn't got wasted, if, just for once in your miserable life you'd done as you said you would, if you'd thought of someone else rather than yourself? Do you ask yourself whether, maybe, just maybe, if you had done that, Conor would be sitting at the table there, with Jen? Maybe Andrew would have had the life he deserved?'

Lilah's face started to crumple, her shoulders hunched. She reached for the kitchen counter to steady herself, gripping it hard, her knuckles white. 'He'd be a QC by now, not just a teacher in some fucking sink school, and Jen wouldn't be here alone, and I wouldn't have had to live every single day of the last sixteen years in pain. I wouldn't be a fucking cripple.'

*Dear Lilah,*

*I'm sending this care of your mum. I'm not sure where you are at the moment. I hope that wherever you are, this finds you happy and well.*

*I know how angry you are with me, I know you feel that I betrayed you, betrayed our friendship. I did. There's no excuse for that, other than love. I love him with everything I am. I always will. I feel as though we are meant for each other. You may laugh at that, you may dismiss it. It's how I feel, Lilah.*

*It's not enough, I know it isn't, nothing I can say will ever take the sting out of what I did. The only thing I can hope for, and oh God, I hope for it fervently, is that you have found someone who loves you so much and makes you so happy that you can forgive me anyway.*

*I don't only want that for myself, I want it for you, of course, and I want it for him. He's had so much to struggle with the past few years, he carries so much guilt with him. If you could find it in yourself to forgive him, I can't tell you what it would mean.*

*You may be angry with me, angrier still for reminding you, but none of us is faultless in this, Lilah. Perhaps mine was the greatest fault, but you must remember that you were, you once told me, 'all but done with him'.*

*I will never be done with him, and I desperately hope he feels the same about me. We're getting married. It's just a registry office job, in Reading on 27 July. Please come. I want so much for you to be there. I miss you, Lilo.*

*With love,*

*Nat*

## Chapter Twelve

~

There was a part of him, a terrible, shameful part of him, which sat there breathless, like a member of an enraptured audience. Dan listened to Natalie spit out her venom, watched Lilah break down, making the journey from drunken, defiant bravado through to virtual collapse; he marvelled at how perfect the lighting was from where he was sitting, the two protagonists back-lit by the snow-white light from outside, the orange glow from the wood burner adding a touch of warmth to the scene. He admired the staging, the group sitting around that solid table in a cosy kitchen interior in the foreground, contrasting perfectly with the chilling, stormy exterior, the white-out behind.

The worst of the scene (the best of it?) was over, ending with Natalie's final, bitter accusation and then her exit, stage left, and up the stairs. Lilah, half held up by Andrew, sobbed with her entire body. She struggled to put on her boots, fell, pushed Andrew away from her when he tried to help her up, got to her feet and walked out of the room and into the snow.

After that, no one moved: there was silence, and the silence stretched out.

Had Dan been directing, he thought he might have wanted some music here, something stirring, orchestral, or possibly 'You Can't Always Get What You Want'. He might have had the camera pan around the room, beginning with Jen's face, pale to the point of ghostly, going around the table, 360 degrees, coming to rest once again on Jen, Jen gripping Andrew's hand so hard her knuckles had turned white. After that, an exterior shot, the lonely house and the mountains behind, and finally, in the garden, Lilah – the beautiful, broken blonde, standing alone in the snow, looking out over the valley as the blizzard hits.

But Lilah wasn't standing in the garden looking across the valley, she had marched off down the driveway towards the road. She was no longer even visible. Dan waited for Zac to run after her, but he didn't. The big lug just stood at the window, watching her go. Andrew got to his feet and grabbed his coat from the stand by the door.

'Come on, Zac, I'll come with you,' he said.

Zac shook his head.

'What, you're just going to let her go? You're going to let her walk out in this? For Christ's sake, she could slip and hurt herself, she could fall down the mountain, get lost – Jesus, she's drunk, alone in a blizzard. Anything could happen.'

Zac puffed out his cheeks and exhaled loudly. 'No. You know what she's like. Or maybe you don't any longer, but I do. She'll get a couple of hundred yards down that hill and realise that she's freezing, and that she has no coat and no money and that she's being silly. She'll be back in ten minutes, fifteen tops. If she's not back in twenty, then I'll go and get her.'

Andrew threw his hands in the air, a gesture of exasperation. Jen got to her feet.

'I'll come with you, Andrew,' she said. 'We can take my car. I've got snow tyres.'

'You're not going anywhere,' Dan said, getting abruptly to his feet and knocking a wine bottle over in the process.

'I'm the only sober one,' Jen said, quietly. 'Plus I know the road better than you do.'

'You're also the only pregnant one,' Dan said. 'There is no way you're going out in this.'

'No one should be going out in this,' Zac objected.

Dan was seized with a sudden, irrepressible rage. What on earth was this huge hunk of beef still doing here? Lilah was his responsibility. If anyone was going to risk life and limb to fetch her, it should be him.

'For God's sake, what is wrong with you? If you'd just run after her straight away, like any sensible man would, we wouldn't even be having this conversation. She's your girlfriend, for God's sake, she's drunk, she's upset, and you've just let her run off into a blizzard. Who does that?'

'I *know* Lilah . . .'

'We all know Lilah. We care about Lilah . . .'

'Oh, hang on a minute, aren't you the guy who completely humiliated her in glorious technicolour?'

'What the fuck has that got to do with anything?' Dan yelled, flinging his arms into the air. 'You're saying because I made a film – a work of fiction – more than a decade ago, that I don't care about her? You're an idiot, you know that?'

The front door slammed. Dan turned and watched as Andrew

strode out to Jen's car. Jen made a move to go after him, but Zac caught her arm and stopped her.

'Dan's right,' he said. 'You shouldn't go.' Instead they stood motionless as Andrew opened the car door, jumped inside and began reversing slowly down the drive. The three of them watched the yellow halogen lights fade out and finally disappear as he swung the car into the road.

*Hi Dan,*

*Thanks for your message. I am sorry that things turned out the way they did. I know it was a big night for you, I hope it wasn't ruined.*

*You must understand, however, that was not easy for us to watch. Yes, it's fiction. Yes, you weren't responsible for the final cut. But you were responsible for most of it, Dan, and I think we can both agree that it was only very thinly fictionalised, wasn't it? And you could at least have warned us of the content.*

*We all believed – were led to believe, I think – that this was going to be a fictionalised account of your childhood. And to some degree, it was just that. You should have warned us that it was going to involve the tragic death of a friend, and the consequences of that, because you know very well that that isn't just about your life, Dan, it's about ours, too.*

*I'm not saying you had no right to make it, to 'use' Conor's death. It's what writers and filmmakers do, I suppose. Tragedy being more dramatic than most things, it lends itself to this kind of treatment. I just think that, if you wanted us to respond well, you should have let us know what we were walking into.*

*And let's not kid ourselves too much: you can call it fiction, but there were certain people and situations which were very recognisable. Your 'Lilah' character was a horrible caricature, a hatchet job. I'm not surprised she was hurt. I suppose that it's natural that as it's your story you would cast yourself as hero, I don't mind that too much. What did get to me was that little love triangle you put in. Call that fiction a thousand times, Dan, but this is what I saw: I saw your fantasy of Jen in love with you, Jen rejecting Conor for you, Jen ending up with*

114

you. That was offensive to me, to Nat, to all of us. It was an insult to Conor's memory. Can you imagine what Conor's mum would have felt, watching that? Or his brother? Can you imagine what Jen felt? I only hope that she hasn't seen it, I imagine she would find it most offensive of all.

I suppose on some level I've always known that you had feelings for her over and above friendship, but she isn't yours, Dan. She never will be.

I don't think meeting up right now's a very good idea. Nat's still pretty raw about the whole thing. She's not very keen on the rewriting of history. I'm still pretty pissed off, too.

Maybe in a few months' time. I do wish you success, Dan. I only hope it doesn't cost you too much.

Andrew

# Chapter Thirteen

~

There was snow on the road, but it wasn't too bad. Visibility was poor, very poor indeed, which was obviously a minus, but on the plus side, the likelihood of there being much traffic on this particular stretch of road in the middle of a blizzard was pretty low. The other minus, of course, was that he'd had three glasses of wine. The thought made his throat close up, he struggled to swallow. How could he be doing this again? On the other hand, what else could he do? They couldn't just leave her out there. Zac was probably right, she probably would turn around and come back, but what if she didn't? What if she slipped and twisted an ankle, and she was lying out there, in pain and afraid? What if she was hit by a car? It was Lilah. She couldn't be left alone, he wouldn't leave her alone.

He was driving very, very slowly, the speedometer barely touching fifteen kilometres per hour. What was fifteen kilometres per hour in miles? He racked his brain for the conversion rate. It was probably around ten. Ten miles an hour! This was ridiculous, he could run faster than that. Gingerly, he pressed down a little harder on the accelerator. He'd never driven in heavy snow before, but he remembered being taught about driving in snow and ice on the course he'd had to attend when he got his licence back. If you drive too slowly, they said, you'll lose momentum and get stuck. Not much chance of that on this hill. You don't want to be going too fast, because you don't want to have to use your brakes. Just take your feet off the pedals and steer. And allow much longer stopping times. There was a bend coming up ahead. He took his feet off the pedals and felt the car coast.

There was a car accident. I was driving too fast. I was over the limit. That's how he tells the story, when he has to. He doesn't tell it often, but sometimes it's inevitable. In job interviews, for example, when he has to explain his criminal conviction.

This is what he doesn't say, what he never says.

He never mentions that it was a celebration, that weekend, it was *his* celebration. He'd finished his articles and had been offered a job at Fineman and Hicks, a leading firm of criminal justice and human rights lawyers. It was the dream job, the opportunity he'd barely dared to hope and pray for, and he had got it. Natalie's parents were away somewhere; it was a hot weekend in June and they'd all taken Friday and Monday off. They'd have the run of the house for an entire long weekend.

He never mentions, because it doesn't seem particularly important, that Dan had recently purchased his first ever car: a red 1976 Alfa Romeo Spider Veloce. Jen and Natalie (Nat crammed into the tiny back seat with her knees up by her chin), were riding with Dan. Andrew was driving the other car, a rather less racy dark blue Vauxhall Nova which used to belong to his mum. His girlfriend, Lilah, was at his side, with Conor in the back seat.

The plan was that he would drive as far as Weyhill, where they were going to stop for lunch. After that, Lilah would take over the driving, because it was his celebration after all. He should be allowed a pint or two.

He never tells anyone about the atmosphere around the table at lunch, which was odd, strained, with everyone either talking a bit too loudly or not at all. Conor hyper, Jen a bit subdued, Dan showing off, Lilah veering wildly between silence and shrieks of laughter.

He never mentions what Natalie has just said, that she caught Lilah doing a line in the toilets and got her to admit that she hadn't been drinking orange juice after all, that she'd got the barman to sneak in a couple of vodkas, too. He doesn't say how he and Lilah ended up in an argument when he said she couldn't possibly drive. He was in a better state. After all, he hadn't quite finished his second pint.

Lilah was furious with him, insisting that he was over-reacting. Fucking Captain Sensible. She let him drive but insisted on switching cars: she couldn't bear to sit beside him, the sanctimonious, self-righteous wanker. Conor, could she switch with Conor? She wanted to be in the cool car, anyway. Come on, Dan, let's see what this baby can do.

Heading out of the village, the road wound down a hill. Dan was driving a little too fast given that they didn't know the roads. Andrew, with Natalie by his side, Conor in the back seat, was left way behind. At the bottom of the hill, there was a long, much straighter section of road, running in between two fields of glorious yellow rapeseed. He never mentions Conor telling him to put his foot down, to catch them up. Come on, pedal to the metal, mate. Can't let that flash git get away with this, got to take him down a peg or two. Andrew put his foot down, the old Nova had more poke than he'd thought.

Conor was cheering him on, Natalie was laughing. They were

catching up with the others, speeding along, sixty miles an hour, seventy, hedgerows a dark green blur. Windows open, music up loud. Conor's yelling, come on, come on, you little beauty, as though he's cheering on a horse. Andrew looked over at Natalie and she was looking back at him, doing that thing she does, where she smiles and bites her lower lip at the same time and it just kills him, the way she looks at him. His heart is breaking, his heart soars. He's in love with her, he's in love with her, he can't be, it's impossible, but he's in love with her. He wants to drive, with her by his side, forever. He put his foot down harder, steered out to the right, coasting past Dan's boy racer, Conor hanging out the window, jeering at him as they went.

Once past them, Andrew slowed back down, aware that the buzz he was feeling wasn't just due to the sunshine and velocity and falling in love with his girlfriend's best friend, there was beer buzz in there too.

When he tells the story, he never remarks on how Dan just *wouldn't let it go*, driving right up to his bumper, beeping his horn, messing around, eventually racing past them, blowing kisses as he went. Natalie waved at him, she blew a kiss back. He doesn't mention how Conor just *wouldn't let it go*, goading him from the back seat, come on, come on mate, you've got the rest of your life to be boring, let's go.

There was a bend in the road, Dan raced around it, Andrew following. After that, there was another straight section. They'd left the farmland behind them now and they were driving through forest, an emerald canopy above. Come on, mate, come on. He was thinking about the kiss that Natalie blew to Dan, wondering if she meant it. There was a cassette in the car stereo, a mix tape that he made years ago, second year at college maybe, all Lemonheads and Suede and Nirvana. 'Sodajerk'

119

came on, by Buffalo Tom, and Natalie gave a little yelp. Oh, I love this song, I haven't heard this song in forever. She turned the stereo up louder, louder, started singing at the top of her voice. Andrew looked at her and grinned and put his foot down.

They almost made it. At the end of the straight section of road, there was a bend, and around that bend came a Land Rover. They almost made it. Almost is nothing, though, when you're doing seventy-five miles an hour and there's nowhere to go. Andrew never talks about how it felt, the moment he knew it was all over, when there was nowhere to go: Dan's car to the left, the Land Rover in front. He had to swerve right, steer through the trees. He was never going to make it, there was no way. But there was nowhere else to go.

It felt as though everything in the world were made of metal. He was made of metal, he was breathing metal, every sound he heard was the scrape of metal, the crunch of it. Hard, sharp, unyielding.

The car had stopped moving.

Andrew's hands were on the steering wheel, he was still holding the steering wheel.

He turned his head.

Natalie was looking at him; her lips were moving, but no sounds were coming out. There was blood on her face, blood in her mouth. Had she bitten her tongue?

His neck hurt, and his leg. He looked down, there was blood soaking through his jeans around his knee.

Natalie? His seat belt wouldn't come undone. Natalie? It's going to be OK. You're going to be OK.

Someone was shouting, he couldn't see who it was.

Slowly, he turned his head. Conor was gone, he wasn't in the back seat of the car. He must have got out already.

Maybe, Andrew reasoned, he'd been unconscious for a while? For how long?

Conor's gone to get help, he said to Natalie, but she wasn't listening. Her eyes were closed and there was blood coming out of her mouth, running down her chin.

Jesus Christ, Jesus Christ.

He had to get out of the car.

Finally, the seatbelt clicked and he yanked it free. He turned back, to his right, to open the door and then he noticed that the windscreen was gone, completely gone, and that there was a pair of trainers on the car bonnet, right at the end of the bonnet. Black Converse, Conor's trainers. He couldn't understand why they were there, at the front of the car, when Conor had been at the back.

His door had buckled, it took him a moment to get it open. His leg was painful, really painful. He pulled himself out of the car. It seemed darker, much darker than it had been when they were driving. What time was it?

Someone was shouting.

He turned around. There were two people on the other side of the car, they were fighting.

Jesus Christ, he couldn't stand, he was going to fall.

It was Dan, Dan and Jen, they were fighting.

Dan was shouting, he was pushing Jen, he was holding on to her. She was screaming.

Dan was crying out, he's gone, Jen, he's gone. Don't look, Jesus Christ. No, Jen, don't.

Don't look, don't look, don't look.

When he tells the story, he never mentions any of that.

*24 May 1996*

*Email exchange between Andrew and Conor*

*Andrew to Conor*

*Got it!*

*C to A*

*Got what?*

*A to C*

*The job! Fineman & Hicks. Got the letter this morning.*

*C to A*

*Result! That's brilliant, mate. Awesome. You totally deserve it. Many, many beers later?*

*A to C*

*Definitely. Greyhound, eight-ish?*

*C to A*

*Sounds good. I think this deserves a proper celebration, though. Party?
Weekend away?*

*A to C*

*All partied out. Lilah hasn't stopped entertaining for weeks . . . I'm
exhausted. Weekend away sounds good, though. Shall we aim for
something mid-June? Because once I start the new job I'm basically
going to have no social life for about three years . . .*

*C to A*

*Mid-June works for me. I'll liaise with the others and set something
up. This really is amazing news, man. You're going to do great things.
Proud of you!*

## Chapter Fourteen

~

If she walked fast enough, she'd warm up. There was a B&B in the village, which couldn't be more than a couple of miles away. Three, perhaps. Natalie used to walk there and back almost every morning, although of course she never did it during a snow storm. Lilah could manage, she'd be fine. She could run six miles in under an hour, though probably not in Ugg boots through the snow.

She picked up her pace and tried not to think about how cold she was. Why hadn't she gone back for her fucking coat? She tried not to be frightened by the fact that the snow was falling heavily now, that she risked getting caught in the centre of the blizzard. She tried not to think about avalanches, or the fact that visibility was worsening and that she was wearing dark blue jeans and a grey sweater and would be completely invisible to motorists until they were right on top of her. Most of all, she tried not to think about what Natalie had said to her, and about the look on Jen's face as she said it.

She thought she heard a car behind her and swung round, almost losing her footing, but there was nothing there. Just the wind, whipping her along, helping her down the hill. She skidded along on icy patches, just about managing to keep herself upright. Her heart was thundering in her chest, fuelled by adrenaline and anger. She clenched and unclenched her fists, wishing she could stop crying – it only made visibility worse. Her suede boots were soaking, her feet squelching in her socks. She wished she'd remembered to put her gloves on. She knew exactly where they were, in her mind's eye she could see them on top of the chest in Jen's guest bedroom; lovely, soft, dark green lambskin gloves from Chanel that her mother had bought for her last Christmas. Not last Christmas, the Christmas before, *her* last Christmas. Her mother's last Christmas.

Apart from Natalie and Andrew, Lilah's mum was the only person who knew what happened on the day of the accident. She *had* been the only person, anyway, but now she was dead, and now Jen knew, and Zac knew, and Dan knew. They knew that it was her fault.

Did she ever think about what might have happened, if she hadn't had that drink, done those lines? That was the question Natalie put to her. And the answer, the honest answer? Not very often.

She didn't deny it. If she questioned herself, honestly, if she examined her behaviour that day and subsequently, she knew that she was wrong, that she was at the very least a contributing factor, perhaps the most important one. She knew that, and she couldn't live with it. So she didn't question herself. She didn't examine her behaviour. She lived with it the way she lived with everything, she simply put it aside.

She put herself first. She had, her mother once said, a narcissistic personality. It didn't stop her mother loving her, forgiving her. Many years before, one of her lovers, a doctor, had told her that her narcissism was so extreme it could be called a disorder. She was selfish, he said, to the point of mental illness. It stopped him loving her. It stopped Andrew loving her, too. He chose someone who gave a bit more, over someone who only knew how to take.

Now, if ever she questions herself she still manages to find a way to blame Andrew for the way she was that day. Not just that day, but for a long time coming. He stopped loving her, and she felt it. She felt him leaving her, slowly, by degrees. He should've done the honourable thing, ripped the Band Aid off, made the clean break. He probably thought he was being a gentleman, letting her down easily. To Lilah, it looked like cowardice. At least it did after the event, with hindsight. At that time, though, she did what she always did, she set it aside. So while Andrew spent his evenings studying, Lilah went to private members' clubs and drank all the champagne and took all the drugs that were offered her with her new glamorous friends. She sought solace where it was offered too, most often in the beds of male colleagues, sometimes in their cars.

She didn't know how much Andrew knew about the infidelities. She told Natalie about one or two of them. It seems stupid now, reckless, but back then they were best friends, they confided in each other. Even about things they felt ashamed of. Lilah could remember Natalie's shock, her outrage; she could remember saying to her, you know, I think it's almost over for Andrew and me anyway, I think I'm done with him. She didn't mean it. She never meant it. She was just getting her retaliation in early. Thinking back, she realised that all she had done was give Natalie a green light to take him away from her.

Lilah stopped walking. She stood by the side of the road, shivering so violently that her entire body shook. It was getting dark. She could barely see a few feet in front of her. Suddenly, she wasn't just upset any longer, she was terrified. She had done a very stupid thing, walking out like that. She needed to go back; she had no idea how long it would take her to get to the village. How long would it take her to get back to the house? How long had she been walking? It seemed as though she'd been drowned in white forever. She turned and started to walk back up the hill, but now she was walking into a wind that cut into her skin like a knife. She kept slipping, the road was steeper than she'd remembered. She fell, tried to get up, slipped again, crawled blindly to the edge of the road. There was blood in the snow, her blood. She'd cut her palm; her hands were so cold she didn't feel it.

She got to her feet, decided she couldn't go back up to the house. It was too hard, too much. She couldn't face them. She'd have to go to the village. She started walking down the hill again, tried to pick up the pace a bit. Panic began to rise in her, from her stomach to her chest, she felt vulnerable, weak; in her mind's eye she pictured herself falling, head cracked open on the ice. No way to die, not out here, alone. And yet she wasn't sure she was alone – she looked up at the side of the road and she felt sure, she *knew* that just behind the treeline there was something waiting, for her. Underneath the screaming wind she could hear something else – a voice, or voices, angry, accusatory, or perhaps it was someone calling for her, someone come to help? She kept feeling that there was someone following her, someone right behind her, so close they could reach out and touch her, stroke her hair, grab her around the throat. She whirled around, but there was nothing there. Nothing and no one.

In front of her, the road started to descend more steeply towards a sharp hairpin bend. She wondered if she should stray off piste, whether she could climb directly down the hill instead of following the road. It was probably no more dangerous and it might be quicker. Shuffling her feet in order to minimise the risk of slipping, she began to make her way across the road. At the very moment she reached its centre, two headlights appeared to her left. She panicked, froze, not knowing whether to return or go over, but the car was travelling so slowly that it came to a halt a couple of feet away. The door was flung open and she heard a voice, yelling over the wind, 'Lilah! What the hell are you doing?'

It was Andrew, come to save her.

*Dear Jen,*

*Your mum insists she's forwarding our letters on to you, wherever you are, so we're all going to keep writing. I do wish you'd get in touch.*

*The hearing was on Thursday. As we expected, he got community service, a fine and a driving ban. He's not going to be a human rights lawyer any longer, but I guess we already knew that. I don't know what he's going to do. Work with his dad for a while, I think. He's going to move back to Reading next year.*

*Dan and Lilah were in the court for sentencing, Maggie and Ronan came too. Andrew took it as you would expect, on the chin; stood up straight as a soldier and looked the judge straight in the eye. The only time he faltered was when they read out Maggie's letter, but then that pretty much floored everyone.*

*I'm OK. It takes me a while to get from A to B, but I've left the chair behind and I hardly need the crutches any longer either. There's some memory loss, but I don't think I've lost anything vital. I can still recite the St Crispin's Day speech, which is always useful. I remember almost nothing about that day, although they tell me some of it might come back to me. I hope it won't. I remember your voice, though, in the hospital I think. I remember you crying.*

*I have dreadful trouble concentrating, I find myself reading the same page of a book over and over and over and at the end I still couldn't tell you what I've read. I'm hoping to go back to work in the new year. They've been so patient, holding the job open for me, but I don't think they can do so much longer. Mum is desperate for me to stay here with her, but I can't stand it, I just can't. I have to get back to my life, whatever remains of it.*

*I was hoping to maybe share a place with Lilah, she'll need a* flatmate once Andrew's gone. I don't know if that'll happen though. To be honest, I've hardly seen her since the accident. She hasn't been to visit much. She's busy, I suppose. I think it's hard for her to see me like this. We're not what we once were.

Oh God. My heart breaks for us, Jen, for all of us. It breaks for you most of all. Please, please get in touch. For Andrew's sake.

We miss you.


Love,


Nat


P.S. Forgive me for going on and on about me, but I don't know where you are or what you're doing, so it's necessarily a one-way conversation.

## Chapter Fifteen

~

Jen crouched over the toilet in the downstairs loo and tried to vomit quietly. She would have gone upstairs, only she wasn't sure that she would have made it, and the sight of her puke dripping glutinously down the stairs would probably have been even less edifying than the sound of her throwing up. In any case, there was only Natalie left to hear her now. Everyone else was gone.

She finished throwing up and hauled herself to her feet. Her head swam. For a moment, she couldn't focus properly; she felt as though the ground were moving beneath her feet, rocking side to side. Instinctively, she brought her hand to her belly, placing it on the underside of the bump, for comfort. She stood there, head down, breathing steadily. The dizziness passed. She washed her hands, rinsed her mouth out, splashed water on her face, glanced up at herself in the mirror.

She looked bloody awful, not so much pale as grey, the colour of Dickensian gruel. The sickness had come over her suddenly: one moment she was listening to Natalie's horrible, devastating outburst, the next she was in here, heaving her guts out. It couldn't be morning sickness – she hadn't had that for weeks. Stress, perhaps. She would put it down to stress.

She left the bathroom and went out to the living room, where Natalie sat perched on the edge of an armchair, looking out of the window. There wasn't much to see. The blizzard had hit. It was a white-out. She and Natalie were alone: moments after Andrew had driven off, moments too late, of course, Zac and Dan had scrambled for jackets and outdoor shoes and, still bickering at each other like a pair of old women, gone out into the snow. Dan promised Jen, just as the wave of nausea hit her, that they wouldn't go further than the wall at the end of the garden.

Jen doubted they could even find the wall at the end of the garden in this storm. She really wasn't sure what they imagined they'd achieve by going out there, but she let them go partly because she was feeling too ill to argue and mostly because anything was preferable to listening to them bitching at each other.

With all the drama and the throwing up, Jen hadn't really given herself time to think about what Natalie had said. It was only now, with the house empty, silence filling up the spaces left by her departed guests, that she had time to reflect. And the thought that struck her straight away was that it made no difference. It no longer made any difference who was to blame. Conor was dead, Andrew was punished, Natalie had suffered, they had all done their time. Knowing about Lilah's behaviour changed none of that. It didn't bring Conor back, it didn't give Andrew back the life he might have had, it didn't take away Nat's pain. All Natalie had achieved was to rip open an old wound, deepen the divisions between them, lessen the chances that they – all of them – might find a future together as friends.

Jen walked into the living room and stood at Natalie's side. 'Are you all right?' she asked her.

'What do you think?' came Nat's reply, spoken barely above a whisper. She was leaning forward, her elbows resting on her thighs, head in her hands, furiously rubbing at her forehead with the tips of her fingers. 'I can't believe him,' she kept saying, over and over. 'I can't believe him.'

Jen placed a hand on her shoulder, but Natalie shrugged it away.

There were a lot of things that Jen wanted to say to her. She wanted to point out that Natalie had done no one any good today. She wanted to express her hurt at what Natalie had said about her before she'd started in on Lilah, that her leaving was meant as punishment for the rest of them, in particular for Andrew. She wanted to say that she thought that, right at this moment, Natalie was behaving like a spoiled, petulant child. Instead, she said: 'He did what he thought was best. He always does, doesn't he?'

Natalie exhaled sharply, half laugh, half sigh. 'Yes, he does,' she replied, her tone hard-edged, sarcastic. 'He does what he thinks is best. And apparently, what was best in this situation was not to support me. What was best was to take Lilah's side, your side . . . Jesus. He's always on your bloody side.'

Jen took a deep breath, trying with all her might not to let her irritation get the better of her. 'Hang on, Nat. I don't think he was taking Lilah's side, I think he was trying to calm a difficult situation. And as for *my* side . . . since when are you and I on opposite sides, Natalie? I really don't get this, why are you so angry with me?'

Natalie shook her head. 'Why am I angry?' She sighed heavily, she raised her eyes to look directly at Jen. 'I begged you, Jen. I *begged* you, just to contact him, to let him know you were OK. We heard nothing from you. Nothing. For years. I begged you to come to our wedding, not for me, not because it meant so much to me, but for him. Jesus.' Her head dropped again. 'How can you say you didn't punish him?'

'I didn't mean to,' Jen whispered, her words never sounding emptier. 'I didn't mean to.'

'Jen,' Natalie raised her hand in supplication, all the sting gone from her voice. 'Please. I cannot have this conversation with you. I mean, I literally can't right at this moment. Please. Could you get me my pills from upstairs? They're in the washbag on the counter.' She arched her back for a second and Jen could see the pain flit across her face, a passing shadow. 'Sorry, sometimes it's just really bad.'

The mean and uncharitable part of Jen wanted to believe that Natalie was creating a diversion, looking for sympathy, but the better part of her triumphed, though, because she knew that seeking pity was not Natalie's style. In any case, she'd seen the look on her face, she recognised the shadow that pain casts. And why would she seek a diversion now that she had Jen on the ropes? Jen ran upstairs to fetch the pills and brought them back with a glass of water, a glass of whisky in her other hand as a chaser. Nat had moved from the armchair; she was standing by the window, her shoulders rounded, head down, arms wrapped around herself. When she heard Jen behind her she turned and reached for the pills greedily, gratefully, and took a slug of the whisky straight afterwards.

'Not supposed to drink with these,' she said. 'But I think today's pretty much fucked anyway, isn't it?' She gave Jen a tired, rueful smile. For a moment, Jen caught a glimpse of the old Nat, the one who was always ready to laugh at herself.

She reached out for Jen's arm. 'Give me a hand, will you? I've totally seized up.'

Jen helped her back towards the armchair, but Nat steered her into the middle of the room. 'Sometimes it helps if I lie flat,' she said. Jen sat on the floor next to her as she lay prone in front of the fire. They stayed like that for a while, listening to that wind, its low howl building, rattling at the window, tearing at the tiles on the roof. The fire spat and crackled; Jen hoped they'd have enough wood to last the night.

Eventually, Natalie spoke, her voice low and strained.

'You remember that interview that Princess Diana gave?' she asked.

'Um. Vaguely, I suppose. Why?' Nat raised her head and Jen fed her a sip of whisky.

'Thanks. That thing she said, about there being three people in her marriage. That's what I feel sometimes.' She smiled, then she started to giggle.

'So Lilah's Camilla? I wouldn't say that to her face if I were you.'

'No, no. Lilah's not Camilla. You are,' she said, and she giggled some more. She laughed louder and louder, shrieked with mirth.

'I am not Camilla!' Jen protested. 'How am I Camilla?' She was laughing now too, and for a minute or two they were unable to speak, tears coursing down their cheeks.

When she finally stopped laughing, Nat said: 'You're not really Camilla. It's just that I feel as though I share him with you. Even though you're not there, maybe even *because* you're not there. It's not that you're Camilla, it's the past that's Camilla. You're a part of it, you, Lilah, Conor . . . I want us, Andrew, me and the girls, to have a life without that shadow.' She reached both her arms up above her head, stretching her spine as far as she could, then relaxed. 'I just don't want all that to be a part of us any more.'

Jen took a sip of the whisky, enjoyed the feeling of it burning all the way down her throat and into her gut. The baby probably wasn't enjoying the burn quite so much. She put the glass down.

'The problem, Nat, is that all that is a part of you. There's really not much you can do about that. You can't make it go away. You can't make *us* go away.'

Natalie took one of Jen's hands in hers and squeezed it. 'I know that. I don't want you to go away. It's just . . . You know what the really awful thing is? When I think about everything that happened, the aftermath, the way Andrew and I got together, I can't shake the feeling that he's with me out of guilt.'

'Nat . . .'

'No, listen. He's dutiful. It's like you said, he does the right thing. He feels he has a duty of care to you. It's his job to look after you in some way, because Conor isn't here to do it. Because you're his little sister. And I think' – her voice broke a little – 'that he feels he has a duty to me, too. And I don't want to be part of his penance.'

The front door swung open violently, the metal handle crashing against the wall. Both girls jumped. Zac and Dan trudged in, stamping the snow off their boots, bringing with them an arctic blast. Zac closed the door, leaning his full body weight against it in a fight with the wind.

'No sign,' Dan panted. 'Can't see a bloody thing.'

Natalie sat up, her head in her hands.

'Oh God, what have I done? What have I done?' She started to whimper. 'I didn't mean it, Jesus. I didn't mean it.' She looked up at Jen and there was fear in her eyes, genuine panic. 'What if something happens to him, Jen?'

'Nothing's going to happen,' Jen said, keeping her voice as even as she could, attempting to demonstrate a confidence she didn't feel. 'He won't have got far. He'll be sitting in the car with the heating on, waiting out the storm. There's a bottle of water in there, there might even be a packet of biscuits. Nothing's going to happen,' she said, trying her best to force from her mind visions of collisions with tractors, cars sliding off the mountain into the gorge, Lilah lying freezing by the side of the road. In her mind's eye she kept seeing that spot of blood on the stairs, the one she thought she'd cleaned up and seemed to come back. She got to her feet, went into the kitchen, grabbed a cloth and climbed the stairs, but she could no longer find it.

She was being ridiculous. There was no omen, and it was perfectly likely that, as she'd said, Andrew, and probably Lilah too, were sitting in her car eating chocolate biscuits and watching the snow fall.

'I'll make us all some coffee,' Jen said to her guests, who were standing in the centre of the living room, looking glumly out into the storm. 'There's some cake somewhere, I think. Let's cheer ourselves up. I'm sure they'll be fine. We'll probably get a mobile signal back quite soon. Try not to worry too much,' she said, and turned to go into the kitchen, and at that moment all the lights went out.

*19 April 1999*

*Dear Jen,*

*Andrew got your letter yesterday. I can't tell you how upset he is. I know that you're very busy, I understand that it's hard for you to come back to England and to see everyone, I do understand that, but this is our wedding. Surely you can change your plans! Lilah isn't coming, of course, but Dan will be there; and both my parents and Andrew's would love to see you. I want to see you.*

*But more than that, more than any of that, Andrew wants to see you. Jen, I'm writing to beg you to come, because it will break Andrew's heart if you're not there, and I don't want him broken-hearted on our wedding day. There, I've said it. You can think me selfish if you like, but please try also to think about how he will feel if you say no, the message it sends to him. You know how he feels about you, you know how heavy his burden. Please lighten it.*

*We miss you terribly.*

*With love,*

*Nat*

# Chapter Sixteen

~

Lilah had no idea how long it had been since she left the house. It seemed like hours. Despite the cold and the darkness, despite her fear and wet feet, she was feeling oddly cheerful. At least they were moving again. At glacial pace, granted, but moving nonetheless.

For what seemed like an age, they had been stuck in a snow drift on the side of the road. Andrew, determined to get back to his wife, was adamant that they should turn the car in the road and drive back up to the chalet as soon as possible. And no matter how much she begged, pleaded, cajoled and just plain shrieked at him, he refused to drive her down to the village to the B&B.

She'd got her way in the end, though. His attempts to do a three-point turn failed miserably: they ended up sliding off the road (fortunately on the mountain, rather than the cliff side) into thick snow, and it had taken them until now to get the car back to its original position, facing downhill. Andrew had finally had to concede that there was no way of turning back, so the village was their only option. He wasn't particularly happy about it.

This and the knowledge that Natalie would be worried sick about him, would be feeling horribly guilty about what she'd said and done, had cheered Lilah up no end.

'It would've been quicker if I'd walked,' she remarked drily, scooching down in her seat, arms wrapped around herself, trying to warm up. They had the heating on full blast, but the windscreen kept misting up so they'd had to open the windows a crack.

'I'm not exactly used to driving in blizzard conditions,' Andrew replied. She looked over at him. His jaw was set and he was hunched forward over the steering wheel like an old man. He looked terrified. 'And I'm over the limit,' he said to her. 'Again.'

She didn't reply. There was nothing she could say to that, so she just reached over and placed her hand on his leg. It was supposed to be reassuring, but he flinched. 'Don't, Lilah,' he said.

It was weird, being in this car with him, after such a very long time. Weirder still as it felt as though they were alone in the world, drifting slowly along in the eerie white night, waiting to fall off the edge of the world. She thought about asking him why it was he who had come to get her, rather than Zac, but she knew the answer. Andrew couldn't help himself. Once upon a time, he wanted to be liked, to be loved, to be good; now he wanted to save everyone. Zac wasn't so easily manipulated.

A sharp gust of wind blew a flurry of flakes into the car through Lilah's open window. For some reason this seemed funny to her and she started to giggle. Andrew looked over at her and shook his head.

'I'm sorry,' she said, trying to straighten her face.

'You should be,' he replied, but his voice had softened, his

140

jaw looked less rigid, his shoulders had dropped. The slope of the road was gentler now, the hairpins less terrifyingly sharp. They were approaching the village, it wouldn't be far now.

'Hey,' Lilah said, nudging his leg with her own. 'Do you remember the last time we went for a drive together?'

He gave a little sigh. 'Of course I do,' he replied quietly.

She nudged him again. 'It's OK,' she said, smiling, 'I'm not angry with you any more. I'm still pissed off with her, but I forgave you long ago.'

'That doesn't seem fair,' Andrew said.

'Maybe not, but as a woman you're brought up expecting men to betray you. You don't expect it of your best friend.'

'Lilah, it wasn't like that, Natalie never meant . . .'

'Look,' Lilah cut him off. 'That's between me and her,' she said. After the way he was in the house, the way he supported her, defended her, after the way he came out into the storm to find her, she really couldn't bear to hear him make excuses for Natalie right now. Not after what had just happened. 'The important thing is that I've forgiven you,' she said.

'Well,' he sighed. 'I haven't.' His face was stern, so very serious. 'I haven't forgiven myself.'

'Ah, but you never will,' Lilah said. 'For anything.'

It had been January, a biting cold Sunday night. Lilah had driven all the way to Basingstoke to pick Andrew up from the station. He'd got the train back from Shepton, but there were engineering works on the line, and she knew how tired he was, and how tedious it was to have to take the bus replacement service, so she'd offered to come and get him. At first he'd said no. He'd asked her whether she'd had a drink that afternoon, which infuriated her. Particularly under the circumstances.

They'd made up on the phone, but she wanted to do it for real. In the flesh. So she drove all the way there to pick him up.

He was in an odd mood. He was always a little edgy after his visits to Natalie, but that Sunday he seemed different. He seemed agitated, cagey. Usually, after a visit to Natalie's he'd talk non-stop, about how she was, how much progress she'd made in her recovery, how far she had to go. Not this time. He didn't want to talk, not just about the weekend, but about anything. Lilah prattled away, talking about the party she'd been to on Friday night, about shopping with her mother on Saturday. She was aware that she was talking to herself, but she didn't seem to be able to stop, and somewhere deep down inside of her, panic was rising.

She thought it must be the argument they'd had earlier. He was still annoyed by that, and he was probably also tired. He certainly looked exhausted, the circles under his eyes deeper and darker than they had been even of late. She wanted to make things better, for him, for both of them, and so she fell back on what she seemed always to fall back on these days. Placing her hand lightly on his thigh, she said:

'Why don't we stop somewhere? We can stay in a nasty Travelodge and pretend we're travelling salespeople having a torrid affair.' She turned to give him her cheekiest, most enticing little smile, but he wasn't looking at her, he was staring out of the window. She gave his leg a squeeze. 'Come on,' she said. 'It'll be fun.'

'Eyes on the road, Lilah,' he said wearily, still not looking at her.

'Andrew . . .'

'I just want to go home.'

They drove on in silence. Lilah could feel the tears rising in her throat, there with the panic, and she wasn't sure why she

142

felt like this, but she thought that if Andrew kept drumming his fingers on the dashboard like that she was going to smack him.

'What is it? Please, Drew, just tell me what's going on. Was it a bad weekend with Nat? Was she worse?'

Silence.

'Andrew . . .'

'Lilah, just drive, OK? And watch your speed, yeah, you're doing ninety.'

Lilah pressed her foot down harder on the accelerator. She watched the speedo go to ninety-five, one hundred, one ten, and she could feel a wobble in the steering wheel, and she pressed her foot down harder still.

'Please, Lilah.' No more than a whisper. His face was grey. She relaxed her foot off the pedal, changed lanes, into the middle and then the slow lane, then pulled off the motorway at the next exit. Fleet Services.

In Lilah's mind, Fleet Services on the M3 would forever live in infamy. They parked in an almost deserted car park and sat for a moment, staring at the dispiritingly cheerful yellow of the McDonald's arches, the bright, buzzing strip light emanating from the food court.

'I'll get us some coffee,' Lilah said. She had her hand on the door handle, but she didn't actually move. Andrew reached out, and slowly took her other hand in his, squeezing it tight. She squeezed back, and in that moment she knew, not exactly what was coming, but that she and Andrew were finished.

'Do you think,' she asked very softly, her voice husky with tears, 'that you'll ever forgive me, Drew?'

'It wasn't your fault,' he said. It meant nothing, when he said it. They'd all got so tired of hearing those words over the past six months.

'But will you forgive me?'

That's when he did it. Andrew, the martyr, falling on his sword and letting her turn her guilt to rage.

'I don't love you any more, Lilah,' he said, blunt as a hammer, his voice low and steady. He listened to her start to cry. Then he said: 'I've fallen in love with Natalie.'

He listened to the catch in her breath, the little gasp of pain. 'You knew that. Don't pretend you didn't know.'

'You feel sorry for her,' Lilah sobbed. 'That isn't love.'

Andrew waited a long time before replying. Finally, he said: 'It is love. And the thing I've only just realised is that it's always been her. For me. I'm sorry. I really am.'

Lilah turned to him. She'd stopped crying; the expression on her face was genuine bewilderment, disbelief. 'Always? You don't mean that, Andrew, you can't. We've been together four years, you can't mean that.'

'I'm sorry,' he said again, and he got out of the car, and walked into the service station. Lilah sat there for a few minutes, waiting for him to come back, to tell her it was a mistake, he didn't mean it, it wasn't true. Then she drove home alone.

There were lights up ahead, a cluster of lights. They'd reached the village. Andrew spread his fingers out wide on the wheel, stretching and flexing his hands to release the tension.

'Thank God for that,' he said.

'You never told me,' Lilah said, 'how you got home that night? From Fleet.'

He smiled. 'Does it matter?' he asked, and as he did they heard a noise from behind, the car was flooded with light, there was a thump, not vicious, but hard enough to jolt them both forward against their seatbelts. The car shunted forward suddenly, veering to the right, towards the edge of the mountain. Andrew put his foot on the brake and Lilah felt the back wheels start to slide, propelling the car towards the precipice.

'Don't brake,' she said helplessly, grabbing at the dashboard and at the door handle. 'Andrew, take your foot off the brake.'

He did, but it was too late. Lilah closed her eyes as the car slid from the road.

*Hey man.*

*God, when did things get so fucked up? I hope you're OK, you sounded in bits on the phone.*

*Listen, she's here with me, she'll be OK. I'll take care of her, don't worry. She's drinking like a fish of course, but I'm keeping an eye on her. I've persuaded her to stay at least until her mum gets back from holiday, then I think she's going to move back in with her, so she'll be all right.*

*She's gutted, obviously. But you know what she's like: one minute she's banging on about how you've broken her heart and she'll never recover, the next she's saying that she knew things were over months ago but she didn't want to end it with you because she felt sorry for you.*

*The thing with Nat, though. That's going to be harder. I assume you're seeing/speaking to Nat regularly – if you are, tell her to stop calling. Lilah is not going to be ready to speak to her any time soon. Maybe she should write or something, I don't know. Honestly, I think she should just leave it, for a few months at least. Wait until Lilah's found herself a new guy (don't want to be harsh, but you know it's not going to be that long), wait until she's on a bit more of an even keel.*

*As I say, I'm not going to let anything bad happen to her. I've been trying, as best I can, to persuade her to just stay in and get trashed with me rather than going out on the town where she could get herself into trouble. We've had some good long chats, actually, about you and Conor, Jen, everything. It's been all right. She'll be all right.*

*Best of luck, mate. I'll come to Reading and see you as soon as I can*

146

*(not now though, because Lilah will take that as me siding with you and she'll scratch my eyes out). Love to Nat. I think it's a good thing, you and her. I really do. It's been a long time coming, hasn't it?*

*Dan*

# Chapter Seventeen

~

Somewhere outside, in the darkness, something was making a noise. A banging sound, eerily rhythmic, bang, bang, bang. Like someone hammering on a door, begging to be let in from the storm. Or someone breaking a door down. Jack Nicholson with an axe and a manic grin. Honey, I'm home. The hairs were standing up on the back of Dan's neck.

'What *is* that noise?' he asked.

The four of them were in the kitchen, scrabbling around in the half-light generated by the wood burner, searching through every drawer and every cupboard for some candles.

'No idea,' Jen muttered. 'Where the hell did I put them? I know I bought candles yesterday. I know I did.'

The banging stopped. Then it started again, louder this time.

'Seriously, what is that?' Dan glanced over at Natalie; she was looking nervous, too.

'I think there might be someone out there,' Dan said.

'Don't be ridiculous,' Zac said. 'There's no one out there.'

'I thought I saw a light, actually,' Natalie said. 'A little while ago.'

'Where?' Dan could feel his heart racing. It was ridiculous, but he was starting to feel really creeped out.

'Out back, towards the woods.'

Bang, bang, bang.

It was the perfect horror movie set-up. A group of people go to a house in the middle of nowhere, an idyllic location by day, lonely and menacing by night. A storm blows up. Some members of the group are separated. The lights go out. There are strange noises outside. Jesus Christ, all they were missing was a maniac in a hockey mask with a butcher's knife.

Dan was really starting to freak himself out now. 'Perhaps we should just sit tight for a bit,' he said, glancing around behind him, trying to ignore the uncomfortable feeling that there was someone else there, someone standing in the darkened hallway, watching them. 'Let's just sit by the fire for a bit, have a drink. The lights are bound to come back on in a minute.'

Jen snorted. 'After the last storm the power was off for nearly thirty-six hours,' she said. 'We need to find those bloody candles.'

'Where else could you have put them?' Natalie asked her. 'Is there another cupboard maybe, somewhere in the living room?'

'Oh fuck,' Jen said quietly.

'What?' everyone asked in unison.

'I didn't buy them.'

'What?' Dan yelped, louder than he'd intended.

'I just remembered, I was on my way to get them from the alimentation generale in Draguignan, and then I saw that rug in the window of that design shop . . . Oh, bloody hell. I don't believe I did that. I never got any candles.'

'Do you have a torch?' Zac asked her.

'There was one somewhere . . .' she said, casting around in the darkness.

'Oh, for God's sake,' Dan said, hoping that exasperation might cover fear.

Jen couldn't find a torch, so they lit their way with mobile phones.

'At least they can be used for something,' Zac pointed out cheerfully. 'Since there's no signal, I mean.' Dan had had just about enough of Zac, his bravado, his optimism, his sunny fucking disposition. They moved back into the living room and sat around the fire. Dan had brought a bottle of whisky with him from the kitchen; he poured himself a glass, offered one to Natalie who seized it gratefully. Her hands were shaking, her breathing a little ragged. During the whole candle crisis she'd been holding things together, but he could see now that with nothing to do, no way to contact her husband, the storm still raging outside, she was starting to unravel.

Bang, bang, bang.

'Jesus,' Dan breathed, gulping down a mouthful of Scotch. 'That really is starting to set me on edge.'

'Relax,' Zac said, smiling at him encouragingly. 'I'm sure it's nothing.'

'What do you mean, it's nothing? How could it be nothing? It's obviously *something*. Something is making a banging noise.'

'The attic,' Jen said.

'You think there's something in the attic?' Dan asked, his stomach curling itself into a small, hard ball. 'It's not coming from the attic. It's coming from outside, surely?'

'No, not the noise. There were a couple of boxes of stuff, left here by the old tenant. Some kitchen utensils and things. I put them up in the attic. I think there might have been some candles in there. Those thin, churchy ones. I didn't bother to take them out because I had plenty of my own.'

'Right you are,' Zac said, leaping to his feet. 'I'll go up and get them then. How do you get into the attic?'

'I'll show you,' Jen said, getting up.

'No, I remember,' Dan said reluctantly. 'There's a trapdoor in the ceiling just outside your bedroom, isn't there?'

'That's right. There's a ladder you can pull down. The boxes should be just to the left-hand side I think. There's not much up there, so they shouldn't be too hard to find.'

'It's OK, Dan,' Zac said as Dan got up to go upstairs, 'you stay here with the girls. I'll manage.'

Dan clenched his fists and his jaw. *Stay with the girls?* Condescending wanker. 'No, I know where I'm going. I'll do it.' He took his phone out of his pocket, checked one more time for a signal and then held it out in front of him, lighting his way into the hallway and up the stairs. He was pathetically, shamefully grateful that Zac did not allow him to go alone.

It took them a little while to get the trapdoor open and pull the ladder down. Dan went first but managed to trap his finger in the mechanism, so Zac took over. Dan was constantly fighting the urge to tell Zac to bugger off, although he hadn't quite had time to analyse why he found him so irritating. It wasn't just that he didn't run out after Lilah when she left, and it wasn't the fact that Zac was so good-looking, although he realised that no doubt everyone would assume that was the reason. Watching him clamber fearlessly up the ladder, into an attic that might contain any number of deeply unpleasant things (rats, dead birds, the evil spirit of some long-dead former inhabitant of the house), he decided that it wasn't even his seeming imperviousness to peril. It was the ease with which he'd slipped into the group. He'd known everyone less than twenty-four hours and, already, Dan sensed people looking to him for leadership. Well, the girls, downstairs, they clearly thought of him as the one who could fend off danger or get them out of trouble. Dan was an afterthought. Andrew, yes, Conor, yes. They were alpha, he was beta, the lost boy, Jen called him. That's just how it was back then. But now he was second fiddle to Zac? It was insulting. Terrified or not, he wasn't going to stand here in the hallway, holding a ladder, waiting for Action Man to save the day. He summoned up all the courage he could and climbed up.

'It's all right, mate, I can manage,' Zac said as Dan popped his head up into the attic. Dan ignored him and kept climbing. There was an ominous creaking sound from above, the rafters straining as the wind battered the roof.

'Let's just get on with this,' Dan muttered.

Jen's information had been misleading; there were actually a number of boxes up there. They opened a couple, found them filled with books and papers, all in French. Finally they found one containing some kitchen utensils and one particularly manky-looking candle. They were about to go back down the ladder with their disappointing haul when Dan noticed another box, stuck underneath one of the rafters. It took him a while, but he managed to dislodge it and opened it up.

'Score,' he said, ridiculously pleased with himself, pulling out a box of twelve candles. He threw them to Zac, who was standing on the top of the ladder. Instead of following him straight down, Dan decided to take a quick look through the rest of the box's contents, his curiosity getting the better of him and his fear. There were letters, postcards, all in French, presumably belonging to the tenant. An old bank card, a picture of a very tanned blonde in a bikini, standing outside this very house, grinning from ear to ear. At the very bottom of the box there was a yellowing piece of paper, lined, folded in two. Dan picked it up and unfolded it, turned it over and felt a shiver travel all the way up his spine. It was a list. Written in his handwriting.

*Villefranche, Alpes Maritimes, France*

*Where will we be in the year 2010?*

    *Conor will be married to Jen. He will design furniture which will sell for extortionate prices. Jen will translate great works of modern literature from French to English. They will live here, in this house, with their two adorable children, Ronan and Isabelle. They will throw wild parties in the summer and at New Year, which we shall all attend.*

    *Andrew will be an internationally renowned human rights lawyer, lauded the world over for work in fighting for the rights of political prisoners and confronting injustice wherever he may find it.*

    *Lilah will be very rich. She will have married a billionaire and subsequently divorced well. She will have houses in the south of France, Vale, perhaps a small castle in the Scottish Highlands. She will have several lovers, one of which will be Andrew.*

    *Natalie will be a Booker Prize-winning author. She will be married to an American war correspondent who divides his time between the UK, New York and Beirut. This will suit Natalie perfectly. She will live in a rambling farmhouse in Yorkshire, but will spend a great deal of her time hanging out in Lilah's villa in Cap Ferrat.*

    *Dan's film will win a prize at Sundance. He will live in LA with Winona Ryder.*

## Chapter Eighteen

~

The wind had become a scream. Looking out of the living-room window, Natalie could no longer see anything further than a few feet away, just endless sheets of driving snow. She wondered how many storms this house had seen, how many more it could endure before the roof was ripped off altogether, before the house was once more left open to the elements. She could hear Dan and Zac moving around upstairs, climbing up the ladder into the attic. And that banging sound, that relentless bloody banging sound, ominous, like a drumbeat, heralding disaster. Andrew had been gone for two hours.

Jen had rung the B&B in the village. They weren't there. Give it another hour, she'd said, and then we'd better call the police. Not that they would be likely to do much, not that there was a great deal they could do. There was a part of Natalie that didn't want to ring the police anyway, because she couldn't bring herself to even begin to prepare for bad news. She sipped her whisky, but it didn't help; there was a bitter taste in her mouth, bile or despair, and no amount of Scotch was going to take it away.

The things she'd said, all those things she'd said. She couldn't get the words out of her head now, they kept repeating over and over. 'He would have been a QC by now, not just a teacher in some fucking sink school.' She'd stood there in the living room and called her husband a failure, in front of everyone. She rang his mobile for the hundredth time.

'Please, please, please,' she whispered to herself, biting her lip with frustration and disappointment when, yet again, she got that insolent, repetitive beep. She longed to tell him she hadn't meant it. She'd just got lost in her anger. She longed to talk to her children. She wanted so much to hear their lovely voices, their pealing laughter, to listen to them prattle on about the skinny jeans they absolutely had to have. Christ, she'd give anything to listen to them nag her to let them get their ears pierced. But she couldn't call them. They'd want to talk to Dad (they always wanted to talk to Dad) and what could she say? Could she lie, convincingly, without bursting into tears, could she say he was in the shower? That he'd gone out for a drive? He went out into a blizzard, chasing after his ex-girlfriend, and he never came back.

She put her drink down, walked to the window and pressed her forehead against the glass. She thought perhaps that the screaming of the wind was fainter now, and was the snow easing off? Or was that just wishful thinking? She tried to imagine them, Andrew and Lilah, sitting in Jen's car, the heating on full blast, windows steamed up. Laughing about old times, perhaps? Or maybe they were cursing her, for what she'd said, for what she'd wrought. Maybe they were making up. Kissing and making up, making up for lost time. Natalie tried to picture her husband with his hands on Lilah's still youthful body; she concentrated on trying to conjure up that image, because it was infinitely preferable to the other one, the one that kept forcing its way into her brain, the one in which Jen's car was lying at the bottom of a ravine, a tangled mess of metal, the windscreen smashed out.

When she closed her eyes she could see just that, the windscreen smashed out. No snow drifting in though: it was warm, the car sat motionless in dappled sunshine. Andrew was there, and then he was gone. She could hear someone shouting, someone sobbing, a terrible, desperate sound, and then silence. Then black, and later, Andrew was back at her side, holding her hand. He told her that she was going to be all right, everything was going to be all right. He told her that he loved her. She'd waited so long to hear him say that, hear those words, spoken to her, from his lips. She should have been happy to hear them, but it was all wrong, it sounded wrong. Andrew had blood on his face, he was crying. Someone else was crying, too, a plaintive, keening wail. Natalie could smell burning. Could she smell burning? She was terrified, she wanted to get out of the car but she couldn't move, the door wouldn't open, her legs wouldn't move. The pain was consuming, paralysing, unlike anything she'd ever felt. Andrew kept holding her hand, speaking softly, telling her that it was all going to be all right. It wasn't, though, she knew it wasn't. She knew that Conor was dead, but she couldn't think about that, all she could think about was the pain and the smell of burning and the terrible certainty that she was going to burn alive.

She could smell burning.

'Zac found candles!' She turned around. Jen was standing there, a lit candle in either hand, Zac just behind her. 'Nat! Jesus. You're shaking. Oh, Nat, it's going to be all right. She handed the candles to Zac and hurried to Natalie's side to give her a hug. 'He'll be OK. It'll be OK.'

Natalie smiled and nodded. She was distracted by the appearance of Dan in the doorway behind them, holding a piece of paper in his hand. He looked pale, shocked. As though he'd seen a ghost.

The phone started ringing and everyone jumped.

*Dear Jen,*

*Congratulations! Of course I don't feel strange about it, you deserve to be happy, I wish you the greatest happiness possible. Can't wait to meet him. And I'm not put out at all – elopement sounds like a fine idea to me. I wish more people did it . . .*

*We're good. The girls had their second birthday party last week – fourteen under-fives running around in our back yard – it was absolute bloody chaos, I can tell you. I've never been so exhausted in all my life. It was a fantastic day, though, they were spoiled rotten and thoroughly enjoyed themselves. I will get Nat to send over some pics for you.*

*Nat has decided to leave Murray Books – she's decided she would rather stick to full-time motherhood after all. I hope it's the right thing for her. I suggested that she may find time to write if she's not working full time, but that didn't go down very well – I got a short, sharp lecture on how being a mother to twins is working full time. But I'm sad for her, because I know that she has been trying to write recently and it's just not coming. She has had terrible problems with her back lately, so she's on some quite strong painkillers and finds they affect her concentration. Plus she can't sit at a desk for any length of time otherwise it seizes up. It breaks my heart, Jen – she's so strong, she pretty much never complains about it, even when I can tell it's really bad. And she's amazing with the girls, she never lets them see that she's tired or suffering. She's always ready to run around the garden with them – no matter how hard it is for her.*

*I only wish I could make it better somehow.*

*Sorry. Rambling on. Otherwise, things are good for me. I've finished my teacher training now and will be starting at Greystone Comp in September. Really looking forward to it, actually, although I* am vaguely terrified. I'm sure teenage boys are bigger than they used to be. And I know the girls are certainly more formidable.

How do you feel about coming for a visit? Bring Monsieur Jean-Luc! We don't have to stay in Reading, I know it's not terribly exciting. We could spend a few days in London, or go to the Cotswolds or something. I would love to see you, Jen. I do miss you.

With love,

Andrew

P.S. Almost forgot to say — Ronan came over for Charlotte and Grace's party — he was on fine form. Asked lots of questions about you, he was saying how much he and his mum would love to see you. It was great seeing him: whenever I see him I feel as though I get a tiny glimpse of Conor again. It's good for my soul.

## Chapter Nineteen

～

There was only one room at the inn.

'We have for you the 'oneymoon suite,' the wonderfully moustachioed Monsieur Caron said to Andrew with a wink. 'Fireplace, *grand lit*, is perfect.' He smiled appreciatively at Lilah, who somehow managed to look glamorous even with her hair plastered to her face and mascara smeared across the top of her cheekbones. Lilah left Andrew to complete the formalities while she disappeared upstairs to run herself a bath.

La Petite Auberge was a typically Alpine structure on Villefranche's main street, flanked by the boulangerie and the tabac. It may well have been rather dull and unprepossessing in bright sunshine, but laden with snow, warm light streaming from within, it had appeared, to Andrew and Lilah, like a vision, like paradise.

They'd had to leave the car where it was – jammed up against a tree on the side of the mountain at the entrance to the village. Fortunately, they hadn't been, as Andrew had feared, quite on the edge of the precipice. At the point where they had crashed, there was a small drop from the road, and beyond that a stretch of ten metres or more of land before the ground fell away to the valley floor hundreds of feet below.

They'd been lucky, too, that the driver of the vehicle which had rear-ended them, a ruddy-faced man whose breath smelled strongly of brandy, hadn't been interested in getting the police involved. On the contrary, he'd been hugely apologetic: he'd sworn that it was all his fault and had left them his details, promising in broken English to reimburse them for the cost of the damage to the car.

Andrew realised, as he signed the form in reception, that he had no credit card and no money with him, but fortunately when he explained that he was staying with Madame de Chassagny, up the hill, Monsieur Caron was more than happy to trust that he would be paid.

'Ah! La belle anglaise! Vous êtes son frère?' he asked, peering at Andrew, looking for some hint of family resemblance.

Her brother. 'Oui,' Andrew said with a smile. 'Son frère.'

Formalities completed, Andrew dragged himself wearily up the stairs to the second floor. He pushed open the door and entered paradise: the honeymoon suite was a large room, with a four-poster bed in its centre, a fireplace flanked by two worn armchairs, and a tiny window under the eaves which looked out onto the road. It was warm and clean and smelled of wood smoke and pine. Standing there in his sodden clothes, shaking with cold, emotionally exhausted, he could have wept with relief.

While Lilah was in the bath, he rang Jen's number from the landline, listened to her calling out, 'Nat, he's OK. He's OK!' For the second time in as many minutes, he felt like crying. He apologised about the car, but Jen didn't seem to care. 'Bugger the car,' she said. 'Thank God you're all right.'

Nat came to the phone. Neither of them said anything for a

moment. Then, in the tiniest voice possible, she said: 'I'm sorry. I'm very sorry.'

'It's OK,' he said. It wasn't OK at all, but he couldn't say what he felt, wasn't even sure what he felt, he hadn't had time to process what she'd said. 'I'm OK. I'm at the B&B in Villefranche. It's actually not that bad. Very comfortable. I don't know whether I'll be able to get anything to eat here, but . . . well. We had a lot at lunch. So. Probably no bad thing for me to skip a meal.' He was talking nonsense, rambling on, jovial, covering the awkwardness. 'I'm sorry if you were frightened. Are you all right?'

'I'm fine,' she said, again, her voice barely audible.

Then: 'Drew, darling!' Lilah's voice called out all of a sudden, clear enough to cut glass. 'Do you want me to leave the water in for you?' He closed his eyes, felt his heart sink into his stomach, and prepared himself for the onslaught.

He could hear her breathing on the other end of the line. 'Huh.' A little exhalation. 'She's there, with you? In your room?'

Andrew took a deep breath. 'They only had one room, Nat. The place is full. We have to share.'

With a click, the phone went dead.

'Bloody hell,' Andrew said miserably.

'What's up?' Lilah was standing in the doorway of the bathroom in her underwear, her arms folded across her chest. He turned away from her.

'Did you have to yell like that?' he asked, exasperated. 'Now she knows that we're sharing a room and I'm going to catch seven shades of hell next time I see her.'

'Frankly, my dear, I don't give a shit,' Lilah replied. 'After what she did to me today . . .'

'I didn't do anything to you, though, did I, Lilah?' Andrew said. 'Christ, I wish you two would leave me out of it.' He turned back to look at her. She was still standing there in her underwear, leaning against the door frame, rivulets of water dripping from her hair, her chin tilted up in a pose of defiance, but there was something in her eyes that looked like remorse. Without clothes she was shockingly, painfully thin, hip bones jutting out over the top of her pink knickers, her ribs clearly visible, clavicles sharply defined at the base of her neck. She looked impossibly fragile, breakable. Andrew had the most desperate, overwhelming urge to put his arms around her, he remembered so clearly in that moment what it was to love her. He closed his eyes and turned away.

*12 September 2009*
*Email, from Lilah to Jen*

*My darling Jen,*

*I was thinking about you today, and I literally could not remember the last time we were in touch. Well, I know you wrote to me at Christmas, and I got your card on my birthday, so I suppose it's more accurate to say that I can't remember the last time I got in touch with you. I am a very, very bad friend. I am a very, very bad person. But then you knew that already, didn't you darling?*

*How are you, anyway? I am having the most terrible time. I got fired from my crappy paid job last month and am now struggling to find freelance PR work. Curse this fucking market. Honestly. Why can't it be 2002 when everyone was borrowing money hand over fist and chucking it around? Plus Mum's ill, which is awful. Too awful. She asks after you, she always liked you. You should come and visit.*

*You're not going to come and visit, are you? I don't blame you, I probably wouldn't visit me either. Fuck, there was a point to me writing to you and I can't for the life of me remember what it was now. Yes I do, I remember. I was listening to the radio and 'White Lines' came on, and I remembered Andrew, Dan and Conor doing the most cringe-inducing dance routine at that God-awful charity talent show thing at college, and we laughed until we cried, that's what it was, it made me think about the fact I don't laugh like that any more and I was thinking how much I wished that I did. I miss you, all of you. Even that back-stabbing cow Natalie.*

*Oh, Jen. There are so many things I would have done differently. I'm so sorry. You'll never know how sorry I am for everything I did wrong and all the pain I caused.*

*I wish you lots of love, I hope that you are happy.*

*Goodbye for now.*

*Lilah x*

## Chapter Twenty

~

Jen moved through the house slowly, trailing her fingers along the smooth, cool surface of the plastered walls upstairs, across the rough stone on the side of the stairway. She placed candles in every room. The storm was starting to die down a little, the creaking of the beams in the roof had lessened, the snowfall had slowed. Inside the house, it felt as though they were at the eye of the storm; there was an atmosphere of strange, tense quietude. Natalie sat at the kitchen table, fuming. Zac was working quietly, wrapping jacket potatoes in foil to cook in the wood burner, in case anyone was hungry later. Dan sat in the living room with a glass of wine. He was troubled by something, that had been obvious from the moment he came down from the attic. Jen wondered if it was because of his girlfriend.

'You OK?' she asked Dan as she took the armchair opposite his. He looked up and smiled at her, a very sad smile, an old smile. One she remembered. 'What happened? Is it Claudia?'

He shook his head. 'No, no. It's nothing. It's . . . nothing.'

It obviously wasn't nothing. 'Well, it looks like it's something. Come on. You can talk to me.'

He raised his eyebrows a little, looking directly at her. 'Once upon a time,' he said.

Jen lowered her eyes. 'You think it too, do you? Like Natalie, you think I was punishing you?'

'No, I don't. I don't think that. I wish . . .' he tailed off.

'Is that what's troubling you? I know something's troubling you. It isn't the banging sound, is it?' She smiled at him. 'Because I think that might be the woodshed door. I might have forgotten to close it.'

'It's not the banging sound either. Although good to know that it's just the woodshed. That's a relief.'

'*She said, there's something nasty in the woodshed . . .*' They sang it together and started laughing.

The fire crackled and spat; a fat spark flew clear of the hearth and on to the rug. Dan fell to his knees to smother it. He found himself at Jen's feet. He put his hands around her ankles.

'I missed you,' he said quietly. She reached forward, running her fingers through his cropped hair.

'You too.'

'I wish you'd written.'

'I know.'

'I found something,' he said. He was still kneeling at her feet, his head bowed.

'Found something?'

'Upstairs, in the attic. In one of the boxes.' He delved into the front pocket of his jeans, brought out a much-folded sheet of paper and handed it to her.

'Oh.' Her hand came up to her mouth. 'Oh my God. The list. Your list. It was in the attic?'

Dan looked up at her. 'I wasn't sure whether I should show you . . .'

'Oh, yes. Of course you should.' She leaned forward and put her arms around his neck, gave him a squeeze, inhaled the scent of him. He smelled expensive, like leather. 'I'd forgotten all about it.' She read it and reread it, a smile on her lips. 'We were so hopeful, weren't we? God. So young.' Her laughter bubbled up in her throat. 'It was . . . a couple of nights before we left, wasn't it?' Dan nodded. 'You were sitting just about exactly where you are now. Con and I were on that old sofa that was here, over by the wall. You decided that we had to note down our ambitions, for posterity. You were always writing things down for posterity, weren't you?'

'I always thought it might end up good material.' He flinched as the words came out. 'I didn't mean . . .'

'I know what you meant.'

'I wonder how this ended up in the attic?'

'No idea. I remember looking for it when I got back to England. It wasn't in my notebook. I remember thinking that I'd have to rewrite it sometime, if I could remember it all. Somehow it must have got mixed in with the tenant's stuff.' Jen reread the list, blinking back the tears pricking the backs of her eyes.

'God. You lot were so ambitious! All Conor and I seemed to want was an easy life . . .'

'Well,' Dan got to his feet and took his place in the armchair opposite her. 'You didn't need ambition. You already had pretty much everything you wanted.'

She couldn't meet his eyes then. 'But get you lot – Booker Prize, human rights advocate, Sundance festival. Actually, you've not done all that badly. I mean, Claudia may not be Winona Ryder, but at least she isn't a shoplifter. She isn't a shoplifter, is she?'

He grinned. 'Not that I know of.' Then he said: 'I'm sorry that you didn't get to live the life you should have.'

Jen shrugged. 'No one gets the life they think they're going to have when they're twenty-three, Dan. Almost no one, anyway. If you look at the names on that list, you can hardly say I had the worst time of it, can you?' They both fell silent after that.

Despite herself, Jen was wondering how you would rank them, in terms of bad luck. Conor had to come first, of course, but then was it Andrew, who took all the blame, or Nat, who lived with the pain? Dan and Lilah appeared to have got off easily, but who really knew what they'd been through?

'Do you blame Lilah, Jen? Now you know. The whole story, what Nat said.'

Jen thought for a moment. 'No. I mean, she could have taken some of the pressure off Andrew, couldn't she? She should have spoken up about that. But it doesn't really change anything, does it? And you know, it could have been me driving that car. If someone had suggested I drive, I would've done. Yes, I'd had two glasses of wine, but I still would've done it. Do you remember, what it felt like, that day, that summer, the summer before?' She smiled. 'It was like this list, we thought we could do anything. No one ever thought about anything bad happening. We were going to be friends forever, love each other forever, live forever. We were invincible. I think everyone feels like that when they're that age, don't they?'

Dan nodded. 'I remember driving so fast, that rush, that recklessness. I know exactly what you mean.'

Jen remembered the rush, too. She still had the taste of wine on her tongue when she climbed into Dan's car, the taste of Conor's kiss. The sun shining down on them. Lilah was in the back, sitting sideways with her feet up because it was the only way she could fit her long legs into the car. Jen could remember leaning back in her seat, closing her eyes, willing him to go faster and faster, letting the rush take everything else away.

'Jen?' Dan brought her back, to the darkness of the living room. 'You all right?'

'I'm fine.' She paused for a moment. 'I was just thinking, that list. I didn't write down anything that I wanted for myself. Conor and Jen want this, Conor and Jen will do that . . .'

They fell into a silence heavy with things unspoken. What she wanted at the time she wrote that list, how that had changed six months later, and six months after that, and then, how everything she'd ever wanted didn't mean a thing any longer, because the life she'd known no longer existed. Slowly, tentatively, Dan reached out his hand to her. She took it.

'Not everyone wants the same thing forever,' he said, as though he'd read her mind.

'I know.' There was a moment where she thought she could tell him, what it was that had kept her away so long, a moment where she thought she could explain it perfectly, but then his phone beeped and he said, 'At last, signal!' and the moment was gone.

*My darling Con,*

*I need to say this to you, but I can't say it to you. I can't say it to your face. I can't bring myself to say it and see the look in your eyes, I can't bear it, the thought of how much you'll hate me when you know what I've done. The terrible things I've done.*

*There is no excuse for it. All I can say is that for some reason, some reason I can't even remember any longer, I woke up one day, or maybe it came upon me gradually, I don't know, I don't even bloody know, I just realised that maybe everything we wanted wasn't everything I wanted any longer. And it's not that you aren't enough, it's that I'm not enough. Like this, I'm not enough.*

*I can't say this to you. I can't even write this to you. I have to write the words down but it frightens me to do it, to end it, to put an end to this, because it will be, once you know, it will be the end of you and me. I know it. I did a terrible thing. I betrayed you. I have to say it to your face, don't I? I can't write this down.*

*I can't.*

171

# Chapter Twenty-one

❧

Without being asked, the auberge owner's wife, a large, round lady, living proof of the inaccuracy of the claim that French women do not get fat, brought to their room two plates of stew, a rich boeuf bourgignon accompanied by dauphinois potatoes, and a litre pitcher of red wine.

'I sink you have not eaten?' she said, proffering her tray with a hopeful, toothsome smile.

Andrew and Lilah fell on her like starving wolves. They devoured the food ravenously, in silence, sitting on the floor in front of the fire.

After they'd finished eating, Andrew found that the silence ceased to be comfortable, so he said:

'I called a taxi. It cost me seventy quid to get home.'

'I'm sorry?'

'You wanted to know how I got back. From Fleet. After we broke up.'

'Oh. Well. You deserved it. After all, you did sleep with my best friend.'

'Fair point.'

'It wasn't the first time, was it?' Lilah asked. 'That weekend?'

'Yes, it was. I promise you that.'

'Who . . . was it you? Who initiated it?' She laughed. 'Sorry, I don't know why I'm asking you this. It's just, I don't know, at the time, I spent ages imagining it in my head. Not the sex, but how it started, who made the first move.' She giggled again. 'Somehow I can't imagine either of you making the first move. Or I couldn't then, anyway.'

'Lilah.' Andrew shook his head, embarrassed.

'No, go on. Tell me.'

'I kissed her. It was my fault. I started it.'

Lilah was sitting on the floor, leaning against an armchair, a blanket wrapped round her shoulders. Her legs were stretched out in front of her, toes touching the hearth. She wriggled them in front of her, inspecting the dark red polish on her toenails, the polish she'd applied that morning, post-sex, while Zac was in the shower. Before lunch, before the argument. Before. She hooked one ankle over the other, looked up at Andrew. He smiled at her, but he looked uncomfortable and awkward and very sad. Her heart ached a little.

'Did you do it out of guilt, Andrew?'

'Did I do what out of guilt?'

'Did you kiss her because you felt bad for her, for everything that had happened? You knew she was in love with you, didn't you, that she always had been? And you felt sorry for her. That's how it started, isn't it? Is that why it happened?'

Andrew made a noise somewhere between a sigh and a laugh. He hauled himself to his feet and turned away from her.

'I think it's time to get some sleep,' he said. 'I'm tired. You can have the bed. I'll take the armchair.'

'Drew, I didn't mean . . .'

173

He turned back to her, his face reddening with anger, his voice raised. 'You're asking me if I got together with Nat out of *pity*? You're seriously asking me that? You think I would have married her, stayed with her all this time, raised two children with her because I felt sorry for her? Even by your standards, Lilah, that's pretty deluded.'

She passed her hand over her eyes. 'That's not what I meant . . .'

'Yes, it was. And,' he sighed, dropping his chin to his chest, 'it's ridiculous. Lilah, I don't want to hurt your feelings, but I fell in love with Nat long before that. Years before that. I've already told you that. I told you at the time.' The look on her face was almost unbearable to him. He crouched down next to her, almost losing his balance. He took her hand. 'Don't, please don't look like that.'

'I didn't think you meant it,' she said, her voice small and husky. 'I thought you were just angry with me. Do you really mean to say that you never loved me at all?' she asked. 'Because for the best part of four years you did a really good job of acting as though you did.'

He sat back down next to her, put his arm around her shoulders and pulled her close. She pulled away. 'Of course I loved you, Lilah. I loved you very much. I'm not entirely sure that you ever loved me though . . .' She tried to protest, but he carried on. 'Wait, wait. Do you remember how we got together? Do you remember that you only made a pass at me – hang on, you admitted this – you only made a pass at me because you wanted to piss off Karen Samuels?' Despite herself, Lilah started to giggle. 'She had a crush on me and you found her really irritating, so you decided you'd have me for yourself.' She let him pull her closer. 'That was how our relationship started.

And I did fall in love with you, of course I did. You were – you are – irresistible. But somewhere, in the background, there was Natalie. And for me, for some part of me, it was always Natalie.'

Lilah pulled herself away from him again, pulled her blanket more tightly around her body. 'Mum saw it,' she said. 'She warned me. I said she was talking nonsense.'

Andrew felt an old shame wash over him. 'Oh, God. I'm so sorry. I hate the idea that your mum thought I was messing around on you. Your mum was always so great to me. So welcoming. I always thought she was going to be the perfect mother-in-law.'

'Shame her daughter was so far from the perfect wife,' Lilah said with a wry little smile. 'Don't feel bad,' she went on. 'Not about Mum. She didn't think you were messing around. She just saw something I didn't. Something developing. She tried to tell me that I should be careful, that I should take better care of what we had, treat you better than I did.'

'You treated me fine, Lilah.'

She laughed, loud and sharp. 'Oh, bullshit, Drew. I treated you horribly.'

They settled into silence for a little while, watching the fire burn down. Andrew could hear the wind in the firs outside. Instinctively he moved a little closer to Lilah, the two of them huddling together in the warmth. Safe from the storm. Protected.

'How is she, your mum? Does she still have that flat in Winchmore Hill?'

'No, Drew. I should've told you, I meant to get in touch but . . . well. She died a year and a half ago. Breast cancer.'

'Oh, fuck. Lilah, I'm so sorry. I'm so, so sorry.' He pulled her tightly to him and she rested her head on his shoulder. 'You were so close to her. That must have been devastating.'

'Yeah,' she replied, a little crackle in her voice. 'It was. Thank God I had Zac. I don't think I would have made it without Zac.'

'Really?' He heard the tone in his voice as he said it, that slight note of incredulity. She heard it too and he felt her flinch away from him.

'Yes, really,' Lilah huffed. She got to her feet, gathering the blanket around her as she did. She poured herself another glass of red without offering him one. 'I know you all think he's a pointless himbo just because he's young and beautiful, but he's actually not at all.'

'I'm sorry, I don't know why I said it like that, I just didn't think . . . I don't know, that it was serious.'

'Well, it is.' She sat down in the chair next to the fire. She picked at her nail polish thoughtfully. 'He saved my life, you know. Twice.' Andrew didn't say anything, he waited for her to go on. She held up her left arm, letting the blanket fall away. He couldn't believe he hadn't seen it before: a dark welt, running a good two to three inches from her wrist towards her elbow.

'Jesus Christ, Lilah.'

'Yeah. Stupid, huh? I only did one.' She held up the other arm, for comparison purposes. 'I can't imagine how anyone does both.' She laughed, low and hollow. 'It wasn't the will to live that stopped me, it was the pain. You've no idea how much it hurts.'

'Oh my God, Lilah. Oh my God.' He just kept repeating it, over and over, stupidly, meaninglessly. How could she have done this, how could he have not known? 'Lilah, I should have been there, I should have made more of an effort to get in touch with you . . .'

'Drew, you made plenty of attempts to get in touch with me.' She smiled at him. 'I'm not your responsibility, you know.

We're not all your responsibility.' He might just as well have been talking to Natalie, she said that to him all the time. *They're not your responsibility, Andrew.* 'It was stupid, it was just a really stupid thing. Unforgivable, actually, because I did this when Mum was still alive. I can't believe I did it now, it would have broken her heart if I'd succeeded. I'd have left her all alone.'

Andrew thought, as she said this, that Natalie was right. Lilah was uniquely selfish. Spectacularly selfish. But there was a lot more to it than that, wasn't there? She wasn't just selfish, she was broken. Completely broken. When he'd loved her, because he had, there was no denying, he'd been captivated by her for a time, was she whole then? The cracks had appeared in that final year, that was for sure, but could they have been mended, had it not been for him, for Natalie, for what they did? Was he the one that broke her? He wanted to say the words out loud, he wanted to ask her, but he was afraid of the answer.

'I met Zac at the hospital,' Lilah said. 'This was . . . almost two years ago? Yeah. Anyway. I'd lost my job. I was flat broke, I was drinking, I'd had my heart comprehensively stamped on by some guy, and then Mum was diagnosed with cancer, and one night, I just . . .' she mimed the action, cutting into her wrist. Andrew flinched. 'Anyway, as I said, I only managed one, and being a total fucking wimp I couldn't take the pain and called an ambulance.' She smiled. 'Mum and I were actually in St Thomas's at the same time for a spell. Only, she didn't know why I was there. I told her I'd fallen down the stairs while holding a champagne glass. She believed me, I think. I hope she did.' She paused for a moment, continued to pick at her nail polish. 'So anyway, I was in a pretty crap way, and they kept me in hospital for a few days to make sure I didn't have another go. One afternoon I'd gone out for a cigarette and there was this guy coming out of the main lobby, on crutches, and he smiled at me and told me that I should quit, because I was the most beautiful girl he'd ever seen and that it would be a shame if I died of cancer.'

'And that was Zac?'

'That was Zac.'

'Very smooth.'

'I thought so. He had a . . . ligament something . . . I can't remember, some sort of sports injury, anyway, and he was coming in for physiotherapy. We ran into each other a couple of times, after that, when I was there visiting Mum. He asked me out for coffee, and of course I said no, but he was persistent and . . . Well. He was the best thing, the best possible thing for me. Kind, strong. No bullshit. He took care of me. He enjoyed taking care of me. And you know how much I enjoy being taken care of.'

Andrew nodded. 'I know.'

Lilah slid down off her chair so that once more they were sitting side by side. 'So that was the first time. That was the first time he saved me.'

'And the second?'

She cleared her throat. 'It was a while later. I'd got a job by then, a crappy PR job, and Mum was very ill. I couldn't go in every day, to the hospice I mean, because I was working. Zac was doing bar work at that time, a bit of fitness training in the day, but he was mostly free. So he used to go and sit with her. We'd only been seeing each other properly for about four months, he barely even knew me. And I don't think Mum had a clue who he was half the time, she was pretty out of it by then, but he went anyway.' She started to cry, her shoulders heaving. 'Every day, he'd just go and sit by her side, hold her hand, talk to her about *EastEnders*. For four months, at the end, I was there in the evenings and he was there in the day. She was never alone.' The tears coursed down her cheeks unchecked. 'I will always love him for that.'

Andrew threw the remaining log on the fire. 'I'm so glad, Lilah, that you had someone there for you, that you have someone. I'm so glad that you've found someone who loves you as much as you need.'

She sniffed. 'Me too.' She smiled at him, opened her mouth as though she had something to say and then closed it again.

'What is it?'

'It's not your fault,' she said. 'The way I am. I was always going to be like this.'

She turned her head towards him, big blue eyes lowered under long, wet lashes; up close like this you could almost see the bones underneath her skin. She slipped her hand into his, lightly scraping her teeth over her lower lip.

'It wasn't your fault. But I want to say, because of what she said – I mean, I want to tell my side. To you.'

'What are you talking about, Lilah?'

'Earlier. The thing with Natalie, that day in the pub.'

'You don't have to say anything to me, not now. It's history now.'

'Listen. My mum, she said that you were pulling away from me, that I wouldn't have long. She said it and I told her it was bullshit. Only it stayed in my head. It was in my head whenever the three of us were together after that, it was in my head that morning at the pub. You were sitting next to Nat at lunch, she was telling you about a book she'd read. I don't remember what it was now, but you were captivated.'

'*Alias Grace*.'

179

'What?'

'The book she was talking about. It was *Alias Grace*, by Margaret Atwood.'

'Jesus Christ, you remember the book.' She shook her head. 'I doubt you can remember a single thing I said to you that entire year.'

'Lilah.'

'There was a reason I needed a drink that morning. A reason I needed to do a line. And that's all I did, you know, one line. I'm not justifying what I did, there is no justification, not for what I did then, not for what I did later. I didn't think about it at the time, I don't think I was even aware of it, not consciously, you know? But I was watching you falling in love with her. And I was hurting. Because –' her voice broke a little – 'how could you not, given the choice between her and me? How could you not love her, her spirit, her strength? She's a thousand times stronger than I am. How could you not love what she is?'

'Lilah, please, don't, don't think like that.'

'I miss her, Andrew. I miss her so much. She broke my fucking heart.'

'I know.'

'No one, no man has ever hurt me the way she did. I loved her so much.'

'I know.'

'I miss her much more than I miss you.'

'I know.' He reached around her shoulders again, pulled her close to him, kissed her damp hair. She smelled of almonds and apples, delicious.

'I hope you make her happy, Andrew. I hope you make each other happy.'

For a moment he couldn't say anything, because there was a

hard lump in his throat and he had the feeling that if he spoke, tears would come. He felt like they'd been coming all day. He felt exhausted. He let his body relax against hers, his head sinking to her sharp little shoulder.

'She does. I mean, we do. Make each other happy. Or we did, anyway. We were happy, her and me and the girls.' He cleared his throat. 'Now, though. I don't know. She's so angry all the time. She could literally start an argument in an empty room. I mean it, sometimes I find her, pacing up and down, furious over some future imagined argument she's going to have with the girls, or the gas company or the local council or some journalist who's written a column in the newspaper. I don't seem to be able to do anything about it. She's so bloody disappointed with me all the time.'

'That can't be true,' Lilah said, turning her face to his, lifting his chin with her fingers. 'How could anyone ever be disappointed with you?'

Softly, she kissed him on the temple, and on the cheek, and on his lips.

*Dear Andrew,*

*This is the fourteenth time I've started this letter. I'm not joking. I've decided, no matter what, I'm finishing it, so if I ramble, forgive me.*

*I love you. You know that I do, that I have for a long time. That doesn't change the fact that what happened this weekend was a mistake. And you know what I mean when I say that, not that it felt like a mistake, not that it felt wrong, because it didn't, it felt right, perfectly right, as right as anything could feel.*

*You know what I mean, because you know me, better than anyone has ever known me. I cannot do this to Lilah, we cannot do this to Lilah. We won't forgive ourselves, it will eat away at us, it will make us unhappy, and the thing I fear most of all is that somehow, though it doesn't seem possible at the moment, that unhappiness will damage what we feel for each other. I can imagine few things worse than not loving you the way I do now, or feeling that you don't love me.*

*I love you, but I cannot break Lilah's heart.*

*Know that this is the hardest thing I've ever had to do.*

*I will always be yours.*

*Natalie*

## Chapter Twenty-two

It was a terrible cliché, but Dan felt he was having a crossroads moment, and at these times, the appropriate thing was to absent oneself from the world for a period of quiet reflection. He would never admit it, but he was still too afraid to go outside to the barn by himself, never mind that the banging noise had been explained. Natalie had still said something about seeing a light out there, hadn't she? No explanation for that other than there was a madman about. So quiet reflection would have to take place in the corner of the kitchen recently vacated by an extremely huffy Natalie. She'd gone upstairs to bed. Zac had completed whatever boy scout task he'd undertaken in the kitchen and had gone into the living room to sit with Jen.

The beep on his phone had been a text from Claudia, saying: *Don't be angry baby. I tell him tomorrow. Promise. Love you.*

For a moment he was confused. What was he supposed to be angry about? Then he remembered, oh yeah, the thing about her having sex with her husband. That conversation seemed like it had taken place a very long time ago, and he found it difficult to care about it now; it was like something that had happened to someone else. This, he decided, was not a good sign. He should, by rights, still be burning with righteous anger, fired by jealousy. Why didn't he give a shit?

This crossroads he was at didn't really have anything to do with Jen. It would be easy to allow himself to think that it did, because he was here with her, because she still looked so beautiful and she still had that way of looking at him which made him feel as though he had a metal hook in his heart and she held a line attached to it and she could tug, tug, tug, any time she liked. But if he was honest with himself, this feeling wasn't completely new.

Zac came lumbering back into the kitchen. Dan groaned, louder than he'd intended.

'You OK there?' Zac asked. He was so solicitous. Why was he so solicitous?

'Fine, thank you,' Dan replied, trying to keep the edge of irritation out of his voice.

'You sure?'

'I'm all right, Zac. I'm just ... Well. Girl trouble.' The moment the words left his lips, he regretted them. Why was he telling Zac?

'Ah, right. The actress. The married actress.'

'Mmm-hmmm.'

'I went out with an actress once. She was on *Casualty*, or *Holby City* or something.'

'Really?'

'Yeah. She was mental. Is yours mental?'

'No. She isn't mental.'

To his chagrin, Zac sat down across the table from him. 'Has she changed her mind? About leaving her husband?'

'No.'

'So what's the problem?'

Oddly, Zac's questioning style, utterly lacking, as it was, in finesse, took Dan to the crux of the matter.

'It's me. I feel . . . honestly? I feel like I may have made a huge mistake. Not in being with her, but in suggesting to her, persuading her, even, that she ought to leave her husband. It's a big responsibility, you know.'

'Breaking up someone's marriage, you mean?'

Dan sighed. 'No. I mean, yes. Well. It's complicated.'

'How so?'

'OK. You're making me sound like a dickhead, and I'm not. I didn't get into this lightly, OK? I've thought about it, long and hard. For ages, I agonised over this.'

'Ages.'

'Yes, ages. We met . . . I don't know, five months ago.'

'Five months? That long?'

'Just . . . listen, OK. I saw her in a film last year. *The Hunger*. I don't suppose you've seen it.' Dan didn't imagine that Zac was a fan of German art house. 'Very interesting, very erotic. She was phenomenal and I just couldn't get her out of my head. When I was writing *The Lost Girl* – that's the film we've just finished shooting – I wrote the character of Ofelia with her in mind. I contacted her agent and persuaded her to audition. Not that she really needed to, of course, because I'd written the part for her. But I wanted to be sure, really sure. And it was just as I'd imagined it, imagined her. She was perfect.' Just thinking about it now made his breath quicken. 'There was this instant, fierce attraction between us. Undeniable. Obviously mutual, right from the start. But we didn't do anything. Partly out of respect for her marriage, but also because of the work.' Dan closed his eyes, thinking back to that time, all those torturous hours spent together, close enough to touch, often actually touching (he was known as quite a physical director), the long nights discussing the script and rehearsing, the ache, the physical agony he felt, wanting her so badly. He shook it off. 'It wasn't until the end of shooting, when we realised that we weren't going to see each other every day any more, that's when we realised that we had to be together.'

'Sounds ... great,' Zac said. 'Hot. The whole thing sounds really hot.' *It sounds hot?* Dan's shoulders slumped. What on earth was he doing talking to this man? What insights could he possibly offer? 'Working together, wanting each other, sneaking around ... sounds exciting. Doesn't really sound like real life, though.'

Dan shook his head, gave a wry little laugh. He tried to think of an appropriate way to demonstrate to Zac that what he had with Claudia was very real indeed, but he faltered. Infuriatingly, he was struck by the notion that Zac had a point. It didn't sound like real life. Even as he was telling the story, talking about her, he realised how much it sounded just like that – a story. With a beginning, a middle, an ending. What was the ending going to be? Happy ever after? He couldn't quite picture it. In fact, if he were honest, whenever he pictured Claudia, whenever he imagined the two of them together, they were never in his apartment in London making spaghetti bolognese, they were never walking on Hampstead Heath or going to the cinema. They were always in a hotel room or at the airport, never at home, always elsewhere.

Enlightening as this conversation with Zac had been, it wasn't helping. If anything, it was propelling Dan towards a state of panic. He'd felt this way before: over the past few weeks a sensation of real terror had visited him in the night, startling him awake and keeping him there, even as he lay by Claudia's side, her ivory limbs tangled in the sheets, blonde hair flung over the pillow, pale lips just slightly parted, perfection. Lately he found himself terrified, and the thing that was terrifying him was the final scene of *The Graduate* where Dustin Hoffman and Katharine Ross get onto the bus, breathless from their dash from the church where Ross has just left her husband-to-be at the altar, and then they just sit there, not speaking, uncertainty writ large all over their faces, and you know what they're thinking. Dan knew what *he* was thinking anyway . . . He was thinking, Jesus Christ, what the fuck have I done? So I've got her, she's mine now. Now what do I do?

Zac was looking at him, waiting for him to say something.

'I need a beer,' he said, and Zac obliged, fetching them a couple from the fridge. Not quite cold, but cold enough. 'I don't know what to do,' Dan said lamely.

'If you're not sure, you should tell her. Don't let her leave her husband if you're not sure.'

He was right. The enormous himbo boy scout was completely right. But how would Claudia take that? She wasn't big on rejection, she wasn't used to it. If she sensed him backing away from her, that would be the end of it, he was sure; the affair would be over, the flame extinguished, never to be rekindled. Could he be without her? He was visited by a vision almost as frightening as the *Graduate* scenario: himself, all alone in a thousand-pound-a-night hotel room in Paris on Christmas Day.

His fingers moved over the touchpad of his phone. He watched it light up, but he didn't do anything. He felt paralysed, immobilised, in limbo somewhere between the frying pan of commitment and the fire of chronic, indefatigable loneliness.

'You come from a big family, don't you?' he asked Zac.

'Two big brothers, one little sister,' Zac replied. 'How d'you know?'

'You just have that way about you. People who come from big, happy families have a certain . . . confidence, I find.'

Zac shrugged. 'Maybe. My brothers used to kick the shit out

of me when I was little.' Dan struggled to believe there was ever a time that Zac was little. 'But we get on all right now. Lisa – that's my sister – she's a little sweetie.'

'It must be nice.'

'You? No siblings?'

'No siblings and no parents. Not any more.'

'Shit. Sorry. That's harsh.'

'Yes, it is harsh, isn't it? I miss having a family. Not my real family of course, because that was never really a proper family. Long story. But us,' he gestured around him. 'These guys, they were my family once. Closest thing I ever had, in any case.' He took a long swig of his beer. 'It's why it hurt so much, when everything fell apart. They don't think I lost anything, you know. In fact, they think I *gained*. That bloody film. I never meant to hurt them.' He looked up at Zac. 'Tell her, tell Lilah. It was never my intention. Tell her I mean that. I hate the fact I hurt her feelings so badly.' He shook his head. 'It was my fault, you know. She didn't over-react. I was stupid, I was a fucking idiot – I used stuff that she'd done and said, I took things and twisted them, I created this character . . . it *was* fiction. It *wasn't* her. It wasn't how I saw her, but there were too many similarities, it was too close to the bone. Christ, even the actress they chose – *they* chose, it had nothing to do with me – she looked like Lilah. And it was the last thing she needed, poor girl.' Dan spread his hands out, imploring. 'I tried to contact her, you know. Many times. She wouldn't have it.'

Zac smiled. 'If grudge-holding were an Olympic sport . . .'

'Lilah for gold, Natalie for silver?' They both laughed. 'I wish there were something I could do to make it up to her.' Zac leaned back in his seat, studying Dan's face, his expression inscrutable. 'What?' Dan asked him. 'Is there something?'

Zac shook his head. 'Not for me to say,' he said quietly. He finished off his beer and got up to place the bottle with the rest of the empties on the kitchen counter.

'No, go on,' Dan said. 'Tell me. I won't say anything to her. What is it? She doesn't want to try acting again, does she? Because we tried that at college and it didn't work out. She's got the looks and the sense of drama all right, but the woman can't take direction.'

Zac grinned. 'It's not that.'

'What then?' Even in the half-light, Dan could see from the way Zac shrugged, lowered his lids, that he was embarrassed. 'Money? She needs money?'

Zac puffed out his cheeks, spreading his arms wide. 'I can take care of her. I will. She's broke. She has been for a long time, she ran up a lot of debts. I don't exactly earn a lot, but we get by. Only . . . well. You know Lilah. Getting by isn't really her style.'

Dan was only half listening. He was rather pleased that she wanted to ask him for money. That was familial, wasn't it? When you were hard up, got yourself into debt, you turned to family, didn't you? That's what people did, wasn't it?

'She has this whole thing,' Zac was saying, 'about how you owe her.' He held his hands up in supplication. 'I don't think that. I think she's taken resentment over that film too far. But she seems to think that she deserves something from you. Reparations, she calls it.'

Dan's heart sank then. She wasn't turning to him because she thought of him as family, she saw it as repayment of a debt – worse, punitive damages for what he'd done to her.

'Don't say anything to her, Dan, I shouldn't have mentioned this.'

'No, no,' he said distracted. 'Of course not.' He pulled his phone from his pocket again, ran his fingers over the touchpad to bring it to life. He brought up Claudia's message and tapped 'reply'.

There was a noise from the hall and Jen appeared in the doorway. She was leaning against the arch, her hair falling forward a little into her face. She looked exhausted.

'I'm off to bed,' she said. 'Will you two be OK?'

'Course we will,' Zac said. 'I think I'm ready to crash out myself.'

'Dan?'

'Yeah, fine. You go on.'

'OK,' she said. She walked over to him, leaned forward and kissed him on the cheek. She smelled of vanilla, and a touch of something citrusy. The scent sparked something, a memory travelled through him like electricity. 'I'm sorry,' she said softly, brushing her thumb over his cheekbone, 'that things got so fraught today. I'm so glad you came.'

His breathing was shallow. He brought his hand up to take hers. The room seemed oddly still – the fire no longer crackled, the wind no longer howled, Zac may as well have disappeared into thin air. 'I'm glad, too.'

She let go of his hand and turned away.

He sat in the darkness for a long while afterwards, staring at his phone, looking over at the staircase, listening to the creaking of the house, people moving around upstairs, Zac's heavy footfall, Jen so much softer. When she kissed him, spoke to him in that low voice, when he could smell her and touch her, he was transported. It was a revelation. He had a chance. He couldn't let it pass. He replied to Claudia's message: *Don't tell him yet. We need to talk. Call me.*

*September 1999*
*Email exchange between Dan and Lilah*

*Dan to Lilah*

*Lilah,*

*I called three times yesterday, I assume you're ignoring me. I'm sorry you took offence at some of the stuff in the film. You have to know that while there were aspects of you in the Zara character, it wasn't supposed to be you. Let me take you out for champagne as an apology? Please, I don't want us to fall out over this.*

*Dan*

*Lilah to Dan*

*You're sorry I took offence? Are you kidding me? I didn't take offence, Dan, what you did was offensive. And I don't care about the fact that the character might have had aspects of me or not, you used things I'd told you in confidence, you used my words, my actual words. You used things I told you when I was desperate, broken-bloody-hearted. Tell me, were you making notes when we were having all those chats when I stayed with you? Maybe you were recording me? Did you bug my room?*

*You're an arsehole and no quantity of champagne will make up for this.*

*Dan to Lilah*

*Of course I wasn't bloody taking notes. I'm a writer, Lilah. We use things from life, all artists do. Once again, I'm sorry if I offended you (is that a better sentence construction?). It wasn't my intention, and I have to say that I'm pretty upset that all you saw in the film was a slight against you. There was a bit more to it than that, I hoped.*

*Lilah to Dan*

*Sod off you pretentious wanker.*

## Chapter Twenty-three

Andrew had forgotten how loudly Lilah snored. It was extraordinary how such a delicate creature, so fine-featured and small-boned, could produce quite so much noise, quite so much grunting and snorting, in her sleep. He remembered now that the reason for his lack of sleep between the ages of nineteen and twenty-three was not solely Lilah's voracious sexual appetite but her terrible sinus issues.

He slipped out of bed and walked to the window. The snow had almost stopped. It lay thick on the road, almost perfect, untouched save for a sole trail of tiny prints, weaving this way and that – a drunken fox, perhaps? The branches of the trees opposite sank almost to the ground under the weight of snow and, just outside the window, icicles, some three or four feet long, hung from the eaves, gleaming silver in reflected moonlight. He thought he might take some pictures to show the girls. Quietly, he crept over to the bed and retrieved his phone from the bedside table.

He'd turned it off to save battery and on turning it back on he discovered, with a start, that the signal had returned. The phone beeped at him, angrily and repeatedly, alerting him to missed calls and text messages. He tried to muffle its sound under the blanket he had wrapped around his body, although it didn't actually matter: Lilah wouldn't have been woken by a bomb going off. She could sleep through anything.

There were twenty-four missed calls, mostly from Jen's landline, and a number of text messages, mostly from Natalie. As he flicked through them, he noticed a clear trajectory in tone, from frightened (*r u ok, call me*) to panicky (*Where r u? V worried pls call asap*), before a sudden hairpin bend towards jealous rage, and finally, a long slow drift into incomprehensibility (*u aasvard dont cmmd cabk*).

There were also three messages from his daughters, one from Grace telling him she'd had an 'epic' time at Longleat Safari Park (still so easily entertained, Grace; she hadn't quite tipped over into teenager-hood yet) and one from Charlotte asking if he could persuade Natalie to let them go to Sonja's party on New Year's Eve. Charlotte most definitely was a teenager, and had already developed the technique of waging extended divide-and-rule campaigns in order to get whatever it was she wanted. Andrew was seen as the weaker of the parents so he was always the first point of attack. The third text, also from Charlotte, was a picture of the two of them, grinning happily in the front room of their grandparents' house, with a '*love you Dad xxxxx*' message attached. This sent a few minutes before the New Year's Eve party request, to soften him up. Nobody's fool, that girl, just like her mother.

He took some pictures of the snowy scene outside, his heart swollen: beauty and love, what more could you wish for? His friends (even Natalie, it now seemed), looked at his life and felt sorry for him, but the thing no one seemed to realise about him was that, of all of them, he counted himself the luckiest. He got what he wanted, he got the woman he loved, and two beautiful daughters into the bargain. He longed to see them now, his arms ached for them.

He shivered. He felt a nameless fear, dread, rising up in him. He could tell himself a thousand times that it would be OK, because although Natalie would be angry with him tomorrow (today), and the day after that and possibly a few days more, they would be OK, once the anger burned out. Once his own anger burned out. Things would go back to normal once the guilt was crushed down, shrugged off, ignored. They would be OK. Wouldn't they? After all they had been through together, they could get through this. And yet, he felt afraid. He typed a message to Nat. *Hope this doesn't wake you up, just wanted to tell you how much I love you. Always, A.*

He turned back from the window, smiling despite himself at the girl in the bed, arms and legs everywhere, a beautiful broken doll. He crawled back into bed, trying his best not to disturb her, trying to find some corner of the bed where he could curl up without touching her. He needed, now, to put as much space as he could between his body and Lilah's. He closed his eyes and dreamed of Nat lying next to him: he dreamed of putting his hands on her, feeling her shiver.

*16 January 1997*
*Email, from Andrew to Nat*

*Dear Nat,*

*I got your email yesterday, I called last night but your mum said you were really tired and had turned in early. Perhaps that's true, but if it isn't, I can think of at least two possible reasons why.*

1. *You don't want to talk to me, because, as you said in your letter, you don't want to go on with this thing with you and me, and talking to me will only make it harder.*
2. *Lilah called you, she told you that I told her, and you're furious with me for telling her without speaking to you first.*

*Either way, I understand.*

*Let me explain though, about Lilah. She came to pick me up at Basingstoke, and I realised that I couldn't lie to her, I couldn't just sit there and lie, I couldn't pretend what happened between you and me didn't happen, I couldn't go home with her, go to bed with her, carry on with her. I couldn't. I could have made excuses, told her I was tired, that I wasn't feeling well . . . You say I know you. Well, you know me. You know I couldn't do that, I'm not built that way. So I just told her. I told her that I'd fallen in love with you.*

*The damage is done. By the time I got back last night she was gone, she'd taken some of her stuff and smashed a fair bit of mine. Dan left me a message in the early hours to say she'd turned up at his place – he said she's going to stay there for a while. Did she call you? Whatever she said, you know that she won't have meant it. She loves you, she will forgive you.*

*If you can't be with me, I understand that. But I won't accept it.*

196

*I won't go away. I'm not saying I'm going to hassle you, or stalk you, or call you every night, but I'm not going away. I won't live without you, Nat. I refuse to, not after everything you and I have been through. Perhaps, in the light of everything, I don't deserve to be happy. But you do, and I believe, I know, more certainly than I've ever known anything, that I can make you happy if you let me.*

*There is nothing on this earth that will stop me loving you. Sorry if I sound like a lovesick teenager, but that's how I feel.*

*I adore you, Nat. You are for me, and I'm for you.*

*With love, always*

*Andrew*

## Chapter Twenty-four

~

Jen lay on her back, staring up at the ceiling, listening to the sound of the storm blowing itself out, the creaking of beams and floorboards as the house, having weathered another tempest, settled itself. She imagined that it must feel weary, the way she did – she felt as though she'd run a marathon, climbed a mountain. She longed for sleep, but she knew it wasn't coming, not with her mind running over and over the events of the past twenty-four hours, the wreckage of the reunion.

In the final analysis, the weekend could, it was safe to say, be termed a disaster. A fractious beginning, a vicious fight in the middle and – who knew what end? She didn't hold out much hope for a joyous reconciliation when Andrew and Lilah came back. If they managed to make it back at all. She could only hope and pray that they ploughed the road on Sundays.

Still, she hadn't been lying when she told Dan she was glad he'd come. Maybe she shouldn't have thrown them all together as she had, that was foolish, but she didn't regret inviting them, being able to tell Andrew about the baby, laughing on the living-room floor with Nat, talking to Dan, him holding her hand by the fire.

There was a soft tap at her door and Dan appeared, as though conjured up by her imagination.

'You sleeping, Jen?'

'Not yet. Come in.'

He shuffled in slowly, holding his phone out in front of him to light the way.

'I blew out all the candles save one,' he said. 'I'll take it to bed with me.'

'OK. Are you all right?'

'I'm fine, yeah.'

'Are you still nervous?'

'No. What do you mean?'

Even in the dark, she could tell his face was colouring. She smiled to herself. 'Oh, nothing. I thought you were a bit jumpy earlier.'

'Yeah, all right. I have an over-active imagination.' He squeezed her leg through the blanket.

'I know you do. I find this place creepy, too, don't worry. I've had many a night lying here in the dark, too terrified to move because I'm convinced I can hear someone moving around downstairs, nails scraping at the window . . .'

'Jesus, don't. I've got to sleep out in the barn, remember?'

Jen giggled. 'Sorry. But it does feel . . . I don't know. It's really stupid.'

'What is?'

'You know I don't hold any truck with the supernatural. I don't believe in God, I think that once we're gone, we're gone, but still. This place, there's something about it. I feel him here.'

'That makes sense. This place *is* Conor somehow. There's

199

so much of him in it, every beam, every board, the table in the kitchen . . .'

'It's true. Also, if he was going to haunt anyone, it would be you and me, wouldn't it?' She tried to keep her voice light. Dan didn't reply, he just squeezed her leg again, moving a little further up the bed, so that he was sitting level with her hips. She propped herself up on her pillows, so that she could look him in the eye.

'Have you spoken to your girlfriend?' she asked him. For some reason Jen didn't want to say her name.

Dan shook his head. 'You didn't reply to any of my letters,' he said.

'I'm sorry.'

'It was the guilt, wasn't it? Was it just the guilt? Or was it more than that? Christ. I can't believe I'm asking you this.' He gave a low little laugh. 'For years, years after it happened, I wondered. I just wanted to know, I was desperate to know, whether there was ever going to be a chance or whether I should just forget about you. I couldn't forget about you.'

'I'm sorry, Dan, I'm sorry.'

'You should have replied to my letters, Jen. Even if it was just to put me out of my misery . . .' He was leaning over her, their faces almost touching, their lips almost touching.

'I betrayed him,' she said softly.

'He didn't know.'

'I knew. And I can't ever be certain whether . . .' She broke off.

Dan leaned in closer, kissed her lips. She closed her eyes and breathed him in. His arms were around her waist, pulling her body into his. 'I just want a chance,' he said. 'We never had a chance.'

Jen wavered, caught between the temptation to give in to him and the certain knowledge that it would be a huge, confusing mistake. Gently, she pulled away from him. Her rational side dominated.

'I . . . this . . . you . . .' She was rational, she'd just lost the power to construct full sentences.

'Sorry.'

'Don't be sorry.' She smiled at him, traced her thumb down the side of his face, across his lips. 'I don't think you really want this, Dan.'

'I do, believe me, I do.'

'Right now, maybe. But I can't really act on right now any longer. I'm going to be a mother. I'm almost forty. At some point I have to start acting like a grown-up.'

'But, I do too,' Dan said. 'That's what I want, too.'

'Really? You want to leave your beautiful German film star and start a life with me and my baby in genteel English suburbia?'

'I . . . I . . . Does it have to be suburbia?' he asked. Jen laughed. 'I want a family,' Dan said. 'I don't care where we live.'

'Dan, I know you do, I know you've always wanted that, but . . . you can't just give up everything you have, for an idea of family, for a child that isn't yours, for someone you hardly know any longer.'

'I know you.'

His expression was so earnest – he meant it, this declaration, it was heartfelt. But it was also Dan; he was a romantic, he allowed himself to get carried away. And it was tempting to go along with him, to allow him to carry her away too. Only she'd done that once before, and it hadn't ended well, not for anyone. She had to be the sensible one this time.

'Yesterday you were in love with your girlfriend,' Jen pointed out. 'You talked about how she inspired you, how she made you feel . . .'

'She won't be family. It's not like that with us. She doesn't want kids, she doesn't want to settle down . . .' There was a note of desperation in his voice, real longing.

'And you do all of a sudden? When did you decide this? This afternoon?'

Dan's shoulders slumped. 'You know that's what I've always wanted, what I really wanted,' he said. She heard pain in his voice, anger. He got to his feet and turned to leave.

'Dan, don't go. Please, just wait a minute.'

'It's fine,' he said, and just like that his voice was light again, all earnestness and emotion gone. They might as well have been talking about the weather, or what time he wanted breakfast. 'Sleep well, Jen.'

It was hours before she fell asleep and when she did she dreamed she was lost in the wood behind the house. Night was falling and she was afraid, and the only way to find the path out was to follow a trail of blood.

*Fragments of letters from Jen to Dan, never sent*

*10 March 1996*

*You are in my head and I can't get rid of you. Why won't you go away? I think I am in love with you. How can I be, when I love him so much? It makes no sense, none of it.*

*12 April 1996*

*I'm sorry for the silence. I want desperately for us to be able to talk again, to be normal again, to be friends again. I miss you, Dan. I don't even know how you feel, whether you're sad or angry, whether you care at all. I know that there's no chance I'm going to send this letter, I'm too much of a coward and I'm scared of what you'll say. Still, writing the words down makes me feel better.*

*4 January 1997*

*I can never come back. I cannot see you, I cannot look at you and not think about what I did to him, and when I think about what I did, my throat closes up and I cannot breathe.*

*I hope you are happy, my boy. Lost boy. Now I'm lost too.*

# Chapter Twenty-five

The coffee was rich and sweet and delicious, the pain au chocolat still warm, the chocolate inside gooey and unctuous. Lilah was ravenous. 'I can't believe how much I've eaten this weekend,' she said through a mouthful of wonderfully light, flaky pastry. 'I must have put on half a stone.'

Andrew raised an eyebrow. 'You could stand to gain a few pounds, Lilah.'

'At my age, darling, everything you gain you keep.'

'I am your age, Lilah. And you may have noticed that I've been gaining and keeping for quite some time.'

Lilah grinned. 'You're still gorgeous,' she said, waving at Madame Caron to top up her coffee cup.

Lilah was feeling remarkably chipper given everything that had happened yesterday: the booze, the fight, the blizzard, the crash, more booze . . . Still. It had been a wonderful end to the evening. It was almost, she thought, worth all the drama that went before it, making up with Andrew in front of the fire. It was only now that she was with him that she realised how much she'd missed him, how much he'd been missing from her life. How much he still meant to her.

She wasn't sure he felt the same, though. He was distracted, constantly looking out of the window at the snow which lay thick and undisturbed on the road outside.

'Doesn't look like we'll be getting back to the house any time soon, does it?' Lilah asked cheerfully.

He shook his head. 'Nat's going to be so upset.'

Lilah shrugged. 'Nothing we can do about it now, is there? Do you want the last pain au chocolat?' He shook his head. 'Don't worry so much, Drew. It'll be fine. In any case, this whole thing was kind of her fault, you know.'

'Mmm-hmm.' He wasn't going to be drawn on that.

'It'll be OK. I'll tell her nothing happened.' She bit her lower lip and gave him a wink.

'Lilah.'

'I will! And she'll believe me. I'll be very convincing. You know how convincing I can be.' She fluttered her eyelashes, her mouth arranged into a demure pout.

'Stop that.'

She giggled. 'Oh, lighten up. She'll be so happy to see you again, alive and in one piece, she's not going to worry about one night in a hotel room with me.'

Andrew rolled his eyes at her. 'Oh, yeah. She's going to forget all about it.' He sipped his coffee. 'I don't know what you're so cheerful about anyway. What about Zac? Don't you think he'll be upset about the fact you just spent the night with your ex?'

Lilah laughed, loud and long. 'Drew, darling, I'm really sorry but I just don't think Zac sees you as much of a threat.'

Andrew smiled ruefully. 'No. I remember the days when I had a six-pack like that. There weren't many blokes I was worried about then either.'

'Sweetheart, you never had a six-pack like that.'

'Cheers, Lilah. You're making me feel so much better.'

Monsieur Caron approached their table, beaming at Lilah, his arms slightly outstretched as though he intended to give her a hug.

'Bonjour les anglais! Comment ça va? Vous avez bien dormi?' He winked at Andrew, the subtext clear: if I was in bed with her, I wouldn't get much sleep either.

'Oui, oui, très bien,' Andrew said, his French making him sound remarkably like Del Boy.

'Bon. You are . . . not staying one more night?'

'We might do,' Lilah said brightly. 'It depends.'

'Depends?'

'Will it be possible to get back up – up this road, I mean, to Madame de Chassagny's house – today?'

'Ah, oui. They 'ave the . . . 'ow you say? Chasse neige?'

'Snow plough?'

'Yes, yes, this is it. It will go maybe at lunch time? Maybe later. They will take you, if you wish. I can ask them.'

The expression of relief on Andrew's face spoke volumes.

'OK. I call the man, I ask 'im to take you.'

'That would be fantastic, thank you so much.'

Lilah pouted. 'I was quite looking forward to another night here, away from all the drama.' She shrugged. 'Although I suppose it will be nice to have clean underwear. What shall we do in the meantime then? While we're waiting for the snow plough, I mean? You want to go back to bed?'

*Hi Mum,*

*Thank you, thank you! I adore the dress — and Armani! You're so sweet. I shall be the best-dressed girl in the college bar. Well, I already am the best-dressed girl in the college bar, obviously (there is a woeful tendency towards jeans and Docs round here), but I'll be even better dressed now.*

*I had the loveliest birthday. The new boy, Andrew, took me out for a breakfast at Dino's, which is just this little greasy spoon, but he'd arranged to have them bring over a bottle of champagne with my bacon sarnie (a bacon sarnie! See, I am getting into the student spirit). When I got back to my room later that morning it was full of orchids — he'd surreptitiously nicked my key and got some friends to sneak into my room while we were out and put them everywhere. My room is now so beautiful. I love it.*

*And I love it here. You're going to laugh when you read this, but thank you thank you thank you for making me revise for my A-levels. I can even forgive you for locking me in my room the night before my history exam when Darren Sanders invited me to go to SW1 (VIP room!). I'm just having the best time — I've met the coolest people, honestly: they're so different to my London friends, they're not into money at all, they're clever and interesting, they talk about art and philosophy and shit like that, and I don't know what they're talking about half the time, but they don't seem to care. They like me! There's this girl, Natalie, she's on my course, and she's just amazing, she's read everything there is to read, and she can talk for hours about politics and poetry, and she's funny and adorable.*

*And I'm in love with Andrew! Really. I think I mean it this time. And you're going to adore him, Mum, I promise. He's totally not like*

Darren, he's an absolute honey. He's really clever, athletic, he works hard and he treats me so well. Plus he's drop dead gorgeous. I was thinking of asking him to come to London at Easter – would that be OK?

Anyway, have to go, have a tutorial in twenty minutes. Thanks again for the dress, Mum, and thanks for pushing me so much, and thanks for taking all my shit. I miss you loads, I'll see you in a few weeks.

Love, love, love,

Lilah

## Chapter Twenty-six

~

The silence blanketing the house seemed deeper even than usual. Calm after the storm. Jen slept in after a fitful night's sleep, and yet when she woke all was quiet. She leaned over and flicked on the lamp next to her bed. Yes. She breathed a sigh of relief, turning it off again. The power was back. She could at least provide her remaining guests with hot water and a cooked breakfast.

She swung her legs over the edge of the bed and sat up. Her head swam a little and she thought for a moment she might be sick. She breathed in and out, slowly and steadily, placed a hand on her belly. All quiet and still there, too. She took a long, warm shower, leaning her forehead gently against the tiles, eyes closed. She wished her mind would stop racing, wished she could gain a sense of inner peace to match the quiet outside.

There were so many things to worry about: Andrew and Natalie, the state Lilah might be in, whether or not Andrew and Lilah would be able to get back to the house, that conversation with Dan last night. She felt a fluttering, a slight movement in her belly and then a sharp kick. Her shoulders dropped a couple of inches, she exhaled slowly, relieved. She didn't like the way she'd been feeling the last couple of days, the dizziness, the sickness. But it was nothing: just stress, rich food, probably a glass or two more wine than was advisable.

Downstairs, she discovered she wasn't the first up. Natalie, dressed in tracksuit bottoms and a T-shirt, sat at the table in the dining room, speaking to someone on her phone. Her voice was quiet and calm, so Jen guessed it probably wasn't Andrew. She guessed wrong.

'He thinks they'll be able to get back here around lunchtime,' she said, ushering Jen to a chair and pouring her a cup of coffee. 'They'll come with the snow plough.'

Before Jen could express her relief, Natalie launched into an apology. 'I behaved horribly yesterday,' she said. 'I know I did. And I really regret it, regret causing so much trouble.' Jen tried to say something, to reassure her, but Natalie went on: 'I hope you understand that there were things I needed to say, things I've been carrying around, that have been weighing on me . . .'

'I do, Nat. I do understand.'

Natalie held up her hand. 'This was the wrong time, the wrong place. And the things I needed to say, I didn't even say them right. I just ended up upsetting Andrew. I was supposed to be protecting him.'

There was a throb behind Jen's eyes. She felt suddenly exhausted, she wasn't sure she could bear to go over all this again. 'It's OK, Nat. Everyone was a little overwrought. It's mostly my fault for the way I handled things anyway . . .'

'No. I see what you tried to do, I know your intentions were good. I spoiled everything.'

Jen shook her head, sipped her coffee.

Mercifully, Natalie changed the subject. She asked Jen

questions about her plans, had she chosen names yet (no), would she live with her mother in Tunbridge Wells when she moved to England (certainly not). Jen explained that she'd probably end up in London, or possibly Oxford. There was a possibility of a job at Oxford University Press. After a few minutes, they lapsed into more or less comfortable silence, sipping their coffee, enjoying the stillness of the morning.

They boiled eggs and made toast, chatted about Charlotte and Grace, and life in England, what Jen should expect. She'd been back for days, here and there, when her father got sick, for his funeral, but overall she'd probably spent less than a couple of weeks in her home country since the year of the accident. The chatter felt warm, companionable; this was the kind of breakfast Jen had hoped for when she'd invited them, only she'd envisaged there being six of them at the table, rather than just two.

'The boys are sleeping in,' she said out loud, stating the obvious.

'Yes, well. Zac's not long left adolescence, has he, and you know how teenagers can sleep.' Natalie grinned at Jen, one eyebrow raised.

'He is rather young, isn't he?'

'Young and beautiful. Can't say I blame her,' Natalie said with a shrug. 'I mean, I don't imagine they have an awful lot to talk about, but . . .'

'They seem pretty happy,' Jen said.

Natalie shrugged again. 'What's it like, by the way, seeing Dan again?' she asked. Jen started a little. How did we get from Lilah and Zac to Jen and Dan? What was she trying to say? Did she know something? Jen tried to read her expression, but she looked innocent enough. 'You haven't seen him, have you? Since.'

'No, I haven't.'

'You were so close, for a while.'

'We were.'

'The film, it was . . .'

'I don't really want to talk about that, Nat.' Natalie thought *that* was why they hadn't spoken. She didn't realise that Jen had never seen the film, couldn't care less about the film.

'No, sure. But you and him, it's not difficult?'

'It's fine,' Jen replied, trying to keep her voice light. She could feel her cheeks reddening, felt as though she'd been caught in a lie. She got to her feet abruptly, turning away from Natalie, asking, 'You want another cup of coffee?'

'I'm OK, thanks,' Natalie said. Jen could hear the note of puzzlement in her voice.

Dan chose that moment to make his entrance, suitcase in hand.

'Morning all,' he said brusquely, walking through the kitchen and into the hallway where he left the case. 'Any coffee going?'

Jen looked at him, her expression questioning. 'Sure,' she said, pouring him a mugful and handing it over.

'Cheers,' he said, turning away. He walked to the window and gazed out. 'They'll clear the road today, won't they?' he asked. 'Because I reckon I'll probably need to get going this afternoon.'

'Oh. Yes. They will, this afternoon I think. The driveway, though . . .'

'It's all right. I can do the driveway.'

So that was it. She searched his face for some trace of the tenderness there had been last night, but it was gone. When he smiled at her it was the polite smile of a friendly acquaintance,

212

and his chatter had reverted to the slick, superficial glibness of his first night here. She hadn't given him the response he wanted, so that was it. Shut down, closed off. It was all or nothing with him. She felt desperately sad, bereft almost, to have the glimpse of something, friendship or more, to be able almost to grasp it, and then to have it snatched away, just like that.

It made her feel impossibly tired, her limbs leaden. If she didn't have guests she would quite happily have gone back to bed, she was sure she could sleep all day. But there were things to do, food to cook, people to entertain. She was dismayed to notice that there was barely any firewood left, either next to the burner or in the living room; it meant a steep climb up the hill to the woodshed. The sound of Zac's heavy footfall on the stairs lifted her spirits; she knew very well that there was no way he'd let her do the heavy lifting.

In the end he took Nat out with him – she was eager to get out of the house after more than thirty-six hours of being cooped up. Jen saw the look of panic flit over Dan's face as he realised he was going to be left alone with her and for the briefest of moments she considered letting him off the hook, disappearing upstairs, but the impulse passed.

'I wish you wouldn't go,' she said. He was looking out of the window, he didn't turn to face her. 'Stay until tomorrow.'

'No. It doesn't feel right now,' he said. He still hadn't looked round.

'You've spoken to Claudia?'

'I phoned her last night. And she rang back this morning. She's spoken to her husband. She's told him about us. She'll be in Paris tomorrow.' This was expressed without emotion. He sounded neither happy nor excited. He got up from the table and turned to look at her at last. 'So it's all sorted.' As he walked past her to go back out to the barn, he touched her arm, gave it a squeeze. 'No going back now,' he said.

Zac and Dan spent the best part of an hour shovelling snow off the driveway. They were almost finished when she heard the steady tractor-like chug of the snow plough coming up the hill.

'Nat,' she called out, 'they're back.'

Natalie almost fell down the stairs, yanked on her boots and ran out into the snow. Jen hadn't seen her move that quickly all weekend.

'Andrew!' she called out. 'Oh, thank God you're back.'

Jen stood on the front door step, watching Andrew and Lilah clamber down from the snow plough; Zac scooped Lilah up into the air, effortlessly spinning her around, kissing her on the mouth. Andrew and Natalie just stood there hugging each other. Jen wished she had a camera, they looked so beautiful out there in the snow and the sunshine. Dan, standing next to his car, turned to look at her, and he smiled, a real smile this time, and she felt tears come to her eyes.

'You should stay,' she called out.

'What?'

'I said you should stay!'

He started to walk towards her, Andrew and Natalie caught up with him, Andrew slapped him on the back, they were laughing about something, Jen couldn't hear them though, there was an odd sound, a kind of ringing in her ears, she looked up at the sky and it was blinding, her heart, oh God, her heart was racing, racing, racing, and then the light was gone.

# Part Two

## Chapter Twenty-seven

~

*May 1996*

She'd knocked her head on something. She could feel the lump forming on her temple, the blood already starting to collect in her eye socket. She was going to have one hell of a shiner.

'Jen? Jen, are you all right?'

She looked up. Conor was kneeling down, at her side. She hadn't knocked her head, she'd fallen down. She was lying on the floor.

'Jesus, Jen. What happened? Are you all right?'

She tried to sit up, but her head was throbbing painfully. She felt like she was going to throw up.

'I think I fell,' she said.

'You did, babe, you fainted.'

'Oh. God. Really? I fainted. How melodramatic. How very Victorian of me.' She smiled at him, reached out for his hand. 'Conor. It's OK. I'm OK. I think I'm OK. I hit my head. But I think I'm OK. It's just this heat, I think. And the booze. I shouldn't have had that glass of wine earlier, I haven't eaten anything today.'

Conor helped her up into a sitting position. She was aware, all of a sudden, that she was surrounded by a crowd of people, all peering anxiously down. She could feel sweat at the nape of her neck and on her lower back; she felt as though she were radiating heat.

'Could I just have some water?'

Lilah was crouching down next to her. Jen was aware of an expanse of tanned flesh, Lilah's long legs, bright pink toenails, wedge heels. 'Here you go, sweetie.' A glass in one hand, a tissue in the other. She was dabbing at Jen's head. 'It's not too bad, just a little cut. You don't need stitches.'

Lilah and Conor helped her to her feet. She was standing in the middle of the kitchen in Andrew's flat. Andrew came running in from the garden where he'd been doing the barbecue.

'What happened? Bloody hell, Jen, what happened?' They took her into the bedroom, laid her down on the bed. The pillow smelt of Chanel No. 5. Lilah. Conor was talking about taking her to casualty. Lilah leaned over her, laid a wet flannel on her forehead.

'Don't be ridiculous, Con, it's just the heat,' Jen said. She reached out for his hand again, gave it a squeeze. 'I'll pop down and see the doctor tomorrow if I'm not feeling well.'

Lilah drew the curtains, Andrew went to fetch her another glass of water. Conor kissed her on the head.

'Leave me a minute, OK?' she asked him. 'I just want to lie here for a bit. I'll be out in a sec. OK?' Reluctantly, he left and, just as she'd hoped (or feared or dreaded), it wasn't long before there was a knock at the door.

'You OK, Jen?' Dan was wearing jeans and a black T-shirt, his skin tanned a deep brown following three weeks of relentless sunshine. He shut the door behind him, sat down at her side, leaned over and kissed her on the lips.

'Don't.'

'Sorry.'

He placed his hand, cool and dry, on her waist, slipped it under her shirt, just above the waistband of her skirt.

'Dan, don't.' He stopped, but she didn't want him to. At that moment she wanted desperately for him to lie down with her, for the door to be locked, the flat to be empty, the two of them to be alone. She closed her eyes and felt the tears squeeze out of them.

'You should go,' she said, and he left her.

# Chapter Twenty-eight

~

*September 1995*

Half the boxes were still unpacked. They'd shifted them all into the second bedroom and piled them up against a wall. They had intended to get everything done before the party, but they'd been too busy having sex all afternoon.

'It's better like this anyway,' Conor said, lazily grabbing at Jen's calf as she tried to get up off the floor. 'This way if the party gets really wild then only half our stuff will get trashed.'

Jen laughed, kicking his hand away. 'Yeah. I'm sure it'll get super wild. There's only going to be, like, fifteen people there.'

'True,' Conor conceded, 'but one of those people is Lilah, so frankly all bets are off.'

Jen pulled a T-shirt over her head and slipped her knickers back on. Conor grimaced.

'Ah, don't do that. You're so much prettier without.'

'Oh really? You'd like me to greet our guests at the front door with no clothes on?'

Conor lay back on the floor, stretching his arms above his

head. 'Nah, probably best not, you'll give the old boy next door a heart attack.'

'You want something to drink?' she asked him, walking into the kitchenette. 'Cup of tea?'

Conor propped himself up on his elbows, watching her walk away. He loved to watch her walk. He loved to watch her reach her hands back to the nape of her perfect, pale, graceful neck and twist her long, dark hair up into a knot, he loved the way it stayed there, piled on her head, without a clip. Like magic. The idea that he was going to get to look at her, every day, first thing in the morning, last thing at night, it made him feel as though his heart might burst with happiness.

'I'd love a cup of tea, ta,' he said.

She turned to look at him over her shoulder. 'Are you planning on getting dressed at all?' she asked, grinning, a big dimple opening up in her left cheek.

'Not right now,' he said, raising an eyebrow. 'They won't be here for at least an hour yet. Plenty of time.'

'Oh yeah? Plenty of time for what exactly?' He raised the eyebrow again. She giggled.

'Again? Bit ambitious, aren't you?'

He jumped to his feet and was across the room in a second, grabbing her round the waist as she shrieked with laughter. 'Oh, I'll show you ambitious, babe,' he said, kissing her neck, slipping his hand under her T-shirt. 'I'll show you.'

They were just about dressed by the time Natalie arrived, at exactly eight-thirty. Nat was endearingly punctual, even for parties. Conor poured drinks while Jen gave her the tour, which took all of sixty seconds. The reason there were to be only fifteen people at their party was that you couldn't actually fit more than fifteen people in the flat. In theory, it consisted of five rooms, a living room downstairs with a tiny galley kitchen off to one side, and the spare room on the other, the main bedroom upstairs, with an even tinier ensuite bathroom. It was three rooms really, neither the kitchen nor the bathroom were large enough to deserve the name, and the spare bedroom was actually no more than a box room. There was a small balcony at the back of the building, too, overlooking the gardens of the larger, grander apartments below, and beyond that, a line of trees at the edge of the common.

'So, you're not going to be doing a lot of cat-swinging, then?' Nat asked Conor with a smile as she accepted the drink.

'Not a lot, no. I said we should go for the place down the road with about double the square footage, but Ms Donleavy over there refused.'

'Isn't it great though?' Jen asked Nat, beaming. 'I know it's tiny, but isn't it just lovely? The view out back, and this building, the square . . .' They'd rented about 350 square feet spread over two storeys at the top of a grand old Georgian terrace which extended all the way around three sides of a square, a private garden in its centre.

'It's not the kind of place we'd ever be able to afford under normal circumstances . . .'

'Normal circumstances meaning being able to fit things like, I don't know, furniture or appliances, into our home,' Conor said with a grin. It was true, it was ridiculously cramped, but he didn't care, he cared not one iota when he saw the look on Jen's face as she talked about 'our place'. Their place, the place they shared. The place they would cook and drink and plan holidays, the place they'd entertain their friends, the place they'd spend hours, days, whole weekends in bed together. If his sixteen-year-old self could see him now, he'd think he'd died and gone to heaven.

By ten, everyone who was expected to attend had arrived, and although they had invited new friends from work and a couple of old friends from college, it ended up, as usual, with the six of them hanging out together, crammed like sardines out on the balcony, everyone talking at once.

Lilah: 'I love this job. I don't care what anyone says, PR is fucking brilliant. Basically, I get to take people out to lunch a lot, or out for drinks a lot, I plan parties and get paid for it, and not only that but they give me things. Like, for free. Look!' She held out her wrist; she was wearing some sort of garish beaded bracelet which Conor thought ought to cost no more than a fiver, but from the reactions of the girls (ooh-ing and ah-ing, asking, 'Is that real?') was clearly worth a good deal more.

Andrew: 'It is not a misogynist book! Yes, it's challenging, transgressive even, but not simply misogynist. To say that is to miss the point.'

Natalie (loudly): 'What point am I missing? The point where it's entertainment to torture women? That book is basically a 400-page catalogue of new and interesting ways to damage and degrade the female of the species. It's . . .'

Lilah (even louder): 'Oh good God. I can't believe you two are still bloody arguing about *American Psycho*. You read it, like, three years ago. Get over it.'

Dan: 'The bastards are going to kick me out. I know they bloody are. Bloody yuppie twat who owns the building wants to redevelop it. I'm going to be homeless in a few weeks and I only bloody just moved in.'

'You could move in here,' Conor said to him and everyone started laughing, except Jen, who gave him a sharp look. 'Oh, I'm only joking,' Conor said, putting his arm around her waist and pulling her closer to kiss her. The smell of her sent a jolt through him, direct to his loins; he had the clearest flashback to that afternoon, it made him dizzy. 'It'll just be you and me in the love nest, I promise.' He grinned at Dan, who smiled back, then looked away.

Andrew and Lilah were the last to leave. Conor kicked them out just after four, Lilah protesting loudly that it was way too early to go home yet before falling over on the pavement and howling with rage that it was all Conor's fault. The first taxi they'd called refused to take them, the driver took one look at Lilah, shook his head and drove off. Andrew just shrugged and called another one. The patience of a saint, Andrew had. Conor would be the first to admit that Lilah was a gorgeous girl and a good laugh, but he had no idea how his best friend coped with that level of drama day in, day out.

He was the lucky one. He knew that as they sat together on the balcony, covered in a blanket, Jen in front of him, leaning back against his chest. Her eyelids were drooping but she refused to go to bed; she wanted to watch the sun come up, she said.

'It feels like the beginning, doesn't it?' she murmured sleepily. Beneath the blanket she snaked her arm back behind her and around his waist.

'Yeah, it does.'

She was right. They'd been together since they met on holiday when they were sixteen years old, but this felt different. This – the end of college, moving in, starting new jobs – it felt as though life were starting for real now, no more rehearsal. He was lucky. He kissed the top of her head, said it out loud.

'I'm so lucky, beautiful. So lucky.'

'Not as lucky as I am.' He squeezed her closer. 'I can't think of anywhere on earth I'd rather be right now.'

'Maybe the French house?'

'Not even the French house. This is too perfect.' The sky was turning pale on the horizon, the merest hint of warmth in the grey. 'In any case, we'll be back there in no time.'

'Yeah,' Conor said. He hadn't told her yet, wouldn't tell her now. There was no way his ma was going to let him skip family Christmas to spend it with his friends in France. There had already been an argument about how he'd spent all summer there and how Christmas was a time for family. And going to church. He'd tell her later, closer to the time. Who knew, he thought, he might even be able to change Ma's mind? The thought of ever being able to change his mother's mind made him laugh out loud.

'What's so funny?' she asked him.

'Nothing,' he said softly. 'You are falling asleep there because you want to watch the sunrise. You going to watch it with your eyes closed?'

He helped her to her feet and took her upstairs to bed.

## Chapter Twenty-nine

~

*November 1995*

Andrew stood like a soldier, Natalie thought, his back straight and chin raised; she could almost picture him in uniform. She tried not to picture him in uniform and listened to his speech instead.

'I remember the first time she ever spoke to me,' he said. 'I was in the library, right at the very back, head deep in *Blackstone's Statutes on Public Law and Human Rights*, and I looked up and there was this girl walking towards me, this *goddess*. She seemed about eight feet tall, she was just legs and blonde hair and bright red lips . . .' Lilah giggled, she had the good grace to blush. 'I knew who she was, of course, because everyone at college had heard of Lilah Lewis. Lilah Lewis was famous . . .'

'Infamous!' Dan interrupted.

'Well, that too. In any case – and I'm not joking, now – I watched her walk towards me and I could feel my insides turn to mush because she was smiling at me, *right at me*, it had to be at me, because there was no one else around. She came up to me, she perched there on the desk, nudging my books aside with her gorgeous arse, and without any preamble she said, "You're not seriously taking Karen Samuels to the Freshers' Ball, are you? Because, sweetheart. You can do *so* much better."'

'Oh, God, she's shameless! She's utterly shameless!' Conor laughed. Everyone was laughing, Lilah batting her lashes and smiling coquettishly at them all. They'd heard the story before, they'd heard it a dozen times, but it was one of those tales that didn't get old, one of those first meeting, first kiss stories that you never tire of hearing.

'Then she took my pen out of my hand,' Andrew went on, 'and scrawled her room number in large print, all over my neat and detailed notes, then she leaned forward and gave me a kiss on the cheek, then hopped off the desk and walked away, *strutted* away, and left me there, speechless, breathless.' He raised his wine glass, inclining his head a little. 'And you would have thought that after all this time, after four years, I might have got used to it, but she can still do it. She can still leave me breathless.'

Conor and Dan rolled their eyes exaggeratedly, they made fake gagging noises, but they raised their glasses too, they all did. 'Andrew and Lilah,' they chorused, and Natalie brushed the heel of her hand across her cheek bone.

'Oh my God, you're actually crying,' Lilah was laughing at her. 'You are the sappiest, sappiest . . .' but she couldn't finish her sentence because she was too busy kissing Natalie on the mouth.

They were sitting around the dinner table in Andrew's living room, which had recently become Andrew and Lilah's living room, as her unpacked boxes strewn around the place testified. It was their moving-in-slash-fourth anniversary celebration, a lazy Sunday lunch on a dark and bone-chilling November day.

They were already three and a half bottles of red down and they had no intention of stopping.

'OK, Lilah's turn,' Conor said, topping up their glasses. 'What are your earliest memories of the great man?'

'Oh, God. I don't know.' She shook her head. 'He was just this hot guy that Karen Samuels fancied and I couldn't bear her, she was just so impossibly vain . . .' There was uproarious laughter from Conor and Dan, which Lilah ignored: 'And so I decided that I was going to thwart her.' She smiled sweetly at Andrew over her glass. 'And it was the best thwarting I ever did.'

She leaned forward and gave him a kiss and Natalie got up to go to the loo because she felt as though she might start crying again.

As she was washing her hands, she looked at herself in the mirror and noticed the flush in her cheeks, the pink stain of her lips, not just from the wine. It was one of those days, one of those rare moments when you're not just happy, but you catch yourself feeling happy, when you acknowledge it, and she almost felt afraid, as though if she weren't careful, her happiness might slip away from her. It was painful, too, an exquisite sort of agony, but she chose to ignore that, because admitting to it was dangerous, and in any case, what good could it do? There was a gulf, a yawning chasm, between what she wanted for herself and what she wanted for her closest friend, and it could not be bridged.

Back in the living room, they'd cleared away the plates and Andrew was opening another bottle and Conor was telling the story of the first time he'd met Dan, at a party in the first year.

'I'd gone into the kitchen to get drinks and I literally can't have been more than three minutes, tops, and when I get back there he is, he's moved in, he's got Jen cornered, the bastard, I'm gone three minutes and he's hitting on my girl, and she was enjoying it!'

'I was not!'

'You're a liar, Jennifer, I remember it well, you were all enchanted with whatever patter he was giving you, you were twirling your hair around your finger, the way you do . . .' Jen was laughing and blushing and Dan just shaking his head.

'It's all lies. It's all lies,' he was saying. 'She was the one came on to me, wouldn't leave me alone . . .'

They pushed the dining-room table back against the wall and sat around the fake fire. Dan put on *Automatic for the People* and he grabbed Nat's hand and pulled her closer to him on the sofa. Lilah was lying on the floor, her head in Andrew's lap, asking to hear the Jen and Conor story again.

'Go on, I love the Jen and Conor story.'

So Jen told it, how the summer she turned sixteen she'd been sent to stay with her Aunt Ruth in Baltimore, West Cork and how, in her second week, she and her cousin, Kay, had dared each other to go skinny dipping in a sheltered little cove a mile or two from the town.

'So we decided to have a race to this buoy which was, I don't know, a hundred metres or so from the beach, and when we got there and turned around, we realised there were people on the beach. And it was like, the horror, the horror! We were just bobbing around out there, and Kay's saying, don't worry, they're just going for a walk, they'll be gone by the time we get back. So we swam back, slowly, slowly, and it was bloody freezing, I was desperate to get out, and the closer we got we realised that it was two blokes and they weren't going anywhere. They were sitting down. About ten metres from where our clothes were.' She passed her hand over her eyes. 'God, it was a nightmare, we were just getting colder and colder and it wasn't bloody funny any longer, I could see Kay's lips going blue, so I just thought, fuck it, and I ran, as fast as I could, out of the surf and up the beach . . .' she was laughing, shaking her head.

'And I was sitting there,' Conor took up the story, 'with my brother, Ronan, and he sees this girl and he's like, bloody hell, she's starkers, and he's just pissing himself laughing but Jesus, I was just sat there, mouth open, my eyes out on stalks. Couldn't believe it. Never seen anything so gorgeous in my whole life.' He was grinning at Jen, she had her hands over her face. 'And the next day, I saw her in the town and she saw me, and she blushed, deep red – the colour she is now, actually. And that was it. I was in love.'

Lilah and Andrew slow-danced to 'Nightswimming' while Conor and Jen snogged like teenagers on the sofa, so Natalie and Dan found themselves in the kitchen, doing the washing up.

'I hope they're not going to be at it all the time when I'm staying with them,' he said, jerking his head back in Conor and Jen's direction.

'Oh, is that happening? I thought Jen had vetoed.'

Dan raised an eyebrow. 'Oh. Well, as far as I know, it's happening. Con said it would be OK. She'll get used to me,' he said giving Natalie a wink. 'I can be quite loveable when I try.'

'Of course you can, sweetie,' she said, proffering her cheek, not her lips, when he bent down to give her a kiss.

'Is he hitting on you again?' Andrew was standing in the doorway watching them, his dance over. 'Honestly, can't leave you alone for a second.'

'No, you can't. Here,' Dan threw his dishcloth at Andrew's head. 'You'd better take over, I need to change the music.'

Andrew stood at her side. 'Don't do it all,' he said, 'I'll finish up later.'

'Don't be silly, I'm here now.'

He slipped his arm around her. 'What would I do without you?' he said, giving her a squeeze.

'All the washing up, probably, because I don't think you'll catch Lilah with a pair of Marigolds.'

His arm still draped around her shoulder, she felt it again: happiness, and the faintest shadow of fear.

'We need to hang out more, you and I. I miss the talks we had, on our walks in France.'

'Yeah, I miss them too.' She looked up at him and he smiled at her and she felt tears sting the backs of her eyes.

'Oi!' Lilah came bouncing into the room, two shot glasses in hand. 'Here. Tequila!'

'I'm working tomorrow, Lilo,' Natalie said.

'We're all working!' She pressed the glass into Natalie's hand. 'Come on. You have to. It's my anniversary.'

'Our anniversary, actually,' Andrew said.

'Yeah yeah, whatever. Drink.'

Natalie took the glass and downed its contents, swallowing as fast as possible, pulling a face. 'Bleugh.'

Lilah gave her a kiss on the cheek and grabbed her soapy hand. 'Come on, Drew can finish that. Come dance with me.' She pulled Natalie into the living room and they leapt around the room, Dan, Conor, Jen, Lilah and Natalie, to 'Disco 2000'.

# Chapter Thirty

~

*December 1995*

'He's driving me mental. MENTAL,' Jen said, suddenly aware that she was talking rather loudly and that the people on the next table were looking. She'd almost finished her third gin and tonic and they'd only been there an hour. She really ought to eat something. The bar, dimly lit and heaving, did not look a likely place to get a snack.

'He'll be gone in a week or so, won't he?' Lilah asked, scanning the room. 'At least you're not stuck with him.' Jen looked at her quizzically.

'Not Dan,' Nat said, rolling her eyes. 'Aren't you listening? She's talking about Conor.'

'Oh. Well, then you are stuck with him. As I am with Drew. Jesus Christ! Living together is not what I expected. It's so much less . . . It's just *less*, don't you think? Less going out, less presents, less sex, less fun.'

'Fewer presents,' Natalie said.

'What?'

'Nothing.'

'Are you correcting my grammar, Natalie?' Lilah threw a piece of lemon rind at her. 'I've warned you about that. God, have you seen that one? At the bar, dark hair, jeans, black T-shirt, right over there, at the end? Oh my word, I *so* would.'

'Lilah!' Natalie threw the lemon rind back.

Jen's head was swimming a little, due to gin combined with Lilah's peripatetic conversational style.

'I'm only joking. I would though, honestly. Look at his arse. There's this guy at work who has the most amazing body I've ever seen. Seriously. I could spend all day looking at him. But . . . what was I saying? Oh yeah. Living together is kind of shit, isn't it? I don't know, I just feel like the fun's been sucked out of everything and we argue now. So much. Like, all the time. Do you argue all the time?' Jen opened her mouth to answer but Lilah wasn't listening. 'I'm seriously considering moving back in with Mum. That's how crazy Drew is making me at the moment. Crazy enough to make me consider living with my *mother*.'

'Your mother's great, though,' Natalie said wistfully. 'Living with your mother would be like living with Marianne Faithfull or Greta Garbo; she'd be able to give you sage advice about men and what to wear. Living with my mother is like living with Felicity Kendal.'

Jen and Conor weren't arguing. Not much. Not *all the time*, anyway. She was happy living with Conor. Very happy. It wasn't exactly how she thought it would be, Lilah was right: they did go out less, but that was a good thing, because neither of them had money to burn, and London was so expensive. And, yeah, OK, apart from the first few weeks, they did have sex less often than before, but that was probably just because they felt awkward with Dan sleeping downstairs and they were always both knackered anyway because they weren't used to having to work for a living.

So, he got on her nerves a little more than he used to. That was normal, wasn't it? She'd shared a house with Lilah in the second year of university, and there were plenty of occasions, daily occasions, on which she'd wanted to kill her with her bare hands. To say Conor was driving her mental was a bit strong. It was just . . . different to what she'd expected. But it was fine. It was better than fine, it was good.

'We don't argue all the time,' Jen said softly, speaking to the dregs of her gin and tonic, but the others weren't really listening.

Lilah was back on the guy at work with the great body.

'He's not my boss as such, but he is senior to me in the company, obviously – everyone is senior to me because I've only been there five minutes. So it wouldn't be, like, a problem from a sexual harassment point of view or anything like that . . .'

'Lilah, why are you even talking about this? You're not actually considering this, I know you're not. So just stop it, because it isn't funny.' Natalie's face had reddened, she wasn't joking around any longer.

'Oh, Nat!'

'She's right, Lilah, it isn't funny. Andrew's our friend, he's my boyfriend's best friend and it really isn't cool to go on and on about how you want to cheat on him all the time.'

'Oh girls!' Lilah got to her feet and hugged each of them, long and hard. 'You know I'm joking! Fuck! Aren't we here to get pissed and talk rubbish? I just like to look, that's all.' She pouted at them, looking up from beneath lowered lashes, couldn't hold the pose for more than a second or two before starting to giggle. 'I'm off to the loo. And when I come back I want you both to have chilled the fuck out.'

They watched her weave her way towards the ladies, turning heads as she went. Natalie and Jen looked at each other, indulgent smiles on their lips.

'Is she OK, you think?' Jen asked.

'A bit all over the place. Andrew says she's caning it pretty hard with people from work.'

'She'll be all right,' Jen said. 'She'll settle down. It's an adjustment period, that's all. That's what Conor keeps telling me. An adjustment period. If he says it one more time I think I'll beat him to death with a frying pan.' Natalie giggled. 'How are *you* anyway, Nat? God, you haven't got a word in for all our whingeing. How's work? How's your love life?'

'B plus for the former, D minus for the latter,' Nat said with a laugh. 'Andrew tried to fix me up with this guy from his work last week but it was pretty disastrous.' Her laughter had turned brittle: she looked down at the table and then away. Jen felt a pang for her, reached over and squeezed her hand. The elephant wasn't so much in the room as sitting right there with them at the table. Jen thought about saying something, tried to think of something she could say, something that wouldn't sound patronising, that wouldn't embarrass her. She tried and failed, and then Lilah reappeared with more drinks, so she changed the subject.

'I'm sorry about France,' she said.

'It's OK,' Nat said. 'It's understandable that Conor would have to go home. Big Catholic family and all that – Christmas is a big deal.' She was trying to be reassuring, but she looked a little forlorn.

'I know, but I know you were all looking forward to it. I

was looking forward to it. But you guys could still go, you know, there's no reason to cancel just because Con and I can't come . . .'

'It wouldn't be the same,' Nat said firmly, shaking her head.

'In any case, I've got loads of parties on around Christmas, work things, you know, so I'm OK to stay in London,' Lilah said, with a little shrug.

'Oh. Well . . .'

'Christmas in Ireland will be fun, though, won't it?' Nat asked her. 'You get on well with Conor's family, don't you?'

'I do. I do. It's just . . .'

'What?'

'Nothing. It's nothing. I'm just a little annoyed. And I promise you I'm going to stop complaining, any minute now, but the thing that bugs me, the thing that drives me mental, is that he didn't even ask me. I was just told: we're not going to the French house, we're going to Cork! Just presented to me, fait accompli. It was the same with the thing about Dan, it wasn't even a discussion, it was just: Dan's coming to stay for a couple of weeks, fait accompli. It's just . . . infuriating. I mean, I don't even mind Dan staying. I like having Dan around, but it's the way the decision was just made for me, you know?'

Natalie and Lilah exchanged a look. Jen wasn't quite sure what the look meant, but she was sure she didn't like it.

'What? What?'

'Well . . .' Lilah shrugged, giggled, drank some more of her drink.

'It's not really such a new thing, is it?' Nat said, playing with the cocktail stick in her glass.

'What do you mean?' She couldn't imagine what they were talking about.

'He's always been like that,' Lilah said matter-of-factly. 'He takes control. He's an alpha male. You like that about him. Well, you used to like it anyway. You've always let him make decisions for you.'

'I have not. I absolutely have not.' Lilah didn't know what she was talking about, she was wasted. But Natalie was nodding, a half smile on her lips, as though she agreed with what Lilah was saying.

Jen stomped off to the loos, irritated. Had she always let Conor make decisions for her, she wondered, grumpily and rather sloppily reapplying her lipstick. She didn't feel as though she had. She wasn't that sort of person, was she? She wasn't some meek little girl running around after her boyfriend. It was absolute bollocks.

By the time she got back to the table, they'd bought yet another round. Jen felt a little sick – she hadn't eaten anything since lunch, it was probably time to call it a night.

'You can't go now!' Lilah protested when she said as much. 'It's quarter past ten. There's a thing later, some people from work are going, it's at a club somewhere . . .'

She leaned forward and tidied up Jen's lipstick with the edge of her thumb.

'Don't be cross, sweetie,' she purred.

Jen could feel the eyes of the blokes at the next table on them, watching Lilah touch her face. She smiled.

'I'm not cross, I'm just knackered. I think I ought to just go home.'

'Oh, all right then,' Lilah said, pouting. 'Give my love to your annoying boyfriend. And to Dan. How has it been with Dan, anyway? Is he driving you mental, too?'

'Weirdly, no,' Jen said. 'It's been nice having him there.

Conor's working ridiculous hours most of the time, so it's been fun to have someone there to hang out with, go to the cinema, watch *ER*.' She started laughing. 'He does this hilarious thing where he dances to the *ER* theme music . . . you kind of have to be there. And I cook for him, because, you know, he's totally undomesticated, can't do anything for himself. It's nice. It's like looking after a stray.' She was babbling a little and she wasn't sure why – she really was drunk, she could feel a prickle of heat at the base of her neck, Jen and Lilah looking at her intently, quizzically, a slow grin spreading over Lilah's face.

'Oh, so that's it!' Lilah said, giggling. 'That's how you do it. You get two boyfriends, that way when one of them pisses you off, you just bring the other one off the bench. Bring them off? Pull them off?'

'Jen, Dan and Conor, sitting in a tree . . .' Natalie sang happily.

They had been joking. Everyone was pissed. So why was she sitting in the back of a taxi, fuming? Why had she had a complete sense of humour failure, stomped out of the bar in a huff? She could feel herself blushing just thinking about it, she'd been ridiculous, and they would be wondering why she'd been ridiculous. Something about their teasing just stung, and in the back of her mind there was a reason. She wouldn't let it come to the fore, so she left it there, to prick and to fester.

The flat was in darkness when she got home save for the blue flicker of the television. Dan was on the sofa, an ashtray at his side, a beer bottle at his feet.

'You're back early,' he said, his voice low. 'Good night?'

'All right,' she said. She could feel her anger slipping away; she was relieved to be home. 'Where's Con?'

'He's in bed,' Dan said, 'party animal that he is.'

'Right. Well.' She hovered in the doorway for a moment. 'What are you watching?'

'Nothing, really. Flicking around.'

'OK.'

He looked up at her and smiled. 'You look nice.' He patted the sofa next to him and shifted up a little. 'Join me? There's another beer in the fridge.'

She shook her head, kicking off her high heels. 'I think I've had enough.' Still she stood in the doorway, just looking at him.

'You all right?'

'I'm going to bed,' she said, ''night.'

''Night, Jen.'

Conor was asleep, his body spread out over the bed, arms flung wide. The curtains were still open, light from the street lamps bathing the room in an orange glow. She pulled the drapes shut and undressed as quietly as she could, slipping beneath cold sheets until she was close enough to him to feel his heat. He stirred, reached one arm around her body, murmured something quietly, she couldn't make out what he'd said. She was wide awake. She could hear the faint sounds of the television below and thought for a moment about getting up again, going downstairs and sitting on the sofa with Dan. She knew that it wouldn't be long before he said something to make her laugh, made her feel better. She closed her eyes and listened to Conor's breathing, slow and rhythmic. She could feel his heart beat against her back. She thought about how good her life was, how lucky she was, and how it made no sense at all for her to feel so sad.

# Chapter Thirty-one

~

*March 1996*

The plane pitched sharply to the left and Conor felt his stomach lurch. His hands gripping the arm rests, he kept his head down, listening for changes in the tone of engine noise. He glanced to his left; the middle-aged woman sitting at his side was smiling at him reassuringly. He wasn't afraid of flying. He'd never been afraid of flying. Now he was filled with dread.

'It's just a little turbulence,' the woman said to him, and he nodded and smiled and felt like a fool.

He was a fool. He should never have walked out like that. He could still picture her, sitting up in bed, holding her hand out to him, knowing that even if he was angry, even if they had had a horrible argument, he wouldn't just walk out without saying a proper goodbye, without a kiss. He could see the expression on her face change, the moment he turned to go, when she realised that he was leaving, just like that. He could picture the hurt, and he felt wretched.

If this plane fell into the freezing Irish Sea, he'd never have the chance to tell her he was sorry.

It had all started over a takeaway. He'd been packing for his trip to Ireland, a week-long trip this time, not just a weekend, to help with the renovations on his brother's house. He'd been going over quite a bit lately and he knew that Jen wasn't happy about it, particularly since Dan had moved out. She was feeling a little lonely in the flat on her own. Everyone was so busy these days, they didn't see each other so often.

They had been planning to go out for dinner, but he was just dog-tired, he'd been working long hours all week, so he suggested a takeaway instead. Jen was fine with that, or at least she said she was. She wanted a curry, but Conor fancied a pizza. It was as simple and trivial a matter as the choice of menu. They bickered about it a bit, until Jen said, fine, OK, pizza, and went downstairs to order it.

It should have been over then, it wasn't a big deal. Only when the pizza arrived, she sat there, plate on her lap, then took one bite and set it aside, her face hard as granite, jaw clenched. She was fuming. It was ridiculous. He said so.

'For God's sake, Jen, do you want me to call out for a biryani for you? Is that what you want? I'll do it! Christ, it would be preferable to sitting here looking at you with that face on.'

'Just forget about it, OK?' she said, getting to her feet and taking her plate into the kitchen. She stood there at the counter, her back to him, as though she couldn't bear to look at him.

'How can I forget about it, with you standing there, I can almost see the steam coming out of your ears!' He laughed. 'You're being ridiculous, Jen, it's just a bloody pizza.'

She turned to look at him, pure hell in her eyes, and he wished he hadn't laughed.

'It is not. About. The bloody pizza!' she yelled and he ducked as a slice of the offending foodstuff came hurtling right at him.

It landed tomato sauce-side down on the sofa. He could feel his mouth fall open; he was astonished, he'd never seen her behave like this, so petulant, so childish.

'Jesus, Jen, what the hell is wrong with you?'

And then she burst into tears, which really got his back up – he couldn't stand it when girls did that, behaved badly and then cried to make you feel bad. That was Lilah behaviour, it just wasn't like Jen. He strode past her into the kitchen, not reaching out for her or trying to comfort her, grabbed a cloth from the counter and returned to clean up the mess.

'It's not about the pizza,' she was sobbing, 'it's not about that.'

'Well, tell me what it is about then, for God's sake,' he muttered, scrubbing furiously at the sauce stain on the sofa, grinding the mess into the fabric. 'I'm not a bloody mind reader.'

And then she went off on this unbelievable rant; it came out of nowhere, he could scarely believe what he was hearing.

'It's about you,' she cried, 'always getting your way. No matter what the issue, from deciding what we're having for dinner to deciding where we're going to spend Christmas, when and where we're going travelling, when we're going to get married, how many bloody children we're going to have, it's all about you. *Everything* is about you. I feel like I don't have control over anything any more. I feel like your bloody wife!' She spat the last word at him, stormed out of the room and up the stairs, slamming the bedroom door as hard as she could.

He sat there, stunned. It wasn't just the unfairness of it, it was the vitriol. His bloody wife? She felt like his *bloody wife*? As though that were something abhorrent. He picked up his plate with its half-finished pizza slice and carried it with shaking hands to the kitchen, dumped it in the rubbish bin. He couldn't eat another thing, could barely swallow. He stood there for a moment, hands gripping the kitchen counter, and felt his shock turn to anger.

He stormed up the stairs and flung the door open, the handle smashing into the bedroom wall. She was sitting on the bed, looking out of the window. She didn't look round, didn't even flinch.

'I thought you wanted to be my bloody wife,' he said, trying his best to keep his voice low and even. 'I thought you wanted to have my bloody children. I thought you wanted me, to be with me, to marry me. Now you make it sound like a prison sentence.' She didn't say anything, still didn't turn around. Silence stretched out. But as he stood there in the doorway with his hand against the frame, steadying himself, anger falling away, he felt desperately sad. He felt afraid.

'Do you not love me any more, Jen?' he asked her, but he couldn't bear to hear the answer, so he turned quickly away, closing the door behind him. He grabbed his coat in the hallway and left the flat.

She was in bed when he came home, after the pubs had shut. Her eyes were closed, but he was pretty sure she wasn't sleeping. He slipped into bed and lay beside her, his eyes fixed on the tiny mole between her pale shoulder blades, that place he loved to kiss. He willed her to turn around, to put her arms around him, to apologise. She didn't. Eventually, he fell asleep.

He got up early to finish packing; he needed to be at Gatwick by nine. He brought Jen a cup of tea, placing it on the bedside table. Her eyes remained closed. When the time came for him to leave, he stood there for a long time, in the doorway, just as he'd done the night before, when he asked her the question she still hadn't answered.

'I'm leaving now,' he said, and she sat bolt upright with a start.

'Conor,' she said softly, 'please, I'm sorry. Don't go yet. I'm sorry. I'm so sorry, I was just feeling . . .'

'I'll miss the flight,' he said abruptly, cutting her off. He was irritated, because she knew he had to leave, and if she'd wanted to talk, if she'd really wanted to make up with him, she could have done so earlier.

'Please,' she said again, her voice small and tight.

He shook his head. 'I don't know what's going on with you, Jen. It seems like I'm the one putting in all the effort here. And it seems like no matter what I do, it's wrong.' He picked up his bag and turned to go and saw the look on her face and knew that she was going to cry and in that second decided that he wasn't going to comfort her.

He left without kissing her goodbye.

The second he got into Cork airport, he was going to call her at work and tell her how sorry he was, that he loved her more than anything, that he always would. And he would apologise for asking her whether she still loved him, because he knew that she did, he knew it in the core of him, how could he have questioned it? It was insulting to her, it was hurtful. And though he still felt that she'd been unfair, now, in the cold clear light of day, up here at 30,000 feet with danger of death imminent, he could admit that he had perhaps taken decisions that, just maybe, he ought to have discussed with her. Like going to Cork for Christmas, for example.

And thinking about it, he knew full well why she said what she did about marriage and children, he knew that she'd overheard him talking to his mum and his aunties after Christmas lunch, when they'd been asking when there would be a wedding, and grandchildren, and all that, and he'd been saying soon, within a year or two. He knew she'd felt a bit put out about that, but he'd only been saying it to get them off his back. Only, it struck him that he'd never really explained that to her, not in so many words.

If only they'd talked through it. And there was the problem, in a nutshell, they hadn't been talking the way they used to. That was probably his fault too, or mostly his fault, in any case. He was working all the time, he was going to Ireland a lot, plus there were those months when Dan was staying (which was another decision he'd taken without really talking it through with her), when they didn't have much time to themselves.

As long as he could talk to her, as long as this plane didn't pitch into the sea, he'd make it right.

## Chapter Thirty-two

She called in sick, and she didn't even feel guilty about it, because she *felt* sick. When she heard the front door close, when she realised he'd really gone, that she wouldn't be able to see him, hold him, make it up to him for a whole week, she felt physically ill.

She pulled the duvet over her head and lay there, replaying the argument over and over. She'd been unreasonable. She'd been unkind. She'd thrown a pizza slice at his head. She'd said terrible, awful things. Bloody wife, bloody children. She kept hearing him ask her over and over again, whether she still loved him. She curled herself into a ball. If she stayed here all day, that was all she would hear, it wouldn't stop. She had to get up, she had to do something.

She showered, dressed and went downstairs to make herself a cup of tea. She rang Lilah, with whom she didn't really want to spend the day, and was relieved when she said there was no way she could pull another sickie. She didn't bother to call Nat or Andrew, because she knew very well that it would take Ebola fever or a severed limb to get either of them to call in sick. And in any case, she didn't really want to spend the day with either of them.

She wanted to spend the day with Dan. She just didn't really want to think about why she'd rather be with him than with any of her other friends. The thought unnerved her. She couldn't remember exactly when this sense of being closer to him than all the others had started. It crept up on her, barely noticeable at first, and then there was that night out with the girls when they were teasing her about him and she got so angry, and suddenly it was all she could think about, these feelings she was having that she shouldn't be having.

If only he hadn't come to stay. Being around him all the time, that was what did it. Seeing him first thing in the morning, his hair sticking up and his pale skin still creased with sleep, tall and skinny with big, mournful grey eyes, eyes alive with light when he looked at her. It was his hopelessness, his general crapness, the fact that he couldn't boil an egg, that if it weren't for her he'd live on takeaways and Pot Noodles. It was all those long nights on the sofa talking, when he told her about how it had been for him, growing up, motherless and then fatherless, when she realised how hard he'd had it and how, compared to him, the rest of them were blessed, spoiled. He'd had to struggle so much, and yet here he was, funny and kind and when he looked at her a certain way it gave her butterflies.

She didn't like thinking about it, didn't like arriving home at night and looking sadly at the spot on the sofa where he always sat, one leg crossed over the other (surprisingly elegant), cigarette in hand, laughing at something on the television. She didn't like how much she thought about him. She especially didn't like the way in which she'd come to make comparisons between him and Conor.

She knew that it was a bad idea to call him. She dialled his number. She put the phone down. Then she dialled it again.

He was on the train within the hour and she met him at Liverpool Street at midday. They had lunch in Shoreditch, went to White Cube on Hoxton Square, wandered down Commercial Street and had a couple of drinks at the Golden Heart. They hopped on the tube and went to the Barbican where they saw an incomprehensible and highly erotic Japanese film. They went back to the flat. There were three messages on the voicemail. She didn't listen to them. She and Dan sat, facing each other on the sofa, feet almost but not quite touching, drinking red wine.

## Chapter Thirty-three

~

Her toenails were painted dark red. Almost black. She had perfect, pale, neat little feet, the kind a fetishist might get excited about. Not that he was one. But Dan did realise that when he was with her, he focused on the small things. He thought about how she would look on camera; he looked for her best angles. He'd yet to find a bad one.

He wanted her so badly, he'd never wanted anyone like this. You could write songs about this girl, you could make a film about her face, about her laugh, and her long, elegant neck and the contour of her lips. His blood was rising, he had to stop it, he bit his lip, hard.

It wasn't new, this thing with her, but it was getting worse, so much worse, every time he saw her, spoke to her. Kissing her hello was the most exquisite agony he had ever felt. It wasn't new, but he'd allowed it to escalate, he indulged himself now, with thoughts of her, he thought about her in a way he hadn't permitted himself to do for years, not since they'd first met and he'd realised, within a short space of time, that she would never look at him the way she did at Conor.

Only lately, he wasn't so sure. It wasn't exactly that she'd given him reason to hope. She hadn't really encouraged him. Not until now anyway, if you considered inviting him to stay with her while her boyfriend was away as encouragement. Which it was, surely? Only he couldn't be sure. He'd been in love with her so long he could no longer tell whether he was simply inventing motives for her, putting meaning that wasn't there into her words and the way she looked at him.

Thinking about it led to writing about it. Not that Jen knew what it was really about. The girl in the story, the one the boy loves but can't have, was well disguised. Dan had let Jen believe that it was based on a girl from college called Cara Nicholson who'd left him for an Old Harrovian with a trust fund and a family chalet in Chamonix. Jen wasn't to know that he didn't give a toss about Cara Nicholson; that there wasn't a single one of his girlfriends or casual flings at college for whom he felt one tenth of what he felt for her.

He wanted to talk to Jen about the screenplay, but he wasn't sure he'd be able to keep up the pretence, whether she'd see straight through it. So when she'd asked him that afternoon, 'How's the writing going?' he'd answered, 'Oh, yeah, not so bad,' and then changed the subject. She'd given him a bit of a funny look then (or had he imagined her giving him a funny look?) because he never passed up an opportunity to talk about his writing, but she'd let it go.

He wanted to talk to her about it because she'd become his sounding board for the screenplay. Somehow, he just couldn't get the second part of the film (unrequited love) to gel with the first (a thinly fictionalised account of his childhood, his mother's death from cancer when he was eight, his chaotic upbringing by a father who suffered from bipolar disorder). He was pretty sure it *could* work, only for some reason the tone of the first part jarred with the second.

But he couldn't trust himself to talk about the fake-Cara real-Jen girl without giving himself away. The conversation had long since moved away from work in any case, it had moved on from their friends and their plans for the summer and now it drifted into even trickier territory.

She was talking to him about having problems with Conor, about the fight they'd had, and how she'd been feeling frustrated with him lately, how she felt as though everything was moving a little too quickly all of a sudden, how it scared her, how she felt as though she were losing control.

It wasn't the first time she'd complained to him about Conor, and he wished she wouldn't. He didn't want to hear it, because it made him hopeful, and it also made him wretched, because he loved Conor. He was the kind of friend who would walk across hot coals for him, for any of them.

She shouldn't be talking to him about Conor. Only, she *should* be talking to him about Conor, because he was her friend, and that's what friends are for, isn't it, to listen to you bitch and moan about your relationship when everything's not going so well? She wasn't to know how she made him feel. There was nothing between them, there never had been.

Now, toes touching, there was literally nothing between them, no space, no distance: he could reach out, if he dared, and touch her face, run his thumb along her luscious lower lip, slip his hand around the back of her beautiful, long, ivory neck, pull her face towards his, kiss her.

'Dan? Am I boring you?'

'What? No! Sorry, I was just thinking, you know, that . . .' He couldn't touch her, he couldn't kiss her. 'I was thinking that maybe you need to cut him some slack.'

She frowned at him; she had the most perfect frown. 'I thought you'd be on my side, I know he drives you mental sometimes too.'

'He does not!' Dan lied with a laugh. 'No, seriously, the thing is, you've got to think about how it is for him. He was the big man on campus, wasn't he, at college? Him and Andrew, rugby team, student council, all that crap. For some people it can be a bit tricky to adjust to life after that, in the real world, when you're nothing special any longer, not that I'm saying he's nothing special . . .'

'That's what he keeps saying,' Jen muttered, beautiful lower lip plumped out. 'Adjustment year, blah blah. But that only makes me feel more anxious, as though I have just one year to adjust, and that year's almost finished now. And I don't feel adjusted yet! I don't feel ready to go off travelling yet, I feel like I need to settle into normal, working life first. And as for marriage . . .'

'He's talking about marriage?' Dan asked, and hoped that she couldn't hear the note of despair in his voice.

'Well, not dates or anything, but it's . . . It's what we've always thought, you know. It's what we wanted.'

Dan cursed himself for being such a coward, for not having the courage to ask: 'What you wanted, or what you *want*?' He knew the answer anyway, he knew she would marry Conor, he'd always known. Only, now, she was sitting opposite him, resting her chin on her knees, looking up at him, just a touch of blush in her cheeks and a smile on her lips and he didn't know any longer, he didn't know anything.

'What are you smiling at?' he asked her.

'Nothing.' She laughed (her laugh was like music, the soundtrack to the film he'd make, about the contours of her lips).

'Go on.'

She took a deep breath and puffed her cheeks out. 'OK. This sounds ridiculous. And it's kind of embarrassing . . .'

'Come on,' he said, poking her toes with his own, a jolt of electricity bolting right up his spine at the merest physical contact. 'You can tell me.'

Another deep breath. 'Right. Well, you know I've been with Conor since I was sixteen years old, right? That's one third of my life. One third! And the thing is . . .' she tailed off. The hint of a blush in her pale cheeks deepened. She looked perfect, she *was* perfect – he had to look away, he had to sit on his hands to stop himself from reaching out to touch her.

'The thing is, what?' He could almost feel them drifting into uncharted conversational waters, dangerous waters. 'You can tell me,' he said again. 'You can tell me anything.'

She laughed. 'It's nothing.' She wrapped her arms around her knees, bent her head down to hide her face. 'It's just that, if we stay together, if we get married, like everybody's always thought we would, then he's going to be it for me. And me for him. There's never going to be anyone else.'

Her voice was muffled, he wasn't sure he'd heard her right. Was she really saying this, was she really talking about being with someone else? He laughed, nervously. 'I, uh, didn't think girls worried about things like that,' he said.

'Yeah, well, we do.' She was still hiding from him, but after a moment, she looked up, her face bright red. 'It's ridiculous, isn't it? I mean, it's a good thing, to only ever be with one person. It's a good thing to only ever want one person, isn't it?'

'Well . . .' They both started laughing.

'Oh, for God's sake,' she said, shaking her head. 'I'm being so stupid. I don't know why I'm saying all this. I've had way too much to drink.' She got to her feet and went into the kitchen, carrying their empty wine glasses with her.

He didn't let himself think about what he was doing, he just got to his feet and followed her. She put the glasses down and turned around, looking up at him, and he knew she wanted him to kiss her, so he did. She didn't pull away at first, not right away, but when she did her eyes were lowered, she wasn't looking at him, and she placed her hand against his chest and pushed him, gently, away from her.

'Dan,' she said, her voice low, husky, 'don't.'

She didn't say another word, just smiled at him and shook her head, then she went upstairs and he heard the bedroom door close.

He thought about leaving, about calling a taxi and going to the station, but it was after midnight and there wouldn't be a train until morning. He wasn't even sure if Liverpool Street was open all night. He turned off all the lights and sat in the darkness, looking out at the almost full moon in the night sky, knowing that there was no possibility of sleep, not tonight. He doubted he would ever sleep again, he'd just lie in bed replaying that kiss, and that hand against his chest, and her saying his name, her telling him no.

It must have been half an hour later when he heard a creaking sound, and then the squeak of a door handle. He held his breath. He heard a footfall on the stairs; she was coming back down. He could hear his heart thudding in his chest.

'Dan?'

'I'm here,' he said, 'I'm sorry.'

She was standing in front of him, wearing a vest and little shorts, her pale legs pressed against his knees. She reached out to him and took his hand, she pulled him to his feet and led him into the spare room. It was real, he wasn't imagining it, her lips on his, her hands pulling at his T-shirt, lifting it over his head, her body pressed against his, the smell of her, citrus and vanilla. She was really there, and he couldn't stop it, he couldn't send her away.

## Chapter Thirty-four

⁓

There was a moth in the room, batting against the inside of the window pane, behind the curtain. She rubbed her eyes. The curtain was pale, a yellowing kind of beige. The light streaming in. What was wrong? It came to her and she gave a little gasp, audible, something like shock, or panic. She closed her eyes tightly. She wished for it not to be real, a dream. Please, let it be a dream. But if it wasn't real, why was the curtain that yellowing sort of beige? That was the colour of the curtain in the spare room, not the dark blue in her and Conor's room. She knew then that when she opened her eyes again and looked under the cover, that on the inside of the wrist of the arm flung around her waist, she would see a tattoo. A small dark Arabic character, an ill-advised purchase on a holiday to Marrakech. Not Conor's pale, untouched flesh. She didn't want to look. She scarcely allowed herself to breathe. She opened her eyes. Her robe was on the floor. She pushed Dan's arm away, slipped out of bed, grabbed the robe and pulled it around her shoulders. She left the room as quickly and quietly as she could, closing the door behind her, not once looking back.

She ran upstairs and into the bathroom, locking the door behind her, and sat down on the loo. She wanted to cry, she wanted to be sick, she wanted to hurt herself, to cut herself with something, to feel something other than this disgust with herself, this awful shame. The tears didn't come, the nausea didn't subside, but she didn't actually throw up. She just sat there, holding herself, digging her fingernails into the tops of her arms until she drew blood.

When she'd gone downstairs last night, what she was doing hadn't seemed so wrong. She knew she was being reckless, but somehow she'd managed to convince herself that it wasn't so terrible, one night spent with a friend to whom she had this powerful, undeniable attraction, a man who in different circumstances might have been so much more to her. She'd persuaded herself that in some way she owed it to herself, this moment of recklessness: it would set her mind at rest, she wouldn't worry so much that she was missing out. She persuaded herself that in the end it would strengthen her relationship with Conor.

Thinking about that almost made her gag – she'd somehow managed to tell herself that Conor would be better off as a result of this betrayal. She was stupid and hateful. She'd ruined everything. How could she look at Conor again knowing what she'd done last night? How could she touch him, how could she sleep with him without him feeling it, without tasting treachery in every kiss. She dug her fingernails in harder, squeezed her eyes shut until, finally, tears came, sobs sticking in her throat, choking her.

There was a gentle tap at the door.

'Jen?'

'Please go away.'

'It's OK. It'll be OK. I'm sorry, Jen, I'm sorry. I shouldn't have . . .'

'Just leave me alone, Dan, please.' He was in their room. The man she'd slept with last night was at that very moment standing outside the door, in *their* bedroom. 'Go away!'

She listened to his footsteps retreat and felt even worse. How could she let him apologise to her? It was all her fault. How could she shout at him, tell him to go away when he tried to offer her kindness? She got up and splashed water on her face, trying not to focus on how bloody awful she looked, her face red and blotchy from crying, shadows under her eyes from lack of sleep, her lips still stained dark red from last night's wine. She brushed her teeth and ran a comb through her hair. She took a deep breath and unlocked the door.

Downstairs, Dan was in the kitchen, spooning coffee into the cafetière. When she heard her behind him, he turned and wrapped his arms around her and kissed her on the temple.

'It's OK, Jen.'

'No, it isn't,' she mumbled. 'It's not OK. It'll never be OK.' She was stiff as a board, her hands by her side, balled into fists. She wished that she couldn't feel the muscles in his arms, she wished she couldn't smell him, feel the warmth of his skin. She had the strongest memory of the night before, how it had felt to be with him, how good it had felt, how much better than anything she'd ever felt before. Her stomach flipped, she could feel her colour, her temperature rising.

'You have to go,' she said softly. 'Please. I'm sorry, but you have to go. I don't . . . I can't even talk about it. I can't be here with you, I can't. I can't.'

'Can I have a cup of coffee first?' he asked.

They stood side by side in the kitchenette, sipping their

coffee. His hand was on the counter, next to hers, they were almost touching. If she stretched out her little finger, she could loop it over his. The silence grew, it expanded until it filled the room, filled the flat, the silence was everything.

'I'm so sorry,' Jen said, when she couldn't bear it a second longer. 'That was horrible of me, my reaction. It's not . . . you know. It's not that I regret it. I mean, I do regret it, but not because it wasn't, you know, good or anything. It was good. I thought, anyway.'

Dan smiled. 'Jen, it was amazing.' He put his coffee down, he turned to face her. He placed his hand on her cheek, he let it slip slowly down, to her jaw, to her neck. He traced the tip of his thumb across her collarbone. 'I don't know what to think. I mean, I know how I feel, but I also know that we shouldn't have.' His breathing was quick and shallow. 'I'm finding it hard to regret it, though.' He was speaking softly, moving closer to her, their bodies almost touching. He slipped his arms around her waist, placed his hands on her lower back, pulled her closer, gently tugging at the fabric of her robe. She drew back a little, raised her head, and kissed him, feeling again the rush she'd felt the night before. They moved into the living room, onto the sofa, her robe was on the floor, she couldn't stop this, she didn't want to stop it.

The phone started ringing.

'Leave it,' he said, 'please.'

And then the voicemail clicked in and the second before she heard his voice she knew who it was going to be.

'Jen? You there? I'm starting to worry now. Can you pick up?'

'Fuck,' Dan said. 'Oh, fuck.'

Jen picked up her robe.

'I'll go,' Dan was saying. 'I'll go now.'

For a long time after Dan left, Jen sat on the sofa, watching the light on the answering machine blink. She needed to call Conor back. She needed to do it now, he was worried about her. But she couldn't do it, she was so afraid. He would know, the second he heard her voice, he would know what she'd done, what she'd been doing when he dialled their number, when he said her name.

He didn't, of course. He didn't sound hurt, or outraged or betrayed. He sounded annoyed.

'Jesus, Jen. I was really worried. I called you at work, they said you were ill, I called the house a dozen times, no answer, I left you messages, I called Nat, I called Lilah . . .'

'I'm sorry,' she said. 'I'm sorry, I'm sorry.' It was all she could say.

'Where the hell were you? Why didn't you call me back?'

'I went out,' she said stupidly.

'You went out?'

'Yes, I . . .' the lies just wouldn't come fast enough, why wouldn't they come? 'I called in sick, and then I just . . . wandered around by myself. I went to the cinema by myself. Then I came back and went to bed, I didn't even check the messages . . .'

She tailed off, waiting for him to say something. Eventually, he did.

'You didn't check the messages? You didn't think I might have called you, that I might have wanted to talk to you? You didn't want to talk to me?'

'I'm sorry,' she said again. 'I'm sorry,' and the tears came.

'I've got to go, Jen,' he said wearily. He hated listening to her cry, she knew that. 'I hope you're OK.'

She stripped the bed in the spare room and put the sheets in the washing machine. She cleaned the flat more thoroughly than it had ever been cleaned during their occupancy: she scrubbed every surface, she vacuumed under the beds and tables and wardrobes, she mopped and dusted, she even cleaned the windows, as though trying to rid the place of every trace of her betrayal. But still, she couldn't stop the images from the night before that appalled and thrilled her. The noise of the vacuum cleaner couldn't stop her hearing the things Dan had said to her. And nothing could stop her replaying the scene that morning; she and Dan with their hands all over each other and Conor's voice as soundtrack.

# Chapter Thirty-five

~

*April 1996*

Andrew had never seen Conor like this before. Conor was the most relentlessly cheerful person he'd ever met, his tendency to look on the bright side bordering on the irritating. He had self-confidence in abundance, he knew his place in the world. To see him now, so unsure, so uneasy, was disheartening.

'I feel as though I'm losing her,' Conor said. 'I can't even believe I'm saying that out loud. And I know what happens when people feel like this, they hang on and they get all clingy and weird and it just makes the other person pull away more. I'm trying so bloody hard not to cling on to her, and then I'm worried that I'm not doing enough. That I'm *letting* her go.'

There were sitting in the Greyhound, at the table in the corner behind the pool table, pints of Guinness in front of them. The Greyhound was just round the corner from Andrew and Lilah's flat. Lilah referred to it as 'that miserable old man's pub' and it had become Andrew's place of refuge when his girlfriend was in one of her more difficult moods, which meant he spent an awful lot of time in there. Difficult moods had become

Lilah's default state of late: she was either manically happy, in which case she tended to drink too much and become loud and lascivious, or miserable, in which case she tended to drink too much and become loud and angry. It was exhausting.

But they weren't here to discuss Andrew's girlfriend troubles. This time it was Conor's turn.

'You're not letting her go,' Andrew said. 'And I honestly don't think she wants to go anywhere. Last weekend she was talking about the summer, about how much she was looking forward to going back to the house. She was saying you guys had been talking about maybe converting the barn out back?'

'Yeah. We did talk about that,' Conor said, his face brightening a little.

'Seriously, she wasn't talking like a girl who's about to walk out on you. And I ought to know, because I live with a woman who threatens to walk out on me twice a week.'

Conor shook his head. 'Seriously, man, I don't know how you live with it. It would do my head in.'

Andrew shrugged. 'I know she doesn't mean it. Well, I know she doesn't mean it all the time. Not even half the time, probably. It's just Lilah being Lilah.' He didn't say it, because they weren't here to discuss his troubles, that Lilah being Lilah wasn't quite so much fun as it had once been. 'I think you're right, though, the thing about being clingy.' Conor gave him a sharp look. 'Not that I think you're being clingy, that you've ever been clingy. It just sounds like it would help her if she felt, I don't know, like she wasn't under pressure.'

'She *isn't* under pressure.'

'I know she isn't. I know.'

'The odd thing,' Conor said, taking a slug of his drink, 'is that after I got back from Cork and we talked about everything, things were going better. It seemed like we were back on track. It was like being on honeymoon.' He gave Andrew a quick grin. 'But then, I don't know, I feel like I'm second guessing myself half the time now, like we're both being really careful with each other, and we've never been like that. I catch her sometimes, you know, just staring off into space and she looks sad, I mean really sad, and I ask her what's up and she won't say . . . I know something is up. I just don't know why she won't tell me.'

'Do you want me to have a word with her?' Andrew asked. 'Maybe I could get her to open up.'

'Nah, you can't – if you go talking to her now she'll know it's come straight from me and I don't want to spook her.'

'She's not a horse, Conor.'

He laughed. 'You know what I mean. I was thinking of asking Dan to have a word, because they were like, thick as thieves when he was staying, and if Dan asks her what's up she won't think that I'm behind it.'

'That's a good idea.'

'Yeah, if I could only get hold of Dan. He's never bloody around, never returns my calls. And I sent him an email asking if I could come up and see him, thought it might be better if I could ask him face to face, but apparently he's flat out for the next couple of weeks. I don't know. I'm being ridiculous, aren't I? I'm over-thinking.'

'Yeah, pretty much.'

They fell silent for a bit, sipped their pints, and watched the barmaid, who was tall and curvy and had the most amazing tits, bending down over the table opposite to pick up some empty glasses. Conor caught Andrew's eye and they both started laughing.

'You want another one?' Andrew asked. 'I can't face going

home to dragon lady just yet. We had an almighty row about my completely unreasonable desire to watch the rugby when it clashed with the *EastEnders* omnibus. I made the mistake of pointing out that she'd already watched all the *EastEnders* episodes this week, but apparently that wasn't the point. She likes to watch the *EastEnders* omnibus when she's got a hangover. I should know that by now.'

He left Conor, laughing and shaking his head, and went up to the bar. The sexy barmaid gave him a dazzling smile as he ordered the drinks; she was always very friendly whenever he came in here. He cast an eye along the bar: it wasn't that surprising that she was pleased to see him, he and Conor were the only people under the age of forty-five in the entire pub. And Lilah was right, it was an old man's pub, all along the bar they were sitting there, stooped over pints and papers, few of them even bothering to chat to each other. Perhaps it was their refuge from the missus, too.

Oh God, he couldn't believe he'd become one of those sorts of men, the type that runs off down the pub to escape the woman they've chosen to spend their life with. He couldn't become one of those tedious bores who sees women as a necessary evil, something to be tolerated because they provide food and sex and comfort. He wasn't like that. He didn't want to be like that. He picked up the glasses, beamed at the barmaid and walked back to their table, determined that they weren't going to moan about women any longer.

'Tell me about the plans for the French house,' he said brightly as he placed a pint in front of Conor.

'Ah well.' Conor's eyes lit up whenever the house was mentioned, the house and his plans for it. 'Yeah, as Jen said, we were thinking, if the barn's structurally sound, and I'm not sure that it is, that we could convert it, into a studio, but also extra living space, in case we wanted to go when her dad's using the main house or whatever, you know . . .' He was off. They might raze the barn and build a whole new extension – a workshop for himself, a place for Jen to work. He wanted to build an enclosure out back because Jen had always fancied keeping goats. They might even move there next year, earlier than expected, they might not go travelling just yet. It was, after all, the place where they were happiest.

They stayed in the pub until closing. They were in good spirits by the time they left, laughing as they told stories they'd told and heard a thousand times of things they did at college, that summer trip to Italy at the end of their first year, the time they stole Dan's clothes and towel from the shower rooms, forcing him to walk back through halls stark naked. The cold air hit them as they waved goodbye to the barmaid and stepped outside, sobering them up just enough to realise how drunk they were. They weaved their way down the road towards the tube station, Conor's arm around Andrew's shoulders.

'I'll give you a call tomorrow,' Andrew said as Conor fished around in his pocket for his travelcard. 'We can go for a hair of the dog if you like.'

'Yeah,' Conor said, 'that would be good.' He found the card and looked up at Andrew, his eyes glassy, expression unreadable. 'She lied to me,' he said.

'What?'

'Jen. That week I went back to see Ronan, I told you, we'd had that big fight?'

'Yeah.'

'She lied to me. She told me she'd spent the day on her own, she said she'd just wandered around and gone to the cinema.

But then, it was like a week or two later, I was looking for my driver's licence, right, and there were these papers in the spare room and I thought it might have got mixed up with them, and there were some ticket stubs for some Japanese film at the Barbican.'

'She told you she went to the cinema, though.'

'Yeah, but there were two. And she told me she was on her own. And the film was at eight in the evening. She didn't tell me exactly what time she'd been, but I just find it hard to believe she was just wandering about on her own, all day, until eight o'clock at night.'

'Are you sure it was from that day?'

'Sure. It was 8 March, the Friday I went to Ireland. And she wasn't with Lilah, she wasn't with Nat, and she couldn't have been with someone from work, because she'd called in sick that day. And if she had been with one of them, she would have told me, anyway. Why would she say she was on her own when she wasn't?'

Andrew shook his head. He was trying to think of an innocent explanation and failing. 'I don't know, man. I don't know.'

He walked back home disconsolate. He was sure there was an innocent explanation, and the only reason he couldn't think of it now was because his head was clouded with drink. Jen wasn't a liar, she wasn't a cheat and she adored Conor, she would never do anything to hurt him. There weren't that many things Andrew had unshakeable faith in, but Jen and Conor's relationship was one of them.

Back at the flat, all the lights were on, the television too. Lilah was asleep on the sofa, an overflowing ashtray and a half-empty wine glass on the floor. He cleared up, turned off the lights and the TV, covered her up with a blanket, went into the kitchen and poured himself a glass of water. There were two empty wine bottles on the counter. He went back into the living room and sat down at the little table. Lilah was lying on her side, one arm flung out, delicate fingers almost touching the floor. Even passed out drunk and dishevelled, she was beautiful, long lashes resting on fine cheekbones, honey-blonde hair all over the place.

Beauty wasn't enough. He was no longer in love with her, he hadn't been for a while now. She made him sad and anxious. Still, he couldn't leave her. She threatened to walk out on him all the time, she might even do it one day. He looked forward to that day and he dreaded it. He knew that if they stayed together, they would end up despising each other and that was the last thing he wanted. But he worried what would happen to her when he was no longer there to calm her down, take her home, to pick up the pieces. He worried what she would do when she was free, free to leave any bar with any man she chose. Andrew worried that Lilah wouldn't choose well.

But as well as this, he worried that the end of Andrew and Lilah would be the beginning of the end for their little band of friends. When you're at university, you think it's going to last forever, it is inconceivable that there will come a day when you don't see each other all the time, talk to each other every day. But less than a year after graduation, Andrew could see how easily they could drift apart. Already, it felt like Dan was going his own way; they rarely saw him these days, he never seemed to want to come and visit. And if he and Lilah split he wouldn't see Nat any longer. If she had to pick a side, she'd pick Lilah's. And then, bit by bit, Nat would drift out of his life, and that scared him more than anything.

On the sofa, Lilah stirred.

'Drew?' she croaked.

'Sorry, didn't mean to wake you.'

'No, you didn't.' She looked up at him and smiled. Her teeth were stained a deep red from the wine, she looked as though she had blood in her mouth. 'You didn't wake me. Come here,' she said, stretching out her arms to him. 'Come and lie with me.'

'Let's go to bed,' he said, getting to his feet.

'I can't move,' she moaned. 'Carry me?' He picked her up and she wrapped her arms around his neck. He could smell cigarettes on her breath and in her hair. He carried her into the bedroom, placing her down on the bed. She pulled the duvet over herself without taking off her clothes.

'You love me, Drew?' she asked him.

'I love you, Lilah.'

## Chapter Thirty-six

~

Lilah threw up on the way to work. She actually had to get off the tube at Angel to vomit on the platform. It was humiliating, people were walking around her, staring, faces contorted in disgust. Some people laughed. A nice middle-aged lady in a black suit crouched down next to her, put her hand on her back and asked, 'Are you OK, love? Are you pregnant?' and Lilah thought, yes, that's it, that's a good excuse. That's less embarrassing than puking in public because you only stopped drinking four hours ago.

'I think I am,' she said, accepting the proffered Kleenex.

'You poor thing. You ought to go straight home and lie down. Morning sickness is just awful.'

Lilah nodded and smiled bravely. 'Oh, I couldn't do that. I've got an important meeting this morning,' she said.

'Your boss is a bloke, right?' the woman asked and when Lilah nodded she tutted sympathetically. 'You'll get no understanding from him then.'

She couldn't bear to get back on the train so she took a taxi the rest of the way to work, which meant she arrived twenty-five minutes late and twelve pounds poorer and she was already pretty much up against her overdraft limit. Everything was such a mess, such a bloody mess, she just couldn't seem to get her head straight.

She flung her bag down at her desk, tossed her coat over the back of her chair, straightened out her skirt, checked her breath one last time (she'd had four sticks of chewing gum) and ran as quickly as she could to the conference room. Everyone looked up as she pushed the door open.

'Nice of you to join us,' the boss said.

'Sorry, tube,' she said, taking her seat, flashing him an apologetic smile. It wasn't returned.

'Yeah, we all take the tube, Lilah, and yet somehow we all manage to get here by nine.'

You don't bloody take it, she felt like saying, you drive in from Surrey in your big, fuck off Range Rover.

'I'm sorry,' she said again, eyes lowered, contrite. When she looked up again, Martin was watching her, the one with the great body, the one she'd told the girls about, the one who had the power to turn her insides to mush with the merest raise of an eyebrow. He winked.

It was all his fault, her head being in a mess. It seemed like every time she turned around, there he was, smiling at her, brazenly looking her up and down, his gaze lingering on her legs. He was driving her mad, she couldn't stop thinking about him. And it wasn't like she even liked him. He wasn't especially bright or funny, he was, to be perfectly frank, a bit of a dick, but she couldn't help herself. Every time she looked at him she wanted to rip his clothes off. She thought about him all the time, she daydreamed about him at work, she thought about him when she was in bed with Andrew. Which was horrible, she knew it was horrible.

271

She was being awful to Andrew, she knew that, too. Some days she couldn't stand to be around him; the sight of him, smart and clean and sober in his suit from Marks & Spencers, made her want to throw things. She found him boring and she didn't bother to hide it. And then on the mornings after, when she couldn't remember what had happened the night before or how she'd got home, when she felt shaky and afraid and filled with dread, the thought of being without him terrified her. She would reach out to him and he would go to her, no matter how horrible she'd been or how badly she'd behaved. He'd make her breakfast and hold her when she asked him to, and sit with her on the sofa watching rubbish TV, holding her hand. She'd ask him if he loved her, and he'd say he did, and she'd know he was lying.

Martin asked her to go for a drink after work.

'You fancy one at Bar Cosa?' was what he said, casually, as he walked past her desk at the end of the day. He made it sound as though he were offering something other than alcohol. For the briefest of moments she considered calling Nat to cancel their dinner that night, but in her head she could hear her mother's voice: 'Never, whatever you do, ditch a friend for a man. Men will always let you down. Friends won't.'

Lilah spotted Nat as she walked into the restaurant. Sitting in a booth over in the far corner, she was leaning over the table, deep in conversation with a man, laughing at something he was saying. Lilah grinned to herself – about time, she thought as she picked her way through the tables, and then she realised that the man was Andrew.

'What are you doing here?' she asked as she got to the table.

'Nice to see you too, darling,' he said, getting to his feet. He kissed her, quick, perfunctory. 'Nat asked me if I wanted to join you.'

Lilah smiled at Nat, kissed her on both cheeks. 'Lovely,' she said, but she was disappointed. She'd wanted to tell Nat about Martin. She'd wanted an opportunity to discuss and to analyse and to obsess about him. She wondered if that was why Nat had invited Andrew? To avoid another conversation about Lilah's crush?

She was glad, though, in the end, that the three of them had spent the evening together; they had a good time and Andrew seemed so happy. He told funny stories and made them laugh, he seemed brighter, more relaxed, more his old self than he had been of late. After dinner, Lilah didn't want to carry on drinking, she wanted to go home with him, straight home. She couldn't remember the last time she'd wanted to go home before the pubs were shut.

They walked to the tube together, arms linked, all three of them, then parted ways. Andrew and Lilah were north-bound, Natalie south. They stood watching her as she walked away from them, small and neat in her black pencil skirt and grey v-neck jumper, a little unsteady in her heels. Lilah turned to Andrew and smiled at him. He watched Nat for a moment longer then turned to look at her.

'Right. Home,' he said, giving her a kiss on the head.

'Home.'

They sat side by side on the tube, her head resting on his shoulder.

'We should hang out with her more often,' Andrew said quietly. 'I think she's lonely living by herself.'

'Nat? Not at all. She loves living alone. It suits her. She just needs to find herself a man, that's all. Don't think she's had a shag since, like, November.'

There was a pause, just a beat, then Andrew asked: 'Who'd she shag in November?'

'That friend of Dan's, remember, the guy he was working with? Dark hair, high cheekbones, skinny, angsty, a bit of a geek. You know how Nat likes them.'

He fell silent then; he didn't talk at all for the rest of the way home, and when he got there, he seemed like he was somewhere else. Lying in bed at his side, she didn't fall asleep, but for once, she wasn't lying there thinking about Martin from the office. She was thinking about how Natalie and Andrew were sitting when she arrived at the restaurant, their heads so close together. And then later, when they left Nat at the tube, was it just affection, that look in his eyes as he watched her go? Because when she thought about it now, she wasn't sure it looked like affection, it looked a bit like longing.

The next evening, when Martin asked her to go for a drink, she said yes. The look on Andrew's face when he watched Nat go, the way he withdrew into himself the moment the two of them were alone, was still playing on her mind when they got to the dimly lit basement bar just round the corner from the office. It was on her mind when she agreed to have the second cocktail, and the third. It was on her mind when she agreed to go back to Martin's place, and when she had desperate, disappointing sex with him on his living-room floor.

On Saturday morning, two days later, when she walked back to their bedroom from the bathroom in just a towel, Andrew asked her, 'Lilah, what happened? Did you fall?' She had marks on her knees, carpet burns. Andrew gave her a smile and put his arms round her. 'Those heels you wear, they'll be the death of you one day,' he said, then he kissed her lightly on her bare shoulder and she burst into tears.

'Please can we go away,' she asked him, when she stopped crying. 'I'm so tired, I just want to go away for a bit, just the two of us? Please, Drew? It doesn't have to be anywhere special or expensive, we can just go to the French house, even if it's just a long weekend?'

He said no, of course, there was no way he could take time off now, not the way things were at work at the moment. He'd understand, though, if she needed to get away. He knew that she was tired, that she'd been overdoing it a bit. Perhaps she should suggest a trip with her mum?

That afternoon she went round to Nat's tiny little flat in Vauxhall. It was on the second floor of one of those stout Victorian townhouses, with a view over four lanes of traffic. In the corner of the living room, she'd set up a little home office: computer and printer, books piled to waist height on the floor, newspaper cuttings and postcards and other little snippets ('inspiration', she said) pinned to a cork board above the desk. And a photograph, too: Natalie, Lilah and Andrew sitting on the lawn outside the French house. Lilah grinning at the camera, Andrew at her side, his face turned a little towards Nat, and Nat looking back at him. Lilah had seen the photo many times before, but she'd never really thought about how they would look to a stranger. Andrew and Natalie together, Lilah the outsider.

'I love that picture,' Nat said to her. She was standing at her side, proffering a cup of tea. Lilah took the tea and turned to look at her.

'I slept with Martin,' she replied.

Nat was furious.

'How could you, Lilah? How can you do this to him? And you don't even like this Martin guy, you said so. He's a prat. I don't understand why you're being like this, it's like you're trying to break everything . . .'

'Sometimes I feel as though I am, as though I do want to break everything, smash everything to pieces. Start over.'

'Why, Lilah? What is wrong with your life? Your good job, the nice flat, the amazing boyfriend . . .'

Lilah gave a little yip of laughter.

'What? You're going to tell me now that Andrew isn't a great guy?'

Lilah shook her head. She wanted to ask her straight out, are you in love with him? But she knew the answer and it would be cruel to make Nat say it out loud. They stood there, just looking at each other, Natalie's anger subsiding. She couldn't stay angry with Lilah for long, she just couldn't. Eventually, she took the mug from Lilah's hand, went into the kitchen and brought back a bottle of wine and two glasses.

'So, what was he like?' she asked, the ghost of a smile on her lips.

'Crap,' Lilah said with a grin.

'So, you're not going to do it again?'

'God, no.'

'You'd be sorry, you know, if you lost Andrew.'

'I would, wouldn't I?'

Natalie turned away. She had her back to Lilah as she said: 'You don't know how lucky you are.'

## Chapter Thirty-seven

~

Natalie had got herself into a routine. The alarm went off at seven, she hopped into the shower, made coffee and, sitting in her dressing gown, spent an hour writing. Then she got dressed and by 8.40 exactly, she'd be on her way to work. It took her twenty minutes from her flat to the office, and though it might not have been the prettiest of routes – it was grim most of the way except for the bridge and a short stretch along the river – she liked it. It gave her time to think about the words she'd just written, to jumble them around in her head.

She was working as an editorial assistant to a junior editor at a publishing company. It was about as lowly a position as it was possible to get, and she didn't care. She worked surrounded by books all day. They were piled high around her, stacked on shelves and under her desk, she could smell them and caress them and take them home with her. She chatted to editors in the smoking room, she stood next to authors, including famous ones, in the lift. It wasn't quite the dream job, but she was on her way.

If she hadn't been cajoled into going to the pub with

colleagues, Nat ate lunch alone, with a book. She'd sit at the same table at the back of the same café every day, eating a salt beef sandwich with gherkins and drinking a bottle of water and she would read. Completely undisturbed.

She left the office at six, and unless she was going out (and she tried to keep nights out on weekdays to a minimum), she'd walk home, hopping straight into the shower when she got there, and then she'd make dinner and write for another hour.

She wasn't lonely. Everyone thought she was – well, everyone except Lilah, who understood her better than anyone else. She wasn't lonely, she was happy. She liked her routine. If she had been asked, in her first year of university, where she'd want to be when she left, she'd have said: I want to live in London, work for a publishing house. I want to write. And here she was, doing exactly that. She'd had a short story accepted for an anthology by new writers under thirty, the letter confirming it pinned to the little notice board above her desk. Every morning when she looked at it, she could feel her heart race, the smile come to her face, she couldn't quite believe it. Published! Already! She'd never dreamed it would happen this quickly, that her second submission would be accepted. She was exactly where she wanted to be, she felt as though the starting gun had just gone off and already she was racing ahead.

She was standing at the kitchen counter eating cottage cheese out of the tub, when the phone rang. She let the answering machine get it.

'Nat. What's up?' It was Dan. 'Seems like ages since I saw you. You fancy coming up to Norwich some time in the next few weeks? Would be great to catch up. I . . .' There was a long pause. 'I've been . . . I don't know. It would be nice to see you. Give me a call, all right?'

Nat stood there for a moment, then went into the living room and replayed the message. So now even Dan thought she was lonely? Unless he had some ulterior motive. You never could tell with Dan. She listened to the message a third time. He sounded nervous, edgy, as though he had something to say but couldn't bring himself to say it. Perhaps *he* was lonely. He used to try, rather half-heartedly, to sleep with her at college every now and again. Were they back to that? She thought about ringing him back, but she wasn't in the mood to be charmed and cajoled. She didn't want to sleep with Dan, she didn't want to sleep with anyone at the moment. She liked things the way they were. *That* Lilah could not understand. Neither could Jen. How could they? They'd never really been single. They didn't understand how liberating it was.

Dinner at Conor and Jen's on Friday night took a little of the gloss off her cherished liberation. She watched them, side by side in their tiny kitchen, chopping and sautéing and nudging each other out of the way with their hips, laughing at each other's jokes, finishing each other's sentences; she watched them after dinner when they sat side by side on the sofa, fingers loosely interlaced; she saw how Conor looked at Jen when she got up to get them more wine, how Jen looked at Conor when he was telling Nat a story about work. Adoration piled on top of friendship. It made Nat happy to see them like this, back to the way they used to be, the way she knew them.

It hurt her heart a little, too, when she got back home and pushed the front door open, welcomed by darkness and silence. She sat next to the window smoking a cigarette, reminding herself that she liked the darkness and the silence. That she liked the solitude, that she wasn't lonely, even if they thought she was. She was just about to go to bed when she noticed that the light on the answering machine was blinking, and she clicked.

'Nat. You there?' A little pause. 'Are you screening? Don't screen me, you know how I hate to be screened.' It was Andrew, she could hear the laughter in his voice, she could feel the grin spreading across her face. 'All right. You're not there. Out living the high life. Listen, I phoned to say congratulations! Lilah told me about the short story. Can't believe you didn't call me. That's amazing, Nat. It's bloody brilliant. Can't wait to read it. Anyway. We're going to have a little party, in your honour. Can you do the tenth? We were thinking we'd have a barbecue at ours, get everyone round. Send us your guest list! If there are people from work you'd like to invite, or, you know, a guy maybe?' There was a little pause and he laughed. 'I'd better get off your answer phone now, before it runs out of tape, or whatever. Well done. You're a clever girl, you know that? You're amazing. Call me soon. Sleep tight.'

She lit another cigarette and replayed the message, over and over. She listened to the warmth in his voice, she could imagine his smile as he said the words. She could see him, standing by the window in his living room as he called her, tall and broad-shouldered and straight backed, the way he always stood, like a soldier. She listened to him laugh after he mentioned her bringing a guy to the barbecue. Was she imagining it, or did that laugh sound a little hollow, a little nervy? She listened again and again. She wished she could stop feeling like this. She kept waiting for these feelings to go away. She was beginning to wonder, a little desperately, if they ever would.

# Chapter Thirty-eight

~

*May 1996*

Dan listened to *Music for the Jilted Generation* on the way to London. He hadn't heard it for ages but that day it felt appropriate somehow. He played 'No Good' over and over, louder and louder, until the woman sitting opposite on him on the train got up and moved away. Dan didn't blame her. He was aware that he wasn't looking his best, might even have looked vaguely threatening, sitting there in black T-shirt and jeans, bags under his eyes, five o'clock shadow, a plastic bag full of cans at his feet.

The train was crowded and airless, it smelled of sweat and smoke. He picked up one of the tins and held it against his forehead for a moment, letting the cold transfer to his skin before pulling open the tab and taking a sip. He leaned back in his seat and closed his eyes, feeling the beer slip down his throat and the disapproval radiating from his travelling companions.

He arrived at Andrew and Lilah's just after seven. Everyone was out back, in their little garden, gathered around the barbecue. It struck Dan that perhaps he ought to have brought some food with him, rather than just the tins of beer.

'Nonsense,' Lilah said, flinging her arms around him and giving him a kiss. 'There's way too much food. There can never be too much booze.' She winked at him and took his hand. 'You look knackered, Parker. You burning the candle at both ends up there?' Lilah was wearing a bright green halter neck, denim mini-skirt and high heels; she looked like a supermodel. Or an expensive hooker. 'I hope you brought something for Nat, though?' Shit. This was Natalie's celebration, the story thing. He was supposed to bring something for Nat. He fished around in his bag and pulled out the Prodigy CD. Lilah rolled her eyes.

'Oh, you are fucking useless,' she laughed, linking her arm through his and leading him out into the garden.

He had butterflies in his stomach, his mouth was dry. He was dreading seeing her and dying to see her. He scanned the garden and spotted Andrew and Nat, perched on the trestle table, laughing about something. There were a few guys from college who he'd known vaguely and had no great desire to talk to, there was Lilah, pouring the drinks and flirting with everyone in sight. No sign of Conor, no sign of Jen. He felt disappointed and relieved at the same time.

Grabbing himself a beer he joined Natalie and Andrew at the table.

'My parents are going away,' Nat said, 'some time at the end of June. We should all go. It'll be fun, we'll have the place to ourselves. We can have a pool party.'

Dan grinned. 'Sounds good,' he said and then, realising he didn't sound as enthusiastic as he was supposed to: 'Sounds great.' It took him a moment, but he remembered. 'Congratulations, Nat,' he said, giving her a kiss on the cheek. 'Brilliant news on the story.'

'Thank you,' she said, and she smiled at him and then looked at Andrew, who slid his arm around her shoulders.

'She's a star, isn't she?' he said and Natalie blushed.

Dan looked up. He saw Lilah, standing in the shadow of the house, watching them, and behind her, Jen and Conor, coming down the kitchen steps, hand in hand. He felt something then that he hadn't felt in a long time, an anger and envy that he thought he'd left behind. Conor came towards them, leading Jen by the hand, head held high, a wide smile on his face, shoulders dropped, relaxed, confident, Jen just a step behind him, long legs in low heels, grey skirt, crisp white fitted shirt, her hair tied back. She was lovely. Her eyes were lowered, she didn't look at him when he shook Conor's hand, she didn't even look at him when she stepped forward to accept his kiss on her cheek. He had an unbearable urge to grab her by the shoulders, to shake her, to shout, look at me!

Instead, he turned to Natalie and said: 'So, this weekend at your place? Can I bring someone?'

Jen looked at him then: just for a moment, her eyes met his before her lids lowered again. Her cheeks flushed, she took a long slug of her wine.

'Course you can,' Nat said. 'Who is she then?'

They were all looking at him, smiling, expectant. Dan kept his eyes on Jen's face. 'Haven't decided yet,' he said. 'Couple of options.'

Jen's lips parted a little, as though she was about to say something, then she turned away, kissing Conor lightly on the cheek as she did. 'God, it's hot,' she said, and she walked away.

Conor and Andrew were in control of the barbecue. Men's men, slinging slabs of meat onto hot coals. Dan sat to one side, sipping his beer gingerly, listening to Natalie and Lilah chattering away about films they'd seen, a dress Lilah was planning to buy. He tuned out, let his mind drift, but he kept his eye on the steps leading up to the kitchen, waiting for Jen to come back outside. He thought about going in there to find her. He wanted to confront her, he wanted to apologise to her, he wanted *something*. He wanted to be close enough to smell her skin. He finished off his beer and was about to get up to go inside when the girls decided they were going to make some Pimm's, and the chance to be alone with her was lost.

Natalie came back out a few minutes later carrying a pitcher and some glasses. She poured him one and perched by his side on the table, asking him questions about Norwich and the girls he'd mentioned, but all the while she was watching Andrew and he felt heartsick for her, for both of them. They were alike, the two of them, they'd never get what they wanted. He looked at her, petite and pretty, hair cropped shorter, making those green eyes seem bigger than ever. He thought about the times he'd tried it on with her at college; he couldn't do that now, it would feel wrong, it would feel weird. But he felt a kinship between them, a connection, a closeness.

'Poor Nat,' he said, putting his arm around her shoulders.

'What d'you mean, poor Nat?'

'You and me, sweetheart . . . Oh, it's nothing. It's nothing.' He leaned down and gave her a kiss on the cheek, squeezing her closer, and at that moment Andrew turned to look at them and something passed across his face, quick, fleeting, a shadow. Anger. Dan smiled at him, quizzically, asking a question, wordless, but he didn't have time to get an answer, because there was a crash from inside. Andrew rolled his eyes.

'That'll be Lilah, smashing the crockery,' he muttered.

It wasn't, though. It was Jen. Andrew and Conor went into

the house to see what was up. They re-emerged a little while later.

'She fainted,' Conor told him. 'Just clean away, apparently, she hit her head. She's lying down now. She'll be all right. I think it's just heat and booze and not having anything to eat. She's been feeling a little under the weather the last week or two.' Dan must have looked upset because Conor smiled and clapped him on the arm. 'She's all right, mate. She'll be out in a minute. We'll just leave her to rest for a bit.'

Dan waited for a few minutes, until Conor was once again busying himself with the barbecue, until Andrew and Natalie were once again deep in conversation. He slipped into the house, down the corridor and into Andrew and Lilah's bedroom. He knocked softly and pushed open the door. The room was dark, curtains drawn. She was lying on her side, her back towards him.

'You OK, Jen?' he asked her, and she rolled over to look at him. She didn't say anything. He approached the bed, slowly, his breathing shallow. Her eyes were on his face; she smiled, but there were tears on her cheeks. He sat down at her side, leaned over her and kissed her.

'Don't,' she said. He couldn't help himself, he had to touch her, to feel her skin beneath his fingertips again. He put his hand on her waist, all the time keeping his eyes on hers, but she shook her head.

'Don't,' she said again. She said his name. 'Dan, don't.' He wanted to say something, he needed to tell her that he loved her. He hesitated for a moment, he was trying to find the words, it was so stupid, it was the simplest thing in the world, to tell her how he felt. She turned away from him, rolling back onto her side. She asked him to leave, and he did.

He bumped into Conor outside in the hallway.

'What are you doing?' Conor asked him.

'I just wanted to see, you know, if she was all right.'

Conor was standing in front of him, barely a foot away from him, blocking his path.

'I told you to leave her to rest,' he said.

'I'm sorry,' Dan said, and he hated himself in that moment, for lowering his eyes, for submitting.

Conor took a deep breath, exhaled. 'Yeah, no. I know. Me too, sorry. Feeling a bit tense, you know. I'm worried about her.'

'Of course,' Dan said, and he looked up at him and smiled. Conor smiled back, but his eyes were searching Dan's face; he was looking for something. 'You go on in and take care of her,' Dan said and the smile slipped from Conor's face.

'Yeah,' he said. 'I'll do that.'

Dan and Lilah got drunk that night, drunk and loud – they were out there dancing in the back garden long after the others had called it a night. He couldn't remember, when he woke up the next morning, exactly how the evening had ended. He didn't recall saying goodbye to Conor, couldn't recall seeing Jen at all after he'd been into the bedroom and kissed her. He remembered Lilah telling him something, a secret, something he absolutely must not tell the others. He couldn't anyway, because he couldn't remember what the secret was.

# Chapter Thirty-nine

~

Jen went to the doctor on Monday, three days after the fainting incident. It wasn't her usual doctor, it was a private place in a smart townhouse near Lincoln's Inn Fields, where they asked her questions and gave her a form to fill in. They debited her card to the tune of £390 and handed her a box containing four pills, two to take straight away, two to take twelve hours later. It started in the middle of the night. She left Conor sleeping, took a blanket and sat on the loo while the baby bled out of her.

She'd expected to feel something, she'd expected to cry, to feel bereft, but instead she was oddly numb. It was as though she had nothing left to feel; she was spent, finished, the past six weeks had taken everything out of her.

The night she spent with Dan seemed so very far away now – that night, and the day afterwards and the day after that, when she'd tried to picture what the world would look like if she left Conor for one of his closest friends. When she pictured her life like that, it was a bleak place, one where Conor was left angry and heartbroken, where her friends shunned her, where a relationship with Dan would pretty much be ruined before it started because everything they felt for each other would be tainted with guilt. She wrote letters to Conor and to Dan, she ripped them up. She thought of how the conversation would go, with Conor, when she told him about what she'd done, when she detailed for him the ways in which she had betrayed him.

She thought about the letter from Conor, the one he'd written in the middle of the night, after their fight and that conversation on the phone, love and joy in every line. She remembered his words, when he talked about all the ways she made him happy, when he told her that her laugh was the most beautiful sound he'd ever heard, when he told her that he ached for her.

She'd read it the first time through tears, her guilt amplified a thousand times. But it brought her back to herself, back to the place she was supposed to be. It was as though someone had pressed a reset button. She had clarity. She was no longer confused. She wasn't happy, it didn't take away the guilt, it didn't change what she felt for Dan, but she read Conor's words and they calmed her. She loved them both. Anyone who said that you couldn't be in love with two people at the same time was an idiot: it wasn't like there was a finite amount of love it was possible to feel. So, she loved two men. She had to make a choice. Unless you want to lie and cheat and hurt people, you make a choice and you stick with it. Jen chose Conor.

All she had to do once the choice was made, was tell Dan. They met the day before Conor came back from Ireland; Jen emailed him asking to meet him and Dan came running, no questions asked. She stood outside Richmond station waiting for him. It was a beautiful, crisp spring day, the sky cobalt, the perfect day to wander along the river and have lunch in a pub somewhere, to go for a walk in Richmond Park and watch the deer. Jen was nervous, worried that Dan wouldn't show and dreading the moment that he would. When she saw him, loping out of the station with his hands shoved into his pockets, his coat collar up, James Dean after a rough night out, slight and pale and a little bit lost, she felt her heart twitch. When he caught sight of her and smiled, she thought she wouldn't be able to do it, she thought that she wouldn't be able to stop herself from kissing him.

But she did. She couldn't tell him that she was in love with him, because who knew where that would lead? She did the right thing: she lied. She told him that she'd only ever been in love with one person and that she only ever would be. And Dan was perfect, he wasn't angry and he didn't beg, he just hugged her and told her it was OK, that he understood, and she couldn't look at him, she couldn't look directly into his eyes because she couldn't bear to see his expression; it would break her heart if she had hurt him, it would break her heart if she hadn't.

All that seemed as though it had happened to someone else, because that was before she realised just how badly she'd screwed everything up, when she thought that things could go back to normal. She thought that so long as she could just get to the summer, to the French house, and have some time alone with Conor and apart from Dan, then it would all blow over, and when she and Conor came back to London, Dan would be with another girl and she wouldn't love him any more and everything would just be normal.

She believed all that was possible until one April afternoon, following a dressing down from the awful bitch of a boss, she half-walked, half-ran to the ladies loos and wept. And she didn't even know why she was crying, because her boss was always a total bitch, this was just a day like any other day.

Back at her desk she looked at her desk diary and smiled to

herself. PMT. Obviously. She was due, that was it. She flicked back through to March, looking for the tell-tale red circle around a date, usually somewhere around the twentieth, which would give her a better idea of exact dates. She couldn't find the red circle.

All of a sudden she went completely cold. Her stomach contracted into a hard little ball. She was looking at the time at which she should have had her period the previous month, but her eye was drawn, over and over, to the weekend two weeks prior to that, the weekend that Dan came to visit. She ran back to the ladies, ignoring the quizzical looks of her colleagues, and threw up.

It just wasn't possible. She was on the pill. Yes, she sometimes missed a day or two here and there, but she made it up. It wasn't possible. It was just the stress of that difficult time with Conor, the thing with Dan, her shitty job, all the late nights and the drinking and the bad diet. It had to be.

And that's what she told herself, all that afternoon, and as she tried to fall asleep in Conor's arms that night; she told herself that on the tube on the way to work next morning, she kept repeating it to herself as she tried to concentrate on her work. She went to the loo about 500 times, just to check it hadn't started. It hadn't. By the time she left the office she could stand it no longer. She stopped by Boots on the way home and bought two boxes of pregnancy tests. She completed all four tests once she got home. She sat on the floor of the bathroom, staring at the crosses on the pee-sticks and trying to cry herself out before Conor got home.

And now here she was, a few weeks later, sitting in the bathroom again, not crying this time, not desperate, not panicking, just numb. Baby gone.

Things were not going to go back to normal. She knew that when she saw Dan at the barbecue, when she saw the flash of anger in his face, felt the sting of jealousy when he talked about other girls, when she endured that desperate moment when he came to her in a darkened bedroom. She didn't know how long it would take, six months or a year, or forever, but she knew that for her and Dan, normal was not a realistic prospect for the immediate future.

She had to let that go to focus on the one thing that was left to her, which was to make it up to Conor. She would never tell him because he would not believe that it was acceptable to get rid of a child. Instead, she swore to herself, that night, in the bathroom, after the baby had bled out of her, that she would spend the rest of her life making him as happy as she possibly could. He would never know what might have been, and she would carry this awful, wretched guilt. She would find a way to atone for it.

## Chapter Forty

On the morning of 21 June, Dan awoke with a shocking hangover, the kind that makes it difficult to move. He couldn't move much anyway, because there was a girl lying on his arm. She had mousy dark hair and a chubby face, a little mascara smeared over her cheekbones. She was nice, they'd had a good time. He was buggered if he could remember her name, though.

He lifted his head off the pillow (pain, nausea), propping himself up on his left elbow, his right arm still trapped under the girl. He didn't recognise the room he was in, they must be at her place. He had no idea where it was. He could remember leaving the club, getting into a taxi, he could remember arriving at a block of flats, tripping on the stairs, but he had zero recollection of what happened in the interim.

Gingerly, he tried to withdraw his arm without waking the girl. As he pulled, she rolled away from him. Mercifully, she didn't wake. He swung his legs over the end of the bed, squinting into the sunlight (terrible pain, overwhelming nausea). The girl stirred a little, she made an odd sort of chewing noise, but still her eyes remained closed. As carefully and quietly as he could, he retrieved his clothes from the bedroom floor and crept, naked, out into the hallway. There was a bathroom just opposite. He padded across the hall, slipped into the bathroom, locked the door behind him and threw up.

He got dressed, splashed his face with water, ate a dollop of toothpaste and crept back into the hallway. He hesitated there for a moment. The front door was right in front of him, he could slip away unnoticed. She might even appreciate it, she probably didn't want to have the awkward morning-after-the-night-before conversation either. That's what he told himself as he walked down the road outside her flat, the throbbing in his head exacerbated by every step.

The chubby girl from last night was the ninth since Jen. Ninth or tenth. Who's counting? He knew a guy, one of the blokes they'd been at college with, who kept a notebook next to his bed. He wrote down their names, if he could remember them, or their notable attributes if he couldn't. He gave them scores out of ten. Pathetic. Dan wasn't going down that route. He was just getting it out of his system. Getting *her* out of his system. And in fact, after the initial booze and girls binging of late March and early April, he'd been a bit better in recent weeks. It was just seeing her again that had set him back.

All the good work, the staying away, the telling himself that there could never be anything between them, that there wasn't anything between them, was undone, in those few brief moments, in that hot half-light in Lilah and Andrew's bedroom. In his more deluded moments, he imagined a secret life with her where they got to be lovers and somehow everyone still remained friends. He dreamed up romantic gestures, lavish gifts, stolen weekends away. He even made her a mix tape. It was pitiful. And when reality bit, he wrote to her and told her that he just wanted her to acknowledge that there had been something between them, but he never sent the letter. He couldn't bear for it to be ignored. So he was back to square one, to sleeping with random girls whose names he wouldn't remember, to drinking too much. He'd even bought a car, a dark red Alfa Romeo Spider. It was like a mid-life crisis twenty years early.

It took him the best part of half an hour to walk back from the chubby girl's flat to his own. It was a warm, close day and he could smell the alcohol in his sweat as he stripped off to get into the shower. It turned his stomach. He had to get himself back together. He had to get through the weekend. Then the others would be off to the French house for the summer, and he, having got an internship with a film production company in London, had the perfect excuse not to join them. And maybe by the time the summer was over he wouldn't feel this way any longer, he wouldn't ache for her so much. All he had to do was get through the weekend at Nat's parents' place.

The weekend had turned from a pool party to a celebration for Andrew, who had landed a job with Fineman and Hicks, a firm of criminal justice and human rights lawyers. It was the dream job, the one he'd been working towards for years. It was a Very Big Deal. Dan couldn't just call up and say he was busy, or that he wasn't feeling well. There was a three-line whip on this one.

He drove to London that afternoon, arriving at Andrew and Lilah's flat around seven. He and Andrew sat outside in the garden feeling the smoggy London air start to cool. It was just the two of them – Lilah was out somewhere and Andrew didn't seem to know where she was or when she'd be back.

'She'll turn up,' he said with a little shrug.

Dan was pathetically relieved that they were alone and that

Andrew was quite happy to just sit and drink beer and talk about nothing of substance.

'So, turns out Conor's Mini's finally given up the ghost,' Andrew told him. 'So I'm having to take my car – I assume you're happy to take yours?'

'Looking forward to it,' Dan said, 'although back seat space is a little tight, so . . .'

'Yeah, I thought about that, but we don't really have another option, other than going out to hire a car, which is a total pain in the arse. You can fit one in the back, can't you?'

'Oh, yeah. Course.'

'Great. So, if Lilah and I pick up Nat, would you be all right getting Conor and Jen from Clapham?'

'Um.' He would mind. He really would mind. 'Maybe I should get Nat? And then the four of you can go in your car, there's more space in the back.'

'Conor and Jen won't mind about being a bit cramped,' Andrew said, getting to his feet. 'I think Conor's looking forward to seeing the Alfa.'

There was something about Andrew's tone that told him that was the end of the conversation.

Dan lay awake half the night trying to think of convincing reasons why he could no longer go away with them for the weekend. He failed.

He parked outside Conor and Jen's building at nine-thirty. He didn't even have to go upstairs; they must have been watching out for him.

'Now that is nice!' Conor exclaimed as he bounced out of the front door. 'That is a proper motor. Can I drive?' He gave Dan a friendly shove on the shoulder as he walked up to inspect the car.

'No, you can't,' Dan said. It came out harsher than he'd intended. 'Sorry mate, you know, insurance.'

'Yeah, I know. I was only joking,' Conor said with a brittle laugh. Dan kept his eyes on the door, waiting for Jen to come out. She emerged a moment or two later, head down, a bag slung over her shoulder. She looked up at him for just a second and his heart stopped. She looked pale, tired, hair scraped back, shadows under her eyes.

'Hi,' she said softly. 'How's it going?'

'Good, thanks,' he said. 'You?'

'Yeah, good.'

'Sure? You feeling better?'

'Better?' She gave him a sharp glance then looked away.

'The other weekend. The barbecue?'

'Oh, God. That was nothing. Heat, tiredness.' She wouldn't look at him. Once again he felt that urge to grab her, to put his hand on her chin, to pull her face towards him. Instead, he put his hand on her arm. 'I'm fine,' she said, pulling away, 'honestly.' She flashed him a quick smile, polite, sterile. Empty.

'Come on then,' Conor called over to them. 'Let's see what this thing can do.'

When they set off Dan found himself gripping the wheel so tightly his knuckles turned white.

He relaxed a little as the journey went on. He and Conor talked about their plans for the summer. 'Sorry you're not going to make it to France,' Conor said.

'Yeah, I know. It's a bugger, but it's a good job, the internship. Plus I'm flat broke, I can't afford to go away.'

'You could come for a while, couldn't you? Get away for a week or two?'

'Well . . .'

'Don't bug him, Con,' Jen said flatly. It was the first thing she'd said for the entire journey. 'If he has to work, he has to work.' She was pleased that he wasn't coming. She was happy that she wouldn't have to see him, to deal with him.

'Shall we put some music on?' Dan suggested to Conor. He didn't want to talk any more. He didn't want to hear her voice.

He hadn't felt like this before. For the past few months, all he'd felt for her was love, longing, then sadness. But now he was bloody furious. This was her fault. She made him feel like this. She made him want her. She came to him that night, she kissed him, she led him into that room and put her hands on him. And now she was just cutting him off. She took what she wanted, a little holiday from Conor, a little glimpse over the fence to see if the grass really was greener, and then she went back to her man, discarded him as though he were nothing. Conor put a CD on, *The Holy Bible* by the Manic Street Preachers. Dan turned it up to ten.

## Chapter Forty-one

He'd been looking forward to this weekend. Four whole days off work, nothing to do but drink beer and go swimming and hang out with his best friends. And now here they were and everything just felt weird. Jen seemed withdrawn and a little sad, and Conor couldn't fathom why. He just never knew any longer when she was going to be her old self, laughing at everything, laid back, relaxed, and when she was going to be tense and anxious. There seemed to be no rhyme or reason to it. Only today, of all days, seemed to be a tense and anxious day.

And what, Conor wondered, was up with Dan? He was so touchy. That thing about driving the car, so obviously a joke, and he'd bitten Conor's head off. And now he clearly didn't want to talk. They hadn't seen each other in weeks and yet the moment they were on the road he'd turned the music up so loud they could barely hear themselves think, let alone have a conversation.

The whole thing was making him uneasy. The aggressive way that Dan was driving, slamming the car into gear, accelerating until he was a foot away from the car in front, Conor was almost tempted to ask him to slow down, but he didn't want to seem like a wuss. It was, after all, a new car. Dan had the right to show off a little bit. He just needed to relax and enjoy it. He leaned back in his seat. Enjoy the ride, he thought to himself.

It was a beautiful day, clear skies and warm sunshine, the weather forecast predicting one of the hottest weekends of the year. He could picture them all, messing around in the pool, music on, cold tins in hand, sausages on the barbecue, the girls in their bikinis . . . He thought for a moment about Jen in her bikini, wondering whether she'd brought the black one or that deep red one she bought last summer and just thinking about it brought a smile to his face. He turned to look at her and as he did he noticed that Dan was looking in his rear-view mirror, and he didn't seem to be looking at the traffic. He was looking at Jen, and just for a fraction of a second, before she turned her head, Conor could have sworn that she was looking right back at Dan. Then her eyes moved to Conor's face and she smiled at him, her face flushed.

Conor turned the music down a little. Dan glanced at him for a second but didn't say anything. He wasn't imagining things. Something was up. What, for example, was going on just before they got into the car? He couldn't be absolutely sure, because he was busy checking out the car itself, but he could have sworn that as he looked up at them, Jen was pulling away from Dan. Jen was angry with him. They must have had a row. That had to be it: that's why Dan put the music up so loud, why Jen was so quiet, why they were eyeing each other angrily in the rear-view mirror.

It was probably something about the screenplay that Dan was writing. Jen had been his official reader since last summer; apparently she was his most perspicacious critic. Presumably

299

she'd said something he didn't agree with. Jen wasn't a great puller of punches when it came to things she liked and didn't like. Conor immediately felt better having figured this out. A falling-out over artistic differences? It would blow over by this evening.

Conor leaned his head against the window and watched the scrubby embankments and service stations of the M3 whizz by until they became a blur. His head drooped, his chin nodding towards his chest. His mind, though, kept ticking over.

It was a little odd, though, that Jen hadn't mentioned falling out with Dan. It was the sort of thing she would usually have told him about. Whenever she had a row with Lilah or got pissed off with Andrew about something, Conor got the blow-by-blow account. More detail than he needed, to be honest. So why hadn't she mentioned this?

When he thought about it carefully, he wasn't entirely sure it could be something about the film script. Or at the very least, not something trivial, because, now he considered the matter, things hadn't been right with Dan and Jen for a while. When Dan was staying with them, those two were thick as thieves, and then when Dan left it seemed like every time Conor got home from work late, Jen was sitting on the sofa, legs tucked up beneath her, nattering away to him on the phone. But he hadn't come home to that in a long while.

He sat up straighter in his seat, opened the window a crack to get some air. Outside, the motorway roared. How could he not have noticed this before? Something had happened between Dan and Jen, and not recently either. Something Jen had never told him about. That sense of unease he had earlier grew, started to morph into something else, something which felt like dread.

Conor shifted a little in his seat, sliding over to his left so that he was up against the passenger door. From that position he could just about see Jen's face in the side mirror. She was looking out of the window, her expression blank, but her hand was clasped around the base of her throat. She was feeling nervous, vulnerable. He *knew* her.

He shut out the music, trying to remember the last time he talked to Jen about Dan, the last time he could remember her even mentioning Dan's name. It wouldn't come to him. He couldn't believe that he'd been so caught up in himself that he hadn't noticed a change like this. Conor's mouth felt dry, his lower back damp with sweat. He rolled the window down a little further, took a deep gulp of hot, dirty air. Pure carbon monoxide.

It wasn't true, was it, that he hadn't noticed a change? He *had* noticed a change in Jen, he just hadn't connected it to Dan. Earlier he'd thought about how Jen's moods, her slide from happiness to sadness, had no rhyme or reason. Maybe he was wrong about that. Maybe the rhyme and reason was sitting right next to him in the driver's seat.

He looked across at Dan, who glanced back at him, cocking his head a little, quizzically. He smiled, but the smile died right there on his lips.

'You OK?' Dan asked, and when Conor didn't reply, Dan looked back at the road, but Conor could still see the expression spreading across his face. Defensiveness? Guilt? What did Dan have to feel guilty about? Conor kept staring at him, saw Dan swallow hard, looking as though he'd been caught doing something wrong, as though he'd been caught red-handed. He'd seen that look on Dan's face before, not all that long ago. The barbecue, when he caught Dan coming out of the room, just after Conor had asked him to leave Jen to rest; the expression on his face was exactly like the one he wore now. And when Conor went in to see Jen he could tell that she'd been crying.

Something was not right.

It seemed to Conor that, where before he'd only been able to see puzzle pieces, now he was beginning to see a picture. Jen had lied to him. They had had a row, and the next day, when he was gone, she went to the cinema, and she lied to him about going alone. She went to the Barbican, she saw a Japanese film. Dan was the only person he knew who really enjoyed Japanese cinema, who could talk for hours (pretentious wanker) about Kurosawa. And since then, Conor couldn't remember Dan and Jen saying two words to each other.

Conor felt hot and cold at the same time, as though someone had poured petrol over him. He felt sick, breathless, his head swimming, he wanted to get out of the car. The sun was beating down outside and yet he couldn't shake the feeling that a storm was coming, he could sense it, dark clouds gathering somewhere just out of sight. He needed to talk to Jen, to look her in the eye, to ask her what happened, to ask her why she lied. He wanted to put his hand around Dan's throat and squeeze.

'Are you feeling all right, Conor?' Dan was looking at him, a little frown on his face. 'You feeling sick? You want to stop?'

Conor looked at Dan's face, at the genuine concern in his eyes, and he couldn't believe the thought that had just run through his head. Dan was his friend. Jen loved him. And Conor trusted her, he trusted them both. This was ridiculous. He was wrong, he had to be. Dan would never do that. Jen would *never* do that. She would rather die than hurt him like that. He let go of the door handle and slipped his hand back between the door and his seat, he reached back for Jen and she took his hand and squeezed it, and he felt breath come back to his lungs.

## Chapter Forty-two

~

They couldn't get there too soon. Jen wanted to tell Dan to drive faster, faster, faster. She couldn't wait to get out of the car, to get out of this ridiculously cramped, uncomfortable back seat, to stretch her legs and put some physical space between her and Dan, because she couldn't bear this proximity.

She couldn't stop looking at him. She tried, she focused on the service stations and the scrubby embankment, the stitching coming undone on the back of Conor's seat, the dark red varnish peeling from her fingernails, but no matter how she tried her eyes were drawn back to him, to the muscles in his tanned arms, flexing as he changed gear, to that little scar, a tiny crooked white mark on the nape of his neck just below his hairline. A knife fight, he told her the first time she asked him how he got it. Attacked by a vicious dog. An unfortunate forklift incident. He had a different story every time, they got more and more ridiculous. In the rear-view mirror she caught his eye and she realised she was smiling.

Her face felt hot. Everything felt hot. God, she wanted to get out of this car. Conor opened his window a little and there was a moment of relief as the air rushed in. She breathed deeply: exhaust fumes and the faint tang of petrol.

She wanted to get out of the car and yet she was afraid, because once they were out of the car she would have to face them both, and she wouldn't know how to behave, she'd forgotten how she used to be with the two of them, back when things were normal. She couldn't remember how she used to look at Dan, but she was sure that when she looked at him now, she did so differently, and Conor would know. He would see something in her face, in the way she couldn't quite hold Dan's gaze, and he would know.

Just then, with perfect timing, Conor reached back and took her hand, and the guilt came over her in waves. She felt as though she were drowning. She bit down hard on her lip, she squeezed his hand tightly, she felt Dan's gaze, still on her, watching her face, and she closed her eyes.

They stopped in Weyhill for lunch, where they had arranged to meet up with the others. Jen clambered out of the back seat as quickly as she could, almost falling over in the car park.

'Steady,' Conor said to her, catching her arm and pulling her closer. 'You all right?'

'That car's a bloody nightmare,' she muttered, pushing her hair out of her face.

'Hey!' Dan protested. 'She can hear you,' he said, patting the bonnet.

'Yeah, well, it's not built for three, is it?' As she said it she wished she hadn't, she felt as though she were pointing out the awkwardness, the *wrongness* of the three of them.

They got a table in the beer garden. Jen perched on the edge of the bench with Conor at her side, Nat to his right. Across the table from her sat Lilah with Dan to the right, as far away from Jen as he could get. Andrew appeared with a tray of drinks, placing it down in front of her with a wide grin and sliding onto the bench beside Lilah. They clinked glasses – 'Congratulations!' – and a little cheer went up and Jen took a long slug of ice-cold, bitter gin and tonic and she felt better.

Conor's hand rested lightly on her lower back. Opposite her, Andrew sat sipping his beer and holding court, sitting there in the bright sunshine, his smile broad. He was golden, victorious, all that hard work rewarded, everything he'd been striving for over the past few years achieved. Next to him sat Lilah in a vivid yellow mini-dress, hopping up to sashay across the lawn to fetch more drinks, every man in the place turning his head to watch her go. Natalie was laughing at something Conor said, laughing until the tears streamed down her face. Conor turned to her, he smiled and held her eye.

'You OK?' he mouthed, soundless.

'I'm good,' she said softly, and gave him a light kiss on the lips.

Conor's gaze held hers for a moment or two. 'You sure? You seemed . . .'

'Just tired, Con,' Jen said, and she kissed him again and wished she couldn't feel Dan's eyes on them.

She wished too that she was a little further away from Dan so that she wouldn't be able to overhear his conversation with Lilah, which lurched at breakneck speed from cars to parties to mutual contacts in London to hangovers to girls, to the girl he'd met last night, to the one last weekend and the one before that, lovely legs, fantastic tits, blonde, brunette, redhead. What was the redhead's name? He couldn't remember. Fun though. Jen wished she could stop herself from wondering how, if he ever bothered to do so, he would describe her to someone she'd never met? How would she match up to all the others? Did she figure in the top ten, the top twenty? She wondered if it were all true, if he were trying to make her jealous, or if he really didn't care at all.

She finished off her gin and tonic and gratefully accepted a second. Conor was smiling at her, he pushed a stray strand of hair from her face.

'Steady,' he said. 'You didn't have breakfast.'

'I'll be all right,' she said, and allowed him to squeeze her closer. She let her head rest on his shoulder. Three weeks. Three more weeks and they would be at the French house. If she closed her eyes she could see them there, working side by side in the barn, sunbathing on the front lawn, or spending all day in bed just because they could.

'Told you to take it easy,' Conor said, nudging her knee with his. 'You're falling asleep already.' He was grinning at her, his blue eyes warm, freckles across the bridge of his nose a little darker in the sun. Her heart swelled. 'I was dreaming of France,' she said softly.

The perfect moment was marred, though, because when she looked up she saw Dan watching them, face expressionless, cool grey eyes on her face, the slightest twitch around his mouth. He was looking at her face, her neck: hungry, predatory. Jen got to her feet.

'Just going to the loo,' she said, and walked away as quickly as she could without breaking into a run.

She sat in the stall for a moment, breathing deep, waiting for her heart rate to slow. She heard the ladies room door swing open and slam shut. Someone rummaging around in a handbag, a sharp intake of breath. The door again, and Natalie's voice saying, 'Lilah! What the hell?' Then there was whispering, then the door banging again, then nothing.

Jen washed her hands and splashed water on her face, pinched her cheeks to put some colour back into them. She left the bathroom and headed back through the pub towards the garden. Just before she reached the back door, someone grabbed her by the arm, pulled her roughly into a little alcove.

'I can't stand this,' Dan said to her. He was gripping her arm too tightly.

'Let go, you're hurting me.' He didn't let go, but he loosened his grip, he ran his thumb up and down the inside of her wrist.

'I can't stand this,' he said again. They were standing opposite each other, very close together, close enough that if she stood on her toes and leaned forward she could kiss his lips.

'I'm sorry,' she said. 'I'm so sorry.'

'Can we just . . . I don't know. I don't want this to be it.'

'It has to be. I'm sorry. It has to be. It was a mistake, Dan. I made a mistake, and I'm sorry.'

'It wasn't, it wasn't a mistake.' He let go of her arm and reached up to touch her face. She pulled away. 'I'm in love with you,' he said.

'No.'

'Jen.'

'You're not. You're not in love with me.' He was in love with her. She knew it, he was telling the truth. A shadow passed over his face, not just exasperation but real anger. He started to say something to her but then he stopped, shook his head.

'This is bullshit,' he said, his voice low and gentle. 'You know it. We both know that was more than just a mistake.'

'I don't love you. I don't. I won't.' The lie slid off her tongue, bitter, acrid. Dan put his thumb at the base of her throat and looked into her eyes; he leaned forward and put his mouth on hers.

'Yes, Jen. You will.' He turned and walked away from her, leaving her standing there, in the alcove, leaning against the wall, her eyes closed, heart banging against her ribs.

'Jen?' Conor had appeared in front of her. The world went silent. She thought her heart might break her ribs, burst through her chest. She stared at him, unmoving, her blood ice water. She opened her mouth to speak, but nothing came. 'Are you OK, Jen?'

She gathered herself, wiped the tears from her eyes, forcing her face into a smile.

'I'm fine, I'm fine. You were right. Gin and tonics at midday without any breakfast. Bad idea. Plus I think I might be getting hay fever. My eyes are bothering me.' She was babbling a little, she could feel that her face was red.

Conor gave a little nod, took a step towards her and reached out his hand, his eyes never leaving hers. 'OK,' he said. 'You OK to go back out?'

'Yes, of course.'

He led her back outside, gripping her hand so hard it hurt.

In the car park after lunch, Lilah and Andrew were having an argument.

'Jesus Christ, Lilah,' Andrew was saying, 'you couldn't hold out until this afternoon? We agreed . . . You said . . .'

'Oh my God, Andrew. I'm fine! Just give me the keys. Give me the bloody keys!'

'No, no. Look at you, you can't . . .'

'For fuck's sake, you are driving me up the bloody wall!' Lilah walked away from Andrew, stomping towards Dan's car.

'Conor!' she called out. 'Switch cars with me, will you? If I have to sit next to *him* for five more minutes I'm going to bloody strangle him.'

Conor hesitated. He looked at Jen. For just a moment, Jen thought about volunteering to go in Andrew's car instead, but she was afraid – she was afraid of leaving Conor and Dan in the car together, she was afraid of what might be said. She shrugged. Conor took a step towards her, he smiled and reached over to touch her face. 'I'll go with Andrew,' he said. 'Keep the peace.'

'OK.'

He didn't go right away; he just stood there, smiling at her, then he slipped his arms around her waist. 'My beautiful girl,' he said, giving her a kiss, pressing his face against hers. 'Do you have any idea how much I love you?' Her cheeks were wet, but she wasn't crying. Conor kissed her again, and again, one more time, then he walked away.

# Part Three

# Chapter Forty-three

⁓

*July 2013*

Dan could feel his eyelids starting to droop. The gentle drone of bees in the lavender was making him soporific. That and the heat. He was working in the barn, the sliding doors wide open to let in the faintest of breezes, the warm air carrying with it the scent of the herbs outside. He'd bought pots of lavender and rosemary to place in the courtyard – the bees loved them, as did the cat, which had appeared from nowhere three weeks ago. It lay, jet black and sleek, beneath the lavender blossom, occasionally stretching out a paw to bat at an insect, or raising its head to sniff the flowers. The cat was wild, wouldn't let Dan anywhere near it, but it happily ate the leftovers he put out. Dan found its presence soothing, he'd never had a pet. He was thinking about getting a dog, but, he wondered, would that mean the end of the cat?

He took a swig of lukewarm coffee and considered making some more, but it really was too hot for coffee, it must be well over thirty degrees and not quite ten thirty in the morning. Maybe Lilah was right, maybe he would need to build a pool.

There was a perfect spot for one, just in front of the oak trees to the south of the house, a flattish piece of land which got the sun all afternoon. Not this year, he thought, although if not this year, it wouldn't be much good for Lilah, would it? He shook his head, rolled his shoulders back a couple of times, went back to his script.

It was going well. It was, he didn't mind saying so himself, the best work he'd done in a very long time. And it was flowing out of him – he'd been writing solidly for days, for weeks, without stopping, without wanting to stop. He honestly couldn't remember feeling like this about work, not for years, not since – well. Not for a long time.

The work was cathartic. Rejuvenating. He felt stronger than he had in ages, he was living better than he had in years: getting up early, running, drinking less, eating well. Eggs, milk and chickens from the farm up the road, game birds from the hunters.

'This thing you're writing,' Lilah said, 'I hope it's not a year in fucking Provence.' It wasn't, but it could have been, the way he was feeling. He was in love with the countryside, with the quaint hilltop villages, with the broken-down stone farmhouses. He loved buying cheese and oil and wild boar sausage from the market, he was even trying to learn French.

He bought the house on a whim. He woke up one morning, roughly four weeks after Claudia left him, walked around his flat in his boxer shorts, counted the empty bottles of Scotch in the recycling bin (four, with two days still to go until collection day), checked his phone and discovered that he had dialled her number eighteen times the night before between the hours of twelve-thirty and two. If things carried on like this, he was either going to fall drunkenly down the spiral staircase and break his neck, or Claudia was going to report him for harassment. Neither was an attractive prospect.

So he rang Jen. She'd sent him an email when she moved to Oxford in January. He'd ignored it. Now, in late March, he dialled her number.

'Have you sold it?' he asked her. 'The house, I mean. Is it gone?'

'Not a chance,' she said. She sounded weary. 'There was one offer, 50,000 euros below the asking price. The weather's been bloody awful over there, I don't think the agent's had more than three people to see it. I think they're just going to forget about it for a few months, try again in the summer.'

'I'll take it,' he said. 'I'll buy it. I want to buy the French house.'

'What? Don't be ridiculous. I'm not desperate for the cash, Dan. Not yet anyway.'

'No, I want it. I want to live there. I'll take it.'

At first she refused. Perhaps she thought he was buying it out of pity for her, or perhaps she thought he had some other, darker motive. A way to get a piece of her, an unbreakable link to her. He upped his offer, which only strengthened her resolve not to give in to him. Then he told her, 'This isn't for you, Jen, I'm not doing this for you. I want it, I feel as though I need it. I'm desperate to get away. Please.'

And she gave in.

He moved into the house on 1 May. It was a different place to the one he'd left in December and so like the one he'd left sixteen or so years ago. The day of arrival was spent in a daze, walking from room to room, in shorts and T-shirt, bare feet on cold stone tile, gazing out of the windows. He kept expecting to see the others, to catch snatches of conversation, to hear laughter ringing out from upstairs. He understood what Jen meant now, when she'd talked of ghosts. It was uncanny.

He found it so unnerving that he moved himself into the barn right away, a place that hadn't existed back in those days, and so could not be haunted. It too had a completely different character in summer than it had in winter, flooded with warmth and light and the occasional waft of the farm yard. He moved into the barn and he started to write, and he'd barely stopped since.

He was still required to go to London from time to time, to speak to his agent or to producers, to go to parties. He kept the socialising to a minimum, though; there were so few people he wished to see and so many he wanted to avoid. At the last thing he'd attended he'd ended up with a glass of champagne in the face and a two-inch scratch on his throat, courtesy of Claudia.

And there were disruptions here, too. The biggest one was heralded three weeks after he moved in by a phone call from Zac of all people, asking for a favour. And that was how he found that the place he'd escaped to, to be alone, turned out to be the place he started to build something like a family.

*Dearest Dan,*

*Ça se passe bien à Villefranche? I hope you're all settled in. If there's anything you need, Monsieur Caron is the man to go to. His English is not bad at all and he's an absolute sweetheart, plus he knows all the local tradesmen and will negotiate good deals for you if you need anything done. Don't try to organise anything directly, they can smell a naïve Englishman a mile off.*

*And so for the big news: the baby arrived on Wednesday. A girl, her name is Isabelle, she weighed six pounds and four ounces. Ten fingers, ten toes, brown eyes and a surprisingly thick head of dark hair. I will email you a picture soon.*

*Andrew and Nat came to visit me at the hospital and Nat is staying with me for a few days while I get used to the whole motherhood thing. Because obviously in a few days' time, I'll have it licked. It's quite shocking how exhausted I am. I know everyone always says you'll be knackered, but I didn't expect this. Still. It's wondrous, too. No matter how many times everyone tells you what you'll feel, you're still not quite prepared for it. And I know everyone always says that, too, but it's true. Which is why they all say it, I suppose. It's indescribable.*

*I hope being up there in the mountains is giving you what you need. It is so beautiful, so peaceful, but also pretty lonely. I do hope you're all right.*

*With lots of love,*

*Jen*

## Chapter Forty-four

Lilah had 'The Ballad of Lucy Jordan' stuck in her head, had done for days, couldn't stop humming it — she wanted desperately to sing it but she couldn't quite remember the words. Something about driving through Paris in a sports car, about getting old, about missing out on the things you always thought you were going to do.

She couldn't remember where she'd heard it last but it was making her more melancholy than it ought. Of all the things she'd missed out on, driving around Paris wasn't one of them. All right, it was the back of a motor bike, not a sports car, but that wasn't the point. The point was to be nineteen, racing along the Quai des Célestins with the sun setting, or rising, or whatever, with a handsome man wearing a leather jacket. That she'd done. It was all the other stuff she was going to miss out on.

They were driving back from the beach. Dan had lent them his Audi, they had the top down. It was a beautiful hot day; when she closed her eyes the world was orange. A soft, warm breeze rushed over her, her skin felt tight from the sand and the salt – she could be anywhere, at any time. She could be seventeen, with everything still ahead, including the guy with the motorbike and the leather jacket on the Quai des Célestins.

She would keep that. She'd just do everything else differently, everything since. 'You all right, babe?' Zac reached over and squeezed her thigh. She opened her eyes for a second and smiled at him, as reassuringly as she could. Well, maybe not everything. If she had her time over, she'd still want Zac. 'You warm enough?' he asked her. 'I can get the blanket from the back if you want.'

'I'm fine,' she said, covering his hand with hers. 'Sleepy.'

'You sleep, baby. Couple of hours yet.'

They'd been to the beach at Menton. They'd left early the previous morning, spent all afternoon lying in the sun and all this morning too. She'd even swum in the sea for a while. The Med was colder than she'd remembered, colder and clearer; diving in was a shock. She gasped and gulped air and kicked her weak legs, flailed in surprise, but after a while she relaxed and floated on her back, eyes closed, Zac circling her like a friendly shark. When she'd had enough she found she no longer had the strength to walk up the beach and he'd had to carry her.

She'd never been to Menton before, but she'd go again if she had the time. It lacked the glamour of Cap Ferrat, but God knows she wasn't feeling all that glamorous. Menton was a proper seaside resort, bustling and busy and about as Italian as France gets, just a mile or two from the border – friendlier, somehow, than most of the Côte d'Azur, although Lilah suspected she just thought that because she was feeling more sentimental than usual.

They stayed in a B&B, a listing terracotta terrace with a balcony overlooking the Place St-Michel and a view of the sea.

She would have stayed another day, two or three, but she hadn't brought all her pills, and she feared one of the bad headaches.

'We'll come again,' Zac said to her. 'We can stay longer next time.'

She opened her eyes and looked over at him, a slight frown on his face as he squinted into the sun. She'd grown accustomed to that frown, he wore it all the time now, it seemed as though he never looked at her except with concern. It was heartbreaking to watch, but no matter how she tried, she'd not been able to chase him away. He loved her, loved her like no one ever had, and there was nothing to be done. He wasn't going anywhere. Lilah consoled herself with the thought that, young and beautiful as he was, he'd recover.

It was Zac's idea to come to France. When she got the final diagnosis, the big one, the bad one, he'd said: 'We can go to the French house. We can spend the summer there, it'll be so much better than staying in London. Dan owes you, you said it, and he knows it. We even had a conversation about it.' Lilah told him it was out of the question, she hadn't told anyone yet, she wasn't ready for that. Zac went ahead and contacted Dan anyway. Lilah was furious: there was a terrible argument, the worst they'd ever had, it went on for days. She refused to speak to him, she threw him out of the apartment, she took away his keys. He slept in the hallway outside their flat. She said terrible things and told him she didn't love him, never had. He bought flowers and groceries and told her that no matter what she did he would be there with her. She gave in, in the end. His will was stronger than hers, who'd have thought it?

She drifted off. When she woke, the car was no longer moving. It was parked in shadow on the side of the road, a small road, not the motorway.

'Zac?'

'You were shivering,' his voice called out from behind her. He was rummaging in the boot and appeared at her side with a woollen blanket in hand. 'Here you go. Won't be long now. Half an hour or so. Shall I put the top up?'

'No. Leave it down.'

'OK.' He leaned over the door and kissed her gently on the lips.

She snuggled down under the blanket and they set off again.

'When do they arrive?' she asked Zac. 'I've forgotten.'

'Thursday.'

'Today is?'

'Monday, sweetheart.'

'OK.'

'You nervous?'

'Yeah.'

Andrew and Natalie would be joining them in three days' time, with their daughters in tow. And a while after that, she couldn't remember exactly when, Jen would be arriving too, with the baby. She couldn't remember the baby's name. She kept forgetting things, they just vanished out of her head, and when she was told again it was like discovering something for the first time, there was no familiarity, no comforting flash of recognition. She hated this feeling of confusion most of all, it was like fear, worse than the headaches, worse than the exhaustion. It reminded her of the blackouts she used to have when she drank, the sense of losing time forever, never to be recovered.

She squeezed her eyes shut and opened them again, rocking her head back, gazing up at the sky, still deepest azure and completely cloudless. Count your blessings, Lilah. A man who loves you, who will stay with you, no matter what. A roof over your head, and not just any roof either. Friends.

She wasn't quite sure what to expect of her friends. She'd written to Natalie, telling her about her illness and the fact that she was staying with Dan, asking her to come. There were things they needed to get straight, things they had to resolve. She couldn't do it over the phone, she couldn't do it by letter or email, it had to be face to face.

The sun was just dipping behind the brow of the hill as they drove up the driveway; Lilah could see Dan standing at the kitchen window, he was waiting for them. He emerged within seconds from the front door, his brow furrowed, too.

'I was starting to worry,' he called out. 'Did you have a good time?'

'Marvellous,' Lilah called out, her voice little more than a croak. She coughed. 'It was lovely. You should come, next time.'

Next time. They made plans, all the time, her and Zac. Zac hadn't given up on her. And why not make plans, Lilah thought. She knew that Dan found it disconcerting, but what was the point in *not* making plans? It wasn't like they had an exact date, a deadline. There might be time for another trip to the beach, there might be time for several.

Dan opened her car door, helped her out.

'You've caught the sun,' he said, giving her a kiss on the cheek.

'I should hope so,' she said, smiling at him, her most reassuring smile. She could tell that he was searching her eyes, her face. How was she feeling? Was she really OK? He did this every time they were apart for more than a day or so. Zac did it too.

That was normal when it came to Zac, but it was funny coming from Dan, because they hadn't been close for years, not for such a long time, and she'd forgotten how sweet he could be, how caring. In her anger over that stupid bloody film, Lilah had completely forgotten how good Dan was to her after Andrew dumped her, after Natalie betrayed her, when Jen was gone and she was left all alone.

Dan was the one who persuaded her to come to France. He'd written her an email, asking her to come, and then when she'd said no, he'd called her up and begged her, which in itself was gratifying. And when she refused him still, he ended up making it all about him, telling her how he was going mad there all by himself, how lonely he was – didn't she remember, he asked, how he hated more than anything to be all alone? At the time she believed him, although once she and Zac had arrived it became clear that he was perfectly happy here, he wasn't lonely at all. Still, she liked that he'd made the effort.

And she did feel sorry for him. Poor old Dan, he'd never get what he wanted, and when he did, he wouldn't want it any more. He was just one of those people, he wasn't built to be happy.

They'd decided this, the pair of them, one night not long after she and Zac arrived. Zac had gone up to bed, Lilah and Dan stayed up drinking wine and talking about how hopeless they were and all the things they'd done wrong, and how some people were simply not capable of happiness, it just didn't come to them like it came to others. Then they decided that that was bullshit and they were being self-pitying and ridiculous, and if they weren't happy then it was all their own fault. They talked about how, given the chance, they'd do everything differently, or most of it anyway. Then Dan put on 'Je Ne Regrette Rien' and they danced around the living room and laughed until they cried.

*Dear Natalie,*

*This is a hard letter to write, for so many reasons. As a result, I'm keeping it short. I need to see you; there are things that you and I need to sort out. You may think that there's nothing left to say, but I have a feeling that if you read to the end of this note, you'll change your mind.*

*I don't mean to be melodramatic or anything, but I'm dying. No seriously, I am. Don't laugh.*

*Don't be sad, either. Just come and see me. I'm at the French house, with Dan. I'll be here for a while, a few weeks more at least. Please come, bring Andrew, bring your daughters. I'd love to meet them. If you don't come, I'll only end up turning up on your doorstep in Reading, and just think how inconvenient that would be.*

*I need to see you, Nat. I really do.*

*Love,*

*Lilo*

# Chapter Forty-five

❧

*August 2013*

Déjà vu. The airport, the car park, the endless search for a silver Citroën. Just like last time, only worse, because this time they were travelling in close, clammy, suffocating heat with two miserable teenage girls dragging themselves along behind them, every movement an effort, every expression a snarl, every response to every question a shrug or an eye roll. And Andrew was in no mood to appease anyone, not his daughters and certainly not Natalie.

He snapped at her three times during the short but fraught trip from the airport to the motorway. He complained bitterly, not for the first time, about the fact that she'd chosen, once again, to book flights to Marseilles when Nice was a much more convenient destination. She'd told him four times that the fares to Nice were double those to Marseilles, but he hadn't been listening. This was the new dynamic. No more softly, softly from Andrew, no more tip-toeing around her.

Natalie concentrated on the map, she tried not to get things wrong. The car was insufferably hot from hours of standing in an unshaded car park; the blast of cold air from the air conditioning seemed to have little effect other than to make her hands cold, leaving the rest of her overcooked, sweat trickling down the nape of her neck and into the small of her back. Now that they were on the motorway and there wasn't much direction to give, silence weighed heavily, oppressively, on all of them.

Or perhaps the others hadn't noticed, perhaps it weighed only upon her. In the back seat, the girls, plugged into their phones, sat in identical, mirrored poses: heads leaning against windows, gazing out onto the parched scrub, expressions somewhere between boredom and disdain. They hadn't wanted to come. Two weeks in the French countryside with *nothing to do*? No *television*? Not even a *swimming pool*?

Andrew, as was his wont of late, took their side. Privately, of course. They don't need to come, he'd said, they can stay with your mother, or with friends. Natalie got upset: is that it then, we don't have family holidays any longer? The girls do their own thing? They're about to turn thirteen, Andrew, not eighteen. They have a whole lifetime to go off by themselves. She got tearful and he got pissed off, but in the end he conceded the argument.

She didn't win them as often as she used to. And even when she did, he no longer took defeat gracefully. This was the way things had been for six months, since their last visit to France. Things had turned around: now he was the angry one, and she was conciliatory. It seemed extraordinary to Natalie that after everything they'd been through, that one weekend could shift the balance of their interactions so seismically, change their relationship to each other so fundamentally.

It was just one thing on top of another, she supposed, all concertinaed together: her outburst on the day of the storm, the night he spent with Lilah, the fight they had the next day, after the doctor came.

When he'd first arrived back, she'd been so happy to see him she'd run out to greet him in the snow. They'd held onto each other for a long time, and he seemed happy to be back with her, too, although there was a little stiffness in the hug, and he was first to break away. Then Jen collapsed and everyone started panicking, Andrew especially, as though he were somehow the cause of it.

Jen was fine. It was just low blood pressure, which isn't all that unusual in pregnancy. As Natalie pointed out quite a few times, not that anyone was listening. But once the doctor came and saw to her, everyone calmed down. Jen went straight to bed, and Dan left, saying he needed to make a start on the journey to Paris, which obviously wasn't true because why would you leave at four in the afternoon when it was getting dark and there was snow on the roads when you had an eight- or ten-hour journey in front of you? He just wanted to get away from them all. Lilah and Zac went up to bed, too, so Natalie turned on the radio in the kitchen as loud as it would go so they wouldn't have to listen to their sex noises. Andrew turned it back off.

'Jen's trying to sleep,' he said crossly, glaring at her as if she were a particularly thoughtless child.

'I know, I just . . . didn't want to have to hear . . . Lilah.'

'Oh, grow up, Nat,' he said. 'It's just sex.'

Just sex. She let it go, she made them both some sandwiches which they ate in front of the fire, plates balanced on their knees. It had started to snow again, nothing like the night before, but still falling thick and steady.

'I wonder if we'll be able to leave tomorrow,' Natalie said. 'The snow, I mean.'

Andrew shrugged. 'Perhaps we'll have to stay another night. We could go down to the B&B if necessary. I imagine Jen is probably keen to be rid of us.' He looked up at Natalie as he said this; there was something in his face, a look of disappointment that she hadn't seen before.

'You're angry with me,' she said softly.

He shrugged again. 'Did you apologise to Jen?' he asked.

'Yes. We spoke last night. It's all right.'

'Is it really,' he said, looking away from her now, staring into the heart of the fire.

They finished their sandwiches in silence. Natalie took away their plates once they were done. 'I am sorry, Andrew,' she said. 'I made a mess of things.' He shrugged, *again*. She was getting a little tired of this. 'I'd had too much to drink,' she said. 'We all had . . .'

'Yes, but you were the only one standing in the middle of the room yelling accusations at people,' he said flatly.

'I was trying to show them . . .' Her voice broke a little, she cleared her throat. 'I wanted to help you, to show them that it's not fair, this guilt you've borne, it isn't yours, it shouldn't be . . .'

'Of course it should be, Natalie,' he snapped, voice raised. 'This constant need to absolve me of all guilt is ridiculous. It's tiresome. Do you honestly think it helps me when you excuse what I did? It doesn't matter what Lilah did. It matters what *I* did. I was behind the wheel, I was driving too fast, I was over the limit. Christ. It was my fault. The fact that you . . .' He tailed off suddenly.

'That I what?'

He got to his feet and turned away from her, stood in front of the window. Natalie couldn't tell whether he was looking out

328

at the snow or at his own reflection. 'The fact,' he said quietly, 'that you are a "fucking cripple" as you put it, and that I have a shit job, the fact that I'm clearly such a total disappointment to you, that is my fault. It isn't Lilah's. The fact that Conor is dead, that Jen is alone, these things are my fault. It doesn't matter what Lilah did.'

'Andrew,' she said, standing behind him, reaching her hands around his waist. 'You're not a disappointment to me, you could never be.'

'Well, you certainly made it sound like I was, Nat. You made it sound like you were ashamed of me. I never realised until yesterday that you think our life is small, that it's less than it should be, that *I'm* less than I should be.'

'Andrew . . .'

'Let me finish! It's shocking enough to discover that the woman you love thinks like that, but to discover it in the way I had to, with everyone watching, with Jen watching, with Dan watching? That was unconscionable.' Natalie rested her head against his back, she started to cry. He didn't comfort her, he disentangled himself from her arms.

'I don't think that, I don't.'

'Well, in that case, Nat, you shouldn't have said it. And if you don't really think that, then I believe that the only possible reason you could have for saying it is that you wanted to hurt Lilah as much as you possibly could, you wanted to twist the knife as hard as you could. Do you think that was necessary?' He moved her, gently but firmly, out of his way and walked to the doorway.

'Wait . . .'

'I'm going to check on Jen.'

She sat alone, in front of the fire, feeling wretched, utterly

329

adrift. She'd never seen him like this before, not with her. They'd had minor bust-ups, but she'd never seen him disappointed in her. She felt as though she'd lost his respect. She felt as though she deserved to lose it. And she felt that there must be something else wrong, something other than the things she'd said the day before, because when he'd got back to the house, he'd seemed pleased to see her, as though she was forgiven, as though they would be all right.

She could hear laughter upstairs. Lilah. How was it that she managed to let everything roll off her so easily? Everything Natalie had said to her, the way she'd been exposed yesterday, she just shrugged it off and carried on as if it were nothing. As if nothing had consequence. It rankled with her.

There was something else, too. Something he'd said in the kitchen an hour or two ago. It was like a bug, it had burrowed under her skin and it was crawling around under there, making her itch. Oh, grow up, Nat, it's just sex. Just sex.

By the time Andrew came back downstairs, offering to make her tea, a very small attempt at reconciliation, the itch had got to the point when it needed to be scratched.

'What happened last night?' she asked him. 'At the hotel?'

His shoulders rose and fell, he exhaled slowly. 'We got to the B&B, went to the room, they brought us some food, we went to bed. We were both pretty worn out,' he said.

'You didn't talk?'

'Of course we talked.'

'About?'

'Ah, Natalie!' He threw his hands up in the air. 'We talked about a lot of things.'

'Me?'

'Yes, you, she was really upset about what you said.'

330

'Oh, poor Lilah.'

'Yes, poor Lilah. Jesus. She's been through a hell of a lot, Nat.'

'*She's* been through a lot? What has she been through? What has she lost? Can you hear her up there, shagging and laughing? She doesn't give a shit. She only ever thinks of herself. I can't believe you're defending her.'

'I'm not defending anyone, Nat, but I think you're being unkind . . .'

'What happened last night? What happened?'

'Hey, hey.' Natalie turned around. Zac was standing behind her in tracksuit bottoms and a T-shirt, his hair sticking up at the back. 'Could you keep it down, yeah? I think Jen's trying to sleep.'

They simmered in silence for a few moments, but the argument wasn't over.

'You're not going to tell me, are you?' Natalie whispered at him. 'You're just going to leave me to wonder . . .'

'Oh for Christ's sake, Nat. I shouldn't have to dignify this . . .' He broke off, shook his head. He was bright red in the face. He got to his feet and walked towards the doorway. 'I think it's time we went to bed, don't you? This isn't getting us anywhere, we're both tired, and you're in pain, I can see that . . .'

'Don't use my pain. Don't make excuses for me. And don't tell me what you see when you can't even look at me.'

'I can see when it's bad, Natalie. I've lived with you through this for sixteen years . . .'

'Oh, congratulations,' she said, her voice cracking. Something inside her broke, it just twisted and broke. 'You've lived *through* this? Through what? This is my life, I'm not living through it, I'm just living it. And there you are, rising above, being good,

331

taking all the hits, playing the martyr. I am tired of feeling like *I* am your penance, Andrew, like I'm the price you had to pay for what you did.'

She'd never seen him look at her the way he did that night, she never wanted to again.

They left the next day. They didn't speak on the journey to the airport and they barely spoke on the plane. The second they touched down in England they started dealing with practicalities, picking up the girls, shopping, Christmas. They never talked about that fight again, they just left everything unresolved. They let life carry on, a new life, a smaller one than they'd led before, darker, with sharper edges.

But that bug was still there. It lived under her skin, burrowing away, keeping her awake at night. She might always have to live with it, there was nothing she could do about it now. She couldn't ask him and she couldn't ask Lilah. Not because Lilah would be angry with her, or because she wouldn't answer, but because she would. Lilah might tell her the truth, and then what? She couldn't be angry with her now, she couldn't hate her. There wasn't time.

They arrived at the house around five, the sun still high in a pale blue sky, the heat showing no sign of abating; if anything, it seemed to have intensified. The lawn was parched, faded to a pale yellow. The grey stone walls reflected the light, and from outside the interior of the house looked inky black, cavernous. Who knew what lurked within?

'Is this it?' Charlotte asked. Natalie, reapplying lipstick, caught a glimpse of her daughter in the sun-visor mirror: her face was set in the same disdainful expression it had worn since the airport. Andrew looked over at her, raised his eyebrows. His expression said I told you so. They shouldn't have brought the girls.

They clambered out of the car, stretching legs and arching backs, breathing in the scent of summer. Natalie was hit by a rush of nostalgia for the French house as it once was, as they had known it way back then. It was the smell of the rosemary and lavender, the sound of bells somewhere, the buzz of insects in the flowerbeds. She looked over at Andrew and he was smiling. His smile faltered just a touch as the front door flew open and Dan appeared, beaming and suntanned in board shorts and a T-shirt, his arms thrown open in a gesture of welcome. The genial host, the lord of the manor.

Natalie had expected Andrew to be delighted about Dan buying the place, but in fact he wasn't. It made him uneasy, for some reason. When Jen first rang him to tell him that Dan had offered to buy the house, he laughed it off.

'It'll never happen,' he said to Nat over dinner. 'You know what he's like. When we saw him at Christmas he was talking about the Italian Riviera, remember, or was it Costa de la Luz? And next week it'll be Croatia, or an island in the Caribbean or something.' Then when Jen rang and said it was all finalised, contracts exchanged, money in the bank, he was pissed off. 'He'll ruin the place,' he grumbled. 'There'll be plasma screens in all the rooms, skylights in the roof. A bloody hot tub. Just you watch.'

There were no plasma screens in the living room or the kitchen, and no immediate evidence of a hot tub. Dan did seem to have had a speaker system installed, because Natalie noticed that you could hear the strains of Adele wherever you went. It was very tidy and very clean, tidier and cleaner, Nat thought, than when Jen had been staying here. Nat wondered whether he'd got himself a maid.

Dan looked well, too, tanned and slim. He pressed cold

333

drinks into their hands and fussed over the girls, going into charm overdrive, telling them how lovely they looked, just like their mum. The pair of them looked happier than they had since Heathrow; meeting the film director was pretty much the only thing they'd been looking forward to about this trip.

Natalie sipped her drink and listened to her daughters chattering excitedly at Dan, asking when was he last in Hollywood and had he really met Robert Pattinson? She listened for about three minutes. She couldn't just stand here pretending everything was normal, that they were just here on holiday.

'Where is she, Dan?' she asked.

'She's upstairs, taking a nap. Zac went down to the village to the butcher's, we thought we might barbecue tonight. That suit you, girls? You're not veggie, are you?'

'Dan . . .'

'Go up if you like. She's in Jen's old room. Don't worry about waking her – she'd want you to. She's been looking forward to seeing you.'

Halfway up the stairs, Natalie stopped. She took a deep breath, resting her hand on the cool stone wall, preparing herself. She could feel her heart racing, beating much too fast. She felt afraid. Andrew, behind her, slipped his hand into hers.

'Come on,' he said gently. 'We'll go up together.' Her breath caught in her throat, it was little moments of kindness like this that made her want to cry, because it brought home to her what she'd lost, a time when moments like this were commonplace, when they were kind to each other all the time. She squeezed Andrew's hand and continued up the stairs. She knocked softly on the bedroom door and pushed it open.

The room was warm and dark, the window open, curtain

fluttering in the breeze. Lilah lay on her side, facing away from them. Natalie turned back to face Andrew.

'Maybe we should leave her to sleep,' she whispered. Andrew's eyes held hers, he shook his head.

'Come on,' he said, placing his hands on her shoulders. 'Let's say hello.'

In the bed, Lilah stirred, moving her legs about, rolling over onto her back. Natalie took a couple of steps towards the bed and Lilah propped herself up on her elbows.

'There you are,' she said, her voice no more than a croak. 'Come here and see me.'

Natalie could feel the smile fixing on her face as her eyes adjusted to the light, as she moved a little closer.

'Hi, Lilo,' she said. Her hands were screwed into fists at her side, fingernails digging into her palms.

'Hi, Nat.'

She was like a spectre, sitting there in the half-light, so emaciated she seemed almost insubstantial, her cheeks hollow, her lips grey, her skin dry as paper. Her long blonde hair was gone, replaced by a short, wispy mop which only served to emphasise her gauntness. For a moment or two, Natalie couldn't speak, could hardly breathe; she sat down next to her on the bed and tried to smile, but she couldn't. She took Lilah in her arms and held her, whispering, 'Oh, Lilo. Oh, my poor girl.'

When eventually Lilah pulled away from her, she was smiling. 'So,' she said, smoothing Natalie's hair and wiping the tears from her cheeks, 'it turns out you *can* be too thin.'

*Dear Dan,*

*Lilah wrote to me. She told me. I spoke to Jen, she told me it's true, it's really true. I cannot think straight. I can't process that.*

*I'm writing to you because Lilah asked me to come and stay, and I'm aware that it's not actually her house and not her invitation to give. I wanted to check with you. Andrew said of course we can go, don't be ridiculous, you don't have to ask Dan, but I think I do.*

*I don't know if you've forgotten what I said to you that first night at the French house in December, but I've replayed it many times in my head, along with a lot of other terrible things I said that weekend. I told you that we weren't friends, that you had no place in our lives, and I feel wretched for saying that.*

*I have been doing quite a bit of soul-searching these past few months, and I find myself remembering things that I'd long since forgotten. Like how, in those early years after the accident, you were very kind to Andrew and me, the way you maintained your neutrality when everything fell apart between Lilah and Andrew and me, the way you sought to hold us all together. I remember how, even after we all fell out about the film, I thought of you often – the girls would do or say something funny and I'd imagine how much you'd laugh if you'd seen it or heard it.*

*You are and were always a part of us all, integral just like any one of us, and I realise that to say otherwise was very hurtful of me. So, before I ask you if I can bring my entire family to stay at your house (your house! I can hardly believe it!), I must ask your forgiveness first.*

*Take care of Lilah for me, for all of us.*

*Love,*

*Natalie*

## Chapter Forty-six

~

They were lying in the hammock, Jen and Lilah with Isabelle tucked up neatly in between them. Late afternoon, the sun just starting its slide down behind the mountain, the shadows long. Isabelle and Lilah were sleeping, the baby's breathing light and steady, Lilah's ragged, whistling, wheezing. Jen lay propped up on a pillow, her book on her lap. She wasn't actually reading, she was content just to watch them.

The hammock was enormous, bright red and brand new, bought by Dan as a gift for Lilah. It hung between the oaks on the north side of the house, the perfect place to shelter from the heat of the afternoon, shaded by the trees and catching the best of the cool breeze blowing in from the coast. Since they'd arrived a week before, Jen and Isabelle had taken to joining Lilah in her hammock; they spent the afternoons there, sleeping or talking or watching the baby sleep. Some days the cat joined them; it climbed into the oak tree and looked down on them from on high.

Lilah was in love with Isabelle, she couldn't get enough of her. She reached for her at every opportunity, she was constantly slipping her skeletal fingers into Isabelle's chubby ones, or grabbing at her fat little toes, tracing circles on the baby's perfect porcelain skin with her fingertips. Jen couldn't believe it, Lilah was pretty much the least child-friendly person she'd ever met.

'I like babies,' Lilah informed her. 'Babies are easy, provided they're not your own. They just sleep, and you cuddle them. You don't have to think of clever things to say to entertain them, or play endless games. They're like puppies, really.' She got on very well with Charlotte and Grace, too, which Natalie said was because she still had the mind of a teenage girl, always had.

Natalie and Andrew scurried around the house like servants, rarely if ever stopping to relax. They seemed curiously detached from each other, focused almost entirely on their children and Lilah. Natalie had assumed the role of nurse; she quietly and efficiently stripped beds and brought food and administered medicine, then she would disappear into the kitchen to prepare more food or put on the washing. Andrew was constantly fixing things, replacing door knobs and oiling hinges, driving Dan to distraction.

'It's my bloody house,' he kept muttering, which made Jen smile, because it wasn't really, it was never going to be his house, it belonged to all of them.

Jen was too exhausted to be properly helpful, instead she and Isabelle became Lilah's constant companions, going for very slow, very short walks in the mornings, lounging in the hammock in the afternoons, occasionally taking brief excursions to the village to visit Monsieur and Madame Caron at the B&B and to have café and pains au chocolat at the pâtisserie in the square.

Lilah stirred, she stretched one arm up lazily, she opened her eyes.

'There you are,' she said, smiling at Jen. 'We were wondering where you'd got to.'

'Were you?' Jen asked. She reached out and touched Lilah's wispy hair.

'We were looking for you everywhere.' Lilah was often like this when she woke, confusing dreams with reality. 'Conor said you'd gone to the village to get food for the party, but I told him you did that yesterday.'

'Conor?'

'Yes. He's in the woods. We were walking in the woods.'

'Oh. OK.' Jen bit down hard on her lip and lay back so that Lilah wouldn't see her welling up.

They tried, as far as they could, not to go to pieces in her presence, but it wasn't always easy. The confusion was to be expected. Severe headaches, nausea, memory loss, speech difficulties, loss of appetite, all to be expected. Jen had read up on the subject. They didn't know how long it would be, but the tumour was very aggressive. For now, her pain could be managed at home, but eventually she would have to go to a hospice. They talked about that in whispers so as not to enrage her.

'Don't worry,' Lilah said. She was smiling up at Jen, her finger ever so gently tracing circles on Isabelle's cheek. 'He isn't cross. He's happy about the baby.'

'I'm glad.'

'And he thought we should have the party out here, he thought that would be best.'

'That's a good idea,' Jen said.

The party was the following day, a surprise party, for

Andrew and Natalie's fourteenth wedding anniversary. It was Charlotte and Grace's idea. The sad thing was that had the girls not mentioned it, it was unlikely that any of the others would have remembered. Possibly not even Andrew or Nat.

As it was, Zac took Andrew to look at some new tiling for the upstairs bathroom while Charlotte nagged her mother into taking her all the way to Nice to do some clothes shopping. Jen, Dan and Grace put up decorations and set up the barbecue, they made salads and marinated lamb chops, they built a bonfire next to the hammock, hung lanterns in the trees, put out rugs and cushions, set up speakers so they could listen to music.

When they were ready, Jen and Dan sat out on the rugs with Isabelle lying between them, while Grace went inside to wake Lilah. It was the first time since Jen had arrived that she and Dan had found themselves completely alone. They sat in awkward silence for a few moments before they both started speaking at exactly the same time.

'I'm not sure this is such a good idea,' Jen said.

'Have you heard from Nicolas?' Dan asked.

They laughed awkwardly, then both fell silent again, waiting.

'Not sure what's not a good idea?' Dan asked at last.

'This party. Things seem a bit off with Nat and Andrew. Don't you think? I just don't know whether it's a great idea to spring this on them.'

Dan shrugged. 'I don't know. I assumed it was just about Lilah. I didn't think it was something between the two of them.'

Jen shook her head. 'It's not just Lilah. It's . . . I don't know. When things are bad, Andrew and Natalie lean on each other. I know that, from things he's told me, in letters, over the years. But they aren't leaning on each other now. Or rather, it looks like Natalie's trying to lean on Andrew and he's pulling away from her. I don't recall seeing him like this before. He just seems different.'

Dan looked up at the oaks, the multi-coloured lanterns hanging from the branches. 'Bit late to call the whole thing off now,' he said.

They fell quiet again. It was a lovely evening, cooler than it had been of late, a breeze blowing up from the valley, wisps of cloud scudding across the sky.

'I spoke to him before I left Oxford,' Jen said eventually. 'Nicolas I mean. He hasn't called since.'

'Sorry,' Dan said. He covered her hand with his.

'I don't care,' she said. 'I mean, not for me. I think it's shitty that he's shown so little interest in his daughter, but it's not a major shock. We've barely spoken since I left Paris a year ago, and he always made it perfectly clear that a child was not in his plans. He's offered financial support,' she said, with a wry smile. 'But I'd rather do without. To be honest, I think we'll be far better off without him.'

'You'll do fine,' Dan said, giving her hand a squeeze. It sounded like a platitude, but when she looked at him he had an expression on his face which suggested that it wasn't.

The party was a success. Jen needn't have worried. Lilah was on wonderful form, she'd been sleeping all day and she was as bright and funny and loud as Lilah could be. She lounged in the hammock, sipping champagne and telling them stories about a rich vintner in Barcelona, a photographer with a leather jacket and a motorbike in Paris, the time she got arrested for being drunk and disorderly in Berlin and ended up having a passionate three-week affair with the arresting officer. Charlotte and Grace were captivated, awestruck. Jen overheard Grace talking to Andrew in the kitchen later.

'I think I want to learn Spanish, Dad,' she was saying. 'So I can live in Barcelona.'

'Good idea,' Andrew said.

'And I'll take many lovers,' she added, appropriating Lilah's antiquated turn of phrase.

'You bloody well will not.'

But he was laughing – he laughed all night, Jen hadn't seen him like that for ages. He and Natalie threw themselves into the spirit of the thing, they relaxed, they held hands. They stopped attending to everyone else for a few hours and were tender with each other instead.

Dan told them all about the Claudia debacle. 'It was miserable from the start,' he said. 'I'd planned this whole romantic – and really bloody expensive – Christmas at the Ritz in Paris, which turned out to be pretty abominable, really. Christmas in a hotel is bad enough, but when your companion spends her entire time either sobbing hysterically or screaming over the phone at her husband – in German, remember, not the most melodic of languages – it's ghastly. Anyway, I thought everything would settle down once she'd moved in with me in London, but it just got worse. We fought about everything, from the weather to work, it was constant. Relentless. And terrifying: one night, I'd been out to the pub with a producer I was talking to about work – I came back a bit later than I'd planned, to find that she had smashed every single piece of crockery in my kitchen. Every single piece.'

'Bloody hell,' Andrew said.

'Exactly. The whole thing, the whole unmitigated disaster lasted five weeks, then she went back to the husband. He wouldn't take her back at first, he told her to get lost, so then she had the gall to come back to me! She only lasted about ten days that time.'

'Oh dear,' Natalie said, giving him a little pat on the back.

'You know, we were utterly, completely unsuited for each other. I've no idea how I couldn't have realised that before.' Jen thought she caught a half-smile on Zac's face, but then he looked away. 'She was so bizarre, said she couldn't live in my place the way it was. She wanted the entire thing redecorated, she wanted every stick of furniture sold. For no good reason at all! Christ, she was self-absorbed.' Then everyone tried not to smile, apart from Lilah who laughed out loud. Dan looked around at them, threw his hands in the air. 'She's *much* worse than I am,' he muttered.

After cake, Jen went inside to prepare a bottle for Isabelle. She was just testing the temperature when Natalie appeared at her side. She slipped her arm around Jen's waist and gave her a squeeze.

'You'd better not do any of the washing up,' she said. 'Mothers of infants should never have to do the washing up.'

Jen smiled at her. 'I wasn't doing it,' she protested. 'But I don't want to see you cleaning up in here either. Those celebrating their fourteenth wedding anniversary certainly shouldn't be doing the washing up.'

'True,' Natalie said. She leaned against the counter and took a swig of wine. 'Dan should be doing this,' she said, and they both laughed. 'Can't believe it's fourteen years, though. Fourteen years! It seems like . . .'

'Yesterday and forever ago at the same time?' Jen asked.

'It does.' She smiled to herself. 'It was a great day . . .' she started to say and then stopped. Jen dried her hands on a dishcloth and turned to face her.

'I'm sorry,' she said, but Nat was holding her hands up.

'No, no. I didn't mean to go there again. We're OK now. We're all OK now. Aren't we?'

'I hope so.'

'Bit of a different atmosphere from December, in any case.'

Jen laughed. 'Tragedy and small children,' she said. 'That's what does it. Brings people together.'

'Except for when it rips them apart,' Nat pointed out.

'It's too stupid, isn't it?' Jen said. 'One death to pull us all apart, one to put us back together?'

'She's not gone yet,' Nat said with a small, sad smile, and she took Jen's hand and together they went back outside to the party.

Night fell and the temperature with it. They wrapped themselves up in blankets and moved a little closer to the bonfire. In her carrycot, Isabelle snuffled away gently, her fingers stretching every now and again into little starfish and then balling back into fists. Jen wondered whether you dreamed at ten weeks, and if so what about? Breasts, she assumed. What else was there?

Lilah drank more champagne than was probably advisable on her medication. Her speech became slurred and it was increasingly difficult to understand what she was saying. Zac said it was time to go to bed.

'Can't we sleep here?' she asked him and when he said no she told him to bugger off; she demanded to listen to Marianne Faithfull and when Dan fetched it she insisted on 'The Ballad of Lucy Jordan' on repeat. After she'd heard it the third time, Zac got to his feet, put his arms around her and lifted her to a sitting position.

'Let's go to bed, darling,' he said, scooping her up easily as though he were picking up a child.

She was reciting poetry as he carried her into the house, misquoting Sylvia Plath.

'The art of dying,' she proclaimed, 'I do it so very ... exceptionally ... what is it? I do it exceptionally well. Ex-theptionally. Ex-sheptionally.' She was stumbling over the word, Zac trying to hush her, Lilah starting to giggle. 'I do, though, don't I? Ex-cep-tion-al-ly well.' They could still hear her as he carried her up the stairs. 'I die much better than I lived, don't I, darling?'

Natalie took the girls to bed then, and Andrew started folding up blankets and collecting glasses.

'No, no, leave it, Andrew,' Dan told him. 'Definitely not your job. We'll do it in the morning.'

He and Jen lay back on the rugs looking up at the stars.

'It's a good thing you're doing,' Jen said.

'What is?'

'Having Lilah and Zac to stay, having us all to stay with you in your new house.'

'It's not *my* house,' he said, giving her a little nudge. 'And in any case, it's not exactly a hardship,' he said softly. 'I've loved having her here. I've loved having her back, you know? It's obviously the most awful of circumstances, but the spirit she has ... And Zac!' Dan laughed. 'God, when I met him back before Christmas I thought he was so ... vapid. Just shows what a shitty judge of character I am.'

'Well, I think we might all have been a little guilty of judging books by covers.'

'He is so strong, and I don't just mean the biceps. He never lets her see him break, you know? I've seen it, once she's gone to sleep and he's had a few beers, but he keeps it away from her. All he does is try to make her happy.' Dan's voice was husky, he laughed to cover it. 'It's inspiring.'

Her eyes on the stars, Jen reached for Dan's hand. 'I wonder what will happen to him,' she said, 'after.'

345

'Don't. I don't even want to think about it.'

They lay in silence for a while, side by side, hand in hand. Then Dan spoke. 'I owe her.'

'I'm sorry?'

'It's not why I want her here or anything, but it was about time I did something good for Lilah.'

Jen let go of Dan's hand, rolled up onto one elbow, peered over the side of the carrycot. Isabelle was fast asleep. She touched her forehead gently to see if she was cold, but she felt perfectly warm, a little piece of toast.

'I don't think you owe anyone anything, Dan,' she whispered. 'I think it's probably time everyone stops thinking about paying for stuff they did, don't you?'

'Nope,' he said, shaking his head a little. 'You don't . . . you don't really know what I did.' He fell silent for a while. Jen hovered between pressing him to explain and letting it go. 'I used her,' he said. 'After she and Andrew broke up, she came to stay. She did stuff, told me stuff . . . I used her words. I used things she did.'

'In the film?'

'Mmm-hmm. It wasn't necessarily stuff that people would recognise and go, oh yeah, Lilah did that. Not many people, anyway. But she knew. I took things from her when she was at her lowest, her most vulnerable. It was a shitty thing to do.' Now he raised himself up, propped himself on the opposite arm so that they were facing each other. 'And now,' he went on, 'now she wants me to write about her. She keeps telling me all these stories, says she wants me to immortalise her. Sometimes she's only joking about it, but sometimes I think she's serious. She goes on about what a wicked woman she is, how her life should be seen as a cautionary tale.'

Jen smiled at him. 'Well, she has got some good stories to tell,' she said.

'Yes, she has.'

'And we were all wicked in our way once, weren't we?'

He leaned forward a little, their faces were just an inch or two apart.

'Were we?' a voice said, and they looked up, and there was Andrew, standing just a few feet away, watching them.

*Letter, from Dan to Jen, dated 18 May 1996, never sent*

Jen

*I hope you're feeling better. I worry about you.*

*I still worry about you. I care about you. I can't fucking bear this, how I can't speak to you any more, one night and that's just it. We're done.*

*I love you.*

*I know, like you do, that even if you felt the same way, us being together would be a disaster, for you and for me. I'd lose my family — because that's what you guys are to me, the only thing remotely close to family I've ever had. So I know, we can't be together.*

*But this is killing me. You know what's killing me, it's when I look at you and you won't look back, you barely fucking acknowledge me, you deny me.*

*I love you.*

*I don't want to end up hating you.*

*So, yeah, I talked about other girls in front of you, I was trying to hurt your feelings.*

*Did I? Do you care?*

*You do, don't you?*

*I love you.*

*I'll find someone else, I will.*

*Only in the meantime I want to hear you say it, say that you loved me, even if it was just for a little while, I want you to acknowledge that there hasn't only ever been Jen and Conor, there was Jen and Dan too, once.*

*I want you to look me in the eye and tell me I was good enough for you to love.*

*I love you.*

Dan

## Chapter Forty-seven

~

Dan had bought bicycles, two of them, from a shop in Draguignan. One for himself, one for guests. And not just any old bikes, either. Expensive ones. Andrew found the extravagance mildly irritating, it looked to him like showing off.

'A guest bike?' he said to Natalie. 'It's ridiculous.'

'I don't know,' she said, shrugging. 'He has plenty of money, why shouldn't he spend it? Anyway, you like cycling. Now you can actually do some.'

A few days after the anniversary party, Dan suggested they take the bikes down to Villefranche.

'There's rugby on, isn't there? France versus England. We can watch that and have a beer, leave the girls to fend for themselves for a while.'

'You don't like sport,' Andrew pointed out. 'You've never liked sport.'

'I can watch rugby while drinking beer, Andrew. *You* like sport, that's the point. I thought we could just go down and hang out for a bit.'

Andrew wasn't sure why Dan's obvious effort to do things

that Andrew might enjoy was irritating him, but it was. It was as though he were trying too hard to be the sporty, back-slapping, blokey sort, it came across as fake. It *was* fake. Dan had never been like that. Dan didn't like rugby. He liked art galleries and Japanese films. Still, Andrew could at least be pleased that the sort of activities Dan was proposing were those that didn't require one to talk much. He wasn't feeling particularly conversational. He couldn't actually remember the last time he'd felt conversational.

They set out at around midday on a scorching Saturday, coasting easily down the hill, arriving at the bar in the village in no time. Andrew considered, as they sipped their beers, that the return journey – up the hill at the height of the afternoon heat with beer in their bellies – would be a lot more taxing. Dan was pretty fit, he probably didn't weigh much more now than he had at twenty-three, he'd probably find it easy. Andrew found himself wondering, rather meanly, whether that was the point. Is that why he'd bought the bikes, why he'd suggested going to watch the rugby match? He noticed that Zac hadn't been invited. Zac would have made short work of the uphill cycle. Zac would make short work of the mountain stages of the Tour de France. Andrew couldn't escape the feeling that Dan was saying something to him: fitter, richer, the man of the house. Not just any house, either, the French house.

They sat on the terrace; the bar's owner had hung a plasma screen at one end.

'You thinking about getting one of those for the house?' Andrew asked Dan.

'What? A plasma? Maybe in the barn. Not the main house. I want to keep the house as it is, you know, as I remember it. As we all remember it.'

'The way Conor intended it to be?' Andrew said, and it came out like a sneer and he wasn't sure why. Neither was Dan, who looked at him quizzically.

'Yeah, I suppose. I just want it to be ... the French house. Lovely and old and rustic and smelling of rosemary. Comfortable.'

'A nice place for a family.'

Dan laughed uneasily. 'Well, not sure I'll be able to furnish it with that ... My relationship record, you know. I don't exactly have pedigree, do I?'

'No, you don't.'

He knew he was being unkind, but anger had been building, and not just since he'd seen Dan and Jen almost kissing at the party. It started before that, when Dan bought the house. He'd turned it over in his mind a thousand times and he couldn't fathom it: why the French house? Why not the Riviera, so much more Dan's speed? Why not somewhere he could surf, or go out on the town, meet girls? Why here? He kept returning to the same thing, to Jen, and to a much older anger that dated way back to that stupid film in which (fiction, my arse) Dan ended up with Conor's girl.

That was why he'd bought the house. It was a piece of Jen. It tied him to Jen.

The rugby kicked off, but Andrew wasn't really interested. He ordered two more beers, lay back in his chair, feeling the hot sun on his arms and his neck. He closed his eyes; it was too bright even with sunglasses, the glare was starting to give him a headache.

'You feeling all right, mate?' Dan asked him.

Shielding his eyes from the sun, Andrew looked over at Dan who was grinning at him, conciliatory. Appeasing. Andrew could feel his hackles rise.

'Tell me something,' he said. 'Why did you buy it?'

'Why did I buy . . . ?'

'The house, Dan. Why'd you buy the house?'

'Ummm. Well. You know, I had kind of a hard time after Claudia left, and I thought . . .'

'Yeah, I know, you wanted to get away, but why *this* house, Dan? Why the French house?' His tone was short and nasty and he could see from Dan's expression that he didn't understand why Andrew was being so aggressive, but Andrew couldn't stop, if anything it just made him angrier: little diffident Dan, playing the sensitive card – what was it Jen used to call him? The lost boy.

'I like it here,' Dan said. 'And I thought . . .'

'You thought that if you owned the house, you'd have a link to Jen, an unbreakable one.'

Dan looked sadly down at his beer. 'Well, not just Jen. All of you.'

'Right.'

Andrew decided to drop it. He was getting pissed off, and he was hurting Dan's feelings, it was pointless. He looked up at the screen, tried to focus on the game. The French scored two tries in quick succession. The young men at the table a few feet from theirs cheered, and one of them turned around and raised his glass in their direction. Andrew glowered at him, waved at the waiter, ordered another beer.

'It sounds stupid,' Dan piped up, 'but when I was thinking about things, after Claudia left, I realised that I'd done a lot of writing the summer I was here.'

'Of course, the masterpiece,' Andrew said.

Dan gave an exasperated little sigh. 'It wasn't that just, I had loads of ideas while I was here, it just felt like a good place to me, a place of inspiration.'

352

'Was it the place, though, was that the inspiration? Or was it the people you were with?'

Dan shrugged. 'Well, the people, I suppose, but the place as well, it's conducive . . .' He gave up, sighed again, spread his hands out. 'I thought you'd be pleased that I'd bought it. I thought you'd be happy that you could still use it – because you can, you know, any time you like.' Andrew nodded and sipped his beer. 'What is it you're so pissed off about? You think that I'm somehow going to spoil it? Or neglect it? What is it that's bothering you?' Dan was starting to get annoyed now, no longer quite so conciliatory. 'Or maybe this has nothing to do with me or the house – maybe this is something about you and Natalie, because it's obvious there's a problem there . . .'

Andrew leaned forward abruptly in his seat, his face close to Dan's, his voice low.

'You don't know the first thing about us, so don't fucking go there. You have no idea what a real relationship is like, what it takes. You've never had anything but fantasy.' Dan put his hands up in conciliation, but Andrew wasn't finished. 'Since you ask, what's *bothering* me about it all is that I don't think I like your motives for buying the place. You know it was always Conor and Jen's plan to live in the house, don't you? You remember how they talked about it?'

'Yeah, of course I do. It was on that list we wrote . . .'

'Exactly. They were going to live here and raise their kids here, and now you're here, and Jen's here, with her baby, and why is it that I get the feeling that you're trying to step into his shoes? That you've been trying to take his place ever since he died?'

Dan put down his beer, pushed it to the centre of the table. 'I honestly don't know what your problem is,' he said. He got to his feet and walked away.

Andrew slumped further down in his chair. The French were now eighteen points ahead, the English were having a nightmare. He wished someone would turn the television off. He wished he hadn't come, he wished he hadn't drunk three beers in forty minutes. He wished he hadn't been so unpleasant to Dan, he wished he could look at Jen the same way he used to, but something about the other night just made him feel uneasy. He wished he could find himself again, because he appeared to be lost. Mid-life crisis, perhaps? Maybe he should buy a car like Dan's. Well, not like Dan's, of course, because he couldn't afford that. Or have an affair? With whom? Ms Gaitskill, head of English? Miss Turner, the twenty-something French teacher? The problem he had, the problem he'd always have, was that he loved his wife, no matter what. He'd realised that back in December, in a room in a hotel not far from where he was sitting right at that moment.

He ordered another beer. He could feel the skin on the back of his neck starting to burn. He re-angled his chair so that he was sitting with his back to the rugby match. He noticed that Dan's bicycle was still there. He wondered where he'd gone. Beyond the buzz of the commentary and the crowd, he could hear church bells, the chugging of a tractor somewhere in the distance. His eyelids drooped.

A shadow came over him, someone kicked his foot.

'Come on then,' Dan was standing in front of him, blocking the light. 'Let's go back. Don't know about you but I could do with some of that mac and cheese Zac made last night. I think there's still some in the fridge.' He reached out his hand and Andrew took it. His head swam as he was hauled to his feet, his T-shirt clung to his back and belly with sweat, his mouth felt as though something had crawled in there and died. He was parched.

'I've got to get something to drink before we head up the hill,' he said to Dan. 'Not beer, water I mean. And a coffee.'

They left the bar and pushed the bikes across to the little café on the opposite side of the square, ordered expressos and glasses of water.

'I'm sorry about earlier,' Andrew said. 'I don't know what the hell's wrong with me these days, can't stop rubbing people up the wrong way.'

Dan sipped his coffee, didn't reply.

'Seriously, Dan . . .'

'No. Don't. There's part of what you said . . . some of what you said isn't right, exactly, but it wasn't exactly wrong, either.'

Andrew rubbed his eyes with his fists, blinked hard, looked up at Dan. 'OK,' he said.

'It's not really any of your business,' Dan went on, his voice flat and even, devoid of emotion, 'but since it appears to bother you so much and since . . . Well. Since I'd rather there not be bad blood between us, since I want for us all to be able to be in each other's lives again, I may as well set the record straight.'

'OK,' Andrew said again.

Dan cleared his throat and Andrew resisted the temptation to shout, 'Just bloody get on with it!'

'I am in love with her. I have been, I suppose, on and off, for a long time. Since university. I don't see that that's anything to be ashamed of, I don't see that I should have to apologise to you for that. She's been married, for God's sake, she's had a child. I know you'll always see her a certain way, but it's been a long time since she was Conor's girlfriend.'

Andrew said nothing, there was nothing he could say. All he knew was that those words sounded wrong coming out of Dan's mouth.

'I'm sorry it bothers you that I bought the house. I'm sorry it bothers you that Jen and I . . . well. Actually, there's nothing going on with Jen and I, so I don't really see what you have to be bothered about. There's nothing going on right now, in any case. I'm not going to sit here and pretend that there isn't part of me that hopes that one day there will be something between us. As for the house, Andrew, I didn't buy it because I wanted to *be* Conor. I bought it because it means something to me, and yes, it means something to Jen, it means something to all of us. I didn't want to let it go. Neither did you, as I recall. The difference is that I had the means to do something about it. That's all. Is that all right with you?' Andrew said nothing. 'You know what, I don't really care if it's all right with you or not. You ready to go?' He got to his feet and walked over to the bikes before Andrew had a chance to answer him.

Dan set off at a gentle pace, but once the gradient started to increase, he attacked the hill like a pro, standing up on his pedals and pushing hard. Andrew tried to keep up, but with every turn, with every hairpin, he was aware that Dan was pulling further and further away from him. His legs were leaden, sweat poured into his eyes, his heart beat fit to break his ribs. Ahead of him, the road shimmered in the heat. He felt nauseous, breathless, paranoid. He was going to die of a heart attack, here, on the side of the road, eating Dan Parker's dust. He dismounted and pushed his bike into the shade of a tree. From somewhere way above him, a voice called out, 'You all right down there?' and he had to summon all his willpower not to pick up the bike and hurl it over the edge of the mountain.

Sunburnt and hung over, he slept fitfully that night and rose at dawn feeling sheepish and desperately thirsty. He slipped out of bed, leaving Natalie sleeping, and crept downstairs to make coffee. He found Jen in the living room, dozing off in the armchair with Isabelle in her arms.

'Oh, sorry,' Jen whispered when she saw him, 'did she wake you?'

'Not at all, didn't hear a thing. Has she been crying?'

'Mmm. Not a good night.'

'You want a coffee?' he asked.

'Actually I was thinking of taking her for a little walk, seeing if I couldn't get her to sleep for a few hours now. You want to come?'

They popped a weakly protesting Isabelle into the pushchair and set off down the driveway. The sun was rising across the valley, but the air was still cool, the grass wet with dew. The world smelled fresh. They walked down the driveway, turning right at the road. They trudged up the hill in silence for the first couple of hundred yards or so, the steeper section. Once the road levelled out, they stopped for a moment to get their breath back and Andrew asked: 'Did you talk to Dan last night?'

'Not really. I was in Lilah's room when he came back. He popped in for a moment. She had a pretty bad evening, so I didn't really chat to him.'

'Oh. Sorry, I hadn't realised she'd had a bad day.'

'S'OK. She fell asleep in the end and slept pretty soundly after that, I think. I was up quite a bit in the night with Isabelle and I didn't hear her.' She turned to look at him. 'Why do you ask? About Dan, I mean?'

'We had a bit of a row.' He thought he'd better tell her, give her his side before she heard Dan's, which was bound to be imaginatively embellished.

'Did you? What about?'

'About you, actually.'

357

'About me?' she laughed. 'What have I done?'

Andrew shrugged. 'No idea. What have you done?'

Jen stopped walking for a moment. Andrew turned and looked at her. 'Andrew, what are you talking about?'

'We had an argument about you. About him and you, the way he feels about you . . .'

Her eyes widened, she looked shocked.

'I don't want to talk about this with you,' she said bluntly, then she turned around and walked briskly away from him, the pushchair almost running away from her as she marched down the hill.

He called after her, a little half-heartedly, but she didn't respond, so he carried on alone. He walked for a long time, all the way up to the very top of the hill behind the house, then he turned and walked back down, slowly, turning everything over in his mind as he went, the things Dan had said, Jen's bizarre reaction, her over-reaction, and in the pit of his stomach something gnawed at him like a rodent. *Dan doesn't like rugby, Dan likes art galleries and Japanese cinema.* He'd walked about three quarters of the way back down the hill when he met Jen walking up to meet him. She was alone, without the baby, carrying a flask.

'I thought you might like a cup of coffee,' she called out when she saw him. 'And I thought maybe you and I should talk.' They left the road and climbed up the verge together, walking across a field and into the woods. They walked until they found a clearing where they sat down, each leaning against a tree trunk. Jen poured them both a mug of sweet black coffee.

'She talked about him again, last night,' Jen said. 'Lilah. She keeps talking about Conor being in the woods. I've no idea where that comes from. He didn't even spend much time up here, did he? None of us came up here much, did we, except maybe to look for firewood.'

Andrew shook his head. 'Not that I remember. I think she just sees shadows, sees things move. You do, if you stare at the trees for long enough, especially at night.'

'Yeah, I used to freak myself out doing that.'

'And being here, with us . . . Conor's going to be the one she thinks of, isn't he? The one she imagines.'

'I suppose so.' She sipped her coffee. Her head was bent, hair falling forward, and when she looked up at him again her mouth was set in a line, determined. 'Sorry about before, running off like that. I was a bit . . . taken aback. I didn't realise. That you knew. About that. Me and Dan.' There were two spots of colour in her cheeks, a deep, blooming red.

Her and Dan. It was quiet then, just the gentlest of breezes pushing a few dead leaves around the forest floor, the occasional chirp of birdsong. Jen and Dan. Dan who likes Japanese cinema. Jen who lied.

'I don't know,' he said. 'About you and Dan. What is there to know?'

'Forget it, Andrew,' she said, shaking her head. 'Just forget it.' She got to her feet. 'Shall we get going?'

'No, hang on. What did you think I knew?'

'Look, I don't even know why we're talking about this. You said something about having an argument with Dan about me. Maybe I misunderstood you. It doesn't matter. Let's just go home now, OK? Dan's watching Isabelle, I shouldn't leave them too long.'

'Playing Daddy is he?'

Jen gave him a look he hadn't seen for a very long time. The last time he'd seen it she'd been looking at Conor; it usually meant he was dangerously close to crossing a line. 'Don't be childish, Andrew.' He was still sitting at the foot of his tree, looking up at her, towering over him.

'So, you and him. You and Dan. When did this happen?'

'Andrew . . .'

'When? College? Here? When?'

'London,' she said quietly.

'London? When? *Jennifer*? When?'

'A few months before the accident.'

Andrew felt as though the ground were shifting beneath him, he actually put his mug down, put his hands on the clammy earth next to his legs as if to steady himself. Right then he had a flashback, the clearest possible memory of standing outside a tube station after an evening in the pub, Conor unsteady on his feet, looking over at Andrew, expression wounded, saying, *She lied to me, Andrew, she lied to me.*

'You're telling me you cheated on Conor?'

'It was a mistake.' Her voice was tiny, broken. She was standing a few feet away from him, staring at the ground; perhaps she felt it moving too.

'Did he know?' She shuffled her feet, turned away from him. Andrew leapt up, grabbed her arm and pulled her roughly round to face him. 'Jen, did he know? Did he know when he died?'

'No,' she said, 'no. I don't think . . . No, he didn't.'

'You don't think so, or he didn't?'

'Andrew, Jesus. What does it matter now?'

She started to cry. For a fraction of a second he felt the old impulse to go to her, to help her – this was Jen, his little sister, the girl he was supposed to protect. Just a fraction of a second and the urge was gone.

'What does it matter? How can you ask me that? Fucking hell, all this time,' he was shouting at her, 'all this time, I've felt so sorry for you, knowing that your heart was broken, that you lost the love of your life, that you lost him because of me, and it wasn't true. It wasn't true! You don't think that matters? It matters to me, Jen.'

He started to walk away from her, out of the woods; he could hear her crying behind him and it made him want to slap her. She ran after him, grabbed his hand, but he yanked it away from her.

'I *was* heartbroken,' she said. 'Of course I bloody was. And I did love him, you know I did, don't you dare suggest that I didn't. Dan and I made a mistake, one stupid mistake, that was all it was. Do you not think that mistake cost me? Do you not think it just made everything worse?' Andrew stopped at the treeline, looking out into the dazzling sunshine of a perfect August morning. She was standing close behind him, he could hear her breathing, quick and ragged. 'I'm sorry, Andrew. I know it's a horrible thing that I did, I know you must be disappointed in me.'

'We have . . . all of us . . . behaved despicably, haven't we?' he said. 'Not one of us is innocent.'

She let out a sharp breath, exasperated. 'Of course we aren't. Did you really think you could get to this stage in life and be innocent?'

He shook his head. 'Maybe I thought we could be better than this.'

'Oh, Andrew. Better than what? You've lived a good life, so has Nat. So has Dan, for that matter. Christ, the mistakes we made twenty years ago are just that, mistakes we made a long time ago. They're not indelible stains, are they?'

He turned to face her, looked her directly in the eye. 'You might think that I'm stupid, or naïve or something, but the truth is that I am disappointed. I am disappointed in you. In myself. I'm disappointed in all of us.'

Jen pushed her hands through her hair, she looked different, tired, ten years older.

'Did *he* ever disappoint you, Andrew? Tell me, did Conor ever do anything you thought wasn't good or honourable? Was he a saint? Because I think that somewhere along the line you canonised him. Did he always behave impeccably?'

'No. No, of course not, but he didn't betray you, Jen.'

She took his hand, squeezed it, and dropped it.

'No, he didn't, that's true.' Her head dropped, her chin almost to her chest. 'I'm sorry I haven't lived up to your standards, Andrew. But sometimes I wonder whether anyone could have.' He started to object, but she stopped him. 'I never asked you to be responsible for me. I think it's time you stopped thinking of me as your little sister. I don't need you to be my protector. And I don't need you to judge me, either.' She walked past him and out into the sunshine, turned back to look at him. 'You know that's why I left, don't you? I couldn't be around you all, feeling sorry for me, feeling I was deserving of sympathy, after what I'd done. My entire life since then has been defined by two things, by a mistake and by an accident. I believe that it's time that changed, that I start doing the defining for myself.' She walked off down the hill, flask in hand, long hair swinging down her back, and she was young again. He blinked the tears from his eyes and squinted a little, he might just as well have been looking at her twenty years ago.

He stayed in the forest for a long time, staring into the heart of the woods, into the darkness, hoping (ridiculously) that like

Lilah had he might catch a glimpse of an old friend. It was cool in the shade, and if you sat still for long enough, other life started to make itself known, creatures scurrying in the undergrowth, birds calling overhead, insects pottering along across the leaves. It became meditative, mesmerising. He wasn't sure how long he sat there – he wasn't wearing a watch and he didn't have his phone – but it seemed like a long time. He could feel his blood start to cool, some of the anger and guilt seeping away. He was left with the remnants, which felt something like sadness, unease. And a feeling of foolishness, too, that he'd been naïve, idealistic – worse, a hypocrite. He'd been looking at everyone through rose-tinted spectacles and he'd had them ripped off and now the world just looked grey.

Eventually, he heard footsteps approaching and he became quite afraid, perhaps he was going to see the ghost after all. It was Nat, come to look for him.

'I was starting to get worried,' she said, easing herself down gently beside him. 'Jen said I might find you up here. She didn't say why.' He couldn't bring himself to explain it, he didn't want to tell her. 'You thinking about Lilah?' she asked, slipping her arm through the crook of his, pulling his body a little closer to hers.

'No, it's not that.' He took a deep breath. 'I was thinking I should go back home with the girls on Monday.'

'Oh.'

The plan had been to send them back to their grandparents for a week, then Andrew and Nat would join them the following week for the start of the school term. But he wasn't sure he could stand it now, he wasn't sure he could bear to be around Jen and Dan for another day, let alone another ten.

'I'm not sure we should be sending them back on their own,'

he said, his eyes firmly ahead, not looking at his wife. 'It's been difficult for them, don't you think? I know they've coped well, meeting everyone and dealing with the situation here, Lilah being so ill and everything, but I think it would be best if I went back with them, got them settled in at home before term starts.'

'You're probably right. We'll go on Monday. I'll explain to Lilah, she'll understand. I can always come back on weekends to spend time with her.'

'No,' Andrew said, disentangling himself from her arm and getting to his feet. 'That's not what I meant. I mean I think *I* should go back with the girls. You stay on here. It's best that way.' He'd never been any good at lying to her, he may as well tell the truth. 'I could do with some time by myself,' he said.

'Oh.' The silence seemed to stretch out for days. 'You mean, some time away from me.' She looked up at him, big green eyes beseeching.

'Yes,' he said, and he saw her flinch, it felt like a knife in his chest. 'I need some time away from you.' He reached out his hand to pull her up, but she waved it away. He could see the pain in her face as she got to her feet. They walked back to the house in silence.

He took Lilah out to lunch the day before he left. They drove all the way to Digne-les-Bains, and sat on a sun-drenched terrace overlooking the Bléone River, eating oysters. Lilah drank three glasses of champagne and after lunch insisted that she felt like a walk, so they ambled along the road beside the river, she leaning heavily on his arm, pausing every ten paces or so to catch her breath. After a few hundred yards they came to a bench, where they sat down and watched a mother duck solicitously ushering her ducklings from the bank into the water.

Lilah rested her head on Andrew's shoulder and slipped her

bony little hand into his. Her skin felt dry and papery, like old parchment.

'What's going on, Drew?' she asked him, and before he had time to reply, she went on: 'Don't say nothing, because I'm not stupid. Things are all wrong with Nat, they have been since you got here. And now you're leaving early, without her? And don't think I haven't noticed the thing with Jen, either, the fact that every time she comes into the room, you walk out. And every time Dan comes into the room the muscle in your jaw tenses and your hands ball into fists. You're pissed off with everyone. Everyone except me, which makes a nice change.' She snuggled closer to him and closed her eyes. 'But I don't want you to leave like this, so angry. Tell me, please?'

He poured it out, all of it. His irrational anger over Dan buying the house, which now didn't seem irrational at all, because he had been right about ulterior motives. The thing with Jen, which, he knew, was none of his business, but he couldn't help but feel the betrayal as though it were his own, he couldn't help but feel aggrieved, furious, on Conor's behalf. And on his own, too, because he felt as though he'd been duped, as though somehow he'd spent all these years caring about a woman who didn't even exist. Lilah opened her eyes wide and laughed at that.

'You thought Jen was perfect, did you? Come on, Andrew.'

'You knew?'

'No. Christ, I didn't know *that*. I knew that Dan was a little bit obsessed with her . . . He used to talk about her all the time – you probably don't remember this, but after you and I split up, I went to stay with him for a while.'

'I remember.'

'Well, he was constantly banging on about her then, he

talked about her all the time. It didn't seem that weird, though, we were all worried about her then, and it was obvious that he'd always felt *something* for her. I didn't think it was reciprocated though. I never thought she would . . . you know. I understand why you're shocked, why you're upset, I would never have thought that Jen would have strayed. But still. She did. She made a mistake.'

'That's exactly what she said.'

'And she's right. Drew, my darling, you know how I love you but you do set impossibly high standards . . .'

'That's what she said too,' Andrew replied. 'But frankly, I don't think it's actually an "impossibly high standard"–' he found himself making bunny ears with his fingers – 'to ask someone not to cheat on their boyfriend with one of his close friends.'

Lilah looked up at him with a lazy smile, raised an eyebrow.

'That was different, Lilah.'

'Really? Was it better or worse?'

'There were circumstances.'

'Drew. There are always circumstances. And even when there aren't circumstances, haven't you ever made a really stupid mistake?'

'You know very well I have.'

'Well then. I have, too, as you well know. I've made hundreds. Thousands, possibly. So really, is it so terrible, what she did? Think about it, if it hadn't been for what went after, losing him like that, we might all have seen things in a rather different light, mightn't we? And, of course, Jen didn't know, did she, what was coming? Just try and imagine, will you, how much worse it is for her.'

He looked down at her, her wispy blonde hair and her tiny,

angled features. 'When did you get so wise and rational?' he asked.

'Impending doom,' she said with a smile, 'gives one perspective.' She was shivering a little; he took off his jacket and laid it over her.

'You want to get going?' he asked.

'No,' she said, 'I don't. I want to sit here with you, in the sun, until we've got this all sorted out. Actually, I'd quite happily sit here, in the sun, forever, if that were an option.'

He felt tears pricking the backs of his eyes. Blinking them back, he pulled her closer still, he kissed the top of her head.

'The important thing about all that, Andrew, the really important thing, is that Conor never knew.'

'She wasn't sure about that . . .'

'But we'd have known if he'd known, wouldn't we? He would have kicked the shit out of Dan, for starters. And he would have told you. Don't you remember,' she asked, opening her eyes again, looking up at him, 'the day of the crash, we were at the pub, and they were kissing in the car park, I yelled at Jen to hurry up? Remember that? They wouldn't have been like that, he wouldn't have kissed her like that . . .' She was right, of course she was. He didn't know. He couldn't have known. 'So, you're disappointed and angry with her, but he isn't. He died thinking she loved him just the way she always had. And even if she didn't – and we don't know whether she did or not – but even if she didn't, it doesn't matter. All that matters is what he knew.'

'So,' he said, leaning back on the bench, tilting his face up to the sun, 'it doesn't matter what you do, it only matters if you get caught? That's what you're saying?'

'That's exactly what I'm saying.'

She was joking, but there was a logic to what she said, a peculiarly Lilah-ish sort of logic. All that mattered was that Conor didn't end this life feeling that he had lost her.

'In any case,' Lilah said, her voice starting to slow a little, a touch of slur on her s's, 'all this is a sideshow. You'll sort things out with Jen and Dan, and even if you don't, it won't be the end of the world. But whatever it is with Nat, that's real. That's what matters.'

They sat there for a while longer, until she fell asleep. Andrew picked her up and carried her to the car; she didn't wake until the moment Zac lifted her up at the end of the journey.

It was Zac who came down to fetch Andrew later that night.

'She's asking for you,' he said.

Her room was dark, illuminated only by a sliver of moonlight coming through the window. Lilah lay propped up on her pillows, blankets and throws piled on top of her.

'Don't turn on the light,' she whispered as he entered the room, 'my head hurts.'

'Lilah,' he said softly, 'we can talk in the morning, before I go.'

'No,' she whispered. 'No, no. I might not wake up.'

'Lilah . . .'

'I don't mean I'm going to die, you idiot. I just mean that sometimes it takes me ages to get going in the morning, and you have to leave early, and I don't want to leave things as they are. I want you to tell me what you plan to do about Natalie.'

His head dropped. 'I don't know. Something is broken . . . I, we, broke something. Her and I, I mean, not you and I. We broke something and I don't know . . . I don't know if I have the strength to fix it. I feel like all my fight is gone. Just like that. I

368

used to hold things together, you know? I'm not sure I can any longer.'

'Andrew.' Lilah's voice was a breath. 'You don't have to be so strong all the time. You aren't responsible for everyone.'

'She says that, you say that, Jen says it. I don't know . . .' His voice cracked a little, he felt as though he were going to cry and he wasn't sure why. 'I feel as though I lost myself, somewhere that weekend before Christmas, and in the weeks that followed. I think that so much of me was caught up in how Nat sees me, in what our life is together. Do you know what she said to me, Lilah? That she didn't want to be my penance any longer. I don't know what to do with that. She says things like that, she talks about our life as though it weren't a good one, and I just don't know what to say, it's as though we haven't been in the same marriage all this time, as though we haven't been living the same life.'

'Some of those things . . .' Her voice faltered a little, her head dropped, her fingers pressed to her temples.

'Lilah?'

'It hurts.'

He moved closer to her, put his arm around her shoulders and pulled her to his chest.

'Some things are said in anger. But Andrew, there is a side of you . . .' She stopped talking, breathed deeply.

'Lilah, you need to lie down, you need to rest now. We'll talk again tomorrow.'

'No, no!' Her voice was a hiss, a harsh whisper as though from an old woman. 'We have to fix this, you have to fix this. Some part of you is only about atonement, she sees that. You've done enough. You have paid your price. Now stop. You're done now. You've done everything right. You married a woman, such a woman! And she loves you. You raised beautiful, clever girls. They are the best of you both, those two, they're spirited, they're clever, they're beautiful. You worked hard. You have lived a good life.' Her face was pressed against him, her tears soaking through his sweatshirt. 'I envy you. I wish I had lived the life you have. I was always planning to do something right, but somehow I never got round to it. Isn't that silly?'

They sat in the dark, he held her and he talked softly about the things she'd done right: the way she loved people, totally, without restraint, the care she took of her mother, her generosity. He wasn't sure she was listening, wasn't sure that she could even hear him, but at last the crying stopped and her body went limp and she fell asleep in his arms. Afterwards, once he'd disentangled himself and slipped off the bed, he stood in the doorway for a long time, watching her. He was afraid to leave, so sure that he would never see her again.

*Darling Drew,*

*You'll know by now, Natalie will have told you. Don't be sad. Well, you can be a bit sad, but not for too long. As I keep telling Zac, I wasn't making a terribly good go of things anyway.*

*Laugh. You have to.*

*This letter is just for you. Don't show it to anyone and for God's sake if you're reading it out loud to the family at the breakfast table, stop.*

*This is just for you and me. I wanted to tell you this before we are all together again, before I have your wife at my bedside, I wanted to tell you that I'm sorry, but that I regret nothing. That I wouldn't exchange that night in the auberge for anything. OK, that's a lie. I would exchange it for a brain free of tumour or for Conor's life. There aren't many things I would exchange it for.*

*I don't regret it because the way that you and I ended was terribly wrong, and this wasn't. This felt like friendship, it felt like love, it felt like you and me aged twenty-one. And for that, darling Drew, I am grateful.*

*Please don't tell her.*

*I hope to see you very soon.*

*With love,*

*Lilah*

# Chapter Forty-eight

~

*September 2013*

The holidaymakers were gone, the pop-up beach bars had all closed up, they'd packed up their tables and chairs and marquees and gone wherever they all went until next summer. Next summer. The promised land.

Lilah, Natalie and Jen were alone on the beach, save for a handful of pensioners shuffling along the sand or sitting on the promenade, feeding the gulls. They'd found themselves a sheltered spot at the furthest end of the stretch of pale yellow sand, and Jen and Nat had erected one of those windbreaker things, although there was only the gentlest of breezes. Still, it was nice, it gave them the sensation of being alone in the world with just the sand and the water and the birds overhead for company. Lilah sat on a deckchair, a towel flung over her legs. She couldn't bear to look at them any longer.

'Like a chicken,' she said to Natalie. 'I look exactly like a chicken.'

When she'd stepped on the scales the previous morning, she'd weighted ninety-seven pounds.

'And at least three pounds of that is tumour,' she said.

She was already feeling sleepy – they'd got up early to drive to the beach. It was just going to be a day trip, and Jen and Nat weren't even sure that was a good idea. Lilah, however, had insisted. She'd been feeling a little stronger the past couple of days and she had to take advantage of the good days, she was determined to do that. Plus, she wanted to spend quality time with the girls: Zac would be back from London at the weekend, and Nat was leaving on Monday, so who knew when the three of them would be together again? When, if.

Jen looked distracted. She kept checking her phone. This was the first time she'd left the baby for more than an hour or two at a time, and she'd left her with Dan.

'Dan, of all people,' she fretted. 'He'll probably get caught up in his writing and forget all about her. She'll be starving and howling and wet by the time we get home.'

Natalie rolled her eyes. 'Bullshit. He won't do a scrap of work, he's going to sit there making goo-goo noises and funny faces at her all day. I don't think I've ever seen a man so smitten with an infant. Andrew was never that sappy over our two.'

'He'll make a good dad,' Lilah said. Jen looked at her sharply. 'I don't mean to Isabelle, necessarily. God, you're so touchy. I was speaking generally. Although, if it came to it, he'd probably be a good dad to Isabelle. All I'm saying is, he'll be good at it, when it happens for him.'

'I'm not sure it will, though,' Natalie said, giving Jen the side eye. Jen either didn't notice or was ignoring her. Nat waited for a couple of seconds and then asked, 'Do you think it will happen for him, Jen?'

'How should I know?' she asked, grumpily. 'Why are you asking me?'

Nat made a guilty face at Lilah, who just laughed.

'Why do you think she's asking you? You do know that the whole Dan and Jen cat is out of the bag, don't you?'

'There is no Dan and Jen cat,' Jen muttered.

'If you say so,' Lilah said archly, closing her eyes and relaxing back into her deckchair.

When she opened her eyes again, Jen was sitting up dead straight, picking the nail polish off her toes, a deep furrow between her brows.

'Jen,' Lilah said. 'Chill. We were only joking.'

'It isn't funny,' she said.

Lilah looked over at Natalie, who shrugged. 'Oh, come on. What are you so worried about? Andrew? Because, seriously, he's just going to have to get over it.'

'It's not that,' Jen said, shaking her head, squinting out to sea. 'That isn't the problem.' She paused for a few moments, she was looking up at the horizon, she brought her hand up to shield her eyes from the sun. 'It's just difficult. Things are difficult. I do have feelings for Dan, but I just don't know if I can be with him. It's complicated.'

'How so?' Nat asked her. 'Not Nicolas, surely?'

'God, no. If I never see him again for the rest of my life it'll be too soon.' Almost as she was saying the words she shot Lilah an anxious glance. Lilah shook her head with a smile. They did this now. They blushed at references to 'the rest of my life', they got terribly overwrought if anyone said, 'I'd rather die . . .' It was sweet, endearing really, but it was also doing her head in.

'Well then? Is it Isabelle? Because I'm serious, he really does seem to adore her, and it's not just the thing where she's a novelty, and fun to play with.'

'Because let's face it,' Lilah said drily, 'she isn't that much fun to play with yet.'

'Lilah!' Nat admonished her.

'No, it's true,' Jen admitted. 'She really isn't that much fun yet.'

'In any case,' Natalie said with a sigh, 'what I meant was that he's happy to muck in, to do the boring stuff. I can quite easily see him changing nappies and puréeing apples and getting up in the middle of the night if you're too tired.'

'Oh, I know. I know. I think that he'd actually be rather good at all the domesticity. To be honest, I haven't even been considering practicalities, that's not why I'm . . .' She tailed off.

'Conflicted?' Lilah offered.

'For want of a better word.'

'You're not in love with him?' Nat suggested.

'Oh, she is,' Lilah said. 'I've seen the way she looks at him.'

It was a funny thing about being ill, Lilah had noticed that people became less guarded around her. Well, they were guarded about some things – any discussion of health or death or plans for next year were obviously off the table – but she felt as though sometimes they forgot that she was there, that she was watching, perhaps because she was quiet, immobile. A sickly piece of furniture. In any case, she'd seen glances exchanged, between Dan and Jen, the way their hands touched when they passed Isabelle between them, the way Jen watched him when he was sitting at the seat in the living-room window, writing in his notebook. It was unmistakeable.

Jen remained silent, she continued to ruin her pedicure.

'So what is it then?' Nat asked. 'If it's not practicalities, and you do feel something for him, then . . .'

Jen looked over at her, her face grave. 'There are things you don't know. Things no one knows,' she said.

375

'Well, that sounds ominous,' Lilah said. 'But if you're talking about you and Dan, Andrew told me. And I told Nat. So we know all about that. I mean, we don't know the details, I don't think we want to know the details . . .'

Natalie, catching the expression on Jen's face, said: 'You don't have to tell us if you don't want to.'

'Yes, she does,' Lilah said.

'Lilah.'

'If not now, then when? Tell me, even if it's just me. It might help.'

'I got pregnant.' Jen blurted it out so loudly they all jumped. 'Sorry,' she said in a whisper. 'I got pregnant.'

'You mean, other than with Isabelle?' Lilah asked.

'Obviously,' Natalie said, sucking her teeth at Lilah.

'Yes.' Jen hung her head, she put her chin on her knees and closed her eyes. 'Ninety-six. A few months before the crash. I had an abortion. Conor never knew.'

'Oh,' Natalie said.

Lilah was quiet for a moment, then she said: 'Is that it? I don't understand. I mean, I know that's not very nice and everything, but how does it affect you now, how does it affect you and . . .' She broke off. 'Oh.'

'Oh!' Natalie said.

'I don't know,' Jen said. She looked up at them, mortified. 'It sounds like the most horrible thing in the world, the most awful, horrendous thing . . .'

'No, it doesn't, Jen.'

'I didn't know. Who the father was. Fuck's sake, Lilah, of course it sounds awful, it sounds like I should be on the *Jeremy Kyle Show.*'

Lilah laughed. 'You wouldn't get anywhere near Jeremy

376

Kyle, sweetheart, not unless you were choosing between your brother and your cousin as the father of your child. You slept with two men, both of whom you had feelings for, at least one of whom, and probably both, you were in love with. It's hardly the stuff of great scandal.'

Natalie moved back a little so that the three of them could sit facing each other, a tiny closed circle. 'Jen, why didn't you say anything? We could have helped you.'

'Nat, you would have been horrified. I was horrified. I was ashamed,' she said. She took a deep breath. 'And to be honest, I didn't even allow myself to think about it. I found out, I booked the appointment, I got it done, as quickly as I could. I never gave myself the opportunity to think twice about it because I couldn't bear to. But now . . . You know how Dan feels about family, about his childhood, about having missed out on having a family? And now I'm thinking about being with him – can I do that, without telling him? I mean, I think telling him would be a mistake, it would be an awful thing to do because then he'd know, or at least wonder about, this thing, this child he'd missed out on. But not telling him, it seems such a dishonest way to start something . . .'

Lilah cut in. 'Don't you dare tell him,' she said, her voice almost menacing. 'Don't ever tell him. Nothing, absolutely nothing good can come of that.'

A cloud passed in front of the sun, it felt chilly for just a few moments, then the shadow passed and it was warm once more. Jen started to talk again: 'I've wanted to tell you for such a long time. Not because I wanted you all to know about my horrible behaviour, but because I thought it might help everyone understand what happened afterwards, the way I ran.'

'You didn't have to explain . . .' Natalie started to say, but Lilah cut in.

'Nat, let her say it,' she said, and Jen smiled at her and took her hand.

'I thought . . . at the time, I thought there would be time,' she said, shooting another anxious glance at Lilah, 'to make amends. To Conor. To make up for the things I'd done, even if . . . even if he didn't know about those things. I thought there would be marriage, a baby. Another baby. And then there wasn't. Then everything was just gone. The life I thought I was going to have, it was just gone.' She took a deep breath, she flapped her hands around at the sides of her face, the way women do when they're trying not to cry. 'That was one thing, that was bad enough, but the worst part, the thing that I couldn't get past was how casually I'd treated it, how carelessly. Months before he died I betrayed him, and I got rid of his child as though it were nothing. I treated what I had as though it were dispensable. Replaceable. As though *he* were replaceable.' She was gripping Lilah's hand so hard it hurt. 'For years I couldn't get over that. I felt as though I deserved everything I got, that I deserved to be lonely, to be punished. And now I just keep thinking, what if I'd stayed, what if I hadn't run away? Maybe things would have been different, maybe I could have . . .'

'Could have what? Held us all together?' Lilah shook her head. 'No, you couldn't, Jen. You think that if you'd been around that Andrew and Nat wouldn't have fallen in love, or Dan wouldn't have written his film or a million other things wouldn't have happened to pull us apart. We were *twenty-something*, for God's sake. You don't stay friends with the people you love when you're twenty. Or if you do, you're very lucky. I think it's a miracle, quite frankly, that we're all talking to each other now.'

They sat quietly for a minute or two, then Lilah said: 'I meant what I said before, Jen. Don't ever tell Dan about the child. And don't tell Andrew either. It's not the same for them, they won't understand. And Dan will feel it as a loss, no matter that you don't know whether the child was his, no matter that even if it was, he probably wouldn't have wanted it at twenty-four. You don't have to be honest about everything in relationships, Jen. That's a lie, it's a Hollywood lie. If the truth is all that's holding you back, just let go of it.'

Jen went for a swim, Nat went to buy ice creams. Lilah dozed in the sun, watching spots of orange and flashes of purple make patterns in the darkness. Then a flash of blinding, agonising white.

She woke up with what felt like a hangover, head aching, hands trembling, white lines wavering at the edge of her vision. She asked for her ice cream.

'I ate it,' Nat said sheepishly. 'You've been asleep for three quarters of an hour. You want me to go and get another one?'

'Just water would be good.'

Nat handed her the bottle. It hurt to swallow; she wondered whether she was getting a throat infection, or whether she'd just fallen asleep with her mouth open. 'Jen still swimming?' she asked.

'No, she went for a walk, over to the other end of the beach. I think she's gone in search of a place to have lunch. Are you hungry?'

'Not really,' Lilah said. The thought of getting up and making her way to a restaurant made her feel weary. Hell, the thought of having to chew her food made her feel weary. If she could just stay here, in the sun. That would be good.

'Come and sit by me, Nat,' she said.

Natalie shuffled her deckchair over so that they were sitting side by side. Lilah leaned in closer to her and whispered, 'You have to fix it, Nat. This thing with Andrew. You have to fix it.'

'We will, Lilo,' she said, patting Lilah's hand. 'Don't worry about us.'

'Don't patronise me, Natalie,' Lilah said, withdrawing her hand. 'I'm serious.'

'I know you are. I know. I'll . . . well, I can't promise, can I? But I'll do my best.'

'That's not good enough. You have to promise me. You have to fix it for me.'

'Lilah, don't get upset. It'll be all right. We're not going to get divorced. OK? Nothing bad's going to happen. We just have things to work through, and we have to find a way to do it, we have to find time to do it. It's not that easy, you know, when he's working hard, and I'm dealing with the girls, and there always seems to be so much to do at home . . .'

'Don't. Don't do that, don't claim you don't have time to fix this, to fix the most important thing you have.'

'OK. You're right.' Natalie looked nervous; she was looking at Lilah's face, studying it. 'Lilah, do you want to go?'

Lilah shook her head, took another sip of her water. She felt as though the sand were shifting beneath her, the horizon tilting. Head shaking was a bad thing, she should remember that.

'I need to tell you something,' she whispered.

'What's that, Lilo?'

'About that night, in December, at the B&B.'

Natalie smiled at her, a half-smile, indulgent.

'Don't, Lilo. It's all right.'

'I want to tell you . . .'

'I don't want to know.' She held up her hand.

'You were never his penance,' Lilah said.

'What?'

'I said, you were never his penance.' She sipped her water and looked out at the sea. The horizon was level again. Natalie was on her feet, rummaging around in a basket, trying to find

380

something. What was it, what was it she needed? Lilah needed to say something, she couldn't remember what it was.

'Here you go,' Nat said, arranging a blanket around Lilah's shoulders.

That was it, she remembered now. A blanket round her shoulders, only then she was in front of a fire, not on a beach. 'I won't say nothing happened,' Lilah said, 'because that wouldn't be true.'

'Oh, Lilah. Please don't tell me.'

'I tried,' she croaked, ignoring Natalie's plea, 'to seduce him.' She made a noise, half laugh, half cough. 'I know, I'm hateful. Hateful.'

'No, Lilah . . .'

'Yes. I was so angry with you, so angry, Nat.' Natalie was sitting at her side, they were holding hands. 'It was such an emotional day, wasn't it? And then the storm, walking in the snow, I was so cold, so afraid. Such an emotional day, and I wanted someone to be with me.' She brought Natalie's fingers to her lips and kissed them. 'It wasn't just spite. I remembered how much I loved him. I remembered how much he once meant to me.'

There were tears on Natalie's cheeks, or at least she thought there were, but she wasn't sure, because she couldn't see all that well, everything looked out of focus, shimmering, as though she were looking through a heat haze, or warped glass. 'I had too much wine, I wanted to be with him. He said no. He let me kiss him, just once, and then he pulled away. He didn't want me, he wanted none of me.'

'Shhh, Lilah.'

'It's true. He told me he never loved me . . .'

'Lilah! That isn't true, he did love you, I know he did.'

381

Lilah smiled at her. 'Well, he says not.' She felt as though her head were clearing; there was a breeze off the sea and she felt suddenly better, miraculously better, as though she could get to her feet, as though she could run. 'He was quite sure,' she told Natalie, 'he never loved me.'

So it was a lie. As she'd said to Jen and to Andrew, as she kept discovering and rediscovering, truth is overrated. The truth was, that kiss lasted much too long and when Andrew pulled away, he did so only for a moment or two, and then she kissed him again, and that time he let her. Didn't just let her: he picked her up, let the blankets fall away from her body and from his, he put her down on the bed and covered her body with his. That was the truth. It was also a lie, the kind of physical betrayal that happens sometimes when old lovers are together again. It was friendship, it was regret, healing, passion. It wasn't love, it wasn't the sort of love that he had for Natalie and that, Lilah felt sure, was the only thing that mattered.

Natalie huddled closer to her and Lilah took the blanket that was spread over her own legs and flicked it out over her friend; they were like two old ladies, sitting out on the beach, waiting for sunset. They were quiet for a long time before Lilah spoke.

'You have to make it right with him,' she said. 'Don't tell me you can't promise me, because you can.'

'OK.'

She couldn't be sure, but she felt as though the temperature were dropping, as though the sky were darkening. Her mouth was dry, she couldn't remember where she'd put her water bottle.

'Now, where the fuck is Jen? I'm tired, Nat. I'm so tired. I'm ready to go now.'

*Hello gorgeous girl*

*Hope you doing OK. I have work until Thursday, I'm trying to get a flight out Thursday evening, but if not it might be Friday, as early as I can make it. I rang this morning, Dan said you and the girls went to the beach. I hope you're not overdoing it. Save some energy for me, OK, because I have missed you these last few days. I miss your sweet smile.*

    *I love you Lilah, I do.*
    *I'll see you very soon.*

*Zac*

## Chapter Forty-nine

~

Lilah died on Thursday afternoon, a little before four, the sun still high in the sky.

Jen knew something was wrong as soon as she saw Natalie, hurriedly packing up their things, waving at Jen to get a move on.

'We need to go,' Nat called out as Jen raced up the beach to join them. 'Something's not right.' Lilah was still in the deckchair, but lolling to one side, head hanging down, fingers tracing the sand, like a puppet without a master.

'OK, OK. We'll take her to the hospital. It's in the centre of town, we drove past it . . .'

There was a faint moan from Lilah's lips.

'Lilah?' Nat was kneeling at her side. 'Lilo, it's OK. It's OK.'

'No, no, no, no, no.'

'Are you in pain, Lilo? Sweetie, tell me.' Natalie put her hands on Lilah's shoulders, she was starting to cry. Jen was beginning to feel desperate.

'Not the hospital.' She said it loudly and clearly, she raised her head. 'Not the hospital.'

'We have to, Lilah, just to check . . .'

'No! No!' She started struggling against Natalie's grasp. 'Please. Please. Take me home. Please take me home.' Lilah started to sob, her tiny body shaking. 'Please, Nat. Take me home. Take me home to Zac.'

She'd forgotten that he wasn't there.

Jen drove like a madwoman, faster than she'd ever driven in her life, her hands gripping the steering wheel, knuckles white, praying all the way, please, please, please don't let me crash, please don't let her die, not in the back of the car, not like this, not like this, not like this. Natalie sat in the back seat, Lilah's head in her lap, one hand gripping the back of Jen's seat.

'Hurry,' she kept saying, 'we have to hurry.' Natalie, the woman who broke into a cold sweat at speeds of more than sixty miles an hour, was urging her to put her foot down. Jen could only guess at the depth of her terror.

Lilah drifted in and out of consciousness. She didn't cry out, she was calm. The moment they had agreed that they wouldn't take her to hospital, she'd become composed. Almost serene. Jen feared it might be resignation.

'Stay,' she whispered to herself under her breath, 'please, Lilah. Stay.'

Natalie rang Andrew from her mobile. It went to voicemail. She rang Zac. Voicemail. 'Voicemail, voicemail, fucking voicemail,' she yelled from the back seat.

'Ring Dan, Nat. Ring Dan, tell him to try landlines, send emails, whatever. Tell him to get them here.'

Dan was waiting on the lawn outside the house when they pulled up. The three of them lifted an unconscious Lilah out of the car and carried her up the stairs to her room. Downstairs, Jen and Dan fought about what to do.

'You should have taken her to the hospital,' he hissed at her.

'She begged us, Dan. She begged us. You would have done the same thing in our place, you didn't see her. She was desperate. She doesn't want to ... They can't fucking help her now anyway,' Jen said. She slumped against the kitchen counter, sliding down onto the tiled floor, swallowing the sob in her throat. 'She's dying now, they can't do anything.'

'I'm going to call Doctor Hulez.' He disappeared into the living room and came back a moment later with a sleeping Isabelle in his arms. Jen had forgotten all about her.

Doctor Hulez said it probably wouldn't be much longer. He strongly advised them to take her to hospital, for the purposes of pain management. But Lilah was insistent. The doctor shook his head miserably, but allowed her to stay there on condition that they promised to call him or an ambulance if things got very bad. As the doctor was leaving, Andrew rang to say he had a flight first thing. No one had been able to get hold of Zac.

Lilah slept.

Jen, Natalie and Dan stayed up through the night. Dan suggested they take it in turns to watch over her, but Natalie would not leave her side, she would not be persuaded, so Dan and Jen took turns to sit with her, while the other kept an eye on Isabelle, who was in her cot downstairs. They'd moved the baby from the next-door room, they didn't want her crying to wake Lilah.

Because when she woke, it was horrible. She cried out. She screamed. She was sick, she convulsed, she pleaded with them to make it all stop. She asked for Zac. Over and over, she asked for Zac. She yelled at them to get out, to leave her alone, why wouldn't they bring Zac to her? Why were they keeping him from her? And all the while, Natalie at her side – her face white, her hands shaking – didn't once cry, didn't flinch, even when Lilah spat at her, swore at her, scratched her face. Jen stood rooted, horrified, cowardly, in the doorway, but Natalie climbed onto the bed and pulled Lilah's emaciated frame to her, she held her like that, physically restraining her, stroking her hair, whispering to her, words of comfort, words of love. She kissed her head and her face, she talked about the first time they met, the camping trip to Saint-Malo, the summer they went to Ibiza and Nat lost her bikini bottoms in the sea. Lilah laughed. And eventually, Lilah slept.

Jen went downstairs. Dan had fallen asleep on the sofa, Isabelle on his chest. It was just after four in the morning, a tinge of grey just starting to seep from the horizon into the inky black sky. The room was cold; they hadn't had a fire yet, but Jen felt it wouldn't be long now until they needed one. Wouldn't be long now. She wanted to take the baby, to lift her into her arms and hold her sweet, soft warmth against her chest, but she didn't want to wake her, so instead she sat in the armchair watching them sleep, holding a blanket over her mouth so they wouldn't hear her sob.

Isabelle stirred a little before five. Jen lifted her gently away from Dan's body, but the withdrawal of her warmth woke him straight away.

'Is she . . . ?'

'Still sleeping. I think. She was an hour ago. I haven't been up since.'

He went upstairs while Jen fed the baby, came down after a few minutes.

'Still sleeping,' he said with a nod. 'Can I make you a tea?' he asked her.

Jen shook her head and held her hand out to him. He knelt down at her side.

'I didn't thank you. For looking after her yesterday while we were at the beach.'

'You didn't need to,' he said. 'I would look after her every day if I had the chance.'

'Is that really what you want?' Jen asked him. 'Another man's child?'

Dan sat back on his heels, he gave a little sigh. 'But she isn't. She isn't another man's child. She's your child.' He got to his feet. 'Sure you don't want tea?' She shook her head.

'I do love you, you know,' she said softly as he walked to the kitchen, but he didn't turn around.

Dan rang Zac at half past five, but the phone went straight to voicemail.

Lilah was a little better when she woke just after six. She sat up in bed and asked for water. She asked if she could see Isabelle, so Jen brought the baby to her.

'I probably shouldn't hold her,' she croaked. 'In case I throw up.'

'She's thrown up on you enough times,' Jen replied with a small smile. 'She could hardly complain.'

'I might have a seizure,' Lilah said, so Jen clambered onto the bed beside her and held Isabelle for her, up against her body, so she could smell her, feel her warmth. There were tears sliding down her face as she said, 'He isn't here, is he? Zac isn't here.'

They arrived at midday. Zac didn't stop to talk to anyone, he didn't even look at them, he sprinted straight from the taxi into the house and up the stairs to Lilah's bedroom, leaving Andrew standing on the lawn, looking up at the house, as though he were too afraid to go inside.

'He was knocked off his bike yesterday,' Andrew explained as Jen ushered him into the house. 'He smashed his phone and had to go for stitches in his head. He didn't get back home till the early hours, but we managed to get him on the flight.'

Natalie appeared, shuffling down the stairs in filthy tracksuit bottoms, her hair lank about her face. Her face was a dirty shade of grey, like dish water, the circles beneath her eyes the colour of fresh bruises.

'Jesus, Nat,' was all Andrew could say as he went to her. Jen left them there, at the foot of the stairs, embracing. She could hear Natalie crying softly and her husband repeating, 'I should never have left you, I'm so sorry, my love, I should never have left you.'

Jen couldn't believe that just hours ago she'd been thinking of lighting a fire. It was stiflingly hot, humid and close, the air heavy with moisture. She and Dan were in the kitchen, passing Isabelle back and forth to one another. The baby was angry, fractious, she refused to settle. She cried and cried and cried. Jen poured cold water on the back of her neck and tried to soothe her with a cold flannel, but nothing worked; her face became redder and redder, her furious screams tearing the air. Jen drank glasses of ice-cold water, wishing she could have gin and lime and bitter tonic, something to take away the taste in her mouth; she didn't know what it was but no amount of brushing would get rid of it. She had never in all her life wanted so much to be oblivious.

When Isabelle finally, finally fell asleep, Jen loaded a tray with glasses and a pitcher of ice-cold water and took it upstairs. The room was rank, close; it smelt of sweat and vomit and worse. Lilah lay on her side in the middle of the bed, the sheets and blankets stripped back, her skin slick and grey. Zac held her hands, Natalie crouched behind her, pressing a cold cloth to the back of her neck.

'Is she . . . with us?' Jen asked.

'Who's she?' came a croak from the bed. 'The cat's mother?'

She drifted in and out, from lucidity to hallucination; she ebbed and flowed.

'Where's Con, Jen? Is he out back?'

'Conor's not here, Lilah. He's not here, darling.'

'Oh. Are you sure? He was here yesterday. Just out . . .' She tried to raise an arm to point out back to the woods, but could lift it no more than a few inches from the bed. 'Out there. The edge of the trees. You can see him, if you look. Red hoodie. He's wearing that red hoodie, the one he always wears.' He was wearing it the day he died.

'OK, Lilah. I'll go and find him later.'

From downstairs, Jen heard a cry.

'That's Isabelle, sweetheart, I'm going to go down and get her, OK?'

'Give her a kiss,' Lilah said. 'Give her a kiss from me.'

Jen slipped at the top of the stairs. She clawed at the stone walls to right herself, ripping a fingernail to the quick. She bit down hard on her lip to stop from crying out and stumbled down the rest of the way, leaving a smear of blood on the wall where she'd cut herself. Her legs trembled. She was exhausted. She hadn't slept in more than twenty-four hours, she'd barely eaten. She washed the blood from her hands and went to comfort

Isabelle. She didn't want to carry the baby back upstairs to that stuffy, stinking room; she was afraid she might fall again, that she might hurt her daughter.

She took her outside instead, hurrying to the shade of the hammock. She climbed in and lay down, Isabelle hot and angry, squirming against her chest. Jen closed her eyes and they rocked and rocked until eventually she quietened.

Dan and Andrew came out a little while later. They brought cold water with them, and sat on the grass next to the hammock. No one said anything, they sat in silence, listening to the lightest of breezes whispering through the leaves above them, the occasional twitter of birdsong, the low moan, in the distance, of cattle. And then they heard a terrible noise, a cry of agony, like a wounded bear. It was Zac, and they knew then that she was gone.

*27 June 1995*

*Greetings, my darling Nat, from the slopes of sunny Winchmore Hill,*

*Actually it's pissing it down and I feel like I've been here forever. Am so bloody bored. All that time being desperate for finals to be over and now they are and I'm stuck in London with no one to play with, because Drew's in Reading with his parents and you're in bloody Wiltshire or wherever it is and Jen and Conor have gone to Cork to see Conor's mum. Dan's around, but he's got some girl and he's too busy shagging to hang out with me.*

*I cannot wait to leave for France. Even if we do have to spend the summer doing manual labour. And there's no swimming pool. Never fear, we'll get Drew to drive us to the beach (on our days off!) and have the very best time.*

*And (drum roll, s'il vous plaît), I have a job! I will be a low-paid lackey at Red, a PR firm in Soho (woo-hoo), starting from September.*

*And (another drum roll), Drew and I are going to move in. It's decided. I was thinking of staying with Mum to save money but she is driving me crazy – every time I pour myself a drink she tuts and rolls her eyes (like she's not a total lush!).*

*So how bloody great is that going to be? Parties at our place? We will fix you up with a divine young man as soon as you move to London (assuming you don't pull something hot on the beach in France . . .)*

*I am counting my blessings . . .*

*I never have to write another exam again.*

*I have a job.*

*I have an amazing boyfriend.*

*I weigh 117 pounds (yesssss! Only five more pounds to go).*

*I have the best friends, the loveliest friends, and most of all, Nat my*

*darling, I have you. Awwww . . . But it's true, Nat, you are top of my*
*pyramid, my very best friend, forever and ever.*

*We are going to have the greatest summer. It's going to be epic,*
*baby.*

*Lots and lots of love*

*Lilo xoxoxoxoxo*

# Chapter Fifty

～

Natalie slept in the hammock the night that Lilah died, and for two nights after that. She barely came into the house. Andrew brought her food outside, most of which she didn't eat. At night he sat with her until she fell asleep, then went inside, where he lay awake, his heart heavy in his chest like a stone. The heat persisted, draping itself over the house like a thick woollen blanket, stifling, suffocating.

On the fourth day, they scattered Lilah's ashes in the wood. She hadn't been clear, in the end, about what she wanted, whether it was to be taken back to England or to stay here. Zac took the decision that she should stay in France. It was, after all, the place she'd chosen to come to spend her last days. The cremation was organised and carried out within seventy-two hours: it was quick and hassle-free, not at all what Andrew would have expected of French bureaucracy. They invited no one else. They told no one else.

'There's no one else she would have wanted,' Zac said.

The sun shone brightly as the breeze took what was left of her, and they stood in perfect silence, even Isabelle falling mute.

It wasn't much of a ceremony. Lilah might well have preferred a smart London funeral with everyone in black tie and a raucous wake afterwards.

'Funerals aren't really for the dead though, are they?' Zac said. 'They're for the living.'

Zac stayed up in the woods for a while after everyone else had come back to the house. After an hour or two, Andrew went to find him. He was sitting on a fallen tree, calm and apparently perfectly serene, just listening to the forest. He smiled at Andrew when he saw him.

'Are you all right?' Andrew asked him.

He shrugged. 'I suppose. I don't know what I'm doing, really. I don't know what to do.' Andrew sat down at his side. The forest canopy softened the sunlight, the trees were still. 'It's just been the two of us, you know, for a long time. We became quite insular. She became everything to me.' He shook his head a little, a futile attempt to shake off grief. 'And it was good,' he said, raising his head, his eyes up to the forest canopy, 'to have a part of her. For a while. You understand, don't you?' Andrew nodded. He could feel Zac's eyes on him, searching his face. 'She's special. It was something to love her.' He fell silent.

After a long time, he said: 'I know about what happened at Christmas.'

Andrew's mouth went dry, his heart felt small and hard, a peach pit.

'It doesn't matter. I mean . . . It doesn't matter. Fidelity was never her strong suit.'

'Zac, Jesus, I am so sorry,' Andrew said, the words sounding hollow and inadequate as they came out of his mouth.

Zac shook his head. 'Honestly, it doesn't matter. She only told me about it when she was trying to get me to leave her.

She didn't want me . . .' He stopped and took a deep breath. 'To have to watch, you know? To have to be there . . .'

'But you stayed anyway,' Andrew said, and for a horrible moment he thought he might cry; he could feel his throat constrict, his voice starting to catch. Zac put his hand on Andrew's shoulder.

'I'm not telling you this because I wanted to make you feel bad. I know it seems like I am, but it isn't that.'

Andrew couldn't quite believe that Zac was consoling him, that he was letting Zac console him. He got to his feet. 'Please, please don't say anything more. I feel terrible about what happened, I wasn't thinking then, it was such an awful day . . .'

'I know all that, and I know why she did it, and why you did it. That isn't the point. That's not why I'm telling you this. She talked to me, she told me things, about everything that's been going on here, with you, Natalie, Jen and Dan. I just . . .' He broke off, shook his head a little, looked up at Andrew, gave him a small, sad smile. 'It meant something to her, that night you spent together . . .'

Andrew's chin was almost on his chest, he couldn't remember a time he'd felt so ashamed. And then Zac reached out and touched his arm, and the shame deepened.

'It was a good thing for her,' Zac said. 'It . . . gave her something, something I couldn't, some comfort, it went some way to healing a very old wound, one I didn't even know about, one I could never help her with. And I'm glad of that, I really am. I mean it, Andrew,' he said, and Andrew stood there, limp, wordless, taken aback by the depth of Zac's selflessness. All that mattered to him was Lilah. 'I'm glad that you loved her. I'm glad that she knew that, in the end.'

Finally, Zac's head dropped, his shoulders shook. 'What will I do now?' he asked. 'What will I do?'

Andrew tried, as best he could, to put his arms around Zac's enormous shoulders, and held him tight, the way you would a frightened child. He expected resistance, but got none; he sat there, hugging Zac, this big, gentle man whom he had wronged.

'I don't know,' Andrew said eventually. 'I don't know what you do. But you can come here. You can always come here. When you think you can't bear it, come here.'

Andrew understood more than most how important it was to have somewhere to go, even if it wasn't a grave site. The graveyard in Ireland where Conor was buried, lush and verdant and populated with solemn slabs of grey stone, was beautiful and peaceful, but did nothing for Andrew, made him feel no closer to his old friend. For that, he had to come here, to the French house. Still, he visited sometimes; he had been back just a few weeks before, after he left France, after all the rancour with Jen and Dan, after hurting Natalie. He had to go somewhere.

Conor had no answers for him, but Maggie, Conor's mother, had a few things to say. He couldn't tell her, of course, what the nub of the problem was, but he did let on that his marriage, for the first time ever, wasn't the haven it had once been.

'Do you remember, Andrew, that I told you, a long time ago, to find someone who valued you? You remember that? I feel so bad now, because I never much cared for the blonde girl, and now she's not well I feel like a right old witch, but there you go. When you came to visit, just after your girls were born, remember, you and Natalie – well, I saw you then and I thought, that's bloody perfect. He's done exactly as I told him.'

Andrew smiled at her. It was just like Maggie to take credit for something that had absolutely nothing to do with her. She regularly claimed that Conor would never have been the rugby player he was had it not been for her cooking.

'I don't know what's going on, but I know it won't be a lack of respect. She cherishes you, that girl. And you're old enough now – what am I saying? You've been old enough for a long old while, to know that kind of thing is not replaceable. You aren't careless with love like that. You have a partnership, not just a marriage. A partnership. It made me happy to see it all those years back, it would break my heart – break my heart! – to see you throw that away now. And you wouldn't want to break an old woman's heart, would you now?' She poured him another cup of tea, then took it away before he could drink it. She disappeared into the kitchen and came back with a bottle of Bushmills and two glasses. 'I'll tell you what makes me sad, Andrew. It's that Jennifer never found a partnership like you have. And now she's alone with a baby. It's such a terrible thing, isn't it? That beautiful girl bringing up a baby by herself. It's not right, is it? My son would not have wanted that.'

On the way back to England he composed letters to Jen and to Dan, telling them he was sorry for the things he'd said. He'd been a stupid eejit, as somebody once said, and worse than that, a hypocrite, a fool. He didn't send them. He didn't write to Natalie; there wasn't a way of saying what he needed to say in a letter, there wasn't a way to bridge the gap between them unless she were standing there in front of him.

He kept thinking about what Lilah said the night before he left France, when he was sitting on the bed with her in the dark. She hadn't said it in so many words, but she suggested that the problem wasn't really about them, about Andrew and Natalie, it was about him. His need to atone had made Natalie feel terrible, as though she were a price to pay. Only, she couldn't always have felt that way, could she? They wouldn't have been happy, and they had been, for a long time. Only now he thought about it, maybe it came to her, from time to time, maybe it was something she lived with, without ever speaking it, or at least without speaking it until now. It was amazing, he found, what we can live with when we set our minds to it, whether it be pain, or guilt, or ghosts, or the suspicion that the man you are married to doesn't love you in quite the way you want him to.

He realised then that he had to find himself again, to find a way to live without the guilt and ghosts, then maybe she would see how he loved her. He booked a flight to France: he'd go the following weekend, he'd speak to Nat. He had things straight in his head, he'd been straightened out by Lilah, of all people. He drove the girls to school, he worked, he slept. And then he got the message from Natalie, telling him to come as quickly as he could, and he understood that the weekend would be too late.

He was terrified that he wouldn't make it, not just that he wouldn't be able to say goodbye, but that he wouldn't be there for Nat, that in the end she'd have to do it alone and he'd have let her down, again. He felt grateful, for the very first time, that at least when Conor went it was with the brittle snap of a vertebra, quick and clean. But he was there. He made it, and he brought Zac with him, so at least he had got something right.

Andrew walked Zac back from the woods to the house in silence. The light was just starting to fade, and he thought he detected for the first time since he'd returned a coolness in the breeze, just the faintest scent of rain. He found Natalie outside, sitting in the hammock, feet tucked up under her, back perfectly straight, looking out over the valley. She smiled at him when she saw him.

'Please come inside tonight, Nat,' he said. 'Sleeping out here has got to be killing your back. And anyway, I think it might rain.'

Natalie looked up at the perfectly clear sky, then looked back at him, cocked her head to one side. 'You think?'

'Please, Nat?' He sat down next to her.

'OK,' she said. She gave him a very small smile. 'She's gone now anyway. She was here, yesterday, I could feel it. But she's gone now.'

Andrew didn't say anything, he just smiled at her, touched her face. It wasn't like her, to talk like that; she didn't believe in ghosts or afterlives, she was staunchly rationalist. But you never knew how you would feel, until it was someone you couldn't bear to lose forever.

'Are you OK?' Natalie was looking at him, her brow furrowed. She leaned closer to him, brought her hand up to her face to hold his. The hammock rocked ever so gently from side to side. 'You look so tired,' she said.

'I'm fine. I was just thinking about . . . practicalities,' he lied. 'I have to go back the day after tomorrow. I want you to come with me, Nat. I want you to come home now.'

'Of course,' she said, as though there were never any question, as though she had completely forgotten the horrible way he'd treated her the last time he left. 'Of course I'll come back with you. I haven't seen the girls for three weeks.'

He winced a little, he wasn't sure what she meant by that. She was coming back for the girls, or coming back for him? Was it an either/or thing? Couldn't she just be coming back?

'I can't wait to get home now,' she said, 'I just can't wait.' And she smiled at him, green eyes looking up from under lowered lashes, and he knew that it wasn't just for the girls, it was for him, too, and his heart skipped a beat.

Natalie slept in the house that night, she slept soundly at his side. Andrew lay awake again, listening to the noises of the house and the night. He heard Jen padding around in the room next door, shushing the baby. He heard low cries in the distance, strange, ghostly sounds that made him irrationally fearful. Natalie didn't stir once.

When he slept, it was fitful and he woke with a terrible start from a bad dream he couldn't remember. Still, Natalie slept. He slipped out of bed and crept downstairs, where he found Jen in the living room with Isabelle; he had a flash of déjà vu, back to the day when he and Jen had argued, the day Jen had told him about Dan.

'Hello,' he said softly and the pair of them turned to look at him, two sets of enormous brown eyes set in pale, drained, unhappy faces.

'Bad night?'

Jen nodded.

'Can I get you anything?' he asked her.

She shook her head.

He made her some tea anyway, brought it to her and sat down in the armchair opposite hers. They hadn't really spoken since he got there, not about anything other than Lilah, in any case. It hadn't been the time. Now, perhaps, in the chilly early morning, just the two of them and the baby, he could apologise to her, tell her he'd been wrong, judgemental, unkind, a hypocrite. But he couldn't find the words, so they sat quietly, just the occasional fretting from Isabelle breaking the silence.

'It's harder than you think it's going to be, isn't it?' Jen said eventually. 'Babies, I mean. And you had two at the same time. I've no idea how you coped.'

'There were two of us, too, that makes a difference. You can't do it alone. Well, you can, I suppose, people do . . .'

He had nothing for her but platitudes – it was so long since the girls had been that age, he barely remembered what it was like. He remembered great happiness, wonder, that constant sense of astonishment that they were really *there*, after all the waiting, and they were so small, so impossibly tiny, so fragile. He didn't remember exhaustion, he didn't remember Natalie ever looking like this. She probably had done, all the time, but all he recalled now was the happiness.

Jen smiled at him, a slow, watery smile. 'It's ridiculous,' she said, 'but I feel as though she knows about Lilah. I feel like she's missing her. She's been so unsettled the last couple of days.'

'It's not ridiculous, Jen. They feel things, don't they? That's what people say, in any case. Your distress, your sadness, maybe she senses it?'

Jen shrugged. 'I'm not sure I believe that. I think it's more than that, it's like Isabelle misses her. You know how Lilah adored her, how she was always touching her. All those afternoons in the hammock . . .' Jen wiped the tears from her cheeks with the heels of her hands. 'I thought,' she said softly, a catch in her voice, 'because we knew it was coming, because it wasn't a shock, I thought it wouldn't be so bad . . .'

Andrew took Isabelle while Jen cried, but the baby protested, loudly, angrily, her little face screwed up and angry red. He got to his feet and tried to calm her, but she only cried harder. Jen didn't move, she clutched the armrests of her chair, her head down. Andrew took Isabelle into the kitchen, he bounced her on his hip, he cooed and ga-ga-ga-ed, and Isabelle screamed. Andrew took her outside, into the courtyard, he walked around and around, trying to distract her, until Dan came out of the barn and took her in his arms, and within seconds, literally seconds, she calmed. Dan looked at Andrew – he looked embarrassed, guilty almost – and he said: 'Sometimes they just need a change of arms,' and Andrew started laughing.

'That must be it,' he said. He put his hand on Dan's arm, gave it an awkward little pat. He turned to go back into the kitchen. Jen was standing there, watching them, her expression unreadable.

*Letter, from Andrew to Jen, dated 17 September 2013, unsent*

Dearest Jen,

I was a fool. I had no right to speak to you the way I did. Please forgive me.

I'm writing this on the plane, I've just been to see Maggie. She set me straight. I don't mean that I told her about anything, please don't think that, but she could see that I wasn't right in my head and she deduced, quite rightly, that it was about Nat, and she talked to me about the way things should be and she set me straight.

But also, she spoke about you. Jen, she talks about you with such love, still, after all this time. You are the daughter she never had, I think. She wishes you happiness, she talked about how much she wished you had a great love in your life, and she shamed me, because I know I should be wishing you the same, instead of judging you and trying to smother your happiness.

I've been a fool. You are not, and could never be a disappointment to me. I've been a disappointment to myself, lately, but I think I know what I need to do now, I know where I need to be.

I wish you love, my girl. And you will always, no matter what you say, be my little sister.

Love, and apologies,

Andrew

# Chapter Fifty-one

～

The heat broke. Overnight, banks of gunmetal clouds blew in from the coast, became trapped above the mountains and burst. The rain was heavy and relentless; it came in cold, driving sheets. Streams of water running down the road became rivers and it was dark even at midday.

Natalie looked for Zac. He was leaving that afternoon; his bags were packed, piled neatly in the hallway, but he was nowhere to be found. He wasn't in the house or in the barn with Dan, he hadn't taken the car out. Nat put on her hiking boots and borrowed a jacket from Jen and walked up the muddy slope behind the house towards the woods. She found him there, in the clearing where they scattered Lilah's ashes. He was sitting on a fallen tree trunk, his hands clasped in front of him, head bowed as though in prayer. His clothes were soaked through.

Natalie sat down at his side, and he placed a sodden arm around her shoulders.

'I keep asking myself,' he said, 'keep asking everyone, what shall I do? She was . . . she'd become everything to me. I just don't know what to do.'

'Go home, work. Lean heavily on your family, on your friends. Lean on us, you have us. Andrew and I are in Reading, the girls would love to see you any chance you have to visit. Honestly, they both fancy you something rotten. They'd *love* to show you off to their friends. Dan will welcome you here any time, you know that.'

He nodded, but he didn't look up at her, he sank lower onto his log. He looked as though he might slide right off it, down into the mud, as though he might disappear and lose the light. It made her fearful, but she had nothing more for him, no more words of comfort, so she got to her feet and reached for his hand and said, 'Please come inside, you'll catch your death out here.'

He looked up at her, and he smiled, she couldn't tell if he was crying or whether it was just the rain. 'I'll miss you,' he said. 'All of you. Which is odd, because if you'd asked me in December, I'd have said I'd happily never lay eyes on any of you ever again.'

He got to his feet, bent down to kiss her cheek. 'I'm so glad,' he said, 'that in the end she had you here.'

On their way back, just as they were leaving the wood, Natalie slipped and fell in the mud. Zac picked her up and carried her all the way to the house.

Dan drove him to the airport that afternoon. It was dark when he returned, the wind picking up, rain battering down, splashing mud up as high as the windows. The house was quiet: Isabelle and Jen were sleeping upstairs, Andrew was reading in the living room. The silence was heavy. Natalie climbed the stairs and walked along the corridor to the main bedroom, what had once been Jen's and latterly Lilah's. The door was closed. She hadn't been into that room for almost a week, not since the very end.

Natalie pushed the door open and closed it behind her. The room was empty – Lilah's things were all gone, packed away into boxes by Jen and Dan or into suitcases by Zac. The bed was stripped. Natalie didn't know where the sheets had gone, the ones they'd wrapped her in. Would they be washed and re-used, thrown away, burned? She sat down on the bare mattress, curled her legs up underneath her and lay down. There was nothing left of her here, no scent of her perfume, no strands of her hair, no echo of her laughter, there was nothing.

Natalie cried until she had nothing left.

She longed to be with her daughters, sitting on the sofa with them, one on either side, a blanket thrown over their legs, Grace's head on her shoulder, Charlotte's arm linked through hers, watching *The X Factor*. She longed for their life, the good one they'd built, for Andrew washing the car on a Sunday afternoon, for walking on the Common after Sunday lunch. She longed for Andrew. She got up and went to look for him.

She got halfway down the stairs and stopped. She could hear Andrew talking, he was in the kitchen, he was talking to Dan. She sat on the stairs and listened. They were talking about Jen.

'Is she going to stay with you?' Andrew asked him.

'We haven't discussed it,' Dan said, his voice clipped and clear.

'It would seem,' Andrew said, 'like a good arrangement.'

'A good arrangement? What on earth does that mean?'

Andrew sighed. 'Fuck it, Dan. I'm trying to say . . . I think you should be with her.' There was a long pause. 'I'm trying to say sorry.'

'Oh? That was an apology?' Dan laughed.

'I'm very sorry for what I said.'

'I know, man. I know where you were coming from, I know

407

how you feel about her, I just know. I was pissed off, but not that pissed off. I know what all this means to you, this place, her, Conor's memory.'

'But it's good, her being here, isn't it? Her and the baby, it seems to work.'

'I hope it does. I hope it could.'

'It would be good to know that she's with someone who loves her, who loves Isabelle.'

'And I do.'

'I know you do.'

It went quiet for a while, then Dan said: 'The thing I worry about, the thing that I keep wondering . . .' He tailed off.

'What? What is it?'

'What if she never looks at me that way? The way she looked at him?'

Natalie could hear the fridge opening, the clinking of bottles. 'Sometimes I'm afraid, you know, that I won't be able to get that out of my head, that it'll hurt us . . .'

The ping of bottle tops landing in the bin. 'Do you remember the way she looked at Conor?' Andrew asked him. 'I'm serious, can you actually remember accurately the way she looked at him? I don't think I can. Is it possible that she won't love you in exactly the way she loved him? Yeah, I'd say so. Does it matter? No. It's what you feel, here and now, the commitment you make to each other, what you're prepared to give, what you're prepared to give up. Not the way you look at someone.'

Natalie's heart was thumping in her chest, she was sure it was so loud they'd be able to hear her. This was what he was like, her husband, the good man, who knew what counted, what love was. This was the way he used to talk, and in that moment she saw how she had hurt him, with her talk of penance, that the giving and the giving up was important to him, it was what made their marriage, it was worthwhile.

She got to her feet and crept down to the bottom of the stairs. She popped her head around the door. They were sitting at the kitchen table, side by side, beer bottles in front of them.

'Hi,' she said softly, and they turned as one, and Andrew raised his arm, beckoning her forward. He got to his feet and put his arms around her waist, he lifted her off the ground and kissed her neck, and he whispered into her hair, 'I think it's time you and I went home.'

*Dear Dan, Jen and Isabelle,*

*Andrew and I would like to invite ourselves to spend Christmas with you in France. Do you think that would be all right? (We're bringing the girls, and Zac, too.)*

*Lots of love to you all,*

*Nat (and Andrew) xxx*

# Chapter Fifty-two

*November*

It was still dark when she woke; through the gap in the curtains she could see that the snow had started to fall. She shifted a little, raised the blanket, carefully lifting the arm which curled around her waist, familiar to her now, with its old stain of ink inside the wrist. She disentangled herself and looked back at him; he was fast asleep. She swung her legs over the edge of the bed and shoved her feet into a pair of sheepskin-lined slippers, then reached for the robe hanging over the back of the chair and wrapped herself up. Outside, the hillside was already white, the storm was coming.

Isabelle's first snowstorm. Not that she'd be aware of it, but still. A landmark, a rite of passage. Her daughter was oblivious, fast asleep in her crib in the room next door. She'd been a terrible sleeper for weeks and weeks and then, all of a sudden, for reasons Jen couldn't quite fathom, she'd settled down and now she slept well, sometimes right through the night. It seemed miraculous, this gift of sleep, it settled over the whole house. Jen felt as though they were nesting, going into hibernation, preparing for the long, dark winter.

She relished it, she was looking forward to it – to cooking hearty stews, sitting round the fire in the evenings, spending days and weeks holed up here without seeing another soul. She told Dan they would stay until Christmas, and then they'd see, but in her heart she knew that when Christmas came, she wouldn't want to leave. There was a job waiting for her, the one she'd taken in Oxford and then left, they wanted her back. She could start in January, they said. She'd have to find a nursery, childminders; she would live in a perfectly comfortable flat in a converted Victorian house somewhere in Summertown or Headington. She would be lonely.

A few days previously, before the weather turned, they'd walked down to Villefranche, Dan, Jen and Isabelle, for pastries and coffee in the square. On the way back, they passed the little village primary school. The children were playing outside at break, shrieking and laughing and running around, and Jen caught herself lingering, watching them. Dan noticed too; he smiled to himself, though he didn't say anything.

Dan knew about the job offer in England, but Jen hadn't told him that the firm she worked for in Paris had been in touch, too. They were eager to get her to work for them on a freelance basis, remotely. No need for nurseries or childminders, no lonely nights in Summertown. She could stay here, with Dan. She wasn't sure why she hadn't told him, she knew he wanted her to stay. Perhaps today would be the day, perhaps today they'd decide it.

They still tiptoed around each other a little. They were still getting used to each other, being here alone, together at last after so long, they were still figuring out whether that thing they had all those years ago, was it really still there or did it just seem like it? When he looked at her, in a certain way, an old way she remembered from long ago, she felt her stomach flip and her heart race, the colour come to her cheeks. It was exciting but it wasn't how she remembered love.

It was a long time since she'd loved anyone, she couldn't remember how it was you recognised it, how it was you knew for sure. She thought she loved Nicolas, but now could clearly see that was just infatuation; she knew she'd never really loved Jean-Luc. So that took her all the way back to Conor, and she wasn't sure she trusted her memory of what that felt like now. Sometimes you had to look from the outside, didn't you, sometimes others could see something that you couldn't for yourself. Lilah saw it, she said it on the beach that day, she said it was plain for everyone to see, that Jen was in love with him.

It happened in the first days they were alone, after Lilah was gone and everyone left. They were sitting in the living room after dinner, listening to music, and a song came on, 'Hey, That's No Way to Say Goodbye', and Dan bowed his head and started to cry. Jen couldn't remember seeing him cry, not ever, not in all the years she'd known him. She knelt at his feet, as he had at hers not all that long ago, and he looked at her and smiled through tears.

'This was on the mix tape,' he said. 'The one I made for you. After. I never gave it to you. Because. But I used to listen to it all the time, all the time, after Conor died. Just brings it back. All that. And now all this. I can't believe it. I can't believe she's really gone.' He shook his head and she put her hands on the back of his neck and kissed his mouth, murmuring softly to him, that she loved him, that she wanted to be with him. She wasn't sure whether it was just comfort,

413

whether it would just be one night, or two, or a lifetime, but they were here now, and they would see. They had their chance.

And it felt like a sign, a good one, when the next day she found a note, tucked into a book, from Andrew. He had slipped it into her well-thumbed copy of the Larousse French-English dictionary, just the way Conor used to, only it was not a love note but an apology, and a blessing. It shouldn't matter whether he accepted her feelings for Dan or not, but it did.

So now, they had their chance, at something like normality. Jen put the coffee machine on and lit the wood burner, she sat down at the table and looked out across the front lawn. You couldn't see further than the stone wall, the cloud had descended so it obscured the view of the valley. She remembered how she'd felt this time last year, when it was just her and the baby in her belly, how frightening she'd found this house, the darkness, the quiet, the smell of cold stone, the wind screaming in the trees, the shadows in the corners. It didn't feel like that any longer: with the fires lit it was as warm and welcoming and cosy a place as you could imagine, it had lost its sense of abandonment, become a home. It was no longer quiet, not with Isabelle chattering and Dan's music playing.

Last year, she'd felt haunted, and though the ghosts remained, she found she didn't mind them quite so much. She'd had trepidations, of course she had, about moving back into her old room, a room she'd shared with Conor all those years ago, the place where Lilah died – was it really a room in which Dan and she could sleep peacefully, undisturbed? They slept fine. She didn't mind so much, the feeling that they weren't entirely alone, that there were shadows, echoes ever present, in dark corners and up in the attic, on the lawn out front by the oaks and in the woods behind. It wasn't such a frightening thing after all; there was comfort in it, the familiar kind, offered by old friends.

# *All I Want for Christmas*

## Amy Silver

**Twelve days and counting . . .**

It is Bea's first Christmas with her baby son, and this year she's determined to do *everything* right. But there is still so much to do: presents need to be bought; the Christmas menu needs refining; her café, The Honey Pot, needs decorating; and she's invited the whole neighbourhood to a party on Christmas Day. She really doesn't have time to get involved in two new people's lives, let alone fall in love . . .

When Olivia gets knocked over in the street, however, Bea can't help bringing her into The Honey Pot and getting to know her. Olivia's life is even more hectic than her own, and with her fiancé's entire family over from Ireland for Christmas, she shouldn't be lingering in the cosy warmth of Bea's café. Chloe, on the other hand, has nowhere else to go. Her affair with a married man has alienated her friends, and left her lonelier than ever.

But Christmas is a magical time, and in the fragrant atmosphere of The Honey Pot, anything can happen: new friends can be made, hearts can heal, and romance can finally blossom . . .

arrow books

ALSO AVAILABLE IN ARROW

# *One Minute to Midnight*

## Amy Silver

**Nicole Blake's New Year Resolutions, 1990:**
1 Start keeping a journal;
2. Lose half a stone;
3. Kiss Julian Symonds

If there are two things Nicole can guarantee about New Years Eve it's that there are *always* fireworks and Julian Symonds is *always* there.

Since she was thirteen, no New Year has been complete without Jules. Through school, university and beyond, as friends come and go, Nic and Jules are at the centre of every party.

Until one year everything changes.

Now, as another New Year approaches, Nicole has bridges to build – with her husband Dom, with her best friend Alex, and with Aidan, the man who broke her heart.

Life is about to change again, and once the fireworks are over and the dust has settled, this time Nicole is determined it will be for the better.

arrow books